AF410388

The BETTER HALF

A NOVEL OF THE NEVADA DIVORCE RANCH ERA

P.W. BORGMAN

CARSON CITY, NEVADA

Jen Carrigan loses her Silicon Valley job—then her home. Desperate, she packs up her dog and becomes a squatter. The squat? An abandoned mansion in the Santa Cruz Mountains. There, she befriends neighbor Stanley Abram, a solitary widower haunted by his own troubled past with the house. Then a mysterious holiday invitation from her sister lures Jen back to San Diego and into the shattered family that exiled her years before, setting the ghosts of the past and her precarious present on a collision course. But as she musters the courage to untangle the decades-long web of lies that's defined her life, the mansion delivers a devastating surprise. An emotional thriller set against the backdrop of coastal California.

To Mark

PART ONE

ONE

BETTYE CHRISTIAN
LAS VEGAS, NEVADA, 1952

had just lifted the flask to my lips when the bomb detonated. The desert dawn flashed to high noon and an enormous fireball leaped into the sky. The spectators around us erupted in a drunken cheer, as the fierce heat and the shock wave from the explosion hit the rise where we'd all parked. A deafening crack split the cool air, as if all the thunder in the world had been unleashed at once. The ground beneath us lurched and danced. I half-jumped, half-tumbled from my perch atop the back seat of the Cadillac convertible, feeling my skirt catch the door handle and tear. Mike scrambled to my side.

Hundreds of birds shot like bullets overhead. Then scores of cottontails and jackrabbits began to flee past us, right under the parked cars and through the legs of the onlookers. Girls squealed and screamed, and men hooted with laughter. I fought the urge to sprint after the animals, but they'd vanished as abruptly as they had appeared.

"It's okay, baby," Mike murmured in my ear, then picked up the flask from the sand, wiped it off with his handkerchief, and gave it back to me. My hands were shaking so hard I almost dropped it again.

I swallowed a big burning slug of whisky, watching a column of filthy gray dust soar into the sky, a muddy, doughnut-shaped cloud boiling upward around it. Behind us, I heard a rosary babbled in Spanish and turned to see Ramona, one of the new showgirls, crouched behind her boyfriend's Chrysler. She had her cheek pressed to her shoulder and her eyes squeezed shut, her powder-blue slacks darkening with piss.

Through this all, Rick sat slouched behind the wheel of his Caddy, elbow on the armrest, smoking—as if he was at a drive-in picture. He tilted his head back to follow the relentless rise of the cloud, which writhed like something alive, violent pinks and oranges twisting into seething, angry purples and browns, as if the blast had bruised heaven itself.

"Damn!" Mike gave me a squeeze. "Isn't that beautiful?" He'd mistaken my horror for awe. A few *oohs* and *ahhs* rippled through the group, the sort of sounds you'd hear at a fireworks display. It was not beautiful. It was horrible.

"Didn't I tell you?" he asked me, exuberant, pounding a kiss onto my cheek. It was the second time he'd been to an atomic test. "God-damn," he declared, grinning. "That's some goddamn American ingenuity right there."

The top of the mushroom cloud began detaching from its stem. Rick shifted in his seat and glanced back at us. "They're making the schoolkids in Las Vegas wear dog tags now," he remarked, watching the cloud's progress toward the city. "That's some American ingenuity, all right."

Mike ignored him. "Bettye, why dontcha enter that Miss Atomic Energy pageant?" As if by watching this catastrophic explosion, I was now qualified. Still trying to regain my breath, I shot him a skeptical glance.

"What? You're way prettier than that skinny redhead who won last time."

"I don't think they want any Italian girls in their contest." I hand-ed Mike the flask with what I hoped was a smile. It was a relief to be with a man who understood so little about me. He took a long swig, then slipped a finger beneath the bateau neckline of my dress, eased it down a half inch, and nuzzled my shoulder.

"They don't know what they're missing." As Mike leaned in for a kiss, a powerful gust of wind hit the rise. Tumbleweeds and sand pelted us like artillery. "Hang on!" He wrapped his body around me. More shouts, more screams. I coughed, feeling grit on my tongue, between my teeth.

The wind suddenly vanished, and a weird calm settled over the rise. "That happened last time, too," Mike said, releasing me. "You okay?"

I nodded, spitting out sand and sagebrush chaff. I was ready to get the hell out of there. Rick leaned over and opened his glove box, produced a small whisk broom from a bag, then carefully brushed debris down the channels in the lipstick-red upholstery onto the floor mats.

"Just washed the fucking thing," he growled, to let me know that this was not for my benefit.

"Can we please go?" I asked Mike, though I knew he was not in charge. I brushed at my face and found grit in my eyebrows, grit stuck to the makeup on my cheeks.

"Looks like the show's over," remarked Rick, replacing the whisk broom and glancing at his watch.

"Dammit, my dress is ripped!" My ears were ringing and my voice came out much too loud.

"Well, Bettye, be sure to submit a claim to the defense department," Rick glanced at Mike. "I told you we shouldn't bring her." He said this as if I wasn't there. And maybe I wasn't. Maybe my spirit had been ripped loose by the blast too, and had vanished with the rabbits and the birds.

"Aww, she's being a good sport," Mike insisted.

I was desperate to get indoors, away from the disbelieving stare of the wounded sky.

"Didn't get your jollies, Bettye?" Rick needled.

"It wasn't my idea to come." Now I mustered my most dismissive tone. "Boys and their toys."

"Toys, huh? Ask the Japs what they think of those toys," said Rick.

"Hell—ask the Reds!" laughed Mike, as if we were just enjoying some good-humored banter.

Mike was the Company clown, its Good-time Charlie and peacemaker. Every group of violent men needs a Mike. It reminded me of the way high-strung racehorses calmed down with goats in their stalls as companions. He seemed to have that effect on everyone but Rick, who was Mr. Ludovico's right-hand man. In a legitimate company, I suppose Rick Russo would have been the Vice President of Operations.

Mike helped me into the back seat. I settled in and fumbled a compact out of my purse. I flipped it open and saw my image shaking in the little mirror. But at least Elizabeth Christian Grafton was still there, staring back at me. I pulled out my lipstick and reapplied it—a reflex.

"We're just gonna mess that up again, baby," Mike warned. He dropped into the passenger seat. "Giddy up!"

Rick started the Cadillac and eased the big sedan down the sandy road and onto the desert highway. We were ten miles from the test site, as close as the public was permitted, but over fifty miles from Las Vegas. A military roadblock lay in the other direction.

I pulled a scarf from my purse and laid it over my hair, cinching it snugly under my chin for the ride back. Then I mustered the courage to glance behind us. To my relief, barely a trace of the horrible, towering cloud remained in the sky. For once I appreciated the relentless desert wind.

I'd been in Las Vegas just over a month. My life in Chicago—even the previous year, and the slow-motion demolition of my marriage—felt just as distant as my childhood in Nevada. Of course, Las Vegas was entirely different than the high desert where I grew up. That was ten excruciating hours north—not that I would ever bother.

I had managed to avoid the desert most of my adult life, with the exception of some miserable golf "vacations" with my husband Peter, in Scottsdale and Palm Springs. But I had come to appreciate the town. Las Vegas was a glaring, blinking, make-it-up-as-you-go-along place. The Mormons and the mob were doing wonders there. Together they were turning it from a bawdy company town for the Boulder Dam construction workers into a glittery playground for people from Los Angeles. They say that politics makes strange bedfellows, but money makes the strangest bedfellows of all. (As well I knew.)

"Remember, darling, I have my riding lesson at two," I called to Mike in the front seat. Rick glanced at him.

"Aw, I'm sorry, baby." Mike screwed his muscular body around to face me as best he could. "We're tied up this afternoon with business."

Naturally, I knew about their big "management meeting".

"Well, I can just take a cab," I huffed. Another glance from Rick. A control-your-woman-or-I-will glance. Poor Mike. I couldn't risk telling anyone where I was going that afternoon.

I'd met Mike Bartosz when I was modeling dresses at Marshall Field's in Chicago. After escaping Peter, I needed money. None of the customers knew that the raven-haired model languidly sauntering past them was thinking about ways she might get her husband to give her a divorce, and on bad days, how she might just kill him instead.

Plan A had been a disaster. I'd had an ostentatious affair with one of Peter's friends, designed to portray me as an unsuitable, whorish wife. I'd been optimistic, expecting he'd throw me out of the house—not throw me against a wall, break my nose, and lock me in a closet for three days. It was a terrible miscalculation on my part. Peter threatened his friend with death and lawsuits, but there was never, ever any talk of divorcing me.

My girlfriend, Rebecca, learned about my plight and took me in. Her husband, Edgar Concannon, was a prominent judge. Peter could not touch me while I was under his roof. I took the modeling job under my maiden name, Elizabeth Christian. It was risky, but I needed cash. Peter hadn't thought to confiscate my jewelry, but trying to pawn my distinctive jewels in Chicago was even riskier. I had a sumptuous collection, each piece commemorating a row we'd had.

Mike came into the dress salon at Marshall Field's with his then-girlfriend, a little poodle-haired gal with the sex appeal of a young Eleanor Roosevelt. She was the sort of girl who still referred to her tits in the singular, as in "my bosom."

I was a good head taller than her, and the cocktail dress she picked out was far better suited for my figure than hers. A week later, Mike returned alone to thank me. His bright, hungry eyes were full of sex and danger. I was in short supply of the former and not worried about the latter. After all, a violent husband is the most dangerous creature on earth. So I let Mike take me out to dinner.

He wasn't quite my type: blond crew cut, blue eyes, and a smile as uncomplicated as sunshine. The quintessential All-American Boy. But he was my type in other significant ways: he was big, with a powerful build—physically intimidating. The biography he offered was brief: he grew up in Detroit, joined the Army, and acquired the breathtaking scars on his torso "in Holland" during the last year of the war. I was still not sure exactly what he did for Mr. Ludovico, but having shot sporting clays with him once, I was certain his talent with a shotgun had something to do with it.

Plan B was a surprise, a windfall. Mike told me he had to go to Las Vegas on an extended business trip. Mr. Ludovico, who Mike refers to only as a "businessman", was hoping to establish a "branch office" there.

The timing was perfect: Mr. Ledyard, my attorney, had told me that a Nevada divorce was my best chance of escaping Peter's grip. Unlike other states, in Nevada, a spouse did not have to "give" you a divorce. After just six weeks' residency, I would have a hearing, provide one of nine reasons why I needed a divorce, and whether Peter agreed to it or not, I would be a free woman. I could make decisions about my life that, as a married woman, I could not make without my husband's approval. Mr. Ledyard referred me to a divorce lawyer in Las Vegas, Wilfred Dodd, who would represent me at the actual court hearing.

When I asked Mike if I could tag along on his business trip, he agreed, elated. The evening of our arrival in Las Vegas, we attended a big dinner with Mr. Ludovico and most of upper management, including Rick. (I should have known he was trouble; he was the only one without a date.) We sat next to "Mr. L" in an enormous circular booth in the Copa Room. It was like something out of a movie: gum-chewing girls spilling out of low-cut, sparkly dresses, loud laughter, booze, dancing.

That evening, I was drunk on my good fortune. I'd escaped Chicago and, like a gunslinger's moll, had holed up in the Southwest with a colorful gang of miscreants. I looked forward to whiling away the days in Las Vegas on my own, since Mike would be occupied with "business". I put on my swimsuit the next morning, and Mike put on his suit and tie. I lplanned to lie in the desert sun, drink icy cocktails, and make my third attempt at finishing Anna Karenina.

Mike escorted me down to the pool, gave me a kiss, and waved goodbye. I was officially installed in the Company's harem of sweethearts and mistresses. And that was where I had to stay.

Monday through Friday, we girls were kept in a little herd by the swimming pool, complete with a minder (usually Donnie) who sat nearby to watch over us. Conspicuous in his pale sport coat and dark sunglasses, he signed for our drinks and sandwiches, and ensured that we didn't talk to anyone outside our circle.

It was hard enough to talk to anyone *inside* the circle. Most of the Harem members were perfect ninnies. One of the girls, a platinum blonde, was reputed to be a starlet "taking a break" from Hollywood. She paged through Variety, hoping that someone would notice. The younger ones, like Ramona, favored the vulgar new bikini bathing suits and scrutinized movie magazines like Peter used to pore over his *Wall*

Street Journal. The "sophisticated" girls read detective novels. The older ones played gin rummy and bitched about their boyfriends' wives.

When the occasional inebriated guest approached, thinking he'd seen a marvelous mirage, a veritable promised land of pussy, Donnie would lead him away with the ease and authority of a good maître d'. (Peter, my much admired husband, a man without a criminal record, had once punched a man in the face after observing him ogling my behind at a cocktail party.)

My one escape was riding, as it had been since I was a girl. I'd found a stable near Red Rock Canyon, and Mike took me there each Wednesday for an hour-long lesson. The school horses were surprisingly good, and there was a covered arena to fend off the blazing sun. The lessons had been the only times on this trip that I truly felt like myself. I wasn't that crazy about the instructor, Philippe Kiehl, but he knew what he was doing.

"Just move the lesson to tomorrow, baby, and I can take you," Mike urged me.

I leaned forward and touched his big, jutting shoulder. "I'll end up waiting another week if I cancel at the last minute. Mr. Kiehl is very popular."

"I can't believe you let her take riding lessons from a fucking Kraut," Rick said. The trainer was an "Alsatian" expat. (No one called themselves German after the war.)

"Aw, he's fine. He's a faggot." Mike tried to light a cigarette.

I actually wasn't sure if Philippe Kiehl was a homosexual, but I was glad that Mike thought so. If there was one thing I couldn't deal with ever again, it was a jealous man.

During my first lesson, Mike stood by the fence, watching intently. Kiehl cut a trim figure in the center of the ring: formal and grave, he wore jodhpurs, a crisp white shirt, and spit-polished boots. Mike, who'd never watched a riding lesson before, found the nitpicking annoying. ("Why did he keep talking about your heels?" he complained as we drove away. "And what the hell was wrong with your hands?")

I'd always admired expertise, so Kiehl's exacting style suited me. Unfortunately, like the other Europeans we'd met at the resort, the man seemed to believe the American desert was a mystical wonderland. He knew his Emerson and Muir—all the rock-worshiping Transcendentalists. During lesson number four, he began banging on about the flooding of Boulder Canyon by Hoover dam, what a travesty it was. He even told me how "sacred" the canyon had been to the Indian tribe who lived there.

"And what is the name of that tribe?" I asked, as I circled the ring and he stood in its center, delicately flicking the bullwhip at the heels of my big gray mare.

"Navajo," he said with authority. "They are an ancient people."

"So were the Jews." It was a foolish thing to say to a German with a bullwhip, but he ignored me. Then I told him I had taken a tour of Boulder Dam and found it awe-inspiring. I told him I adored all the blinking lights of Las Vegas, just to watch his face harden. He's one of those tiresome romantics who thinks he has found his soul in the desert.

It was probably inevitable that, after a European war, people would turn their back on that battered continent and try to justify why they love this one so damned much. I could understand worshiping a land with silky beaches and warm water, trees laden with fruit, and colorful birds. But the American desert was proof that God did not exist, that planet earth was simply a random mathematical phenomenon. There was a damned good reason they blew up H-bombs here.

"I can take a cab to the stable," I told Mike at last. "It's okay, darling."

"Tell her," Rick said.

"Baby, that's not gonna work." Mike's sunny expression had dimmed. Time to be a good soldier.

I sighed and sank back in the seat. I needed a Plan B.

Rick opened up the Cadillac and let its big engine roar. Shadows cast by the rising sun stretched blade-thin across the dull gray high-way ahead of us. Ahead, listing on the sandy shoulder of the road, was a broken-down pickup truck. As we rocketed toward it, I saw two brown-skinned men peering under the hood.

I hardly expected Rick to stop and help, but instead, he crushed the accelerator. The ferocious grille of the Cadillac, with its twin chrome missiles, bore down on them. We blew sand and dust all over the men as we passed, and I saw them fling their arms up and shout in dismay.

"Goddamn Beaners," shouted Rick, "They should take that piece-a-shit truck and go back where they came from."

I couldn't help myself. "They *are* where they came from. This used to be Mexico," I called from the back seat. I could see the angle of Rick's ears shift as he scowled.

"Naw, baby, this is Indian Country!" Mike let out the war-whoop popularized in Westerns. He was right. It had been the homeland of the Southern Paiute, the Shoshone.

I turned around to watch the Mexicans vanishing into the desert. When I faced forward, I caught Rick's glance into the rearview mirror. I understood Rick. Just like my husband, he played a zero-sum game: for him to win, someone had to lose. I knew he was uncomfortable that Mike was keeping company with me. I was worldly, well-read, an obvious mismatch. But reassuring anyone here that I didn't care about "the business" would surely have backfired; I would have been the Lady Protesting Too Much. The truth was, I didn't give a single goddamn about any "business" other than my own, and Mike was my handsome and agreeable means to that end.

"Do not let her go wandering off on her own," he admonished Mike, as we entered Las Vegas.

"Aw, she's fine," Mike replied, as if Rick said this out of concern for my well-being. "Bettye's a big girl." He threw a grin over his shoulder.

"*Mr. L* doesn't want them running around," Rick said. Mike was quiet for a moment, but it wasn't the quiet of real acquiescence.

"Don't screw this up, Mikey." Rick's warning sounded almost big-brotherly.

"Not gonna screw it up," Mike said. I felt a pang of concern for him. Had my attitude rubbed off on him? He turned back toward me. "Babe, how about we go to the coffee shop at the Desert Inn? They got that Eggs Benedic' you like, with the holiday sauce."

"Sounds perfect."

"Well I'm gonna drop you lovebirds off, then. But Mike, we start at ten sharp. Don't be late."

Mike dropped a long arm over the seat to squeeze my knee. "You know how I like my eggs. Raw and dropped right in a double Bloody."

Happy anticipation flooded me. A Bloody Mary sounded wonderful. Two sounded even better. One thing I could say for Las Vegas, no one looked askance at a woman drinking cocktails with (or for) breakfast.

"Easy on the sauce this morning, Mikey," Rick warned. "You need to be sharp today."

"Aren't I always?" Mike replied, with the easy confidence of a favorite son. The long pale Cadillac sailed into the entrance of the Desert Inn Resort & Casino. It struck me then, that when it came to Mr. Ludovico, Rick might be playing Abel to Mike's Cain. I hoped not.

The warm promise of booze coaxed me back into my body. I stopped brooding about attending a dress rehearsal for the end of the world. The gruesome bomb test was beginning to feel like a lousy movie we'd all suffered through.

Under the port cochere, valets sprang for our doors. As Rick shooed away the youngster trying to open his, Mike helped me out. I didn't look back, but I heard the squeal of tires and the roar of the Cadillac's V-8 as Rick took off down Las Vegas Boulevard.

"Rick's got a lot on his mind," Mike said, like the peacemaker he was.

I turned to smile at him and saw the relief on his face at my absolution. It was a lot like horseback riding, keeping just enough tension on the reins, then easing it at exactly the right moment.

Mike grinned and stooped to peck my cheek. Then he slipped his arm around me and we walked into the hotel.

TWO

n the Desert Inn lobby, floor-to-ceiling windows revealed a glimmering pool in the courtyard. It was still early, and the lounge chairs were almost empty. I could see a mother tugging water wings onto her little girl's arms, wearing a determined expression. Nearby sat a large, balding man, reading a newspaper and ignoring them both with the untroubled laziness of a male lion. The coffee shop was working up to a breakfast fever-pitch. A clatter of plates issued from the kitchen, along with the welcoming aroma of coffee and cigarettes.

Mike let me slide into the booth and then sat down next to me.

"Oh darling," I said with a sigh, "Why can't I look at your handsome mug across the table?"

"Sorry, babe, you know the drill." Mike was very protective of me. I found it a little embarrassing sometimes, but it was touching, too.

I glanced around the restaurant, hoping I wasn't being too obvious about it, but Mike caught me.

"Anybody interesting?" he teased.

The very first time we'd eaten there, we'd been seated just two tables from the world's most famous newlyweds, Frank Sinatra and Ava Gardner, who were clearly in the midst of one of their infamous fights. The boys had been giddy with excitement; Mr. Sinatra was their patron saint.

I had often been told that I looked like her, and when we passed their table on the way out, Miss Gardner shot me a murderous glare.

She was known for her volcanic jealousy, and it thrilled me to receive her Seal of Disapproval.

"Not today," I shrugged. "Or at least, not this early."

"They're all looking at *you*, baby. You're the best-looking gal in this whole damn town."

I'd migrated to New York at age fifteen, thinking I could become an actress. After all, I'd been acting most of my life. (*Bettye Christian moves audiences to yawns in "The White Girl".*) But I learned, going to auditions, that I didn't possess the slightest passion for it. Watching girls crammed into dingy Midtown hallways, running lines, I soon realized that there was no thrill for me in acting—it was a survival skill.

Nor did I have the taste for the privations of an aspiring actress' life. A girl who was born rich and volunteered for such things could treat it as a lark. But one who was born into poverty had too much to lose in returning to such an existence. I did not want to live in an apartment with six other girls and eat bean soup. I wanted a lovely home, peace, security, and lots of money.

But the competition in New York for the role of Society Wife was intense. New York was chock-a-block with beautiful and clever girls. Like any sensible bird that did not like the prospects of its current habitat, I left. I flew west for the first time since I'd fled Nevada.

Chicago offered much better husband-hunting conditions than New York, where I was just another pigeon. In Chicago, I was an exotic bird. And thanks to Peter, I got my gilded cage.

"Bettye," Mike began, as the waitress placed our double Bloodies on the table.

"Cheers," I clinked my tumbler to his.

His expression clouded. "I don't want you to get in trouble, baby." He sounded apprehensive. "Don't go to that riding lesson, okay?"

"It's sweet of you to worry." I tilted my glass and took a long, luxurious sip of the salty cocktail.

"I'm serious, Bettye."

My alibi was causing a little too much anxiety for him. The men would be tied up for hours, and I needed Mike to be relaxed, not fretful. As much as I enjoyed antagonizing Rick, I didn't need to draw any more attention to myself.

"You're right. I'll cancel it." I pecked his cheek. There were other ways to account for my absence from the Harem that afternoon.

"You promise?"

"Yes, darling," I told him, blithe and smiling. "Besides, I need to get my hair done if we're going dancing tonight."

Mike, the eternal prom king, took me dancing almost every night. Lucky for us, the Desert Inn had convinced Louis Prima and his orchestra to take up residence there. It was a surreal existence, being under a sort of house arrest, but one with all the comforts. I felt like a deposed queen, kept in grand style in her desert palace.

"You always look beautiful," Mike told me with great sincerity. "And your hair looks fine."

"Nonsense." I took another greedy sip of my drink, a little buzz setting in. "I'm pretty sure the "H" in H-bomb stands for 'hair.' When we get back to the Sands, I'm making a beeline for the beauty salon."

"All right, baby." I heard the relief in his voice. "Thanks."

Poor Mike. He was so credulous, so easy to steer this way or that.

The waitress reappeared with our food. "Ready for another round?" Mike nodded yes, but I passed. After that shot of whisky at the test site, the cocktail had hit me hard.

"My girl tired?" Mike snapped open a napkin.

"I don't normally get up this early."

"Let's have a little siesta before we go out this evening." Under the table, he slid my skirt up and gave the suspender on my garter belt a playful tug. I laughed, and turned to kiss his salt-flecked lips.

. . .

When we parted after breakfast, I headed up to our room. I took off my dress and looked for the rip. To my relief, it turned out to be the hem; it would be easy to fix myself.

I took a quick bath to wash away the sour smell of fear and the clinging desert dust. Toweling myself dry, I contemplated my hairdo in the mirror. There would not be time to fix it, if I was to be on time for my appointment at the attorney's office. I brushed it out and applied some Spray Net.

I stuffed the dirt-smudged dress into a laundry bag as I remembered Rick's little taunt about sending the bill to the Department of Defense. The DOD was indeed footing the bill: it would also be underwriting my divorce settlement. Thanks to my husband's arms business, financed by the generous American taxpayer, I would soon be ensconced in a charming vine-covered villa in the hills above Arles. It wouldn't exactly settle my score with Uncle Sam, but it was a start.

I selected my most conservative suit, a jewel-necked navy-blue serge, and a white silk blouse, its high neckline finished in a soft bow. It was the first time I'd worn the outfit since the day that Mike and I left Chicago on the *City of Los Angeles*. It hadn't stayed on me for long that day. As soon as we checked into our private Pullman berth, he'd untied that chaste white bow like he was unwrapping a present. We'd spent much of the trip west lost in lazy lovemaking, as America slid past outside the window.

That had been just a month ago, but it felt like years. I loved Chicago. I missed the restaurants, the museums, and the shopping. I missed the city's venerable old barmen, who would never be caught dead mixing a Bull Shot or a Pink Squirrel, the "latest" cocktails in Las Vegas. I even missed the Chicago weather, which had been the perfect excuse to indulge my passion for furs. (My collection would have made Madame Karenina weep with envy.) But this was war, and I had surrendered the city to Peter.

I'd met my future husband in a fashionable restaurant on the

North Shore when I was twenty-one. I was dining with another fellow when a handsome, impeccably dressed man stopped at our table, pretending to recognize me. My date endured the brief exchange with a stiff smile, but I saw in his eyes the unmistakable, primal fear of the inferior ape.

When the hat-check girl handed me my mink and I slipped my gloves from the pocket to put them on, I discovered a strange calling card tucked inside one of them. I waited until I was alone in my cab to examine the card. Printed on heavy ivory stock, its engraved letters read:

Peter H. Grafton, Founder and President
Grafton Industries

It was October 1942, the war was raging, and the Grafton Industries factories were booming, churning out aircraft parts. I was surprised that Mr. Grafton was so young, perhaps just in his early forties.

Peter and I were a splendid match. We were equally gifted liars, equally ambitious social climbers, both preoccupied with money and appearance. Everywhere we went in Chicago, people treated him like a hero, a patriot. But my husband was a war profiteer, one of the biggest and one of the worst.

There was a marvelous picture of him and Eisenhower in LIFE magazine, taken in early 1945. They were shaking hands, but you could see in that photo just how much the General despised him, as he smiled through gritted teeth. Peter appeared oblivious, but he was not—he just didn't give a damn. My husband was getting ready to sink his teeth into Korea, whether Ike liked it or not.

Had I a calling card to exchange on the night we met, mine would have read,

Elizabeth "Bettye" Christian
Gold Digger

I came by my calling honestly. In the mining town where I was conceived, people literally dug for gold. Virginia City, Nevada had once been the richest city in the world, with an opera house, elegant hotels, and lavish bordellos. Men made spectacular fortunes over the course of a decade, drained the earth of its staggering wealth, and left. But by the 1920s, when I was born, Virginia City was a pile of ramshackle high-desert nothing populated by a handful of half-mad prospectors and the operators of played-out gold and silver mines. My father (rather, the man who fathered me) was one of the latter.

Before I was born, my mother had worked in Virginia City as a servant. There were few career options for an Indian woman other than that. Mama was like a dry leaf in the Nevada wind, blown from place to place, buffeted by the whims of employers. One of my earliest memories was watching the children of one of these families, including a boy my age, get onto a school bus in the morning while we were doing the washing. I desperately wanted to attend school. Those careless children left their books (books!) lying everywhere, and whenever the family left, I devoured everything, especially the fairy tales. That was how I learned the whole marry-a-prince routine.

I'm sure when Mama secured employment in the Cleary household, she had thought it a stroke of extraordinary good fortune. Daniel Cleary had arrived from Boston after the turn of the century, the proud new owner of a dwindling silver mine. He installed his wife and three daughters in a tall, grim Edwardian house near the top of a windswept hill.

My father's calling card could have read:

Daniel B. Cleary
Metallurgist & Rapist

Perhaps that's harsh. Mr. Cleary must have liked Mama. She was young, beautiful, much too bright to be a servant, and a voracious read-er. She had lovely, expressive hands. He probably believed that a woman in such a low position would accept his attentions with gratitude.

What began as a romantic mystery in my childish imagination eventually revealed itself to be a tired cliché. By the time I was a teenager, I was well-versed in the facts of life: I had learned from experience that beautiful girls often attracted the wrong sort of attention. And I had learned from my teachers that Indian women were considered morally and intellectually inferior.

My mother might have served as a distraction from Mr. Cleary's troubles, an amusement, but she became pregnant with me. The harlot who had seduced poor Daniel Cleary was put out of the house. I believe Mama tried to return to the Pyramid Lake reservation, but things must not have gone well there for her, either. Perhaps word had spread that she was pregnant with a White man's baby. These were things that she never shared with me.

According to my birth certificate, I came into the world on April 17, 1919, at St. Mary's Hospital in Virginia City. I'd always suspected that Mama returned to the town hoping to convince Daniel Cleary to accept me as his daughter.

He died not long after I was born, "of drink", according to my mother. When I was five, she ventured back up to Virginia City to apply for a job as a chambermaid at a shabby hotel. She had no choice but to bring me along. I found the town riveting—it looked like a child had built it. Terraced streets etched its thrilling, steep hills and ornate, improbable houses clung to the side of a mountain. As we hurried along the sagging boardwalk of the main street, I tugged at Mama's hand, trying to peek into the open doors of the saloons, which were already noisy by noon. (The gold and silver may have stopped flowing in Virginia City, but the liquor never did.)

Mama rarely got angry with me, but that stirred her up. "Those places were the death of your father!" she declared, in a tone that suggested I might be next. I added that to the scant collection of facts she'd shared about him: his name, his occupation, and the bewildering idea that he had "another" family. (My avid study of fairy tales had not prepared me for concepts like bigamy and alcoholism.)

Before we left Virginia City, she took me to the cemetery and showed me his grave, which sat high on a weedy, windswept hill. The shiny granite of the headstone appeared newer than anything else around it, but it was quite modest. Just uphill loomed an old grave surrounded by an elaborate iron fence, and crowned by a tall, beautiful marble angel. I asked Mama why my father's grave didn't have an angel, too. She did not answer.

Mama attempted to instill me with pride for my Paiute family, though we seldom saw any relatives. She maintained that my great-great-aunt was Sarah Winnemucca, a famous tribal leader. Sarah had been a national celebrity, an Army Scout and interpreter whose exploits eclipsed those of Pocahontas or Sacagawea. She was an expert horsewoman, a lecturer, and an author.

Even as a little girl, I'd been doubtful about these tales. If we came from such august lineage, why didn't we have a proper home? Why were we so desperately poor? Why did Whites expect us to step off the sidewalk when they approached? And why did women eye me with such visible consternation, while men smirked at my mother?

In time I understood. Our lives clung to a slender thread suspended between two worlds, White and Indian. I was a half-breed child, a tremendous liability. But I could pass—and I had, since the day I ran away from the Indian boarding school.

Still, when I saw Indians in Las Vegas, it made me a little nervous. It seemed like Boulder Dam had floated them up out of their lost, hidden canyons and deposited them on the city's bright new boulevards. The "lucky" ones were chambermaids and gas station attendants. It had been obvious to me even as a girl that there were no happy endings to the stories of Indians. Nothing that I'd seen in Las Vegas almost three decades later suggested otherwise.

I eventually learned that great-great Aunt Sarah, despite her fame, wasn't an exception to that rule, even after she became an international performer. White westerners dubbed her "The Paiute Princess", a nickname that was pure ridicule. Her lectures, shows, and book brought attention to the plight of her tribe, but it proved an exercise in futility.

Was there a family resemblance? Sarah's love life was as big a mess as mine was, though we had different specialties. She fell for charlatans who stole her money and broke her heart. I married a wealthy sonofabitch whom I never loved. Sarah had a fierce temper too, though she was not a manipulator like me—she was a bare-knuckle brawler. Even if I'd inherited her talent for combat, it would not have protected me from Peter Grafton.

Then there was the fact that even after Aunt Sarah became famous, people accused the diehard romantic of being a prostitute. Unlike her, I had indeed traded sex for money. And I was not finished with the transaction: for services rendered, I intended to relieve my husband of a proper slice of his fortune.

Sarah may have had her heart broken repeatedly by men, but mine was shatter-proof, so Peter found other things to break. I had a nose job after the worst of the rows, when he found out about the affair with his friend. The plastic surgeon had to create a new nose from "ground beef" (his words).

"Hedy Lamarr," I told him. I thought that it turned out even better than the actress's. I was still not quite used to it. My nose, my mother's nose, was gone. In the morning, when I first woke up and drowsily confronted the 1952 Bettye Grafton in the mirror, she could still startle me. I was not sure that I even liked her, though I still had the same deep brown, hooded eyes and full, symmetrical lips. My heavy curtain of hair was black and shiny as jet beads. And my "suntan" was the envy of the girls around the pool.

Now I blended in with the assorted European rejects who'd found their way to Las Vegas.

"Northern Italy," I would reply, whenever someone asked where 'my people' were from. "Bologna." *Baloney.*

Elizabeth Christian had become a woman that her mother would never have recognized—but most of that had happened long before my Indian nose was replaced by a movie star's.

This afternoon's meeting with my Nevada attorney called for frosty elegance. I selected a pair of understated gray pearl earrings (understated only if you didn't know that they were large, gem-quality Tahitian pearls). Still exasperated by my H-bombed hair, I fetched a white straw fedora from a hatbox in the closet. Slipping the room key into my purse, I stepped out of my room and headed for the rear stairway. The taxi rank was close to that exit, and I headed toward the last cab of six that sat idling at the curb.

"Downtown, please," I said, as I opened the door.

"Uh, lady—" The cabbie tried to wave me toward the front of the line, but when our eyes met he understood that I was getting into his taxi deliberately. I handed him the address I'd written on a piece of hotel stationery.

I fished out my sunglasses and settled back into the seat. Later that afternoon, after I finished my legal business, I'd return to the Sands, slip on my favorite poppy-red maillot and settle in on a chaise lounge with a drink, close my eyes, and return to one of my favorite fantasies: a balmy afternoon sitting on my flagstone terrace above Arles, watching the sea turn into an aquamarine mirror.

After I tuned out chatter of the Harem—it required several minutes—I would imagine the soughing of wind in the stone pines on that hill, the sun shining on the Mediterranean, a lavender-scented breeze caressing my skin, teasing the tendrils of vines into a gentle dance, and stirring the pages of my novel.

The thought of such exquisite solitude filled my heart with an upwelling of joy. Very soon I would once again belong to a tribe of one.

THREE

The law office was on the second floor of a new, two-story brick building that rose like a carbuncle from a fresh asphalt parking lot. A pretty young receptionist, scarcely older than a bobby-soxer, greeted me.

"Mrs. Grafton," she chirped, "Mr. Dodd will be with you shortly. Can I get you anything? Coffee?"

"No thank you." I settled into a chair of brown leather so new it still smelled faintly like the cow it had previously upholstered.

As I cooled my heels, my thoughts turned to the next evening. When I discovered that Mike had booked a big table in front of the stage at the Copa Room for my "party" I nearly died. Under the best of circumstances, I never wanted a fuss about my birthday. Commemorating the worst day of my life with a party at the Copa Room sounded hellish.

But Mike's bright face fell so hard when I expressed my dismay, I felt like I'd kicked a puppy. After watching him sulk for a few minutes, I had to relent.

"No candles," I warned him. "And no singing."

"Whatever you want, doll," he'd assured me, the grin re-emerging like sun from behind clouds. I let him believe that this was just my female vanity getting the best of me, mortified at the prospect of turning 31 in front of witnesses.

The truth was far too complicated for our relationship. Trying to explain why I did not celebrate my birthday would be like a swan-dive into the kiddie pool. My birthday was the anniversary of the day I lost my mother, and the day that she lost me.

...

My sixth birthday fell on a bright April morning in 1924. The big cottonwood trees that would shade Carson City from the summer heat were unfurling fresh, yellow-green leaves. Exhausted daffodils leaned over neat lawns, and the white petals of fruit blossoms swirled through the neighborhood streets like snowflakes had only a month before.

Mama and I (we were partners) had just found a job, a very good job, with a doctor's family on Nevada Street. The doctor's home on the prosperous West Side was the largest house I'd ever been inside. It contained both the offices where he saw patients and the family living quarters. I remember the mansard roof, which I thought was the height of elegance, and probably had been, back in the late 1800s. My mother's job came with a tiny wage, plus room and board for us both.

The "room" was the drafty utility porch which held a washing machine as well as the sagging cot we shared. "Board" was leftovers and kitchen scraps, and come summer, the doctor's wife explained, we could glean vegetables and fruit from the garden—anything not fit for the family's table was ours to eat. We had the privilege of cooking our meals over an oil-drum fire in the backyard. But it was not a barn, or a shack, and rodents didn't scamper over us at night. It seemed like a palace to me.

I loved to help Mama with her work. Since I could walk, I'd been eager to be useful. I swept, I scrubbed; I pulled weeds and watered. I could shell beans and peas nearly as fast as her.

The morning of my birthday, Mama decided to put me in charge of the doctor's flock of speckled chickens. I was to feed them and secure them in the henhouse at night. (Carson City lay at the foot of the Sierra, so foxes, coyotes and weasels prowled the neighborhoods.) Most exciting to me about my new job was the honor of gathering and cleaning the eggs in the pre-dawn gloom, then placing them in the family's icebox before they were awake, like the Easter Bunny. I would do this while my mother got the kitchen fire started. Mama urged me to keep my presence light and unobtrusive—to speak softly, and not enter a room without checking first to see if the family was present. She was teaching me the way of the servant, the way of invisibility.

The doctor and his wife on Nevada Street were some of the nicest Whites that I'd met so far, but Mama warned me that we could not get too comfortable. The lady of the house, she told me, could not entirely be relied upon. She was a woman of 'enthusiasms'. Enthusiasms, explained Mama, could fly away like birds at any moment. One day our employer might be sweet as pie, and the next, she could pitch us out onto the street.

But that spring morning, Mama was in great spirits. She had just been paid, and decided that we would mark my birthday with a visit to the dry goods store for six new buttons, which she would sew onto my tired old calico dress. She held my hand as we made our way into the fabric department of the general store on Carson Street. The notions aisle was a wonderland to me: the rainbow spools of braids and trims, the shiny fasteners and the glorious boxes of buttons.

A young clerk stocking shelves overheard me talking excitedly about my birthday.

"Here!" she said with a smile, and sneaked me a remnant of blue silk ribbon from the end of a spool. "It's a present from me. Let's put it in your hair."

She drew me toward her, turned me to face a large mirror, and crouching to my level, showed me how to tie it. I watched her deft hands, mesmerized.

"It's the same blue as the Nevada flag," she told me. "Happy Birthday!" She stepped behind me and let me admire myself. I have never forgotten how that smooth, clean, shining ribbon looked in my thick black hair. I smiled proudly at Mama. My obsession with fashion began at that very moment.

An older clerk floated quietly into the aisle and shot us all a scathing look. The young woman vanished. I turned to see my mother, standing still as a doe behind me, holding the six silver buttons we'd selected.

"We'll take these," she told the woman, holding them out. Mama grasped my hand and I walked by her side, beaming and preening, up to the cash register. I was a poor student of invisibility. Attention was attention, and I was a child. After my triumph in the notions aisle, I decided to take matters into my own hands.

"It's my birthday," I informed the pinched-looking man behind the counter, as my mother fumbled out a few coins for the buttons, some needles, and a spool of sturdy buttonhole-twist thread.

"Is that so?" he asked, and stopped what he was doing to scrutinize me. "How old are you, my dear?"

Mama slipped her hand to my head.

"She's five," she replied, just as I declared, "I'm six!"

The man laughed, and so did Mama, but it was a tight, strange laugh.

"She's just learning her numbers," Mama said.

"I can count!" I declared, irate. "Mama, I was five but now I'm six."

"Awful tall for a five-year-old," the man observed, and handed me a piece of horehound candy.

"Thank you," I said. He busied himself behind the counter. Mama grabbed her purchases and swept me out of the store.

"Don't tell anyone else that it's your birthday!" she warned me once we were outside. But the damage was done. The disapproving clerk from the notions department had followed us out of the store.

"Excuse me!" she called after my mother in the loud, officious manner I had come to associate with White speech. Mama grabbed my hand and began to walk quickly away. I stumbled, trying to keep up. Something was wrong. I'd seen my mother alarmed before, even afraid, but there was a terrifying expression on her face now. Her hand nearly crushed mine.

"Mama!" I whimpered. "That hurts!"

"Hurry!" she said, pulling me along.

We turned the corner and headed west, toward the doctor's house. We had been walking less than ten minutes when a drab sedan with official-looking markings on it pulled quickly to the curb ahead of us. It wasn't a police car, I knew, but it seemed intimidating. A couple of large White men got out.

"Good morning!" called one in a friendly tone, stepping onto the sidewalk.

My mother stopped abruptly and tried to push me behind her.

"Can you explain why this child isn't in school?" asked the other man. He didn't sound genial at all. I felt Mama's body trembling.

"She's not feeling well."

"What's your name?" asked the second man. A gust of wind flipped his necktie up over his face, and he yanked it back down, doing his best to maintain his expression of authority. Mama didn't speak.

"You'll both need to come with us." The second man opened the rear door of the sedan. "Please get in the car."

The men took us to the Stewart Indian Boarding School, just south of Carson City. I sat silently in the office as Mama, now composed and formal, told a stern-looking woman my name, that I was six years old (she had finally remembered?) and that I knew how to read and write.

The woman behind the desk examined me. I was familiar with that look, but for the first time, it came with words.

"This child is not full-blooded Indian," the woman observed. On the ranches where Mama and I had worked, farmers discussed their horses, sheep, and goats in a similar manner. My mother turned to look at me, as if hearing this for the first time.

"Half-White," said my mother, in her soft, husky voice.

I looked down at my legs wondering, which half? They were light brown, like the rest of me.

"Her brother is a student here," my mother added. This was news to me. I stared at Mama in amazement. She'd told me that I had a brother, but he was no more real to me than a character in a fairytale. So he was here? This close to us, all this time?

The woman sat up straighter and lay her thin hand atop the blotter on her desk. "Is that so? What is his name?"

"Luke Moore."

The woman made a sour face and coughed over her shoulder. "He's in detention right now," she told my mother.

"As opposed to what?" Mama replied. At this, the woman scowled at her.

"Don't be smart with me. He's a troublemaker!" she snapped. I had heard people speak rudely to my mother many times, but this woman seemed particularly angry.

So did Mama. "What sort of trouble has he made?" Her voice was low and strange.

"He defies his teachers and he gets into fistfights," the woman shot back, with a glance toward me, and regained her composure. "But the girls and boys here at the Stewart School are not permitted to fraternize, and we separate the younger children from the older ones, so his bad influence won't be a problem." She looked at me again. "And since her father is White, I expect the girl will be better behaved."

"My father is Mr. Daniel Cleary," I told her. "Mama says he's in heaven."

"Let's hope so." Mrs. Walters said. I was puzzled by her words.

"Bettye is a good girl," my mother said. "She reads the Bible and goes to church."

The woman glanced at me. "You do?"

For some reason I thought it might be a good idea to genuflect, so I did. The woman peered at me as if I were a curious creature in a zoo.

"My name is Mrs. Walters," the woman said to us, with a wan smile. "It's unfortunate that you took so long to bring Elizabeth here."

"It's her birthday today. We are right on time," Mama replied defiantly. I had never heard her address a White person this way. It thrilled and unsettled me. "And my daughter likes to be called Bettye. Spelled with an 'e' on the end."

Mrs. Walters raised an over-plucked eyebrow. (I was transfixed by her stark, unflattering makeup.) "Everyone knows that's not how you spell 'Betty'. But it doesn't matter anyhow. At the Stewart School, children go by their full, Christian names. You'll answer to Elizabeth from now on."

"That's what Mama calls me when she's mad," I said, annoyed.

"Good." Mrs. Walters took a piece of onion skin paper off her desk and handed it to me. I remember the feel of the paper between my fingers, its delicate and mysterious texture.

"Read it out loud," she commanded, thinking she was calling Mama's bluff about my literacy.

Nervously, I took the typewritten sheet. I glanced at Mama and she nodded.

"Memo," I attempted, but pronounced it "mee-mo." This strange word had not appeared in my Bible or the children's books I'd read. Was it a Numu word?

Mrs. Walters cocked her head, surprised. "Go on."

"It has come…to my…ay…uh?…ten…TI…on…" I stammered, sounding out the syllables the way my mother had shown me.

"That's fine." Mrs. Walters waved her hand in the air to take back the piece of paper. She did not seem pleased at my demonstration.

"Did you make this?" I asked her in wonderment, reluctant to surrender the paper.

"I typed it." She gestured toward a typewriter atop a small metal table next to her desk. "Have you never seen a typewriter before, child?"

"Of course she has," Mama said.

I had seen one of the little machines in the doctor's house. But I had no idea that people could make pages with it that looked like they were from a book. I glanced at Mama. If I went to this school, maybe I would learn to make book-pages too.

"Where on earth did she learn to read?" asked Mrs. Walters.

"I taught her," said Mama.

"Remarkable," murmured Mrs. Walters, as if a cat had taught a chicken to read.

Clearly, she did not know that literacy was a cherished tradition in Mama's branch of the Paiute tribe—it had been great-great-Aunt Sarah's cause. Mama adored the Bible and read it every evening to me. Listening to her read, I'd soaked up the cadence and richness of the words—though I must admit that few of its lessons stuck. (Jesus seemed like a pantywaist to me. I preferred the Old Testament. *An eye for an eye.*)

"Her great-great aunt was Sarah Winnemucca," Mama told Mrs. Walters.

"And my great-great-grandfather was George Washington." Mrs. Walters chuckled. "If I had a nickel for every Indian who told me that..."

I looked at Mama, who suddenly seemed small and defeated.

"Shall we?" asked Mrs. Walters brightly, as if we knew what was next.

It turned out that Mama did. She knelt and clutched me to her. She kissed my cheek, wetting my skin with her tears. "Be good, Bettye," she whispered. "Learn as much as you can."

. . .

When Mrs. Walters escorted me from her office, I caught a glimpse of Mama lingering by the gates of the Stewart School. She waved at me, then turned and headed up the dusty road that led back toward Carson City, her head down.

"Why don't those men give her a ride?" I asked, upset that Mama would have to walk all the way back to town by herself.

Mrs. Walters ignored my question. "First we will get you deloused." She clamped a hand on my shoulder and marched me briskly toward the girls' dormitory. "Indians have lice, and it's important to be clean. Personal hygiene is the first thing that you'll learn here at Stewart."

I had never heard this strange word, *lice*. Or had she said *lies*?

As we cut through the quadrangle between the stone buildings, we came upon a little troop of girl students, walking in two orderly lines behind an adult. They wore uniforms, their dark hair in identical, jaw-length bowl haircuts. As we passed, I saw many pairs of brown eyes cut toward the bright blue ribbon in my long black hair. A bad feeling overcame me.

An hour later, my birthday gift and half my hair lay in the bottom of a garbage can.

FOUR

LAS VEGAS, NEVADA
1952

"Scotch?" offered Wilfred M. Dodd, Attorney at Law, as I took my seat. "I'm sorry about the wait."

I heard ice cubes clink into a tumbler. Despite his ossified name, this fellow was not much older than me and boyishly handsome, with wavy auburn hair and a spatter of freckles that suggested plenty of time on the new Las Vegas golf course.

"Thank you, Mr. Dodd," I replied, "But I'd rather keep my head clear."

"You can call me Will." He threw me what was supposed to be a disarming grin. I could feel him sizing me up, though he was doing an excellent job of pretending not to.

"I'll just stick with Mr. Dodd," I said pointedly.

"Suit yourself." He took a seat at a large mahogany desk, setting down his scotch. The office had the usual trappings of the legal profession. Wood-paneled walls (as if any building in Las Vegas was that old or venerable) displayed certificates and degrees. I noticed an undergraduate degree hanging behind his desk.

He followed my gaze. "University of Nevada," he said, as if I couldn't read it for myself. He pointed to another wall, and a photograph of him in cap and gown in front of a vine-covered brick building. "Looks just like the University of Virginia—built after the same design, by Thomas Jefferson. Hard to believe the school was founded in the 1870s. Barely ten years after the Pyramid Lake War."

I glanced up sharply.

"A big Indian war," he clarified, interpreting my expression as simple ignorance.

"The end of the Paiutes," I said.

He smiled, surprised. "Are you from Nevada?"

"No. Chicago." I placed an unlit Marlboro between my lips and Dodd leaped to his feet, as I expected he would. He walked around the big desk to light it.

"You know your Nevada history, then."

"I certainly do," I said, inhaling. Time to change the subject, before I lost my cool. "How long have you been practicing law, Mr. Dodd?"

"Almost fifteen years." He returned to his chair. "And having grown up in Nevada, family law is my calling."

"Meaning…you're a divorce attorney."

"In the popular parlance, yes." Mr. Dodd settled back in his seat. "So. While Mr. Ledyard was preparing the property settlement, I did some research on your husband. Mr. Grafton is a very prominent businessman."

"Well, thank goodness I found you. I had no idea," I snapped.

He chuckled at my sarcasm, and his blue eyes went a bit flinty and cold. That was better. He understood now that he would not need to handle Mrs. Grafton with kid gloves. And that I wasn't the sort of divorcee-to-be who would collapse in his arms requiring 'comfort'.

"I'm sure he'd prefer to avoid any negative publicity," he intoned.

"Then you obviously didn't do very much research. All Peter cares about is winning."

Dodd took a sip of his scotch and smiled. "Well, in Nevada, Mr.

Grafton has already lost." Not quite smug, but close.

"That's the divorce bit." I waved my hand. "As you're aware, I need to relieve him of a lot of money, as well."

"Certainly, Mrs. Grafton. We're certainly going to do all we can to ensure that you enjoy the lifestyle to which you are accustomed." He made a note on the yellow pad in front of him. "Now. Do you plan to remarry following your divorce?"

"I try to learn from my mistakes, not repeat them."

Dodd smirked. "Many of my clients come to Nevada with…"

"A 'spare'. Yes, I've heard the term."

"I was going to say, 'their intended.'" We briefly shared a cynical smile.

"I have no intention of intending."

"I see that." Mr. Dodd jotted something else on the legal pad. He regarded me for a moment. "Your husband is the sole shareholder in Grafton Industries?"

"That's correct."

"Mr. Ledyard sent me the list of your community property. The homes, the cars, the sailboat, etcetera. While I know it is your intention to reside in Nevada—" at this, he stopped and grinned—"Is there a chance you'll wish to reside in one of these homes as well?"

"Mr. Dodd, I just want cash. I'll be leaving the country."

"That makes things simple. In Nevada, the court expects to see your property settlement at the divorce hearing. It's entered as an Exhibit. So we'll need to have all that concluded shortly."

"That's for Mr. Ledyard to work out."

"So things are progressing well?"

"I haven't heard otherwise," I told him, "But I'm sure he's earning his fee."

"Well then. As to the grounds for your divorce." Dodd leaned back in his chair expectantly.

"There's mental cruelty, abuse, humiliation, and regular physical violence," I said. "Take your pick."

"How violent?"

"Broken nose. Broken wrist, cracked ribs. And cuts, bruises, that sort of thing. He slapped me around quite a bit." I slid the envelope out of my purse and pushed it across the desk.

Dodd examined the color snapshots Rebecca had taken five days after Peter threw me against the wall and punched me repeatedly in the face. Me with two black eyes, cuts on my cheeks, nose mashed to a pulp, cast on my wrist, arm in a sling.

He winced, sliding the photos back into the envelope. "Was there a police report?"

"No."

"Well, these are more than adequate. It's Nevada after all." His smile ebbed. "Does Mr. Grafton know that you're here?"

"I don't think so."

"When did you arrive?"

"About four weeks ago."

"Oh." Dodd paused, his pen poised over the legal pad. "I'm surprised that we didn't meet sooner."

"I've been busy."

"Who's your witness? The person who will vouch for your residency?"

"I've been at the Sands the whole time." I watched him write this down.

"You made arrangements with a hotel employee?"

A lousy feeling started up in the pit of my stomach. "N-no," I stammered. I thought of Mike. There was no way he could get anywhere near a courtroom. The lousy feeling intensified.

"Mrs. Grafton, can you present a witness who can attest, under oath, that they've seen you at least once every 24 hours for six weeks? Didn't Mr. Ledyard explain that?"

I sat there blinking like an idiot. "He did but—" I tried to remember our conversations on the topic. "I just assumed the hotel manager would…"

"Mrs. Grafton, it doesn't appear that you've actually started the clock on your Nevada residency."

How could I have been so stupid? I stubbed out my cigarette in his crystal ashtray.

"Here's what we'll do." Dodd slid a piece of paper across the desk. "Let's get all your pertinent information. My secretary will prepare the paperwork for our engagement. You'll need to secure your witness. They will have to swear under penalty of perjury—

"I know what 'oath' means."

"And we will need your retainer today," he said.

"Mr. Ledyard told me that your fee was five hundred dollars."

"Two hundred today will be fine."

"What will the damages be?" I asked. "I mean, for the whole thing?"

"Well, Mr. Ledyard will have to discuss that with you. That's his purview. It depends on how hard Mr. Grafton fights you over the settlement. I expect the divorce will probably cost about three to five thousand when the dust settles. Though we've seen some that run over ten thousand."

I removed an envelope from my purse and counted out ten twenty-dollar bills. Without touching the cash, Dodd pushed his intercom button.

"Winnie, can you receive Mrs. Grafton's retainer?"

The bobby-soxer entered his office. She collected the bills and wrote out a receipt in a little book. She handed me an engagement letter to sign. Dutifully, I picked up a pen and signed it. I was still furious at myself, disgusted with all the time I'd wasted.

"Could you please call me a cab?" I asked, as we finished the formalities.

"Certainly, Mrs. Grafton."

"It's been a pleasure." Dodd stood up. I stood too, sorry that I was wearing high heels. My legs were wobbly as a newborn foal's. As we shook hands, I realized that my palm was clammy.

I made my way back down the stairs. Six more weeks bored out of my mind by that goddamn swimming pool? The thought filled me with a dull dread. Well, what the hell did I expect? It was my birthday. A black-letter day.

I stepped out of the front door into the glare of the afternoon sun, spotting a patch of shade next to the building where I could await the cab. I took just one step in that direction before I noticed the ivory Cadillac idling across the parking lot, and Rick Russo standing next to it.

FIVE

"Hello, Rick." I walked toward the car, struggling to keep my voice low and casual. Why on earth did you follow me?"

"Hello, Bettye." He opened the passenger door like a valet from hell. "Get in the fucking car."

It was almost a relief to hear him curse. I preferred it to the coiled snake.

"I'm getting a divorce." I tried to sound breezy as I slid into the passenger seat.

"Sure you are." Rick slammed the door and walked to the driver's side. He knew I wouldn't dare try to make a break for it. He got in, put the Cadillac in gear, and headed out of the attorney's parking lot.

"I thought you had a big management meeting."

"We didn't have a quorum." Rick aimed the car south. "What the hell were you doing at that attorney's office?"

"Didn't you hear me?" I shot back. "I'm retaining Mr. Dodd to represent me in my divorce."

"Anything else?"

"Like what?" The lousy feeling that had begun in Dodd's office abruptly got stronger.

"Oh, I don't know."

"For Pete's sake, Rick. What the hell do you think I was doing in there?"

"I don't know, Bettye." I saw an unnerving little flare of his nostrils, "That firm represents our competition. So you tell me." He stomped down on the accelerator.

"I don't know anything about that. Mr. Dodd is a goddamn divorce lawyer." I clamped my hand to the top of my hat to keep it from blowing off.

"Maybe he is," Rick shouted, as we rocketed toward Las Vegas Boulevard. "But he's not the only attorney in that office."

Akers, Dodd, & McCroskey, Attorneys at Law. Which one of them represented Mr. Ludovico's enemies?

"I'm only in this godforsaken state to get a divorce!"

"What do you suppose Mr. Grafton would say about that?"

"As if I give a damn. Mr. Grafton can go to hell."

"He probably will." Rick smiled for the first time that I could remember. "But he's stopping here first."

I turned to stare at him. "Who's stopping here?"

"Your poor, abandoned, heartbroken husband."

"You didn't." A gust of fear and rage shook my body.

"He arrives tomorrow morning on Pan Am." Rick shifted hard and pushed the accelerator down again. "For your joyful reunion." The Cadillac roared into third gear. My hair whirled around my head, whipping my cheeks.

I desperately tried to compose myself. "I have to give you credit, Rick, it's a very creative way to get rid of me," I shouted, hoping the telltale waver in my voice wasn't noticeable over the rush of air.

"Profitable, too," Rick yelled.

"He's paying you?"

"Five large."

"For heaven's sake, I'll pay you seven hundred dollars, Rick, and let's be done with—"

"Five...*thousand*," Rick cut me off. "Got that in your pocketbook, Bettye?"

Jesus. That was a lot of money.

"He'd just outbid you anyhow," Rick said.

He was right. I could not buy my way out of this mess. As we neared the El Rancho, the town's original "resort", Rick stopped for some pedestrians.

"He's going to kill me, you know," I said quietly, now that I didn't have to shout.

"If my wife ran off to Vegas and was screwing another fella, I'd kill her too." Rick's tone was reasonable. He watched the couple cross the boulevard. The man waved his thanks and Rick nodded politely.

"What about your friend Mike?" I demanded.

"Mikey is a big boy," said Rick. "He understands how the world works." He glanced my way. I opened my mouth to protest, but he cut me off. "You're not gonna try to tell me that was true love."

He had me. We all understood how the world worked. We rode the rest of the way to the Sands in silence.

When we arrived, Rick eased the Caddy under the porte cochere and braked to a halt in front of the valet. "We've moved you to the honeymoon suite," he told me.

"I had no idea you were so witty, Rick."

The earnest young valets opened the doors of the Cadillac with a flourish. I stepped out, trying to display my usual hauteur, but panic gnawed away at my composure.

"Welcome back, Mr. Russo," called the valet.

Rick hooked his arm into mine and propelled me into the lobby. "You need to stay put—no monkey business," he continued quietly.

"Whatever you say, Rick." I attempted to sound casually exasperated. "At least you won't be around when I run off the next time."

Rick ignored me. "Until your hubby arrives, Benny will be outside your suite. You know, if you need anything."

They would be guarding the door. I was a prisoner.

He steered me into the elevator and pushed the button for the second floor. As soon as the door slid closed, Rick seized my wrist.

I shrank back.

"For God's sake!" I cried.

"I know you pack." He grabbed my handbag. Yanking it open, he took out the little Colt and removed the bullets, then tossed the gun back in. When he handed my purse to me, I saw the brown envelope. It gave me an idea.

"Take a look at these." I shoved it into Rick's hands. "This is what that bastard did to me. This is why I can't go back."

He withdrew the pictures, shuffled through them, and gave a low whistle. "Mr. Grafton does nice work."

"Go to hell!" I snatched the photos back. He gave me a faint, mocking smile. The elevator door opened, and once again he took my arm. At least I knew that he wouldn't lay a hand on me if Peter was on his way.

We reached the double doors of the Honeymoon Suite. "I have an appointment at the beauty parlor this afternoon," I said as coolly as I could, as I entered the room.

"I'm sure he loves you just the way you are."

I turned, an idea occurring to me. "Well, I need to have the beautician come here to the suite. I can't have Peter see me like this."

If Rick were the sort of man who rolled his eyes, he would have. "Jesus, just shut up." He yawned and indicated the suite's low-slung sofa. "Siddown, would you?"

After a couple of minutes, Benny knocked at the door and Rick admitted him. The two conferred for a moment. Then Rick left.

"Hi, Bettye," Benny greeted me cheerfully as he entered the living room.

"Hello, Benny," I smiled.

"Nice digs you got up here."

So we were going to play make-believe. "Yes, they are." I gave him what I hoped was a disarming smile. "Drink?"

"Not on the job," sighed Benny. "Mister L is pretty strict about that."

"That's a shame." I poured myself a scotch. "Well, thank you for looking after me." I took a long swallow.

"The pleasure's mine," said Benny.

"And you'll be…?"

"Right outside. Mind if I take this?" With a meaty hand, he held up a dining room chair like it weighed no more than my pocketbook.

"Please, go ahead." I watched as Benny opened the door and set the chair down outside on the covered walkway. I stepped toward the door, but tried not to appear too much like I was figuring out if I could make a break for it.

"Lemme know if you need anything, Bettye."

"I'm expecting the beautician," I said. "Will you please let her in?"

"Sure." Benny seemed relieved that I was not making more of a fuss.

"And I'm going to call for some extra towels." I poured myself another drink from the decanter on the sideboard, then thought better of it. I walked to the opposite side of the suite, pushed aside the atrocious royal-blue velvet drapes, and peered out the second-floor window.

The brand-new "Honeymoon Suite" sat on the upper floor of one of the resort's four two-story buildings—all named after famous racetracks. The newly opened Sands was considered the pinnacle of elegance, but to me it looked like a motor lodge with delusions of grandeur. In the desert, there was no reason to build up when you could just build out, forever. All around the hotel lay miles of cheap, naked soil.

How the hell had I ended up in this mess? I'd been so discreet. No one in the Harem even knew that I was married. In my naivete, I'd believed that the only person in Las Vegas who knew that I was Mrs. Peter Grafton was Mike. Somehow Rick had found out. He'd probably been planning to sell me down the river since I arrived.

I shook off the quickening vibrations of panic. Escaping and hiding were two things I was good at. Two things I'd learned at a very early age.

I walked through the suite, inspecting the windows. The drop from the second floor was higher than I expected. I knew how to fall from a horse, but I couldn't fall from a second-story window. The window faced the interior courtyard, where a woman plunging from the second floor would probably not go unnoticed. And then where would I be? Lying in the landscaping with a broken leg.

Could Mike help me? Of course not. He was a company man. Rick was right: he knew how the world worked. If he got tangled up in this, we'd end up in matching shallow graves in the Mojave desert.

I walked back into the living room and stared around me, turning in a slow circle. I had to get out. But how? There was a man with a gun outside my door. And there were plenty more where he came from. I couldn't outrun them. But I might be able to out-think them. I picked up the phone.

"Beauty salon, please," I told the operator.

The salon receptionist answered.

"This is Miss Christian. I'm afraid my hair is going to need more than just a wash and set."

"You'll have to come to the salon for any chemical process."

"I'm afraid I don't have the time for that. Can Clarice bring some wigs up for me to try? Perhaps a blonde one and a red one, too?"

"I'll ask her," said the receptionist. "She can see you at...four p.m.."

"That sounds perfect. And can you make sure that no one sees the wigs? Perhaps...hide them? I'm trying to surprise my husband."

"Sure." This time I could hear a conspiratorial smile in her voice.

"Thank you."

I depressed the cradle, then dialed the phone again. It seemed to take forever for the damned thing to complete its round.

I thought about blurting, "Get me the police!" But doing that would have been futile—or worse. I'd heard the boys bragging that the local cops were on the take. To think that last week, I had found all this so amusing: my exotic vacation among the mobsters.

"Housekeeping, please," I said to the operator. A brief pause.

"Housekeeping department," came a cheerful young voice.

"Hello, this is Mrs. Grafton. I, uh, have a rather funny request."

"Yes?" The voice sounded a bit apprehensive.

"Would it be possible to borrow…a maid's uniform?"

"Oh." She hesitated. "I'm not, uh, sure."

"My husband is coming tomorrow and I'm trying to surprise him," I told her, with a little laugh. "I thought it would be fun to spice things up a bit for our reunion."

Another pause. "Ma'am, I'll need to ask my supervisor."

Dammit.

"There's a twenty-dollar tip in it for you if you don't," I blurted.

A short silence. "Your room number?"

"The Honeymoon suite," I said, relieved. "What's your name, my dear?"

"Miss Woods," she replied, sounding brighter. "I have a couple of uniforms. A medium and a large."

"Could you bring me the large one? I'm rather tall."

"Yes, ma'am."

"I'm going to lie down for a little nap. Do you think you could come in about a half hour?"

"Yes, ma'am."

"Oh, and there's a gentleman sitting outside my door," I told her. "He's part of my husband's security detail. Please don't tell him what you're delivering. I would be terribly embarrassed if anyone found out about my little costume party."

"Yes, ma'am," said Miss Woods. I was sure she'd seen plenty during her time in Las Vegas.

"And can you bring some more towels?"

"Yes, ma'am," she said again.

After I hung up, I stepped to the front door of the suite. "Benny—" I opened the door a crack.

"Yeah?" He sounded friendly, but a little cautious.

"I'm going to order some dinner from room service. Would you like anything?" I poked my head out.

"No thanks, Bettye." Relief warmed his voice. His prisoner wasn't trying to pull a fast one. "I'm actually having dinner with Della after I get off."

"I hope you're not going to make her wait, Benny," I teased.

"Never." He worshiped his fiancée, who had the charm of a water moccasin. "Vince is coming up in a coupla hours."

"Well, let me know if you change your mind. They have awfully good French fries."

"Maybe some french fries," he said. "Thanks, Bettye."

So there would be a changing of the guard. Vince Klein was a recent arrival from Cleveland. The good news: we'd never spoken. The bad news: I'd noticed that the new boys seemed to take a while to relax into the Las Vegas routine. He might be more vigilant than Benny.

I called room service and ordered a steak, medium rare, french fries, a milkshake, and a bottle of French wine. The owner of the Sands was eager to make his new resort seem worldly and sophisticated, and his wine list was surprisingly good. (I'd been running up Mike's tab with Puligny Montrachet and vintage Champagne.)

How exactly would I pull this off? I needed to have the beautician and the maid here at the same time, so the man outside would not take notice of one woman leaving the suite. And if room service showed up at the same time, all the better. A bit of confusion—misdirection—would be ideal.

I would have to convince the maid to spend a bit of time here, so I hurried into the bedroom and tore apart the bedclothes. Then I went into the bathroom and ran the bathtub, scattered fresh towels on the floor. I undressed to my slip.

I stood there for a moment, half-naked. If I didn't get out of here, I knew exactly how it would happen: Peter's arrival. His terrifying calm, and the smile I'd learned signified exactly the opposite of what normal smiles did. The lovely dinner he'd insist on, at the best table in the Sands showroom. The magnum of Champagne. The tiny filaments of ostrich feather drifting down through the spotlight's rosy beam, as the showgirls took their final bow. Applause. The slow walk through the lobby as he let my terror build.

This was the only way. I had no friends here, no Rebecca to take me in. And Mike...Mike was a good soldier. And he knew how the world worked: the strong survived, money talked. Peter Grafton got his way. I had to admit, I admired the brute honesty of it. No one was pretending to be anything but self-interested. No one was telling me it was for my own good, or explaining away their evil as God's will.

As I bundled up my clothes, I realized that there was no hope of getting on a bus, a train or a plane after making an escape. Perhaps a rented car? I knew that if I was thinking about these things, Rick would be, too.

I suddenly thought of my riding instructor. Mr. Kiehl was the only person that I knew in Las Vegas outside the Company. Now I regretted my coldness toward the Alsatian, and poking fun at his idealistic, philosophical blather about Indians. I'd never bothered to make myself likable; it wasn't necessary. Our relationship was simply a series of transactions: he taught me, I paid him.

I yanked open the closet door to toss my things inside, and with a start, found my dresses, my blouses, even my peignoir, hung carefully on perfectly spaced hangers, from long to short—just the way Mike liked. My heart fell. Poor Mike had moved my things, no doubt as part of his penance. My bras and panties, my girdles and swimsuits, had been folded with military precision and tucked neatly into the top drawer of the bureau. I knew Mike. This was how he had said goodbye. He couldn't leave me a note. He couldn't kiss me. So he had lovingly, carefully, put away my things.

Then I felt a stab of panic—where was my jewelry bag? I rifled the drawer, frantic. In seconds, I found it tucked into a back corner. I unrolled the satin bag on the dresser and did a quick inventory—to my relief, everything was there. The diamond watch, the bracelets, my cocktail rings, the brooch, the stunning diamond-and-sapphire collar set, the everyday gold necklace, the pendant with the heart-shaped, two-carat ruby, the chandelier earrings.

I considered this for a moment—it wouldn't make sense to steal Mr. Peter Grafton's property, would it? They might be gangsters, but they respected power. And they would certainly know when they were dealing with a more powerful gangster, one funded by the U.S. Government.

To outwit Peter, I would need to be as cold and calculating as he was. And as determined. There was no way in hell I would let that monster drag me back to Chicago.

SIX

heard a soft tap at the door, then Benny's voice. "Bettye, the gal from the beauty salon is here."

"Thanks, Benny." I squelched the tremor in my voice.

Clarice entered, carrying a tote bag and her portable cosmetology kit. A platinum blonde, she wore a loud, shimmery peacock blue sheath dress under her white cosmetologist's smock, and noisy costume jewelry.

"Hello, Miss Christian! Nice to see you." She shut the door behind her with a quizzical glance, her bracelet jingling.

"Hi, Clarice," I paused. "It's actually...Mrs. Grafton."

I watched her eyebrows rise, her mouth form a silent "O".

I gave a quick mea culpa shrug and she broke into a grin.

"You've been a busy girl," she winked. "Vacation's over, huh?"

"Jesus," I sighed. "That's an understatement."

Clarice took a couple of little steps toward me and asked in a stage whisper, "What's with the muscle outside?"

"My husband is a defense contractor. He always asks for extra security."

"Well, he's got himself one interesting bodyguard," Clarice said significantly. She bit her lip and smiled at me. "Is it kooky around here, or what?"

I gestured toward the dining room table, hoping to redirect the conversation. "Should we set up here?"

"Perfect." She gave a little sigh of pleasure. "It's nice to get out of the salon. By the end of the day, I smell like permanent wave solution. My fiancé calls it Eau de Ammonia."

In minutes, a small beauty parlor appeared in the dining room. Clarice pulled out a chair for me, settled me in, and fastened a cape over my shoulders. Then she brushed out my hair. The sensation was soothing, and I let my eyes close.

"Good heavens, you have a lot of hair," the beautician remarked. "And as black as coal. Do you color it?" I could feel her lean over to inspect my roots.

"No," I told her, as I'd told every beautician I'd ever known.

"What are you? Italian?"

"Uh huh," I said casually.

"Gosh! You are so lucky. I would kill to have hair like this!" Clarice tucked my hair skillfully into a skullcap. "So when was the last time you saw your husband?"

"It's been almost two months," I said. "We—we're trying to reconcile."

"So you came here for a divorce?"

"Yes, that was the original plan."

"Well, good for you," she said. "I mean, good for trying again. I get depressed, you know…seeing all these folks here, husbands and wives just giving up on their marriages. It's such a shame."

Perhaps the gold crucifix dangling between her breasts actually meant something to her. I attempted to appear pious and regretful.

She extracted a wig from her bag, held it up and brushed it tenderly, as if it were a living creature. "So, let's see what you look like as a blonde." She settled the wig on my head, fussed with it a bit, then gave me a hand mirror.

The effect was startling. The luxurious, creamy shade would be more at home on Doris Day than a hotel maid, and it was entirely unconvincing against my complexion—too obviously a costume.

Clarice gave a soft whistle. "Pretty dramatic," she said, in the noncommittal tone of an experienced beautician. "What do you think?"

"I think my husband may prefer something less...artificial." I examined my skin in the hand mirror. Despite my hat, and my insistence on sitting under an umbrella, I'd gotten too dark during those hours by the pool.

"Oh, don't you worry. I have just the thing." Clarice smiled and slid the blonde wig off. She adjusted the skullcap and tugged a wavy, cinnamon-colored wig into place.

I fingered the hair, a bit too close to my own length. "Hmmm," I said. "It might be fun to have something a little shorter."

"I can style it any way you like. I could definitely see you in something shorter."

"That sounds good."

She took out her shears and comb and began to snip carefully at the wig. Bits of hair fell onto the floor. (Perfect—yet a bigger mess for the maid to tidy up.) When she finished, I got to my feet and crossed the room to contemplate my disguise in the large sunburst mirror. Much better.

At the sound of a knock at the door, I startled.

"Room service is here," came Benny's muffled voice.

"Do you mind getting that?" I asked Clarice, stepping into the bedroom and out of sight.

"Not at all!" She gave me another wink. I could hear the room service cart trundling in, and Clarice directing the waiter to set up the food on the sideboard.

"Can you see that Benny gets the milkshake and fries?" I called.

"You bet."

I heard her step outside, and Benny's polite "Thank you!"

"It's like Grand Central in here!" called Clarice. "Did you call housekeeping?"

"Yes. Thank you." I poked my head out of the bedroom. I smiled at Miss Woods, a small, bespectacled girl. She was visibly confused by the entire scene: the makeshift beauty parlor, the bulky man sitting outside my door, the room service waiter opening the bottle of wine, and my casual state of undress.

"Could you tidy up the bedroom and bathroom?" I asked.

Her face fell. "I don't have all my supplies with me. I can bring up the cart." The soft, truncated words and the familiar cadence told me she was Navajo.

"Oh no need to bother, it's in pretty good shape," I said. "Just do what you can." She'd come in with a stack of towels and a small tote. The spare uniform—if she had brought one—was nowhere to be seen.

"Yes, ma'am." I watched her eyes flick in alarm toward the hair on the floor before she disappeared into the bedroom. I gestured to the waiter, added an enormous tip, and signed the check. He thanked me quietly and pushed his cart back out of the suite. Benny's cheerful "Bye now!" rang out and the empty cart rattled along the outdoor walkway toward the elevator.

I shut the door. I poured myself a bit of the Montrachet and turned to Clarice. "Makeup next? I haven't the faintest idea how to do it with this hair color." I sat back down in the chair, gripping the wine glass tightly by its bowl, hoping my hands weren't visibly trembling. I took a long swallow.

"It's easy," Clarice assured me.

"Can you make my skin a bit lighter?" I asked. "You know, like a real redhead?"

"Why not?" She fished through her kit and produced a pancake makeup that was three shades paler than me. "This is the ticket. *Ivory Whisper.* Total coverage."

As she sponged the foundation over my face with rapid little strokes, I listened for the maid's progress. Miss Woods had started in the bathroom. Without her cleaning supplies, there would be little for her to do other than mop up the water with a towel, and polish the fixtures.

"So when you're done," I told Clarice, "I am going to do a costume change and I want you to tell me how I look."

"This is fun!" she declared. "Now for the eyes." She began to stroke eye shadow over my lids with a soft brush.

"Miss Woods," I called, unable to wait a minute longer. "Do you have something for me?"

She stepped out of the bedroom, her face reddening, and sheepishly produced the uniform from between a couple of towels. She shot a self-conscious glance at Clarice. From her tote, she pulled a pair of white uniform shoes. I had forgotten about shoes. "I picked some size nines…they were the largest shoes that I could find. Since you asked for a large uniform."

"That's good thinking." I said, regarding the girl with fresh appreciation.

"Oh my goodness!" Clarice laughed, finally understanding the full extent of my disguise. "What are you up to, you naughty girl?"

"Now." I fixed them with a grave expression. "This is a secret, girls." I fished a twenty out of my purse and handed it to Miss Woods.

She slipped it carefully into her pocket. "Thank you, ma'am," she said. The poor thing looked as if she might throw up.

Clarice grinned like the Cheshire Cat as I handed her a twenty. I wanted to say, *this is for all the shit that is going to rain down on you in an hour or so.* They would grill her, wouldn't they? They would interrogate her. She might lose her job.

"Ready for the fashion show?" I asked, as brightly as I could. I needed to keep the mood light, but the maid's obvious case of nerves was amplifying my own. "One last accessory."

I took the sunglasses from my purse, placed them on the table under a towel, and forced the dark lenses out of the frames.

I put them on, and the cosmetologist's mouth fell open. "Oh my God. You're going to shock the pants off him!"

"That's exactly the idea." I carried the maid's uniform and shoes, along with my purse, into the bedroom. I undressed, put them on, and inspected my reflection in the full-length mirror. Something wasn't quite right. I padded the midsection with a towel to disguise my figure, and that final touch did the trick. I did not look like Bettye Christian, or Mrs. Peter Grafton, for that matter. I was a slightly thick, bespectacled redhead. I rolled my shoulders forward and slouched a bit. That helped, too.

My hands shook as I searched through my wardrobe. I gathered some inconspicuous, casual separates, the sort of outfit that I might wear for a trip to Boulder Dam. Lightweight cigarette pants, a pink cotton blouse, a mousy cardigan that I'd never liked. Flat shoes.

What on earth would I put them in? I couldn't sneak past Vince with a goddamn suitcase. Then I spotted Miss Woods's tote, sitting next to the bathroom door. Perfect. As quietly as I could, I unloaded her cleaning supplies into the cabinet under the sink.

I returned to the bedroom, rolled the clothes into a tight bundle and stuffed them, along with my shoes, underwear, and a handful of essential toiletries and cosmetics, into the tote. I tucked the jewelry bag into my purse, wedged that in tightly, and tossed a couple of crumpled towels on top.

"You need any help, hon?" came Clarice's voice, close to the bedroom door.

"Just a minute!" I called. I was looking at myself in the mirror, yet I looked nothing like myself. I felt like I was hallucinating.

"Ready, girls?" I stepped out, lifted my chin and assumed a model's imperious gaze. I sashayed through the suite as I once had done at the dress salon, throwing in a few little spins.

"That's amazing!" gasped Clarice.

"That's really something." Miss Woods shook her head in disbelief.

There was a knock, and we all turned at once.

"Yes?" I called.

Benny cracked the door ever so slightly. I stood frozen behind it, praying that he wouldn't poke his head inside.

"Thanks for the French fries, Bettye," he called. "Vince is here and he'll take good care of you."

"Thank you, Benny!" I called back. "Say hello to Della for me, would you?"

"Sure thing, Bettye," I heard him say. "Have a good evening." Then his heavy footfalls. I heard the chair scrape as Vince settled into his post on the walkway.

This was good—I'd been expecting to wait a while until Vince arrived. Good, and unnerving. It was time to put my plan in motion.

Clarice approached to tug gently at the wig. "I think I'm a genius."

"You are, sweetheart." I handed her another twenty-dollar bill and her eyes widened.

"Thank you!" she gushed.

I lowered my voice. "I want to test-drive my new look." I tilted my head toward the door. "In a few minutes, I'm going to walk out and see if Vince recognizes me."

"You're so funny!" Clarice giggled, delighted at the idea.

"When I come back, the three of us will have a little nip of Champagne. What say you?"

Miss Woods didn't make eye contact. Did she know something about the trouble I was in? Or did she resent me for treating her uniform like a costume?

"Why don't you order something for us from room service?" I suggested to Clarice, watching her eyes widen slightly. "Pink Champagne would be nice."

. . .

I gave them my most mischievous smile, hoping that my teeth weren't audibly chattering. Every nerve in my body sizzled and spat.

"Okay, here we go," I said. Standing by the door, I called out, "Miss Woods, can you bring up some more towels?" I pointed to the maid, indicating it was her line.

"Yes, Mrs. Grafton!" she said, right on cue. "I'll be right back."

Clarice stifled a giggle.

I'm a hotel maid, I'm just a maid, no one will notice me, I told myself. Slinging the tote over my arm, I took a deep breath and pulled open the door of the suite.

Vince sat on the chair, examining a racing form. I nodded politely as I passed him, and he didn't bother to give me another look. I'd done it.

But just before I reached the stairway, Vince called out, "Hey!"

I stopped, my heart pounding, and turned. I assumed a blank, cheerful expression, praying he wouldn't recognize me.

"Can you bring me back some matches, hon?"

I nodded, then headed down the stairs, my legs dissolving underneath me.

Once out of his sight, I hurried toward the hotel's rear entrance and made my way to the employee parking lot. Stooping between two parked cars, I changed into my street clothes, then placed the maid's uniform in a nearby trash can. I would walk to the Flamingo—it was too risky to get a cab at the Sands valet.

I reached the Flamingo as the "comfortable" flats began to gnaw at my heels. Limping to the taxi rank, I once again chose the last cab in the line.

"I need you to tell your dispatcher a little white lie," I said to the driver, who expressed no surprise when I slid in. "There's a twenty in it for you."

He shrugged his assent and we drove out of the city.

SEVEN

Philippe Kiehl emerged from his stable and squinted at the approaching cab. He wore his customary jodhpurs, but instead of his usual crisply pressed, collared shirt, he had on a dirty white t-shirt and held a rake. I'd interrupted him cleaning stalls.

The cabbie braked to a stop. I took the twenty I'd folded in half lengthwise and held it up between two fingers, ever so briefly.

"You remember our chat?"

"Sure."

"Good." I got out of the cab, slammed the door, and turned toward Kiehl. "Hello," I said.

He stood there for a moment, but I could see that he still didn't recognize me. It gave me a little thrill of triumph.

"May I help you?" the trainer inquired politely.

"Mr. Kiehl."

"Yes." He looked befuddled. "Have we met?"

"We have." I removed my glasses.

"Miss Christian," he said. "This is a surprise."

"Please. Call me Bettye. Can we go inside?"

He glanced after the retreating cab, its cloud of whirling dust. "You have not come today for a lesson."

"I have not." I began walking toward the stable, and after a second's hesitation, so did he. The quiet gloom was a relief after the glare outside. I turned my gaze toward Kiehl. He stood with his arms folded, expectant. Had this been a mistake? We didn't exactly have an effortless rapport.

"Are you all right, Miss Christian?" He was deferential, but clearly unsettled.

"I'm not all right. I'm in some hot water."

"Let me guess. You owe people money."

"I don't owe anyone a thing," I snapped. "But I need to get out of Las Vegas. Quickly."

"Ah." He remained absolutely still. "And do you plan to do it on horseback?"

Was it my imagination, or was he enjoying himself now? Despite the warm afternoon, I felt a sudden chill race down my back.

"I don't know what to do," I said. "I don't know anyone here. Other than…" I stopped myself.

Kiehl glanced over his shoulder. "Your friend?" He sighed. "I'm not sure what to tell you. I am transporting two horses to a buyer this evening." He indicated an open trailer out in the yard.

At that moment, a young girl emerged from a stall carrying a small bucket. She wore a tired pink dress that was too big for her—an obvious hand-me-down—and a pair of rubber boots. She had long dark hair worn in a thin, straggling braid, and blue shadows circled her hollow eyes. I realized with a start that she was an Indian.

"Susan," Kiehl said. "Can you please get the sandwiches and the thermos from the kitchen?"

"Okay." The girl headed toward the house. She could not have been much older than seven or eight.

"Is she…okay?" I asked.

"We think Susan may have radiation poisoning."

I stared at him in disbelief. "How?"

"Many of the local Indians have been eating rabbits from the atomic test site. Her family, most of them are sick. Her grandparents are dead. Her mother may be next." His normally impassive face collapsed, ever so briefly, into an expression of disgust. When he looked at me again, his gaze was hard, challenging. There was nothing cool and reserved about Philippe Kiehl now.

"That's terrible," I murmured. I had half-taunted him when he mentioned Indians during my lesson. Written him off as an ignorant romantic.

Kiehl brushed off his jodhpurs and glanced down at his soiled, sweat-stained t-shirt. "So. Miss Christian. I'm not sure how I can be of assistance."

I forced myself back to the present. "You're taking horses somewhere?"

He frowned. "To a ranch near Lake Tahoe."

"Could I…come with you?" I heard myself say. If I could manage to stay—and stay alive—for six more weeks in Nevada, I could still get my goddamn divorce.

Kiehl gave a short laugh.

"Please," I pressed, my desperation mounting. It had been less than an hour since I had left the Sands, but by now Clarice and Miss Woods would have emerged from the suite in concern and confusion. Vince would have discovered that he'd been duped. And Rick would be hunting me.

Susan made her way across the yard with a paper bag and a large thermos. She came into the barn with a shy smile.

"Thank you." Kiehl's voice was kind as he took them from her. "That will be all for today, Susan. You did extremely well."

He glanced at me again, his cool gray eyes still holding a last trace of tenderness. "Susan is one of my best students," he explained, collecting himself. "We have arranged a trade. She assists me in the barn and I give her lessons after school." He offered the child a rare smile.

"How nice," I said, as she slipped out of the stable like a little shadow.

"She's an extraordinary equestrienne, a natural," he continued. "The horses respond to her in a remarkable way."

I tried some flattery. "Well, you're an excellent instructor."

He gave me a skeptical glance and then I watched his expression shift. "One of the horses I am taking is the stud, Ulysses. He is not easy for one person to handle." During my lessons, I'd heard the stallion trumpeting and stomping in his paddock. He was a huge, restless chestnut Warmblood with hooves the size of tea kettles.

I opened my mouth to thank him, but the trainer held up his calloused hand.

"What sort of trouble should I expect, if I help you?"

There was no point in offering him any nonsense, any lies—I was certain that he could see through just about anything. "I'm not sure, Mr. Kiehl," I said.

"A disguise is not usually a good sign." To my surprise, he reached out and fingered a strand of the wig. There was something to the gesture that seemed oddly natural. "This is quite nice, and your makeup is very well done." Then he looked over at the two-horse trailer and stood in silence for a moment, pursing his lips. "You would need to ride in the hay compartment for a while."

"Oh, please don't—" I began, but once more he held up his hand.

"We shall cover you up with a couple of burlap bags, then the loose hay." Unfortunately, he was warming to this idea.

"You are not going to stick me in a hay compartment for eleven hours," I said.

"Just until we reach the California state line," he said. "I think we can load the horses now." He frowned at my shoes. "There are some paddock boots in the tack room. They might be big enough."

"We have to hurry!" I insisted.

At that, he turned to face me, then placed his hands on my shoulders. "If I am to help you, you will need to do exactly as I say, and when I say." His voice was firm, matter-of-fact, the voice he used in the riding ring. It was as if Philippe Kiehl smuggled women out of Las Vegas every day. "As you know, rushing rarely helps. Let's not make mistakes, or get injured, Miss Christian. We have a very un-predictable horse to load."

Without another word I headed into the barn to find the boots. I didn't want to give Kiehl a chance to change his mind.

Ulysses was indeed a monster. Twice he nearly struck me with one of his massive hooves. By the time we had the stallion in the trail-er—and it was only because he'd had tired of the game—both Kiehl and I were drenched with sweat. I leaned against the trailer panting, my pants smeared with dirt and horse snot.

"Miss Christian," I heard Kiehl say, "Allow me to introduce my sister Ingrid."

I looked up, startled. I hadn't noticed the slender, white-haired woman walk out of the barn with Susan. She carried herself with the poise of a trained dancer, and walked with a pronounced, elegant limp.

As she drew close, Ingrid Kiehl looked frankly into my eyes. Her own were the color of shadows on snow, a chilly violet-blue. She knew that I was trying to figure out how old she was. Her white hair had completely thrown me, as it probably did everyone who met her.

"Hello, Miss Christian," she said, her tone formal. "It's a pleasure to meet you."

"Please. Call me Bettye." I extended my hand. Susan peered up at me.

We shook hands and she studied me with the same penetrating calm that her brother had. She wore the faintest trace of a smile, as if she had smiled a few minutes before, and this was all that remained of it, a palimpsest. Her tanned skin, taut against high cheekbones, was smooth and unlined. She could have been thirty-five, she could have been fifty-five.

Then she and Kiehl walked to the other end of the barn and had a conversation in German. There are few sensations as unsettling as having people talk about you in a language that you don't under-stand—especially German. It took me a moment to realize that little

Susan was standing next to me.

"You're pretty," she said, out of the blue.

"Thank you, darling," I replied, leaning down toward her. "So are you."

She looked doubtful. "But my hair is falling off."

I felt a terrible pang. So much had been taken from this child, from The People. Now she was sick with radiation poisoning. How could it be, that in the 20th century, the U.S. Government was still coming up with new ways to kill Indians?

"Do you want to see my hair fall off?" I asked. She blinked, confused. Her face grew worried.

"It's a magic trick," I reassured her.

"Oh," she murmured then, her fear turning to curiosity. "Show me."

I slipped my fingertips under the skullcap, pulling both it and the wig off in one motion. "Presto!"

Susan's small mouth fell open as my hair was released from captivity. I leaned over, shook it loose and raked it a couple of times with my fingers. Her eyes widened.

"I'm an Indian, too." I crouched down so our faces were level.

"You're not an Indian."

"My mother's tribe was Northern Paiute, Numu. But when I was your age, I had many friends who were Shoshone."

She still regarded me with a dubious, you're-pulling-my-leg expression.

"Eggwo," I said, touching her hair and then mine. It was the first time I'd uttered a Numu word in twenty years. "Toohoo, black, just like yours."

Susan's eyes brightened.

"Can you do the trick again?" she asked eagerly.

I laughed. "I'm giving the magic hair to you," I said. "So you can do the trick."

She clapped her small hands together. "Show me!" she urged. I had her hold the wig while I worked her thin wisps of hair under the skullcap. Then I slipped the cinnamon-colored wig over her head as she wriggled with excitement.

"I want to see!" She scampered off toward the house to find a mirror.

Philippe and Ingrid returned from their deliberation. As they trained their frosty gazes on me, I wondered if they'd decided it would be smarter to send me on my way.

"Hello again," chuckled Ingrid, taking in the spectacle of my disheveled hair.

"What happened to your disguise?" Kiehl asked, surprised.

"I gave it to Susan. She's playing dress-up."

Ingrid glanced toward the house, then back at me. "That will be nice for her."

As if on cue, there was a muffled shriek of delight from the house, and a smile bloomed on Ingrid's face. "Sounds like it was a hit." She turned toward her brother, as if to confirm something they'd agreed upon, then back to me. "Philippe tells me you would like a ride north."

"Yes." I tried to tamp down the urgency in my voice. "If it's...not too much trouble."

Ingrid Kiehl appraised me for a moment, then glanced over her shoulder at her brother. "And here I thought we were done with our smuggling days." When she turned back to face me, a playful sparkle illuminated her eyes.

I looked from her to Kiehl, curious. He gave a very Gallic shrug.

"During the war," he said matter-of-factly, "We transported people."

"We found...creative ways to help people leave Germany," Ingrid added, as if I might be too thick to understand.

"Oh," I managed, glancing from brother to sister and back again.

"Ancient history." Kiehl said dismissively. Then he turned to his sister and kissed her lightly on each cheek. "Be prepared for Bettye's friends to pay you a visit."

"Then I must make some lemonade."

"Be sure to load the Walther and the shotgun," he reminded her, as if saying, *Don't forget to water the plants.*

Ingrid was unperturbed. "I prefer my rifle—you know that," she replied with that unnerving little pentimento of a smile. Her eyes swept over me in one final appraisal.

"I'll call you from Tonopah," he told her.

"I will be just fine," Ingrid reassured him. After the Nazis, maybe the prospect of dealing with some second-tier Mafiosi seemed like child's play to her.

She turned to me. "Bettye, best of luck," she said, extending her hand. "It was lovely to meet you."

"Likewise." I took her hand, noting her firm grip. "Thank you," I added emphatically.

"Shall we?" Kiehl said, gesturing to the horse trailer, as if he were inviting me to slip into a Lincoln for an evening on the town.

The little girl dashed back into the stable yard and tugged my hand.

"Goodbye, Susan," I crouched down so we were eye-to-eye again. "It was very nice to meet you." I gave her a hug. It felt like my throat was closing around an enormous lump.

"Have a nice trip to Los Angeles," called Ingrid. So that was the cover story. "Don't do anything I wouldn't do," she added. I doubted that was possible. She was the most intimidating woman I'd ever met.

The trailer jounced down the driveway of Kiehl's stable. Though he'd laid two folded horse blankets on the hard metal floor, lying there on my side it seemed like I felt every piece of gravel, each little rut. Worse yet was the itchy hay that worked its way into my sweaty clothes. With a final, painful bounce, we turned onto the blessed smoothness of the paved road, and I felt Kiehl accelerating with practiced care. I could tell from the sun that we were indeed heading north.

North, to the high desert east of the Sierra Nevada. To the one place I had never planned to go again. To a place I could never have imagined running to, only from.

I should have known that I was not made to stay in one place, that my life would begin to fall apart if I did. It made sense. Moving around had been part of the Paiutes' annual rhythm. Mama had told me many stories about this, how Grandmother and her tribe went into the high Sierra in the spring, when the rivers ran with cutthroat trout. How, when fall came, they trekked across the valley to the eastern foothills for the pine nut harvest. How they traveled to the wide marshes of the Carson Sink, where they disguised themselves under dripping veils of moss to stalk waterfowl. And in November, how families gathered in long lines and pushed through the sagebrush on their big rabbit drives.

Settling? Staying in one place? You would perish.

The Whites that hurried to the west looked down upon this practice. They were alarmed by The People's lack of enterprise. "Hunting and gathering" was a primitive, un-Christian way to live. Civilized people farmed, they insisted, civilized people owned property. It was the same claptrap they'd been feeding the unfortunate souls they controlled, for generations.

But my mother—she had not stopped moving. I sensed her profound restlessness even as a child. After my world shrank to the handful of acres that comprised the Stewart Indian Boarding School, I would lie in my bed and remember how we had wandered. How quickly we could scoop up our belongings and disappear.

In my early years at the school, as I absorbed the intricate rules of the White world, those memories had filled me with shame. It was vital for us students to "assimilate," the watchword of the boarding school. My mother's peregrinations were evidence of her failure to do just that. But by the time I left Stewart, I could have won a Miss Assimilation pageant.

Now, as I lay sweating and miserable in that bloody horse trailer, bumping northward—back to the place where I started—I began to wonder if my footsteps might simply have been the echo of my tribe's. Something that I could not help, something engraved in my fate. The People were always moving, but each year, they'd returned to the beginning to start again. Perhaps that was happening to me, too.

I hoped like hell it was not.

EIGHT

lay smothered under burlap feed sacks and three feet of loose hay, damp clothes stuck to my skin, miserable with itching. I had no idea how much time passed, maybe an hour, maybe two, when I finally felt the trailer slow, and come to a halt. Had something gone wrong? Were we being pulled over?

Kiehl got out and slammed the door, and I heard the sound of men's voices. I strained to understand what they were saying. I felt my heart begin to pound. Ulysses stomped and whinnied, shaking the trailer. Then I heard a couple of clanks, a ripple of easy laughter, and a gas pump dinging out the gallons. I heaved a sigh of relief, then shifted, trying to move my body into a more comfortable position.

The door to the compartment opened and I felt a welcome rush of fresh air. "How are you faring?" Kiehl's voice was quiet. For a moment I considered playing possum just to scare him.

"I'm dying in here," I hissed. "I need to get out."

"We're near Rhyolite," he said, as if that meant a thing to me. "It won't be much longer, and we'll get you out. Patience, Miss Christian." He shut the door.

I wanted to cry. But he was right. I reminded myself that Philippe and Ingrid Kiehl were doing me an enormous favor. They were risking their lives for an arrogant, pain-in-the-ass riding student, someone they barely knew.

Back on the highway, the truck and trailer roared northwest. I felt the temperature in the compartment begin to drop. The stale air that pressed into my face smelled like manure and exhaust. After a while, I fell into a wretched, fitful doze.

When I awoke, we had stopped again. I braced myself. Then the door to the compartment opened.

"We're in Tonopah," came Kiehl's muffled voice through the layers of burlap and hay. "I haven't seen any vehicles behind us for the last 70 miles." He dug through the alfalfa and lifted the feed sacks. "I think it's safe to get you out of there." Cool air washed over me and with it, the smell of sagebrush, the distinctive, familiar scent of the desert at night.

I groaned, pushed myself up, and clambered out.

"Are you all right?"

"I've felt better."

Kiehl stepped back. In the darkness he was little more than a shadow, and the lone, weak light in the parking lot created a nimbus around his trim form. He lit a cigarette, and the orange glow of the match briefly illuminated his face, carving his features into a mask of dark and light.

"I have some water." He walked over to get it.

As my eyes adjusted, I realized that he'd pulled behind a motel, where we couldn't be seen from the highway.

He returned with a canteen and held it out. "They have a café here, but it's best if you don't come inside."

"Great," I grumbled as I took it from him. I took a long draught of the lukewarm water. "I'm dying for a big, icy Coca Cola. And a bathroom."

"I'll bring a drink back for you," Kiehl offered. "It's too risky to use the washroom. You'll need to relieve yourself out there." He pointed into the desert.

"Lovely," I groaned. I swayed for a moment, my knees aching. I had a vicious headache.

"Ingrid packed some ham and cheese sandwiches. They're on the front seat."

"I want a hamburger."

"Well, I'm glad to see that you're perfectly intact, Miss Christian." Kiehl turned toward the café. "But we do not have time for someone to cook you a hamburger."

I ignored him. "Medium rare. With extra pickles, and some potato chips. Please."

He gave a brief, incredulous snort. "We are not stopping for Tonopah's fine dining. We're stopping so I can telephone Ingrid. Stay here. If you see anyone approaching, get back in the compartment." Then he strode around the corner of the cabin and disappeared.

I headed into the sagebrush and did my business. I broke off two small pieces and used the bundle of velvety leaves in place of toilet paper, the way I often had as a child. The sharp smell of the herb, the distinct night-smells of the desert, reminded me of camping with Mama.

"This is how the taboo'o sleeps," she would tell me, as she helped me smooth a little depression in the loose, crumbled granite soil, and arranged my bedroll. Sleeping in my own jackrabbit nest, listening to Mama's stories by the fire, had been great fun at age five. Only with the distance of years did I realize that we'd had no choice that night but to sleep like rabbits.

I returned to the motel parking lot, where I watched a young rattlesnake glide out of the sagebrush and stretch out to bask on the still-warm asphalt. In Las Vegas I'd seen dozens of snakes, large and small, smashed flat on the dark roads—pale bodies inscribing their morbid calligraphy on the macadam.

"Not a good idea, my friend. You're going to get run over," I told her. I headed back to the truck, took another swig of tepid water, and pulled out one of Ingrid Kiehl's sandwiches. After a few minutes, I heard the crunch of gravel underfoot and Kiehl returned with a bottle of pop in one hand and a paper cup of coffee in the other. I looked at him expectantly.

"Ingrid says that nobody has come to the ranch yet."

My sigh of relief was louder than I expected. "Thank God."

"How are you feeling?"

"Better, thank you." I took the cold bottle from his hand.

He shrugged, peering into the trailer where Ulysses was fussing. The sorrel mare in the adjoining stall whickered softly.

"Not much longer," I heard Kiehl say gently to them. "You're doing very well."

"Isn't it queer that horses can abide whizzing around on highways in a loud, bumpy, rattling metal box?" I mused.

"Indeed." Kiehl began putting the alfalfa that had been covering me into the feed racks. "And now you know exactly what it feels like." I could hear the smile in his voice.

"Where are you taking them?"

"The Red Wolf, a ranch near Lake Tahoe. They want to breed Ulysses, but they also needed a good saddle horse for their daughter. Cinnamon is too inquisitive to spend her days as a school horse. She's a perfect little Arabian for a youngster who wants to explore the Sierra."

"Lucky girl," I remarked.

"And that brings up a very good question, Bettye," he said, starting the engine. "Where am I dropping you off?"

I'd been stewing over this. "Reno. If it's not too much trouble."

His brow knitted.

"There are lots of casinos in Reno," he replied. "And many of them are run by people who may know your…friends."

"I have to stay in Nevada. It's the only way I'm going to get a divorce."

"I see." Kiehl's voice was thoughtful.

"It's just for six weeks."

"That can be a long time when people are looking for you."

"I'll keep a low profile," I shrugged, and rubbed my sore neck.

"I don't imagine that's something that comes naturally to you," Kiehl chuckled.

"Be careful, there's a snake right up there." I pointed to the resting creature now visible in his headlights and he maneuvered the rig around her. The truck and trailer swayed out onto the empty highway.

I glanced at Kiehl, his profile dominated by a slightly large, aquiline nose, a small, firm chin. He looked like some sort of minor aristocrat.

"How did you fall in with these people?" Kiehl asked me at last.

"Fall in?" I repeated, with a laugh. "You make me sound like some sort of wayward teenager. I met Mike back in Chicago. He was nice."

"Nice?"

"Do I need to spell it out for you?" I laughed. "Good-looking, built like a Mack Truck." I took a little breath and collected myself. He'd asked a perfectly reasonable question. "I'd just left a bad marriage. Very bad."

He gave me a sharp glance and then returned his eyes to the road.

"Mike—my boyfriend—made me feel safe," I went on. "So when he told me he was heading to Nevada on business—" I paused to see if the smirk would return. It did not. "I tagged along. The only reason I'm here in this miserable state is to get a divorce."

"What happened in Las Vegas?"

"I didn't hit it off with the Boss' right-hand man. He didn't approve of me and Mike," I explained. "I wasn't the right sort of opportunist. If I was in it for money...he probably wouldn't have given a damn. But I guess I just didn't add up to him. He kept trying to figure out my angle."

"You were a rather odd couple," Kiehl said with a chuckle. "I had a hard time imagining what you two found to talk about."

"Talking was not really our metier."

I would miss the sense of safety I'd briefly enjoyed with Mike.

And yes, the clock on my freedom had been set back six bloody weeks. But there would be no need for a long or messy farewell. I would walk onto the pier in New York perfectly alone and unencumbered. After having just abandoned my entire wardrobe, I might not even require a porter.

"And your husband? What was he like?" asked Kiehl. "You've gone to a lot of trouble to get away from him."

I debated for a moment how much to tell him about Peter. But everyone knows that a long drive and an empty highway act like a truth serum.

"He nearly killed me."

"So he was violent?"

"That's an understatement. Yes, he was violent. But he was also corrupt. A defense contractor, probably the biggest con man in the country."

"What sort of con?"

"Inflating the price of everything he sold the defense department. Double-billing. Billing for things they never shipped."

It was a relief to be able to talk to someone about this, someone who wouldn't overreact, someone who would not be horrified at my complicity. "It didn't really come out until a few years ago. He and his attorneys are still battling them. Just before I left, he opened a new publicity campaign, accusing some of the Pentagon people he dealt with during the war of being Communists."

"That seems to be a popular tactic these days."

"It was a diversion—like tossing raw meat to a pack of starving dogs." I said. "Mike was my ticket out of Chicago. He got me away from Peter. And I'm not going to apologize for that."

"Bettye, I am the last man on earth to question your means of escape," Kiehl replied. "During the war, I made many deals with bad people, to help good people. I found criminals to be the most reliable, the most predictable, because their motives are so straightforward.

So. You don't have to explain yourself to me. Not at all."

"How many people did you get out of Germany?"

"*Tch*. Ingrid knows. She kept track of those things—" he hesitated. "I imagine it was over three hundred. Some before the war, but most after it began. Many, many children."

"That's remarkable." I still wondered if their story was actually true.

"There were many we failed to save. People who died because of my failures," Philippe added darkly. "Others who were badly hurt."

I tried to imagine the Kiehls skulking around the moonlit fields and farms of Alsace, dressed in black, sending coded messages with flashlights, stashing Jewish children in barns and basements.

"Ingrid was wounded in 1942," Philippe went on. "Her leg was broken during one of our operations. She was captured."

"Captured?"

"Yes. They put her in a prison camp." I inspected Philippe's face, which looked stony. "And our commander insisted that I leave the field. So I was sent to England. I didn't see her again until after the war."

How had I spent the war? Attending cocktail parties. Dinner parties. Openings for plays. The only war I cared about had been the one between Peter and me.

We'd all seen the pictures, but those concentration camps seemed distant and unimaginable.

"She was in Ravensbruck," Philippe replied. "A camp for women." His eyes were fixed on the road. "That's when her hair turned white."

"And that's why she limps?"

"Yes," replied Philippe. "Her tibia was shattered. She was not given medical care. It became infected, and never healed properly. It's a miracle she's alive."

I sat back in the seat, digesting all this. I had asked a lot of Philippe Kiehl, far too much. What a pain I'd been to him during my lessons. How scornful I was of his affection for the American desert. It must have felt like the promised land when he and Ingrid arrived.

"I'm sorry."

"It's why I don't like to leave Ingrid."

We both fell silent and rode that way for a while. Our headlights illuminated an empty highway, the low wall of sagebrush on either side, the occasional eerie gleam of a jackrabbit's eyes. We passed no one, no headlights appeared behind us.

Out of nowhere, Kiehl spoke. "I have been thinking," he began, "About where you might go."

NINE

Kiehl rubbed his chin thoughtfully. "The Rocking B is in the Washoe Valley," he told me. "It's a dude ranch."

"A divorce ranch?"

"Yes," he said. "I know the proprietors."

Nevada had gotten into the migratory divorce racket before the turn of the century and had been making hay off it ever since. In 1931 the state reduced the time to get Nevada residency from six months to six weeks, a gambit to bring more money into the state during the Depression. Nevada divorce became a national sensation. People flooded in from everywhere.

Even though we students rarely and barely left the Stewart School grounds, we heard our teachers complain loudly about the divorce trade: how their rents were going up, how hard it was to get into the pictures on Saturday night, and how "loose" the rich divorcees were.

The ranches catered to rich women from the East coast. (Clare Booth wrote a play about it, *The Women*, and that play became the famous movie with Joan Crawford.) But we all heard the rumors about this or that movie star who'd been spotted at the picture show in Carson City, or gambling at the Nugget. Rich girls were carousing in Carson City casinos, sitting on the laps of local ranchers, losing a thousand dollars in one night on roulette! Sex-crazed "Easterners" were seducing all the single men, even leaving Nevada with a cowboy in tow. You'd be forgiven for forgetting that there were perfectly legal bordellos in the neighboring counties, the way they went on about the divorcees.

This was how I came to understand there was a pecking order for White people, too. I had already learned that Indians were at the bottom of the heap, but I didn't realize the heap had so many layers.

"The Rocking B is a working cattle operation too." Kiehl paused, clearly still thinking this through. "Two sisters run it, Dorothy and Floss Walker. Dorothy handles the cattle and Floss handles the guests."

"Sounds swell," I said.

"It's not cheap."

I shrugged. "I'm not broke yet. Have pawn shops, will travel."

Even urbane Mr. Kiehl would probably be shocked at the opulent contents of my jewelry bag. Peter's "gifts" (and there were many) were a ritual of contrition. A slap across the face might warrant a bouquet, but a right hook, a tumble down the stairs—or rape—had been followed the next evening by red roses and a velvet box. Each time I liquidated one of them, the satin bag grew lighter—and so did I.

"I've done business with the Walkers," Kiehl continued. "They treat their animals well and they pay fair prices for horses."

"I will happily trade a chaise lounge by the pool for a saddle," I said, warming to the idea.

"A Western saddle?" Kiehl asked with a smile.

"I rode Western as a girl."

"Summer is their busiest season, but it's only April, so you may be in luck. When we get to Bishop, I will call."

. . .

As we rumbled toward the town of Bishop, California, the snow-covered mountains to the west began to blush against the pale sky. It didn't look like April. It looked like January.

"It was a very heavy winter," Kiehl said, following my gaze. "Do you ski, Bettye?"

"No," I said, remembering the times that Peter had dragged me along to Sun Valley, and Gstaad. He loved to race, of course, but I saw no reason to leave the lodge—or the brandy. Skiing was the Whitest of White people's sports. Luke had once fashioned a pair of skis in the wood shop at the Stewart school, only to have them appropriated by the teacher. A few weeks later, the man proudly showed my brother a snapshot of his son whizzing down a slope above Lake Tahoe.

"Ingrid was extraordinary on skis," Kiehl said. "For us, much of the time, it was the only way to get around. She was never happier than gliding through a forest in the dead of winter."

"But now you live in the desert."

"We are not far from mountains where she could ski, should she ever wish to, again." I heard the regret, the guilt, just under the surface. We both fell silent.

A few more miles passed before we entered Bishop, where I spotted a coffee shop with a cadre of mud-spattered pickup trucks parked outside.

"Can we stop?" I pleaded. "I'm starving."

"Yes, we can stop. But I want to park off the main street. And I need to call Ingrid."

As I stepped out of the truck in the alley, the dry winter air threw its frigid arms around me. I tugged at my thin cardigan, but it offered no protection from the mountain wind that knifed through the side streets. I looked every inch the foolish tourist. Kiehl, by contrast, had put on a fleece-lined jacket and a hunter's cap. We made a very strange-looking pair.

A bell tinkled as we entered the cafe. The place was paneled in knotty pine and all done up with blue gingham curtains, with a couple of decorative wagon wheels hanging over the grill. (The hicks could not seem to get enough of their cowboy décor.) A row of actual cowboys sat lined up at the counter like birds on a telephone line, swilling coffee.

Kiehl walked briskly into the back to find the pay phone. I made a beeline for the restroom and relieved myself. As I tried to clean the dirt off my slacks, I noticed hay in my hair. I brushed it out with care, powdered my nose, and put on lipstick. I still looked absolutely awful.

As I settled into an empty booth, I ignored the glances of the men at the counter. Of the five sitting there, four wore cowboy hats. A waitress bustled up to the table.

"You waiting for your fella, hon?" she asked. She might have been twenty-five, but she had a terrible dye job and even worse teeth. Her uniform had "Gladdie" stitched on the pocket.

"Yes," I said, "But I'll take a coffee, with cream and sugar."

"Coming up," she chirped. The waitress swayed off toward the counter as two of the younger cowboys watched her, like coyotes tracking a wandering lamb.

I looked up to see Kiehl walking toward me, his face grim. For the first time, he seemed tired. He sat down and remained silent for a moment, to my dismay.

"What?" I pressed.

"Ingrid has taken Susan to the doctor."

"What happened?" I leaned toward him.

"She's sick." After a moment, he added, "Nausea. Vomiting." Tears trembled upon his lower eyelids. "But the doctor at the emergency room refused to admit her. He told Ingrid it was the flu." He gave a soft *pfffft* of disgust.

I stared at him. Of course they did, I wanted to tell him. They didn't want an Indian child taking up a hospital bed. No one would miss a little Shoshone girl. No one cared, and especially no one in the government, no one in the military—certainly not the mad scientists in charge of these hideous, unnatural explosions. What would they say about it? *Well, we told the goddamn Indians they're not supposed to be eating those radioactive rabbits.* That's what they would say. It would be her family's fault. I thought again of the fleeing birds and rocketing jackrabbits, racing past us after the H-bomb exploded yesterday morning. Racing past as if we weren't even there. Running for their lives.

Kiehl sat there in silence. The radio blared breathless campaign news over the chatter in the café. It seemed quite possible that Peter's old buddy General Eisenhower would be our next president.

The waitress returned to find us sitting there, still as statues. "You know what you'd like for breakfast?"

I glanced up at her, startled out of my silent boil. We doubtless looked like a typical married couple, unable to think of a single thing to say to one another.

"A Denver omelet, please."

"And you, Sir?"

"Oatmeal and wheat toast, dry," said Kiehl, without hesitation.

"Coming up." The waitress bustled off to clip the order to the rotating rack by the cook's pass-through. He scowled at her as if she'd just flipped him the bird.

"Ingrid…is okay?" Best not to appear too selfish.

"Yes, yes," he replied testily. "No one has been out to the ranch. Yet."

He fell silent, and we ate our meals with nothing more than a "pass the salt, please."

I gazed out the window of the café onto Bishop's main street, which was beginning to awaken. In front of the hardware store, a stout man busily swept the sidewalk. It reminded me of long-ago mornings in Carson City when we were between homes, creeping out from a place where Mama and I had sheltered for the night and encountering the early-rising shopkeepers of the town. Some were kind—I remember an icy January morning, when a woman slipped out of a bakery to hand my mother a little pink cardboard box containing two miraculous jelly doughnuts. But the men would run us off, swinging brooms like battle axes, or aiming boots at my behind, as if I was a stray dog.

The hardware store man stopped sweeping and went back into his store, where he flipped the CLOSED sign to OPEN.

Gladdie the waitress returned. "Anything else for you?" she asked, as she gathered the dishes.

"No thank you," Kiehl said. "We'll take the check."

"Where you folks headed?" she asked brightly. Between my thin sweater and Kiehl's accent, we were obviously Not From Around Here.

"Yosemite," said Kiehl.

"Tioga Pass is still closed," Gladdie chirped, her eyes bright and challenging. She was the kind of frumpy girl who took pleasure in being a know-it-all.

"Yes, so we've discovered," I said with a smile, before Kiehl could respond. "We'll be taking the long way around."

"Well, you'd better bundle up, it's a big year in the mountains." She toted up our check with a pencil stub. "If you need chains, Mr. Emory is open across the street. He'd probably sell you some." She pointed toward the hardware store.

Tearing our ticket off her little pad, she placed it on the table with a wink, then bustled off to another table. I took a ten-dollar bill out of my pocketbook and slipped it across the table to Kiehl.

"That's not necessary, Bettye."

"It's time to call your dude ranch friends." I didn't want to wait another minute.

"Take care of the check, and I will." He headed for the pay phone.

When he returned, we were barely out the door before I asked, "What did they say?"

Kiehl took my arm again. "I decided not to tell them about your…interest in staying there. Not yet."

"Why on earth not?" I resisted the urge to yank myself free.

"They were in the middle of their breakfast service—it wasn't the right time," Kiehl replied. "And in my experience, it's usually better to ask for favors in person."

I knew he was right. It was much harder to turn someone down if they were looking you in the eye.

"But I did tell them I was coming through today with my friend Bettye. So the Walker sisters are looking forward to meeting you."

I had to trust Kiehl's judgment. He knew these people, I didn't.

"You'll need to be on your best behavior," he said. "Floss is lovely, but I think her sister prefers the cattle to the guests."

"I'll be an absolute peach."

As we turned the corner, I caught a glimpse of a tall, broad-shouldered man in a suit peering into the horse trailer. Before I could react, Kiehl pushed me lightly into a doorway. "Stay out of sight." He continued walking, without missing a beat.

"May I help you?" I wasn't sure it was Kiehl's voice at first. His accent had vanished. I froze, straining to hear.

"That's a good-looking animal," came a loud, friendly response, with the unmappable Western drawl typical of the eastern Sierra.

"Thank you." Kiehl's tone was pleasant but aloof.

"He for sale by any chance?"

Ulysses stomped and shook the trailer, trumpeting angrily.

"I'm afraid not," Kiehl replied.

"Beautiful creature."

"Thank you."

"You don't see horses like this around here too much," the man observed. "Lotta the stock around here has mustang blood. Scrawny-looking Indian nags. Better off in a can of dog food."

Kiehl did not reply. My nerves tingled. It seemed like the doorway amplified the sound of my breathing.

"Moe Gladstone." I heard an introduction in progress, the pause for a handshake.

"Steven Clark." Kiehl had not so much as hesitated. It sounded like a well-used alias.

"Mr. Clark, what brings you to our fair city?"

"I'm sorry to say I'm only passing through," I heard Kiehl respond.

"Where you headed?" The jovial voice brightened, but the words were a little too inquisitive for comfort.

"Boise."

"Well, damn," said Moe Gladstone. "That's a long haul."

"I plan to stop near Eureka tonight," said Kiehl pointedly. "The trailer's pretty hard on the horses."

"Well, next time you're heading this way, be sure to give yourself a couple of extra days. There's some damn fine fishing on the Owens River." The man laughed. "Good grief, look at the time. Gonna be late for the Rotary meeting. You drive safe, now."

"Thank you," said Kiehl. "Have a good day." I heard the door of the truck open and slam shut. The engine started.

Now I could hear footsteps, and I stiffened. I turned to try the door behind me. Locked. I fumbled in my bag, pulled out my cigarettes, shook one out of the package with trembling hands, put it in my mouth, and tried to light it. If he passed by, I would look like a woman sneaking out for a smoke. (If I could just light the damned thing.)

The sound of footsteps grew louder, and I struggled to control my breathing. This was nothing, wasn't it? A Rotarian heading to his morning meeting? Though my glimpse had been brief, my well-honed eye told me his suit was not from J. C. Penney, and his tie was a flashy lemon yellow. Perhaps he was a doctor, or an attorney, or some self-important local swell. Thank God he didn't give an Italian surname.

I managed to get my cigarette lit. I inhaled. The first couple of drags delivered a welcome flush of nicotine. I leaned in the doorway and waited, shivering, for the man to pass me.

Bettye Christian delights audiences in her star turn as Loitering Woman.

I heard Kiehl put the truck in gear. He wasn't ditching me, was he? No, he just needed to make good on his little yarn. I could hear the truck and trailer banging away down the alley, which ran behind the buildings on Main Street. Ulysses continued to make a racket, furious at being contained for so long. The stop had been a tease.

The man's heavy feet shuffled to a stop. He was so close that I could hear the sound of him patting his pockets and cursing softly. It sounded like he'd forgotten something. Car keys, cigarettes? I held my breath. Then I heard hard, sharp footfalls, but they quickly faded away.

I waited there for a couple of minutes, shivering. When I finally stepped onto the sidewalk, into the morning sun, I was alone. I walked as fast as I could to the end of the block and looked down the street. No sign of the truck and trailer. I felt a flash of nerves but kept walking. It was all I could do not to run.

And there, idling on the next side street, was the blessed dark green truck. Kiehl sat watching his rearview mirror as I dashed the final few steps and hauled myself into the cab, pulling the door shut behind me.

"Well, I'd say we made a bit of an impression in Bishop," he said. "Let's get out of here."

. . .

I awakened to warmth and brightness. We were in Minden, Nevada, just over the border from California, rumbling down a Main Street lined with tidy bungalows.

I wondered if the six o'clock siren still sounded in the town. When I was a little girl, it was a warning to any Indians who were not yet back on the reservation that their 7 p.m. curfew was approaching. Before her husband Joe died, my mother lived on the reservation and worked in nearby towns. Every afternoon must have been a panicked race against the clock to finish her work and get back to Diamond Valley.

The "sundown" curfew may have been the reason that, as a

young widow, she sought employment with the Clearys up in Virginia City. Being a live-in servant with the security of room and board was a plum job.

She may have thought herself safe in the maid's quarters, but she wasn't safe from Daniel Cleary. Was this my birthright? Being pursued by a brutal man who thought he owned me—just as my father thought he owned my mother?

Ahead towered the flour mill, its familiar silos like fingers pointing up toward the cloudless morning sky. It was hard to believe that the ugly brick pile had survived the post-war vogue for modernization. There was also a spanking-new neighborhood of small, plain houses being built a couple of blocks to the west. The building boom would soon turn the little farming community into another suburb. And perhaps the suburbanites would decide that the fifty-year-old flour mill was an eyesore and have it torn down.

"Does it look different to you?" I heard Kiehl ask. I wasn't sure that I'd heard him correctly.

"What do you mean?"

"You've been here before," he said matter-of-factly. I tried to conceal my surprise, then realized he had been observing me—just as he did when I was a student in his riding ring. "You have a tell," he added with a little smile. "That mill means something to you."

"Yes." I rubbed my eyes. "It does. This is where I grew up."

"Ahh," said Kiehl. It seemed like he was savoring this information. "Why didn't you mention that earlier?"

"It didn't seem relevant."

He glanced at me and chuckled. "You're full of surprises, Miss Christian." He settled back into his seat with an enigmatic smile.

"I haven't been back since I was fifteen. So yes, it does look different. Not different enough, though. My mother and I were chased away from that flour mill when I was very small. We were trying to gather some spilled grain, and a man ran us off."

"You were poor."

"Not just poor. We were Indians."

Kiehl nodded, adding this all up. "Susan told Ingrid you spoke to her in Numu."

"My mother was Northern Paiute. I still remember a few words," I explained.

"Your mother is no longer alive?"

I shook my head no. This was not a conversation I was prepared to have with Philippe Kiehl. "I ran away from the Indian boarding school here. I haven't been back to Nevada since."

The town ended abruptly and flat, open fields resumed. The Carson Valley had been turned into a marsh by the snowmelt.

"And you wound up in Chicago?" Kiehl asked.

"I went to New York first."

"That's very impressive, for a fifteen-year-old girl."

"I didn't exactly look fifteen."

He smiled. "I imagine you were already quite formidable at fifteen."

I had to laugh at that. "I talked my way into a job working for the head seamstress at Bergdorf Goodman's. I was one of four girls who did alterations. They gave me the beadwork, the stuff that everyone else hated. And then one afternoon a model didn't show up in the dress salon, and they asked me to step in. When I moved to Chicago, Marshall Fields hired me as a model. And that was how I made a living, until my ship came in."

"The S.S. Grafton?"

"Yes." I felt tired, suddenly, talking about my past. I turned my head to watch the landscape fly by. Cows and calves stood on soggy little islands of grass, egrets patiently stalked frogs, and hawks stared over the pastures from telephone poles.

"This is such beautiful country," Kiehl said. "It's hard to believe we're still in Nevada. So different from the Mojave Desert."

"How did you and Ingrid end up there, of all places?"

"Well, shortly after we arrived in the United States, Ingrid was diagnosed with tuberculosis. It had been rampant in the camps. She was sent to a sanitorium in Phoenix, so I moved there, too. And a couple of months later, I visited Las Vegas. I wanted to see Hoover Dam. And I met the gentleman who owned the Red Rock Stable in a card game."

I turned to study him for a moment. "And he lost it to you in that card game?"

"Not that one," Kiehl replied.

"Are you a sharp?" Perhaps Philippe Kiehl was not as noble as he seemed.

"I'm always happy to play an honest game with an honest player," he said.

"And how do you know who the honest players are?"

"The same way that you do." His eyes cut from the road to me. "The same way you understand who can be trusted."

We crossed a low bridge over the Carson River. It was close to cresting, filled with the muddy, boiling water of the spring melt-off. On the bank, I saw a brown-skinned teenage boy sitting on a paint pony just a few feet from the chaos, watching it swirl, expressionless. He reminded me of my brother.

I hadn't thought about Luke in a long time. I had always expected to learn, months or years after the fact, that he'd broken his neck in a rodeo or crashed a car. He had just never seemed to me like the sort of boy who would grow up, let alone grow old.

We left the pastures behind as the ribbon of highway ascended. We crested a bare, rocky hill, and Carson City came into view. Even from a distance, I could see the silver cupola of the Capitol jutting above the other buildings. Among the dark smudges of evergreens, trees were leafing out, and a chartreuse cloud of spring foliage hovered above the town.

I couldn't help myself. I peered to the east as we rolled down the other side of the hill. There lay the many-colored stone buildings of the Stewart Indian School, arrayed on impeccable emerald lawns. There were the broad, self-important streets. The water tower. The train tracks.

Kiehl saw me staring. "What's that?" he asked.

"A prison," I replied.

TEN

THE STEWART INDIAN SCHOOL
CARSON CITY, NEVADA
1925-1929

On the night of my sixth birthday I lay on a narrow iron dormitory bed, surrounded by weeping, snoring, mouth-breathing little girls. My body reeked of carbolic soap and disinfectant. I ached for my mother and desperately prayed that she would come back and take me home with her.

That Sunday, all the children were marched in ranks to attend church services. Girls sat in the pews on one side, boys in the pews on the other. Orderlies sat in the rear, to keep an eye on us.

As we emerged from the chapel, there was a brief moment before they marched the older boys back to their dormitory. An older boy wearing a military-style uniform walked up to me. He was tall and gangly but broad-shouldered, with the impassive face typical of children at Stewart. I stared up at him and found myself gazing into Mama's deep brown eyes. I felt my heart surge.

"I'm Luke Moore." He said this in a low voice, as if confiding a secret.

"I'm Bettye Christian," I stammered. "You're my brother, aren't you?"

"Yes," he told me, and glanced around. "I'll get you some butter."

"W-what?" (Had he said *butter*?)

And then he was gone. I stood there, overwhelmed at the shock of meeting Luke for the first time, by his imposing physical presence, by his resemblance to Mama. I was bewildered by his words—was it some sort of code?

Though I rarely saw him in those early days, I began to receive little wax paper-wrapped parcels of butter. They were delivered by children who functioned as couriers for Stewart's elaborate contraband network. Most of us did not get enough to eat in the days before the Indian New Deal; butter was a precious commodity. Though it was produced by the school's dairy, it was sold commercially, and seldom appeared on tables in the dining hall. Butter quickly established my reputation as a girl to know. (The contraband grew in sophistication over time, to include cigarettes and even moonshine.)

On the infrequent occasions that I crossed paths with Luke during that year, he cautioned me against talking about our relationship. As a little half-breed half-sister, I was a liability for him. That changed five years later when, at eleven, I began to get a figure, and he was forced to defend my reputation.

I learned Luke's story in bits and pieces, usually in the few hectic minutes after church. I pelted him with questions about Mama and his father, and if I was lucky, he might answer one of them. It was like an agonizing radio serial. Luke's father, my mother's late husband, was a Washoe lumberjack named Joe Moore. He had been killed in a logging accident at Lake Tahoe. Mama, Joe, and Luke had lived together on the Washoe reservation near Diamond Valley.

Easter morning in 1926 was mild and drowsy. A beehive hummed in one of the locust trees, which was laden with fragrant, grapelike clusters of pink flowers. Copper-breasted swallows dived and darted over our heads, circling the lawns. No one, including the orderlies, seemed to be in much of a hurry, and so we all milled outside for five or six luxurious minutes.

I asked Luke when Mama had brought him to the school. She hadn't, he told me. Shortly after his father was killed—he was only five—he was picked up while playing stickball in the street with some friends. It was a beautiful day, he said, just like this one, and when the wagon rattled into the Washoe reservation, all the children were outside playing.

The little boys were hoisted into the back of the wagon, and before Mama even knew he was missing, Luke was hauled off to the boarding school. Officially, Indian children were not put in the school until the age of six. But Luke had been large for his age, strong and coordinated. He looked like a six-year-old, but more importantly, he could do the work of a six-year-old. So they kept him.

"Will Mama ever come to visit us?" I asked. My brother gave me an anguished look and walked away.

My seventh birthday was just a week later, the 17th of April. I was working in the laundry with the other young girls when the Baptist minister, Reverend Clay, called on me.

"Let's walk to the chapel, Elizabeth," he suggested. "I need to speak with you."

I remember rinsing the bluing off my hands and following him, certain that I was in trouble. He must know about the butter, I thought. I could sense the eyes of the other girls watching apprehensively as he escorted me out of the laundry, his hand on my shoulder.

"We're going to the church."

We headed down the straight path that crisply bisected the lawns, between the new buildings that Hopi masons were teaching older boys to construct with multi-colored stones from the area. I envied the boys, out working in the sunshine. Nearly every job they had us girls doing—laundry, mending, sewing, cleaning—took place indoors.

Reverend Clay's pace was ponderous. I knew it couldn't be good, but it was a welcome relief to be outside.

As we approached the church, I saw Luke sitting on the steps. Had they found the notes that we passed to each other? Had someone intercepted the butter? I braced myself for the punishment I knew was ahead. My brother stood up, his face slack but his dark eyes full of dread.

"Hello, son," said Reverend Clay, and led us inside the church. He continued toward the front, near the altar. He motioned for us to sit down on a hard pine pew.

Then he told us that our mother had died. Is it possible to be stunned, but not surprised? I had come to suspect that I might be an orphan, thanks to the lessons of fairy tales, but the news devastated me.

"The Lord God is showing you a new path, one that will enable you to assimilate completely." Reverend Clay said. He concluded by reminding us that He worked in mysterious ways.

"How did she die?" Luke demanded. The minister looked displeased at his question, as if we should simply accept the fact of our mother's death and leave it at that.

"She committed a grievous sin," the man told him, and glanced at me. "She took her own life." I wanted to scream, but my throat was constricted—my entire body was paralyzed. How could Mama have done such a thing? Was it really true? Did ministers lie, too?

Reverend Clay steepled his hands and gazed toward the back of the church. "Unfortunately things will not be peaceful for her... where she is now."

Luke stood up slowly from the pew. His fist shot forward with startling speed and caught the man square on the jaw. The minister tumbled backward against the altar with a high-pitched cry.

"Our mother is not in hell." My brother took my hand with surprising gentleness and led me out the door of the church.

Luke's own personal hell began within minutes, as he knew it would. We were standing there lost, in the bright morning sun, when four orderlies came charging across the lawn to tackle him.

It was six weeks before I saw my brother again.

. . .

My classmate Dolores and two older girls were detailed with cleaning the school offices, an assignment that enabled them to eavesdrop on conversations between teachers, orderlies and administrators, as well as any other visitors passing through. With scrupulous detail, the girls relayed everything of interest to the students. One day after her shift, Dolores pulled me aside. A sheriff's deputy who regularly hung around the office to court one of the younger teachers had revealed the details of my mother's death.

Her body had been discovered by hunters above Carson Valley, on the slopes of the mountain White people called Job's Peak and that the Paiutes called Wangikudak. My mother had hiked up there not long after I'd been put in the school. Her remains (well, some of them) had been found near an ancient juniper tree.

The very old and large Sierra junipers are noble trees, twisted like a great wrought-iron candelabra, proud and upright. Their wood can look as if riven by the claws of a giant cat. The oldest trees are said to live for thousands of years. Mama's grandparents had used the bark of the juniper to build their huts back when the Paiutes were still permitted to live in such "primitive" dwellings. Mama made me a tea of juniper berries when I got a cold or flu. Her favorite creature was the bluebird, and during the winter, when the silver berries were ripe, those trees seethed with their iridescent blue feathers. It was a special tree. She had chosen it deliberately.

I imagined Mama trudging up a little deer trail toward the summit. I pictured her sitting down under that juniper tree at nightfall and gazing east as the Pine Nut Mountains turned pink in the glow of the sunset.

I learned later that hypothermia is a very sensible way to commit suicide. After the discomfort of the cold passes, one actually feels warm. You simply fall asleep, and it's over. You don't leave a corpse hanging from a beam, or splatter blood all over the wall by blowing your brains out.

Unfortunately, there had been very little of Mama left under the juniper tree when the spring thaw arrived. According to the boastful deputy, my mother's bones were picked clean and scattered about by animals and birds. In an arroyo several hundred yards down the hill, the hunters found her skull snagged in the twigs of a bare willow thicket.

Only much later did I understand the poetry of this. Mama's Paiute name, given to her because of her untimely birth in February when the trees were bare, the winds were high, and there were no flowers blooming, was Red Willow.

I could not believe that she had given up, that she had chosen to leave us. And I could not believe that the tedium of my daily life at the Stewart Indian School continued, that her death was so insignificant. It was as if she was a squirrel run over by a car. I was still expected to work and do my chores. I was still required to study and pray. My world was oppressively small, stuffed into the confines of the campus.

I longed to see Luke more, but the older boys were busy tending the livestock and repairing the school's buildings, the farm's pens and barns. The younger girls were relegated to the laundry, where we mended the students' uniforms and bleached stained bedding; and the mess hall, where we prepared food, scrubbed pots and pans, and cleaned.

Our lives were those of indentured servants, not school children, but the liberal-minded people running the school believed that an academic education would be wasted on Indians, or worse, set our expectations too high. If my mother had begun my education in the ways of the servant, Stewart was the finishing school.

As I grew older and became adept at the students' underground message system, there were some Saturdays when Luke and I could sneak out on a "borrowed" horse. I'd clamber up the corral fence and climb aboard behind him, arms around his waist, and off we'd go, down toward the Carson River canyon or along one of the big irrigation ditches. When we got to an open field, he would slide off and instruct me. That's how I learned to ride.

My friendships at Stewart were limited to the other half-breed children. The full-blooded Indians scorned and bullied us, and we feared them. But I found that it was easy to curry favor with my academic teachers, who sometimes provided special privileges or protections. The teachers who worked on the vocational side were less fond of me.

However, Miss Fisher, who taught sewing and tailoring, discovered my talent with a needle. I was ten when I began to sew frocks for older girls to wear to the school's newly permitted dances. I made new dresses from castoff clothing that Whites donated to the school. If I had a moment of spare time, I embroidered handkerchiefs for some teachers, who gave me a nickel or two for my effort.

One of the matrons asked me to sew a dress for her daughter's first school dance at Carson High. She actually drove me into town, to the very store where Mama had taken me on my sixth birthday, to select the fabric and notions.

I loved being in that store, surrounded by clothes and the sharp, fresh smell of new things. I was impressed by the pretty shopgirls who bustled around, assisting customers. We passed a large woman standing in front of a three-way mirror as a girl knelt to pin the hem of a butter-yellow dress.

"What is she doing?" I whispered.

Mrs. Evans regarded me as if I were dense. "She's hemming her dress, child."

"Is she a servant?" I asked.

"No, dear, she's a seamstress. She works here," Mrs. Evans said, shaking her head at my ignorance.

This girl was doing exactly what I did in my sewing class, but she was working in a store—being paid for it. How thrilling!

"I could do that," I announced in a firm, clear voice.

"Don't be ridiculous," Mrs. Evans snapped. "Respectable establishments don't hire Indians."

She took me firmly by the hand and pulled me out of the store behind her. But a seed had been planted in my mind.

. . .

That summer, along with other girls, most of them older, I was sent by train to San Francisco, where we all worked as domestics. Sending us out to work for affluent families in cities like Stockton, Sacramento, and San Francisco was believed to be better than sending us back to our Indian families—if we still had them. Stewart's administrators maintained that children who summered with their tribe would come back filthy and wild, and that the thankless work of civilizing us would have to begin all over again.

Summer was not a respite from the cruelty of the school. The people who imported Indian children for servants were every bit as bad as the orderlies and teachers, with a similar fondness for ridicule, beatings, and worse.

One summer I was placed with the Rices, a well-to-do family who lived in a handsome Tudor-style house on Pacific Street, built after the Great Fire. Mr. Rice worked at the San Francisco Stock & Bond Exchange, and Mrs. Rice was a clubwoman whose main occupation seemed to be attending and hosting luncheons and ignoring her four children.

At the Rice household, I did what I did at school—endless heaps of laundry and non-stop cleaning. The only kids I had really known before that were my fellow students at the Stewart school: in contrast, the Rice children were astonishingly spoiled, lazy, and slovenly. I was not permitted to fraternize with the children. Sometimes they broke that rule, but only to play cruel jokes or mimic the disdain heaped on me by their parents.

I also worked in the kitchen where the family's Negro cook taught me how to wash and cut up vegetables, make perfect biscuits and roast a chicken. I slept in Cook's small room, on a cot grudgingly furnished for me. The family had been required to provide a proper bed, lest I revert to "savage" ways by sleeping on the floor. Cook (I never learned, or dared to ask, her real name) began to take me with her when she did her marketing, ostensibly to carry bundles. Despite her gruffness, I knew she took me out with her so she could look after me.

We walked through Chinatown as she selected produce and haggled with the merchants. There were hordes of Italians in San Francisco by then, boisterous fishermen, and lively new shopkeepers and restaurateurs. Walking back through North Beach, I would occasionally get my cheek pinched by one of the old men sitting outside the neighborhood's teeming cafes.

"Bella!" one would declare, and a little chorus of "Bellissima!"s would follow. They clearly thought I was an Italian child. The attention pleased me as much as it alarmed Cook. In response, she would pull me along faster. She did not know what they were saying, but she'd learned to presume the worst. I didn't blame her. I had watched well-dressed, seemingly civilized men grab her bottom or catcall her, even in places like Union Square.

Despite such discoveries, I liked San Francisco. I was fascinated by the gray sky, the vast briny ocean. Its residents lived atop the steep hills, not in their shadow, as we had in Nevada. I was impressed by the tall, ornate buildings, but most of all, by the beautifully dressed women and men.

On one of Cook's days off, I was permitted to accompany the Rice family on a visit to Playland, the amusement park on Ocean Beach. I knew they only brought me because they didn't trust me alone in their house. I was not allowed to go on any rides, which suited me perfectly. I stood silently next to my employers as their children spun and dipped, my back to the clattering rides. I was in heaven, scrutinizing the dresses, the furs, the cunning cloche hats, the exquisite little shoes of the women strolling the midway with their beaus.

"Stop staring," the mistress of the house finally snapped, pinching my ear so hard I yelped. "It's rude."

"Oh, leave her be," growled her husband. "She's just a dumb Indian."

...

The year that I turned twelve, my brother "graduated" from the boarding school. By then I'd spent half my life there, but it was time for Luke to move on to the next phase of his life.

He had been hired on as a hand by a sheep ranch near Elko. It was spring 1932, and as an Indian boy, Luke was lucky to find a job. Though many ranchers in Nevada had gone bust during the Depression, his new employer was an old Basque family with a vast spread northeast of the town. They had a practice of hiring boys from the Stewart school, who were cheaper to employ than adult ranch hands.

I didn't know where Elko was, but everyone talked about it as if it was just up the road. "Can I come?" I remember asking.

"You stay here and mind your studies," Luke had instructed me sternly. "You stay in school as long as they'll let you, you hear?"

On the day he left, I was allowed to come along as Mr. Moss, one of the teachers, drove Luke and another boy to Reno. There, they were to meet some other hands for the trip to Elko.

The handsome buildings and well-dressed people on the street impressed me. The state had just passed the law permitting anyone to establish Nevada residency in just six weeks to get a "quickie" divorce, and another that legalized casino gambling. The town was jumping. The Truckee River sparkled through the center of the city, and people buzzed around the Washoe County Courthouse like bees in a spring orchard.

We crossed the river and drove down to the train depot. Men, some young and some as old as Mr. Moss, gathered around a large, open-backed truck. They were grim-faced and dirty-clothed. Mr. Moss spoke briefly with a fellow in a cowboy hat, then came back to the car.

"This is your ride, boys." My brother glanced back at me. He did not dare hug me. I did not dare cry. He got out and climbed up into the wooden bed of the truck, then turned to give me a little nod. His hand lifted slightly, but he didn't wave.

That was the last I saw of my brother. I received three postcards during his first year, with barely a sentence apiece, and wrote long letters in return. Then he moved on, ostensibly to a different outfit, and the postcards stopped altogether. The Stewart Indian School had completed its mission, and washed its hands of Luke. It was a blessing that I was in the throes of puberty, my head full of boys and the petty drama of crushes and dormitory feuds.

Though Luke and I had not been able to spend much time together at the school, it felt like a different place without him. My brother had been at the center of my personal geography, and knowing he was nearby, mending fences or painting the dairy barn, had always been a comfort.

And then, the year I turned 13, the school was a different place. "The Indian New Deal" arrived, the brainchild of more liberal-minded White men. Somehow, the United States Government had decided that what had happened to the Indians was wrong. The corrupt and ineffectual Indian Agents who had presided over the destruction of The People—while stealing us blind—were pitched out of office.

Almost overnight, the mission of the school was changed: it was no longer to turn us into servants and workhorses, but to turn us into "Educated Indians" who could help lift our tribes out of poverty (yes, the very same poverty that the U.S. government had engineered).

Excitement gripped the students at Stewart. The school erupted in a series of strikes and protests. We older students refused to do work, demanding compensation. Heated negotiations took place with the school's administration.

There would be no more indentured servitude during the summer for wealthy San Franciscans; boys and girls would learn academic subjects along with trade skills.

I was fit to be tied. My summers working for families in San Francisco, while grueling, had exposed me to a different world, one I was eager to join. Indians, it was clear to me, were still doomed. I wanted to be on the winning team—the team with the power and the money. I decided I was going to run away.

It took a year, beginning with a bungled escape attempt with two other girls. The next time I knew better—I went solo. I was fifteen, but with the right makeup and the smart tweed suit I'd sewed for myself, I did not look like a high school girl. I had saved enough money from selling contraband and from my sewing to buy myself a purse and a train ticket. I managed to get myself as far from Nevada as I could go. All the way to New York.

ELEVEN

WASHOE VALLEY, NEVADA
APRIL 1952

A poplar-lined driveway and yellow mailbox painted with the Rocking B brand offered the only clues to the location of the Walker sisters' dude ranch. The discretion seemed promising. In pastures close to the road, glossy black cattle grazed belly-deep in lush green grass. A stream coursed through the big meadow, brilliant in the morning sunshine.

Kiehl steered the truck carefully onto the gravel driveway. I could see a large, whitewashed barn in the distance, napped by willow thickets and cottonwood groves, and the mountain beyond, covered with dense stands of pine and fir.

A gust of wind buffeted Kiehl's trailer. The allee of Lombardy poplars that marched alongside the driveway leaned permanently toward the northeast. Ah, the miserable Washoe Zephyr. Like the Mistral or the Santa Anas, the wind that raked this land was infamous enough to warrant a name—it was probably ironic. A "zephyr" was a gentle, salubrious breeze, and the wind that battered and bullied the Washoe Valley was neither.

We approached a closed metal gate, and a couple of old outbuildings. They weren't exactly shabby, but they had a lonesome, disused look. As gaudy as Las Vegas could be, most of it was new, and fresh, and loudly boasted that man had triumphed over the pitiless desert. This land might be picturesque, but the desiccated wreckage of bad luck and disappointed greed lay in little heaps around every corner. It was clear to see that not much had changed.

As we drew closer to the cluster of buildings, I had a sudden memory of approaching a ranch much like this with my mother, of her hand tightening on mine as she summoned her courage to ask if there was work. That day, a man stood on the high porch. He shouted to get off his land and sent his hounds out to intimidate us. I must have been four, and those dogs looked as big as horses to me. As the hounds barked, Mama leaned down and picked me up, carrying me the rest of the way back to the road.

Kiehl braked to a gentle halt and peered around. Then, out of nowhere, a wiry young ranch hand appeared, gave a short wave and hustled over.

"Howdy sir, can I get your name?" he asked in a friendly tone, his accent predictably twangy. I saw a pair of unreadable green eyes flick my way, then back to Kiehl.

"Philippe Kiehl."

"Welcome," said the ranch hand. They were expecting us. "Sir, you just follow this here road to the first barn and you'll see a place you can park right on the other side—plenty of shade under the trees. Floss will be down in two shakes." He opened the gate.

We rolled past the young man, who tipped his dusty straw cowboy hat with an almost unconscious gesture. No one could arrive here without traversing that driveway and getting through that gate. Or rather, no one in a car. There was a lot of open country surrounding the ranch, but I couldn't quite imagine Rick Russo or Peter slogging through a boggy cow pasture to snatch me.

Kiehl halted the truck just past a large hay barn, in the shade of three enormous cottonwoods. I looked around. Where on earth was everything? I didn't see any accommodations. Then I spotted a tall, smiling woman striding toward us.

"Philippe!" she called, with a sweeping wave that required half her body. Kiehl's face burst into an uncharacteristic grin. He launched from the cab, took a couple of strides in her direction, and they collided in a bear-hug.

Good heavens, I thought. I'd never seen the Alsatian so demonstrative. Kiehl double-kissed her in the European manner. I got out of the pickup and smoothed the creases from my clothes.

Floss was a handsome woman, with a long face, sun-crinkled eyes and a square jaw. She was lean and nearly flat-chested, and wore a Western shirt with pearl snaps.

"And who do we have here, Philippe?" Her voice was hoarse and a bit boyish.

"Floss Walker, permit me to introduce Bettye Christian, a dear friend of mine."

Dear friend? Dear God. Thank you, Philippe.

Floss took a couple of steps in my direction. Close up, I saw a face peppered by a startling amount of freckles, and expressive eyes of a warm, bright hazel. A horsey, affable type. She probably donned a dress for a wedding or a funeral, but lived her life in dungarees. The sort of woman I would never have palled around with back in Chicago.

"It's a pleasure to meet you." I smiled and extended my hand. She shook it.

"Likewise," she grinned. "Any friend of Philippe's is a friend of ours."

"This is a beautiful ranch!" I summoned my most dazzled-city-slicker, gee-willikers smile. "You're so…lucky to live here." Might as well go all the way with that whopper.

"Been in the family since 1861. I grew up here with six brothers and sisters. And I agree. It's a little piece of heaven."

1861? That meant her ranch had been in *my* family before it was stolen from us by her ancestors. Probably by force. Perhaps with murder. Or maybe they'd just swindled the Paiutes. That had been a popular sport here too.

"The Rocking B is a working cattle outfit," she said with obvious pride. "Even though we're a dude ranch, we're a real ranch, too. My sister Dorothy oversees the cattle operation."

"You must be so busy!" I couldn't think of anything else to say that would not cause me to unravel.

Floss looked to be about forty, so she would have been growing up here while I was incarcerated down the road at the Stewart Indian School. She would have worn her blonde hair in pigtails while mine was cropped in the official bowl haircut of the institution. I felt another flash of resentment toward her. Toward her family. Toward all these smug, sanctimonious, "history-loving" Whites. (Yes, toward the very tribe I've been pretending to be part of since I ran away from Nevada.)

"We sure are," she grinned. "And our dozen dude ranch guests are ten times the work of two hundred head of cattle." She glanced at Kiehl.

I thought instantly of the loud, demanding girls of the Harem. Was I to experience that all over again? "I can only imagine," I said.

"Philippe, you need to turn those horses out? There's a corral right here," she offered.

"Thank you, Floss, but I'm very close to my destination and Ulysses is extremely hard to load." At the sound of his name, the stallion trumpeted. "I won't be able to stay very long."

"Well, do you have time to see the zoo?" Floss asked with a wink. Kiehl smiled and shrugged.

"That would be swell," I said. "Are you sure? I mean, we don't want to impose..."

"It's no trouble at all," Floss said with a laugh, and to my surprise, she took my arm. We walked into the cottonwood grove. "Now, tell me how you two know each other."

"I've been studying riding with Philippe."

"You're from Las Vegas?"

"No, I haven't been here very long. I came to Nevada…" I paused, adding the right catch in my voice, "to leave a terrible marriage."

"Oh," she said, with what sounded like well-practiced sympathy. "I'm so sorry. I didn't mean to pry."

"It's okay." I hoped that I sounded properly vulnerable. Kiehl walked alongside us on the path. "My husband is…a very violent man."

Her face grew serious. "My father was a very violent man, too," she replied, surprising me. "It was how he was raised. And his father before him. The men who settled this valley were hard men."

I'd never heard a White person say something like this. Their ancestors were always big-hearted heroes who'd "won" the west, not helped themselves to it.

"I actually started the divorce-ranch business in my mother's memory. She never got away. She stayed with my father to the end." There was no bitterness in her voice, just determination. "Our brothers left the ranch as soon as they could, and I went away to college, but Dot stuck around. I came back after Dad died, to start the dude operation." Her tone became cheerful again. "I really hope that Pa is spinning in his grave. He's buried here in the family cemetery, so someday I may just check." She tightened her arm in mine.

Had Floss Walker's father been the man who threatened to set his dog on Mama and me, all those years ago?

"So where will you go now that you've graduated?" she asked.

"Well, I haven't graduated yet. My husband pursued me to Las Vegas. That's why I had to leave. Now I have to start my residency process all over again."

Floss stopped, slipped her arm from mine and turned to face me. Her bright open face was clouded with concern, or anger—or both.

I couldn't quite tell.

"Where are you going now?"

"I was told the Mapes was nice."

She exhaled slowly through her teeth. "I don't mean to alarm you, Bettye, but it may not be safe for you in Reno. Especially the Mapes. It's pretty high profile. If you don't want to be found, the Mapes is not the place to be."

"There are more discreet hotels, then?"

I could see the wheels turning in Floss Walker's head. She glanced quickly at Kiehl. "For heaven's sakes, you're a friend of Philippe's. You should stay here."

This had gone far better than I expected.

"Miss Walker," I heard myself say. "It's not just my husband who is looking for me. I fell in with some less-than-savory people in Las Vegas, men who helped him find me." I glanced at Kiehl, who looked surprised, then gave a tiny nod of approval.

Floss looked around as if expecting them at any minute. Then she turned back to me with a devilish smile.

"This may seem like a casual operation, Bettye, but what you don't see is that our ranch hands are damned good security guards. These fellas grew up with shotguns and rifles, shooting squirrels out of trees by the time they could walk." She gestured back behind us. "That boy who opened the gate? He was a paratrooper. Most of our hands are veterans." Floss took a breath and paused in her sales pitch. "They're protecting everything on this spread, from whatever might want to bother us. Coyotes. Mountain lions. Last week they ran off a bear. Tomorrow it might be two-legged sons of bitches."

She was doing her damnedest to convince me to stay.

"I just wouldn't want my troubles to cause trouble for *you*," I said.

I had figured her correctly. Floss Walker's eyes snapped with righteous anger. "Let the bastards try!" she declared. "You're staying here."

We skirted another barn, and then a tall, whitewashed plank

fence, which bore a "No Trespassing" sign. Floss pushed open a barely noticeable gate and stepped aside for me.

"Welcome to the zoo."

At least a dozen tidy log cabins were scattered around a lush meadow, sheltered by young pines and still-bare aspen. The creek we'd crossed earlier meandered down the middle. Just beyond the little compound sat what must have been the Walkers' ancestral home.

It was a large, plain, clapboard farmhouse that had been added onto several times, with the most recent addition clearly its broad covered porch. I could see rocking chairs lined up in the shade, and window boxes of bright coral geraniums. The incongruous effect was that of a stern matron wearing a girlish flounced skirt.

"We have twelve cabins, most double-occupancy, though some folks pay extra to have one to themselves," Floss said. "And three single rooms in the main house. That's where we serve the meals."

The screen door banged open and a couple of young women trotted down the wooden steps in cowboy boots and jeans, chattering like blue jays.

"Right now we're completely full," she added. "But there's an extra bed in the cottage where our bookkeeper Elouise lives." She pointed toward a little cabin. "Over there. 'Sugar Pine'. It's due to be remodeled later this year, and it is definitely nothing to write home about."

"I really don't want to impose." A bed. I felt like I was back at the Stewart School.

"I won't take no for an answer," Floss said firmly. "You're Philippe's friend, and that's that."

I glanced toward Kiehl, and I saw that he was wearing a smile.

"It's a real bunch of mixed nuts here," Floss went on. "We get everything from minor movie stars to society girls. Currently we have a nymphomaniac or two, a very ugly and very rich heiress, and last month we even had a gentleman who decided to switch teams. If you can handle all that, you'll be fine."

I grinned at her frankness.

"Now. The cowboys." She paused for effect. "There are rules against fraternization. Needless to say, they are completely useless. The rules, I mean."

I laughed.

"Proceed with caution," she said. "There is an evening social hour before supper. Sometimes we have a guest who plays piano. The heiress is pretty good. But I am hoping that Philippe might stay long enough to treat us to *Fur Elise...*"

Kiehl flushed. "I'm afraid I'm a bit behind schedule," he apologized.

"Rats," said Floss.

"My dear, I do have a favor to ask," Kiehl said. "May I use your phone to call Ingrid?"

"Oh. Sure! Come on in." She made a beeline for the main house and we fell in behind her. "Do you have an attorney?" she asked me over her shoulder.

"In Las Vegas."

"Well, we can find you a new one in Reno."

"Thank you." I wondered what might have befallen Mr. Dodd after my visit.

"I'd be happy to make a recommendation," Floss said. "We know who the good ones are. Lots of shysters here, lying in wait for naïve females."

"Thank you."

We climbed the steps to the main house and Floss showed Philippe to the phone. The parlor was appointed in comfortable ranch-style furnishings, including a handful of antiques. A lovely spinet piano sat in one corner. I stepped over to admire it.

"My grandmother played," Floss offered. "She was from Austria, classically trained. How she ended up a mail-order bride, I'll never understand. She taught my mother, and my mother taught me. But

I'm not very good. I'll play in a pinch. Popular tunes." She leaned over the bench and banged out the opening chords of "Take Me Out to the Ballgame."

"Singalong stuff," she shrugged. "But it's swell when we have a guest who can really play."

"Floss," I began. "Can you tell me what your rates are?"

She folded her arms. "For a friend of Philippe's? How 'bout this. It'll cost you the same as the Mapes. But here you'll get three squares. All the activities, horseback riding, trips to the Lake, fly-fishing. Our booze isn't much to write home about, so if you like the top-shelf stuff you can buy your own."

"Oh, you don't have to—" I protested.

"Hush," she said matter-of-factly, and laughed. "And do watch out for the wranglers. They get a little excited when new inventory arrives."

Philippe returned to the parlor. He looked relieved.

"Everything okay?" I asked, scrutinizing his face.

"Susan is improving," he replied. "And Ingrid just sounds a bit lonely." That was probably his way of saying that no one had shown up yet. He consulted his watch. "It's time to get these horses to their new home."

Despite Floss Walker's hospitality, I didn't want to be in Northern Nevada, a place I'd never wanted to see again. I'd be stuck here at the ranch until my "time" was up. But at least, when it was all over, I could leave. And I would. I was heading to the south of France if it was the last thing I did.

"Oh, Philippe, I understand," said Floss. "Perhaps you can stop on your way back?"

"I am afraid that I need to get back to the stable," he apologized. "Ingrid has her hands full. But I will be back this summer for some fishing."

I had been gone about 24 hours, which meant that the search for me would be in high gear. And Peter would be in charge of it now. I'd put Philippe, Ingrid, and perhaps even that little girl in danger.

"Okay." Floss gave a quick smile and a shrug of surrender. There was a wistful look in her eyes. "But please come back soon. We've missed you. There's a lot of catching up to do."

Philippe patted her arm.

"How do you two know each other?" I asked, and instead of answering, they both chuckled awkwardly, and Floss blushed.

"We met skiing," Philippe said. That was it.

"Well, shall we get your things, then?" Floss asked, turning to me, clearly ready to change the subject.

My things? What a laugh. "I left in a hurry," I told her.

"Whatever you might be missing, we probably have here. We have a closet full of stuff our guests leave behind. From evening gowns to cold cream."

We walked back to the truck, where I pulled out my "things" and we said our goodbyes. I wasn't sure what to say to Philippe. "Thank you" seemed ridiculously inadequate for what he'd done for me, but it was all that I could come up with. I threw my arms around him in a brief hug.

As soon as I let go, Floss stepped forward to double-kiss his cheeks.

I resolved to send the Kiehls a large check after my divorce settlement.

And he was off. Floss Walker and I stood there quietly, squinting after him. Sun flickered through the dusty air between the neatly spaced poplars, illuminating the truck and trailer as it rolled down the long driveway, like frames from a silent movie.

"Let's get you settled in, Bettye," Floss declared, her cheer returning. "My sister Dorothy will want to meet you. She's in town running errands. Cocktails are at five thirty, and dinner is at seven, but I'm guessing what you'd really like now is a long shower and a nap. Your roomie Elouise went into Reno with Dot, so I'll introduce you two later. She's our bookkeeper, but more of a Girl Friday. Nice kid, from Georgia."

"That sounds great," I lied.

"Do you want to go by Bettye here?" she asked me, then.

"What do you mean?"

"Some of our guests have aliases," she replied. "You know, loose lips sink ships. The girls go into town and get loaded, someone lets your name drop…"

"Oh," I said. "*Oh.*"

"It's up to you," she shrugged. "A chance to have the name you always wanted."

"Helene," I told her, without hesitation.

PART
TWO

TWELVE

ELOUISE BERNARD
WASHOE VALLEY, APRIL 1952

Jamie, one of the wranglers, asked me if I wanted to go out on a ride at the end of the day. He said he was checking fences because a couple of the calves had gotten out that afternoon. It didn't take much to get me out of the cabin I'd been forced to share with the new guest, Helene. (Like Jamie, I guess I am just the Help, so what could I say?)

Down by the stream we spooked a small herd of grazing deer, and Jamie stopped to let them move along. It was so quiet out there that I could hear the bodies of the deer rustling through that tall grass. They disappeared into the willows, as slow and dignified as a funeral procession.

"Here it is." Sure enough, there was a hole in the fence, big enough for a calf to squeeze through, so Jamie got off his horse and set right to mending it. I wondered, as I always did, how things came to get broken. I sat there quietly on Kinky, the gentle paint pony who was my favorite. I could hear a mama cow lowing. The pasture was full of their rumpled black calves, who they can't seem to stop licking. I smelled something oddly sweet that reminded me of home. All of a sudden I wanted to cry.

"What's that sweet smell?" I asked Jamie, hoping he couldn't hear the wobble in my voice.

"Must be me." He had a foolish grin on his face.

I rolled my eyes.

"That's the desert peach. Little pink flower. They're blooming up on the hills right now."

I laughed. "Peach" was Helene's nickname for me, short for "Georgia Peach." When she found out I was from Savannah she just assigned me that name.

That's when we spotted the coyote. It was trying to sneak around behind us, but the horses got a little stirred up.

Jamie pointed. "Coyo," he muttered, and moved to get his rifle.

"Are they dangerous?"

"They kill Dorothy's chickens, the lambs too. Even calves,"

The coyote slipped into the sagebrush. Jamie walked after him, as smooth as a cat. I decided to get off and hold Kinky's reins. I thought he might spook when Jamie fired the .22.

A shot echoed off the granite mountains. Then another.

"Missed him, dammit." Jamie walked back, shaking his head. I was relieved. I had no desire to see a dead animal. I wasn't really big on live animals either, so it was pretty rich that I worked at a ranch surrounded by cows and horses and dogs and chickens, with all the dust and the mud and the poop. The guests reminded me of livestock sometimes, too. I'd get annoyed at the way they'd gather in a herd to get their evening cocktails or bunch up in the dining room at meal time.

Maybe because of that, (or maybe it was my Georgia accent or maybe it was because I wrote up their bills and charged them for cigarette burns and broken mirrors) a lot of the girls at the Rocking B thought I was a fussbudget and a priss. (I'd sure like to see what *they* did during the war. I'm sure the closest they came to doing their part was buying war bonds at the pictures.)

The only thing I had in common with those guests was that I came to Nevada for a divorce. But I could not afford to cool my heels for six weeks at a Nevada dude ranch to "establish residency" like those wealthy blueblood gals.

When I found out I could divorce George here, I came out on the train by myself, and I found a teeny-tiny room in a boarding house in Reno. One morning a couple of days later, I was sitting in a diner having breakfast, and watched a girl get fired for spilling coffee on a man at the counter. I waited until the fuss was over and when I was paying my bill I said to the manager, "It looks like you've got an opening."

I waited tables there for a couple weeks. Then I got lucky. There was a cattle auction and the Walker sisters came to the diner afterward. I overheard them talking about prices they got for their stock. Floss and Dorothy watched me add up their bill in my head like I can do, lickety-split. Dorothy asked if I was good with numbers.

"Yes, ma'am," I told her. So they told me about their ranch south of Reno. At that point I hadn't even gone beyond the city limits.

They told me they'd turned their cattle operation into a dude ranch eight years before, after their folks passed. Dorothy knew another family making good money mixing cattle ranching and divorce. So the Walker sisters built half a dozen "rustic mountain cabins" in a big grove of aspen trees, near the stream. After the war was over, they put in a couple more. Business was booming, and they needed a bookkeeper.

On any given week, we warehoused about a dozen gals and an occasional fellow. Because Floss and Dorothy were still running cattle, and the big attraction was riding Western style, there were also the wranglers, who had themselves a bunkhouse behind the hay barn. As far as I could tell, most of the fellows did not spend a lot of time there. Talk about the foxes and the henhouse. But plenty of days, I couldn't tell who was the fox and who was the hen. Jamie, my fox, was an amiable fellow who grew up on a sheep operation outside Lovelock, which was a couple of hours east of here. His family had been lucky and hung onto their ranch through the Depression.

Jamie finished up the fence, packed away his tools, and we got back on the horses. The sun had already dropped behind the mountains, and we were in the deep blue shadow that moves across the valley in the evening. Little sloughs full of snowmelt water winked up at the sky. It was a fine evening and I felt almost happy.

"You going back to your people now that you're finished up here?" asked Jamie. "Finish up" was his way of talking about my divorce.

"I don't know," I told him. "I might move on, to California." I had no such plans but it made me sound like I had something better to do than run back home.

"You'd like California." Jamie had somehow guessed I'd never been there. To my ear he sounded a little wistful. "I was in San Francisco for a spell during the war."

"That so?" Poor Jamie kept trying to have these "get to know you" conversations with me. It might work with other girls, but I just wasn't having it. He was tan and handsome, with brown hair turned yellow in the sunshine. He was good at what he did, keen with a lariat. I had seen him giving riding lessons to the girls, and he didn't put his hands all over them like the other fellows. He was older than me, nearly thirty I think, but he looked younger, with a clean-shaven, cheerful face.

"I was there before I shipped out," he went on. I knew he wanted me to ask where he'd served, all those kinds of questions. But I didn't.

We rode along together in the dusk, not talking, just slapping at mosquitoes.

"Can I take you to the movies on Saturday?" Jamie asked finally.

"Oh Jamie…" I sighed.

There was a theater in Carson City, and Floss would drive guests into town in the big station wagon. I could just picture them seeing me there with one of the cowboys.

"Why don't you ask Bertha? She has one big crush on you."

"I don't like Bertha," said Jamie. "I like you."

It was the first time he'd come right out and said it.

"I have a little girl back home, Jamie." That usually makes fellows scram.

"So?"

"So I'm not up for fun and games right now."

"What makes you think I am?" His voice didn't have the teasing sound to it anymore. "You can think about it."

It was nearly dark when we got back to the barn. I unbuckled the cinch, pulled off my saddle and blanket, brushed Kinky's damp back carefully and slowly, and prayed silently that my chatty cowboy friend would disappear. I liked this part of riding. I liked the smell of the alfalfa and the soft muttering of the hens up in the rafters. Most of the girls just wanted to hand their horse to someone afterward, like giving a car to a parking valet at a fancy restaurant. It surprised me a little to see that Helene wasn't like that. She groomed and saddled her own horse, complaining the whole time about the lousy tack. She spent hours every day out on the trails. In the four months that I'd been there, I'd noticed that the guests who really took to the horses were the loneliest girls.

"Well…see ya," Jamie said at last.

"Have a nice evening, Jamie."

He lit a cigarette and walked off toward the bunkhouse.

I was surprised to find Helene already in bed, but not surprised to see the bottle of bourbon sitting on top of the stack of books on her bedside table. She was reading, hair in rollers, in an apricot-colored peignoir, wearing glasses. She took the glasses off right away when I came into the cabin.

"No roll in the hay for you tonight?"

"No, ma'am," I said.

"That cowboy of yours is adorable."

I wondered how she knew I'd been out on a ride with Jamie. Sometimes I felt like I was one of the little rabbits that ran around in the sagebrush while Helene sat up in a pine tree like a big old owl, watching me.

"I'm not here for that," I said. Prissily.

"For what?" Helene liked to be provocative. When she talked, she sounded like actresses in the movies.

"For men."

"We're all here for men." She gave that worldly laugh of hers, which reminded me of Bettye Davis.

"You mean because of men."

"For men, because of men. So you can get rid of the old men and marry the new men." She waved her hand in the air like she was dismissing a whole regiment.

I ignored her and started picking up the cabin. From the looks of the place, Helene had probably never worked a day in her life. We didn't have any vacancies when she showed up, so the Walker sisters stuck her in my cabin, the oldest one on the property. Some sort of favor for the fellow who brought Helene here. I wished I'd been here when they all decided this was a good idea.

"Stop that, have a drink," she said with a loud sigh.

"Give me a minute," I said. (She was a bad influence on me in this regard. I think I'd had three beers in my whole life before I came to Nevada.)

She poured some bourbon into a coffee cup that was on her nightstand, probably because she was too lazy to stand up and walk to the cabinet where the glasses were.

"Heavens to Betsy," I declared, seeing the cup halfway full.

"I'll finish it if you don't want it," she said in her kitty-cat voice. She stared at me with her big dark eyes. "You smell like that little pony of yours."

"Do I?" I felt my face flush. Helene managed to look perfect, smell perfect, all the time. Her dungarees fit her better than anyone else's. Her shirt was unbuttoned one button more than the rest of us. She wore smart little kerchiefs. She looked like a goddamn Vargas pinup of a cowgirl.

When Helene first got to the ranch she refused to ride, and everyone made fun of her (behind her back) because she was so obviously a dude, all gussied up in her brand-new Western wear from Parker's downtown. The wranglers kept trying to get her on a horse.

Then one day, a big old package arrived, special delivery, for Helene. I mean, huge.

"Put it in the barn," Helene told me. The box sat there for two days, and everyone wondered what the heck it might be. Bets were placed. (This is Nevada, after all.)

Then one morning she walked up to the head wrangler, Connie, and asked him what his best horse was.

"You'd better start out with Kinky," he advised her. "We don't want you getting hurt."

"I'd rather not," she said to him in her high-and-mighty voice. "Again. Which is your best horse?"

"Well, the best horse here is Sweet Potato. But she's definitely not for dudes."

"Do I look like a dude? Bring me Sweet Potato."

Everyone knew the wranglers were the only ones who could ride Sweet Potato. The horses the dudes rode were mostly plugs. They didn't even spook at rattlesnakes.

Cowboys love practical jokes, as we girls all learned the hard way, so Connie said, "Yes ma'am," and brought out Sweet Potato, a big Appaloosa mare who was ornery as all get-out. There was nothing sweet about her. She bit, too.

He snapped Sweet Potato into the cross-ties and she stomped and fussed.

"Bring me that box," said Helene.

So Connie lugged it over to her. He had some money on what was inside, like everyone else. She told him to hand her his buck knife and he did. She took it and sliced open the box. She pulled out an English saddle like a rabbit out of a hat.

Connie busted out laughing.

"That is the best five dollars I ever lost!" he howled. He laughed so hard he had to sit down on a bale of hale and just keep going. But all that while, Helene was grooming and saddling Sweet Potato, calm as you please. She even picked her hooves, something Connie himself had never managed.

Connie stopped laughing long enough to snort, "English saddle and Western bridle?"

"You use a hackamore on Sweet Potato, don't you?"

"Yes ma'am."

"Then fetch it for me. Don't just stand there gawping."

"Miss Helene, I can't let you ride Sweet Potato. Miss Dorothy will have my hide."

"Don't be silly," she said calmly. "Just get the hackamore." And he did. He wanted to see the show.

By the time Helene came out of the barn atop Sweet Potato, the corral fence was lined with cowboys. Helene had on her snug little buckskin gloves and she held the reins Western style, in one hand. The wranglers hooted and hollered at her as she walked the big mare around in a circle in the dust of the corral.

"Miss Helene! What's gotten into you?"

"Miss Helene! You know where the brakes are on that thing?"

She nudged the horse with her heels and Sweet Potato went into a nice little jog, smooth as silk. Helene was stuck to her back like she was glued there. She did a few circles, then a couple of figure eights. The wranglers saw that she was for real.

"Open the gate, fellas," she called. They did. And out she went. She kicked Sweet Potato into a little lope and that horse acted just like they'd been together forever. They started down the long, sandy road that goes to the south pasture. Then Helene leaned forward and let Sweet Potato have her head. The Appaloosa took off in a flat-out run to the end of the road. About the time the cowboys were wondering aloud if the horse had run away with her, Helene stopped her on a dime, in a cloud of dust.

Then she reined that big mare up the mountain, and in a twinkling, they'd disappeared into the pine forest.

It would not be an exaggeration to say that every cowboy who was not already in love with Helene fell head over heels for her that morning.

THIRTEEN

"'m thinking about going to Reno tomorrow night," said Helene. "Do you want to go?"

"I don't like gambling," I told her.

"Who said anything about gambling? I need to get out of this cracker box."

"Go to Carson City with Floss and the girls." I kept my eyes on my magazine. I knew she'd turn up her nose at this.

"Oh God." Helene gave one of her big, dramatic sighs. "Not Carson. It's a wasteland, Peach. A girl like me needs some real nightlife."

"A girl like me needs to get up at 5 AM." This was probably the worst part of working on a dude ranch. Things started too damn early. Even for the bookkeeper.

"Live a little," Helene said. I just ignored her. "Fine. I'll ask someone else," she huffed.

"I didn't say I wouldn't go."

Then she laughed. "You are sounding more and more like me every day." I hated to admit it, but I felt like I'd just won the approval of the most popular girl in school. That had never happened to me in Savannah: I was white trash, and the popular girls in my school had a keen nose for trash.

There were plenty of other girls at the ranch who were very well-to-do, girls Floss referred to as "Eastern bluebloods", like they were some sort of bird. But Helene was not impressed with them. She was a snob's snob. She was educated. She had traveled the world. She was tall and beautiful and had even been a fashion model.

And, as far as I could tell, she was heartless. Any time I said anything about my Lucy or mentioned that I'd gotten a letter from Mama, she would just change the subject. Maybe it was a blessing in disguise, because the less I thought about my little girl way out there in Savannah, the easier it was to get through the weeks. But after Helene arrived, I had to go out to the barn after supper to cry.

When I first moved into Sugar Pine cabin, I set my favorite picture of Lucy up on the bureau. A couple of days after Helene checked in, I found the picture lying face-down. I set it back up, thinking maybe it had fallen. Next day, same thing. It made me very upset.

"What's your problem?" I asked Helene one evening. My hands were balled up in fists.

"What's yours?" Helene had herself a bourbon or two by then and was spoiling for a fight.

"That's a picture of my daughter."

"I know." She was cold as ice.

"I have a right to put it up on the bureau."

"A right?" Helene gave me the kitty-cat smile.

"Yes." I knew I was outgunned. This was not a girl used to losing arguments.

"It's just depressing, sweetheart." She shook her head.

"You wouldn't understand, I guess."

"And why wouldn't I understand?"

I didn't like the look on her face. "Because you don't have a child!" I practically shouted.

"I don't have a child because I understand," she said to me, real slowly. "Aren't you depressed enough, Peach?"

What could I say to that? She was right: looking at Lucy's picture made it worse, but I would rather feel that feeling than not. I snatched the photograph off the dresser and put it in my underwear drawer, where it had stayed.

"When I leave, you can put your little picture out," said Helene. She gave me a cheer-up smile, the sort my mother would wear when she was putting a bandage on my skinned knee. "Drink?"

I took the drink. That was the evening she decided to tell me her story. Helene was from a very expensive suburb of Philadelphia. Her family had money. She met an older man, who was rich and well-known in society circles, with a successful company.

They had a huge wedding in a hotel, with orchids that had been flown in on an airplane from Hawaii, which she claimed were a wedding present from Howard Hughes. They lived in a mansion and had servants. I couldn't imagine having a life like that. Well, some parts, I could. Her husband didn't love her. That much we had in common.

After they were married, he got cold and mean. He turned out to be a wife-beater.

She asked for a divorce. He wouldn't give it to her, saying that it would be bad for his reputation. She asked again the next year, and this time he threatened her life. She told him she was going to save him the bother and kill herself instead. (I did know for a fact that she had a gun, a little bitty Colt small enough to fit in an evening bag. Speaking of things hidden in underwear drawers.)

It got so bad, she was checked into a sanitorium. When she got out, she secretly got on a train and headed west with just a small valise. That's why she showed up here nearly empty-handed.

I hadn't the faintest idea how much of that story was true, but I knew a little more about her than she thought. I knew that she actually came here from Las Vegas, and that a man Floss knew, someone who was trailering horses, dropped her off at the ranch. But everyone at the Rocking B had their reasons for telling the stories that they did, and I could not begrudge that.

Helene's husband (or I should say, the private detectives she thought he had hired) did not know she was at the Rocking B. Only her attorney knew her real name. I didn't suppose I'd given her any reason to make me her confidante, but that suited me fine.

So that was how the wife of an auto mechanic from Savannah, Georgia, came to be roommates with the wife of a rich man from Philadelphia, at a dude ranch in Northern Nevada.

The only people getting rich in Nevada were casino operators and divorce lawyers. And maybe some brothel owners, because prostitution was legal in some nearby counties, too. Floss said that had been going on since the 1860s. And just a few miles away from the brothels sat Carson City, with a pretty state capitol building and tidy little houses snuggled into lilac bushes. It seemed so normal—not like a place swimming in sin.

Speaking of sin, I hadn't been to confession since I left Savannah. Our people were originally from France, which sounded high-falutin whenever I said it, but the French just got to Georgia first. So I was Catholic. And getting divorced would get me excommunicated. (George wouldn't be excommunicated for cheating on me with three different women. He'd be Forgiven, capital F, by the same church that was bound and determined to send me to hell.)

The only thing we girls at the Rocking B had in common was divorce. Just as I had, they counted down the days to their official Nevada residency like a bunch of prisoners awaiting their release date. Everyone joked around and called it a "divorce degree" (instead of decree) and we had some jolly times, but no one at the Rocking B was fooling themselves. When they got that piece of paper, those girls couldn't wait to toss their wedding rings into the Truckee River and go their separate ways. Most of them left Nevada on a train that same day.

I had "graduated" three whole months before, but I'd been saving up my wages. As soon as I could afford to leave, my plan was to go get Lucy. I couldn't live in Savannah as long as George was around. Maybe we would go to San Francisco, or maybe to Los Angeles. Floss and Dorothy wanted me to stay on, but this did not feel like a place anyone could set down roots. Even the trees had a hard time doing that here. And I didn't like snow. I didn't like the wind, either, except at night when the aspen trees sounded like ocean waves I used to hear from our little broken-down cottage on St. Simons Island, during the early years when George and I were happy.

"Here, you can borrow a dress," said Helene, as she fished through the cabin's teeny-tiny closet. It was like one of those magician's trick cabinets, where the things just kept coming out, scarves and doves and flowers. She pulled out a pink-and-white number that she'd bought her first week, when she went into town with Floss. She had gone on a crazy shopping spree that day and come back with six bags of clothes and shoes and lingerie.

"No thanks." I wasn't going to Reno on a work night.

"You'll look adorable in this," she said. I glanced at the lacy thing, which was a mistake. She saw that I'd looked.

"Do you have a girdle?" She started rummaging in a drawer.

"Do I look like I do?" I just laughed. Girdles were the first thing girls gave up at the ranch.

"Well, this dress requires a girdle, so here you go." She handed it to me. "Go on."

Pretty soon I was standing in front of the mirror looking at myself. The dress was beautiful, and it nearly fit me, even if it was too long. (Helene was a tall drink of water.)

I had to say, I looked pretty swell. "So where are we going tonight?" I asked, warming up to the whole idea.

"The Riverside Hotel," she told me. "It sounds like the closest thing to glamor as we're going to find in that one-horse town."

"How are we going to get there? Floss is taking the girls to Carson tonight."

"This isn't a grammar-school field trip," she replied. "Mother won't be coming. I've hired a driver."

Helene's "driver" was a gambler from Lake Tahoe named Teddy

who hired himself out as a chauffeur whenever he was on a losing streak. Dorothy and Floss vouched for him, though. He had a nice Packard and wore jewelry. Most important, he did not drink.

Teddy had thinning strawberry hair. He was cheerful and pink-faced and flushed even pinker when he was nervous, probably not a good quality for a professional gambler. Helene seemed to make him very nervous.

Teddy yanked open the rear door and Helene and I slid onto the mohair seat. Teddy sat up in the front seat by his lonesome.

"Where are we going this evening, ladies?" he asked us merrily.

"The Riverside," said Helene.

When we arrived at the hotel, she unfurled herself from the Packard like a flower blooming. The last thing she did was lift up her head to let the light from the entrance fall on her. She looked like a movie star, and I wasn't the only person there who thought so. A boy in front of the hotel opened the tall front door and welcomed us with a wide smile. After that, a man in a dark suit standing just inside the lobby nodded respectfully while he ate her up with his eyes. She was a sight.

Savannah had some nice places, but the rooftop restaurant at the Riverside, which overlooked the whole city and the Sierra mountains, was fancier than any place I'd ever been to. They had an orchestra that night. Right away I saw that all the girls there had beautiful hairdos. I realized that despite my elegant dress, with my long, loose hair I looked like I had just ridden in from a godforsaken ranch. Which I had.

Before we even sat down at our table, though, a man asked me to dance. He was the sort who knew that he had to strike early before gals got the lay of the land—a plain fellow with nicotine-stained teeth. But his suit was neat and his shirt was pressed, and he smelled of shaving cream.

I wanted to say no but Helene smiled a yes for me and gave me a little push. So I went off onto the big dance floor with him. He was actually a smart fox-trotter, but he didn't talk much.

We danced a few numbers and then I excused myself and went to find Helene. She was sitting at a small table, stirring her highball with her fingertip. For a rich girl she had some interesting manners. She stared openly at people and acted like she owned the place. A waiter was fawning over her and she was treating him about as well as she had Teddy.

The poor man leaped to light her cigarette. She waved him off like a shoo-fly.

"You're not bad, Georgia Peach."

"Thank you." I think it was the first time I'd ever heard Helene pay someone a compliment.

"Where'd you learn to cut a rug like that?"

"My husband," I admitted. When I first met George he loved to dance, and we went out two or three times a week, to little cafes and bars around Savannah, not fancy nightclubs like this. But those places sometimes had first-rate musicians, and they pulled in some of the best dancers I'd ever seen. I don't mind saying, I got pretty good as a result.

"Never trust a man who's a good dancer." She blew a plume of cigarette smoke over her shoulder.

I laughed. She was probably right. Then I looked up to see a big fellow heading toward our table. He was sharp-looking, and his suit was the new cut, with a narrow lapel. His hair wasn't slicked but had that sort of effect. Before he even got to our table I smelled his cologne. After all that time in the out-of-doors, my nose was used to the smell of sagebrush and pine trees. This smelled overpowering and kind of nasty.

I glanced at Helene. She looked at him as he got close, and in that split second I watched her face change. It turned into a mirror—all flat and shiny. Then the man stopped, bent toward the table, and put out his hand to shake hers. She took it the way you'd take back your ticket stub from the usher at the pictures.

"Good evening," he said, looking at me too. I gave him a little nod. I didn't much like the looks of him.

"I'm Salvatore, but my friends call me Sal." He looked at her expectantly.

"You have friends?" She blew her cigarette smoke off to the side, but the way she did it, with her eyes on him, let him know she'd rather be blowing it right in his face.

He forced out a laugh.

"Well, Salvatore, my friend and I are waiting for our dates," Helene said. There was a tiny line on his forehead now, between his black eyebrows.

"Allow me to buy you ladies a drink while you wait, then," he said.

"Another time," she said with a hard little smile, but at that very same moment I answered, "Thank you."

I'm from the South. I was raised to be polite. I didn't see any reason that she should be so mean to old Salvatore, even if he seemed kind of creepy.

Helene gave me a look of disdain.

"I'll send over something nice," Salvatore said to me. He must've thought I was his pal now. But he barely took his eyes off Helene.

"That's mighty nice of you," I said. It was actually fun to tick her off.

Helene smiled thinly, as if she could just barely tolerate his presence. "I guess my friend is thirsty," she shrugged.

Salvatore gave a little bow. He called for a waiter, and left. The waiter came over carrying a bucket of ice and a bottle of Champagne ever so carefully, like he was walking into a tiger's den.

Helene looked at the label on the bottle as the waiter popped the cork and people glanced our way. "Italians," she said in a low voice, with a curl of her beautiful lip. I guess it figured she would be a snob.

The waiter carefully filled my glass, stopping just before the bubbles foamed over the top. The last time I had Champagne was at my wedding. And it wasn't real French Champagne like this.

"Cheers!" I smiled. Helene half-heartedly clinked her glass to mine. I was warmed up from the dancing and loved how the bubbles danced around on my tongue. I admit I drank it a little too fast. As soon as my glass was empty the waiter reappeared and topped it up.

"Pace yourself, Peach." Great advice from a gal who drank bourbon from a coffee cup.

I watched Salvatore cruise by our table again like a big old shark. "I didn't like him either," I told her.

Helene smiled and took another long drag. Then she turned to me, cocked her head. "You clean up rather well, Peach."

"Thanks." I recognized the comment for what it was. We Southern women are the queens of backhanded compliments. I wasn't exactly Plain Jane, but everyone knows the difference between pretty and beautiful. Helene was Beautiful, capital B, and she was the most beautiful woman in that room. She was dark, like Ava Gardner or Cyd Charisse. She had high cheekbones and her eyes were set wide and big as a deer's. Her hair was black and shiny, and it tumbled down to her shoulders in perfect waves.

The one thing that didn't fit was her nose. She'd had it bobbed— it didn't go with the rest of her features, which were bold. But even with that teeny, girly nose of hers, she looked like a queen. So it didn't surprise me to see women stealing glances, and men staring like cartoon cats that just got hit with a big mallet.

I could feel her getting more and more agitated as we sat there, her foot tapping nervously under the table. I knew something was going on that I didn't understand, but I didn't much care. I was in the ballroom drinking Champagne and wearing a dress that made my waist look like Scarlett O'Hara's, with a foamy tulle skirt that washed against my legs like waves at the beach. I was out west in Nevada, surrounded by a bunch of rich swells and dressed-up women who were here to get their divorces and gamble and live high. A ten-piece band was playing up on the stage. Corks were popping and couples were necking in the booths and laughing.

A fellow who couldn't have been old enough to drink tapped me on the shoulder and asked me to dance. Without hesitating or looking at Helene, I said yes. He led me by the hand out onto the shiny dance floor. I thought it was strange that no one had asked Helene to dance, but then again she was pretty intimidating.

My partner moved me around the floor in a big, slow loop as the orchestra played *A Kiss to Build a Dream On*. I figured he was more accustomed to the taxi-dance places across the river where it was like an old, sad carousel. The next time we passed Helene I saw the Salvatore fellow had come back. I could see him talking to her, but her face was as still as a mannequin's.

When the song was over, I strolled back to the table. I thought I saw her hand trembling when she picked up her little clutch purse.

"I'm going to the ladies' room," she declared. I noticed the shine of perspiration on her upper lip.

"Are you all right?" She didn't seem haughty or cool now, not one bit.

"I'm just bored." She gave a sigh as if to convince me.

"Well, I need to powder my nose, too." I pushed back my chair.

"Sit," she commanded.

I hadn't seen anyone get under her skin before. "Did he say something to you?"

She was silent, her lips pressed together tightly, her eyes sawing back and forth like she was reading the timetable in a railroad station.

"The nerve!" I started scanning the room for Salvatore. I don't know what I planned to do, but I was tipsy and my dander was up.

Helene put a cool fingertip on my chin and turned my face toward hers. "Listen, Peach. Sit back, relax, and act like you're planning to stay. Then slip out when he's not watching. Meet me outside the hotel."

"What on earth, Helene?" It reminded me of ditching an annoying boy at a high school dance. I started to giggle.

"Some guys just can't take a hint." She gave me a phony smile and drained the last of her Champagne.

I watched, along with half the nightclub, as Helene sashayed through and disappeared into the hallway that led to the ladies' room.

FOURTEEN

nstead of taking the elevator, I took the back stairs. When I got down to the third floor, I practically tripped over a couple necking on the landing, the fellow with his hand up the gal's dress. They didn't even stop when they heard me coming down the stairs. I'd stumbled on wranglers and guests in clinches plenty of times, so it didn't throw me like it might have, a few months ago. It was just how people behaved (or misbehaved) in Reno.

I reached the ground floor, pushed through the exit door, and found myself on the sidewalk. There was Teddy and the idling Packard. He waved me in.

I slid into the back seat, giggling. Helene was busy lighting a cigarette.

"Who on earth was that fellow?" I asked. Teddy put the car in gear and we headed up Virginia Street. I had a sudden thought. "Does he know...your husband?"

"Why would you think that?" She snapped the lighter shut and turned her eyes on me. Then something seemed to occur to her. "Did he talk to you?"

I was annoyed by her bossiness. "Of course not, I did just as you said." I was disappointed to leave the Riverside. "Well, where are we going now?" I asked.

"How about the Cal Neva?" Teddy suggested. It was a casino over at Lake Tahoe. I'd been over that twisting Mount Rose Highway before and didn't much like the idea of doing it in the dark.

"Mr. La Grange's pawn shop."

"Now?" I asked.

"Don't give me that look, sister." Then Helene finally offered me a little smile. "We're going shopping."

"Are they even—open?" Plenty of girls at the ranch made trips into town to hock their jewelry, but this seemed like a pretty strange time to do it.

"If the casinos are open, the pawn shops are open," she said, as if she were the world's foremost authority on the subject.

So that's how we found ourselves looking through trays of jewelry at La Grange's pawnshop a bit after 10 p.m. on a Thursday night in Reno. The proprietor was a small, courteous Frenchman, and they seemed to know each other.

"These are new," he said, and held up a triple strand of pale pink pearls. They looked familiar.

"Those are Maisie's." Helene tossed me a devilish smile. "Miss Maisie DeVere from Charleston. Remember? She wore them when we went to the Lake a couple of weeks back. I think they belonged to her grandmother."

The proprietor looked very embarrassed. I felt like some sort of vulture.

"My apologies." He put the pearls away. Then he took out a large, gaudy bracelet.

"Now, this piece is very special. Unusual stones. From Poland."

I waited for Helene to laugh at it. Instead, she picked it up and tried it on.

"Interesting." A little smile spread over her face.

"It is probably from the 1870s. It was said to belong to a notorious madam in Virginia City."

Now she grinned. "Then I must have it." She slipped it onto her wrist and flashed it at me. "Isn't it just awful?" I wasn't sure what she expected me to say.

"It's very colorful," I managed, and she laughed loudly.

Then she asked if I saw anything I liked. I figured she was just making conversation, so I pointed out a pair of lovely pearl drop earrings that had caught my eye. The proprietor removed them from the display case before I could stop him.

"You have very good taste," he said with a smile. I knew that was just shopkeeper flattery, but it worked. Self-consciously, I held one up to my ear and peered into a mirror that he had set on top of the counter.

"Please, Miss, you're welcome to try them on," he encouraged me, so I did.

"They're beautiful," I said. The pearls had a sheen to them, a depth. Nothing like the little cultured pearl pendant I'd received for my high school graduation from Mama. These had a slight pinkish cast, and there was a ring of tiny diamonds on top of each one, and delicate gold openwork above that.

"They're late Victorian. The benchmark appears to be that of an English goldsmith," he explained.

I had no idea what all of that meant—I just knew they were the prettiest damned things I'd ever seen.

Then I heard Helene say, "She'll take them."

"No—no," I protested, flushing with embarrassment.

"Nonsense," she said. "They're pennies on the dollar of their actual value. Practically free."

"Helene. I can't." I told her quietly.

"Then consider it a birthday present!"

"No. I can't." I could hear my mother's voice in my ear. I could not accept a gift like that from someone I didn't even consider my friend.

"Don't be silly!" She stood there staring at me like I was from Mars. Finally she tossed her head and turned away.

"Just the bracelet, then," she told the proprietor, to my relief. I stood there quietly as he put the bracelet in a blue velvet box. He wrapped the box gently, like it held a baby animal.

"Please put that on my account," Helene told him. (I had not heard the price of anything. Rich people were awfully peculiar.) The proprietor thanked her. He saw us to the door, opened it with a little flourish.

"Merci, Monsieur. Au revoir," said Helene. Her French accent was excellent. I may have been white trash but I was white trash from Savannah, and I knew a good French accent when I heard one.

"Au revoir, Mademoiselle," said the man, and gave the tiniest little bow.

The door closed behind us and we were alone on the sidewalk in our fancy dresses. Even though it was late, there was a lot of traffic, people going downtown to dance and drink and gamble. The desert air had an electricity to it.

Helene started walking very briskly up South Virginia Street toward the Packard. We weren't far from the bridge where legend had it that everyone threw their wedding rings into the river after getting their divorce decrees at the Washoe County Courthouse. (You could also buy fake gold rings at the local dime store for that purpose. Not all of us could afford to throw away a real ring.)

I tried to keep up with Helene's long strides, wobbling down the sidewalk on those heels like a dressed-up baby lamb. Just then a car full of boys, or men, or both, passed us, with all the passengers carrying on and hooting at us. It was awful. I stumbled, and heard a roar of laughter from the car. But Helene, ahead of me, didn't even seem to notice.

Teddy stood leaning against the trunk of his car.

"Ladies," he said, moving to open the passenger door. Helene slid in and I followed. I was still pretty upset about nearly falling down in front of that carful of men.

"Where now?" he asked.

"Virginia City," said Helene, as if we'd already discussed it. What on earth had gotten into her? Virginia City was a tumbledown old mining town high atop a mountain southeast of Reno. It had lots of honky tonk bars but nothing you would dress up to go to.

"Right-o," said Teddy.

"Dressed like this?" I demanded.

"Why not?" She started to re-apply her lipstick.

Teddy hit the gas and I gripped the mohair arm rest. I started to say something, then shut my mouth. Helene casually unwrapped her blue velvet box and slipped on her bracelet.

"What do you think?"

She was right: it was perfectly awful. I decided to take a page from Helene herself. "It's very gaudy."

"Yes, it is." She examined it more closely. "And it belonged to a fabulously immoral woman. Don't you think that's just marvelous?"

"If you say so."

"You should have let me get you those earrings, Peach."

"I wasn't brought up that way," I said. I could hear Mama's scandalized tone now. *We don't take gifts like that, Elouise.*

"They were beautiful," she egged me on. "And you're obviously a pearl girl, Peach."

Hardly, I thought. Savannah had plenty of pearl girls. They wore cashmere twin sets in pastel colors that set off their eyes. They went to Cotillion with polite beaus, handsome college boys who brought them corsages.

"You mean I'm just semi-precious?"

Helene threw back her head and laughed real loud, and in spite of myself I felt a little twinkle of pride at being witty enough to make her carry on like that.

"No, I meant that you're a good girl."

Lord, I was tired of everyone thinking I was Miss Priss, a goody-two-shoes. Even Helene was bound and determined to put me in that box. "Well, that's where you have me all wrong."

Helene raised one of her perfect black eyebrows.

"Good girls don't get excommunicated by the church," I told her. The other eyebrow went up at my heated tone. "Good girls don't leave their husband and child without saying goodbye or leaving so much as a goddamn note. They don't put sand in the gas tank so they can't be followed. And they don't shop-lift candy bars at the train station!"

"You're a regular John Dillinger, Peach." Helene's smile only made me madder.

"Oh, you think I was just some little homebody?" I fumed. "I worked at Hunter airfield during the war. I worked on airplanes. I wonder what *you* did during the war."

"I serviced the rich bastard who sold the U.S. government your airplane parts," she said, without missing a beat. I'd never heard a girl talk like that in front of a man. Then she turned to face me. "I'll be damned. I'm out on the town with Rosie the Riveter."

"What? No. I was a mechanic." I told her, getting hot under the collar. No earrings, pearl or otherwise, for me and the girls on my crew. I wasn't even allowed to wear my crucifix. (We heard dark stories about girls whose necklaces or hair had been caught in a machine. Strangulation. Beheadings. No wonder jewelry still made me a little nervous.)

"A mechanic, huh?" Now Helene held out her cigarette case, a peace offering, and I took one. She cocked her head and squinted at me as she lit my cigarette and then her own.

"That's right."

"And after the war?"

"You know," I shrugged, trying to settle my temper down. "We all went home."

"Back to the kitchen," she said sarcastically.

"Well, it's not as if we had a choice. The boys leaving the service needed jobs to support their families. No one wanted to see women taking men's work."

"See? You *are* a good girl."

"I took apart B-26 Marauder engines and put them back together again. Pilots put their lives in my hands. So yes ma'am, I was a good girl. Good at what I did!"

Helene leaned back to look at me. "Hell, Peach, we should pour alcohol into you more often! I like this spunky side of you." Her eyes sparkled.

I blushed. This was the longest conversation we'd had since she crashed-landed in my cabin.

"Teddy, take us up to the Bucket of Blood," announced Helene. "We're going to drink whisky and tell secrets."

FIFTEEN

The Packard growled up dark, steep Geiger Grade, high into the mountains southeast of Reno. I'd gone up there a couple of times before with Floss when she was looking for cheap antique furniture to put in the new cabins.

Virginia City was not just old and crumbling—I'd seen plenty of that in Savannah, too. Most of the town had fallen down, burned down, or been dismantled and used to build elsewhere. Only the heart of the town remained. But it was the land—lumpy as an old hound—that made it look especially peculiar. Floss said it was heaped-up piles of tailings from the mines. In Virginia City they'd turned the earth inside-out, and it gave you a funny, almost dizzy feeling.

When we reached the top of the mountain, the road straightened out into a narrow main street. On both sides there was a row of crooked two- and three-story brick buildings, hotels and bars and shops crowded together, like they were hanging on to each other to avoid falling off into the canyon below. There was a street above, where the empty windows of old houses stared down at us, and a street below—the rooftops of some of those houses were right next to the sidewalk, like you could just step onto them. Shutters sagged, paint peeled, and dried-up weeds filled the yards. In the moonlight, patches of dirty snow glowed.

I noticed that Helene sat looking at her hands, not out the window. As we crept into Virginia City, I could see that there were bars open, blazing with light. People spilled out onto the plank boardwalks, taking in the air of the spring night. I could hear happy quarrels and laughter and music, at least three different songs at once, a trumpet here, a piano there, and a woman singing. Teddy stopped suddenly for a drunk couple who stumbled out in front of us, laughing. For a ghost town it seemed awfully gay.

"Here!" called Helene. "Stop here, Teddy."

The Bucket of Blood saloon was stuffed with people. The patrons were drinking and singing and shouting to be heard. And to my surprise, no one batted an eye at the sight of two women in fancy evening dresses. We had made a much bigger impression at the swanky Riverside.

I realized that this was the piano I'd heard, but it wasn't the corny old nonsense you'd expect, no *Camptown Races*. Instead, a young fellow in thick black-framed glasses was banging out a boogie-woogie tune and couples were dancing frantically under big chandeliers full of cobwebs and dust.

I followed Helene across the plank floor and she surprised me by walking up to the bar and pulling out a stool. Sit at the bar? Well, why not? I climbed up and arranged the fluffy skirts of the dress as best I could, so they wouldn't touch the patron on the stool next to mine. He didn't notice, because he was too busy arguing with the man sitting at his right, about (what else?) gold mining.

"That claim isn't played out," yelled the older of the two. "You'll see!"

"You were had!" declared the one closest to me.

The barkeep looked like a trapped hornet, moving furiously back and forth behind the huge mahogany bar.

He gave us an impatient look. "What'll it be?" It was as if we were interrupting something very important he had to do. It was the first time I'd seen a man perfectly unimpressed by Helene, and from the smile on her face I could see she appreciated that.

"A bottle of your best whisky, and two glasses." Helene said, like we were a couple of gunslingers in a Western. In a jiffy he set it all down in front of us, just like the barkeep in that movie would. Stone-faced, he poured a finger of whisky into each glass. I couldn't help it; I giggled. It was all so silly, these odd people pretending they lived in the Old West. Helene added more whisky to my glass. I had no intention of drinking it all.

"You don't need ice, do you?" she asked, in the tone I might use to ask Lucy if she needed help tying her shoes.

"No, thank you." I planned to make that damn drink last at least an hour.

Helene poured herself a little more. "Cheers!" She clinked her glass to mine, and just like that, tossed it back. Helene was sure a queer thing: fancy and stuck-up as you please, but with the manners of a sailor on leave.

"That's better." She reached toward the bottle to pour another.

"Allow me," offered an elegantly dressed man standing to Helene's left.

Helene smiled her kitty-cat smile and peered up at him through her thick eyelashes.

Another man, younger and more handsome, sat on a stool next to him, and gave us a charming smile. He had a high forehead and kind face that reminded me of Leslie Howard. He wore a wide-striped, sateen jacket and underneath that, a flowered waistcoat like a riverboat gambler. The pair looked like they'd just stepped out of a Gilbert & Sullivan number.

"Hello!" he said cheerfully. I could see that Helene was intrigued by them, too.

"Ladies, you are a sight for sore eyes this evening!" declared the whisky-pouring man, a very tall fellow. He seemed delighted, as if they'd been anticipating our arrival. He had the face of an accountant, but he was dressed like a dandy. Despite his size, he carried himself as if he'd never heard about the law of gravity. He picked up

Helene's hand and kissed it.

"Lucius Beebe at your service," he announced. "And this is my partner, Charles Clegg."

"Helene," she said in a teasing drawl, as if her first name said it all.

"Cherchez la femme!" Mr. Beebe looked tickled to death. He turned to the younger man, presenting Helene like she was the magician's assistant he'd just made reappear.

"Helen of Troy Ounces," he said with a smile. I had no idea what he meant by that, but the three of them tossed back their heads and laughed like old friends.

"You can't possibly be Lucius Beebe," teased Helene, nestling up against the bar all coy, her eyes gleaming. "He lives in New York."

"He did," said the man, and glanced at his friend. "And naturally, we still keep an apartment there. But as I always say, it's best to leave the party when it's still good. Café society has vanished into the mists, or the soot, as the case may be. Once we discovered that there was a splendid Victorian saloon for every twenty residents of this town, we knew we'd found Mecca."

He said all this in that fancy, too-clear, too-loud voice that you only hear in the movies. They reminded me of large, talkative, colorful birds.

"What a marvelous surprise!" A disbelieving, thrilled expression spread across Helene's face as she decided that the man was who he said. I still hadn't a clue. She suddenly remembered that I was sitting there like a bump on a log.

"Forgive my manners, permit me to introduce my friend." She smiled at me as if I were in on the big secret. "This is Peach."

I blushed, embarrassed and annoyed that she'd used her silly nickname for me.

"Delighted to make your acquaintance, Peach! Lucius Beebe at your service!" He took my fingers gently in his and kissed my hand as well. "And given your exquisite complexion, it's easy to see why they call you Peach."

I must have looked more like a plum than a peach right then.

Charles repeated the ritual.

"Enchanted." He kissed my hand.

"Likewise," I replied. This was all very silly and strange, I thought, but I had to admit—it was not dull.

"Welcome to Virginia City's version of the Stork Club," announced Lucius, with a big sweep of his arm.

"When I lived in New York, I utterly adored your column," Helene gushed, sounding like a schoolgirl.

"Why thank you, my dear."

Finally, a clue. Helene turned to me. "Walter Winchell used to call him Luscious Lucius," she said. "They were the fiercest rivals." I raised my eyebrows. At least I knew who Walter Winchell was.

"Oh that," snorted Lucius. "He was being a jealous bitch."

My eyes probably got big just then, hearing a man talk that way.

Lucius brushed something off his sleeve with a little smile. "But he does have a knack for a clever turn of phrase. Which is essential for the gossip trade."

"*She's been on more laps than a napkin*'," Helene said gleefully. "That was my very favorite." My face turned red once again. I could not imagine speaking with a stranger like that, but obviously it didn't bother Helene at all.

"Well, that was his ghostwriter, you know," Lucius told her. "All his really good lines were Klurfield's."

"How did such a lovely New Yorker find her way to Virginia City?" asked Charles. It was obvious that he didn't think it was strange at all.

"I was born here," replied Helene matter-of-factly.

I could not help myself; I turned and gawked at her. That was a whopper if I ever heard one.

"Born here? In Virginia City?" Lucius sounded impressed.

"Right down the hill in St. Mary's hospital. My mother nearly died in childbirth."

My mouth opened even wider. She had to be spinning a tall tale to impress them.

"You must tell us your story." I could see genuine curiosity in Lucius' eyes.

"Ah." Helene smiled mysteriously, and lifted her glass. "There is not enough whisky in this bottle!"

"Then we'll just have to order another one," Lucius said.

. . .

"And you, Peach," he began, as we settled ourselves at a small round table, the better to converse. "You have a lovely Southern accent. I'm guessing..." he paused, and pursed his lips. "Atlanta."

"You're close," I replied. "I'm from Savannah."

He looked quite pleased with himself. "What year did you debut?"

I stared at him like a goldfish. Who on earth did he think I was?

Now he looked embarrassed. "My apologies, I hope I did not offend!" he murmured. "I realize that's a very impertinent question, as ladies should never be compelled to reveal their age. But I know a few of the old families there."

Now I smiled. "I'm not...a society girl," I said. How I had envied those beautiful girls and their perfect lives. I certainly never expected to be mistaken for one, not even in a fancy borrowed dress.

"Nor are you a gold prospector or a cowgirl, I'll wager," he said. Then Lucius clapped his hands together and glanced at Charles. "Well, of course. Divorcées!"

I felt myself flush again.

"Fallen women," quipped Helene, propping her chin on her hand.

"My favorite kind!" Lucius declared. "The patron saint of Virginia City was a fallen woman."

"Julia Bulette," said Helene. "I believe this was her bracelet." She raised her arm to let the bracelet catch the lamplight.

"It's marvelous!" Lucius and Charles took turns examining it. "How did you come by it?"

"She bought it in a pawn shop tonight," I blurted, because I didn't want to hear her tell another cockamamie story. But everyone just laughed, like I'd said something clever.

"We started our evening at the Riverside. But Peach wasn't ready to call it a night."

"You'll like it better up here," Charles said. "We are an unpretentious lot."

"I can see that." The whisky had made me a little bold. I reached out and playfully tugged his silk cravat. He gave a loud, appreciative laugh, and Helene joined in.

"Peach has a wit on her." She winked at me, then turned to Lucius. "So yes, we're here for what Mr. Winchell called a Reno-vation. And what on earth brings you gentlemen to Virginia City?"

"The past." He turned to Charles, and using the same sort of voice that couples use to tell you they're having a baby, he said, "We purchased the *Territorial Enterprise*."

"And what is that?" she inquired.

"Only one of the greatest newspapers in the history of the United States!" Lucius looked a little crestfallen at having to explain this. "Mark Twain was its most famous editor."

"Really!" I exclaimed. Being a Southerner I certainly knew who that was.

"It had been dormant since 1918," Charles put in. "But we have brought it back to life."

Lucius nodded enthusiastically, leaning forward. "Charles is a splendid photographer, as well as a crackerjack writer and a vicious editor. And you would not believe the pantheon of literary luminaries who have made submissions. The crème de la crème of modern writers."

"We have stepped into history," Charles said. "It's quite thrilling."

So these two high-falutin men had moved from New York to revive an old newspaper? They were apparently wealthy eccentrics. We had plenty of those in the South, too.

For the next hour, the conversation ricocheted from subject to subject, and I sometimes had a hard time following it. The gentlemen had other passions, but all of them seemed to be for old things. Old houses—they were restoring a place called the Piper Mansion. Old trains—they traveled the country in their own restored private railroad car, named the *Gold Coast*. A friend who was a Hollywood set designer had decorated it.

Lucius Beebe had also written many books, most of them about railroads and trains. He wrote a column about restaurants for *Gourmet* magazine. He was now writing a cookbook based on (what else?) old Virginia City recipes.

But soon his attention returned to Helene's story. "So tell me about your parents. Who are they?"

"They're dead," she sighed, sounding bored. She put an unlit cigarette between her red lips, which Charles leaned right in and lit.

"But what brought them to Virginia City? Was your father in the mining business?"

"Mmm hmm," Helene said vaguely, blowing a little smoke ring. "They died when I was very young." But she had piqued my curiosity too. I looked over at the historian and saw that he was getting ready to ask her another question.

"It's late!" Helene declared then, looking at the Madam's bracelet as if it were a watch. I'd noticed her eyelids getting heavier as she drank. "This has been such fun, boys, but Peach and I should probably turn in. Our poor driver is probably asleep in the back seat by now."

"Where are you staying? The Riverside?"

"The Rocking B," I said.

"How delightful." Lucius glanced at Charles. "We've been out there for poker. Dorothy Walker calls us occasionally when there is an...interesting game afoot. There was an absolutely mad night last summer with Mr. Gable and some ranchers."

"We played right through breakfast," Charles said.

"And after all that, we lost our shirts. He is formidable."

I'd heard the rumors about movie stars coming out to the ranch to ride, or shoot, or play cards. I'd yet to see one myself.

"You must be reveling in springtime in the Washoe Valley," Lucius said to us. "An earthly paradise."

"Hardly," Helene said, slurring a little. "Paradise doesn't have blizzards and mosh-quitoes at the same time. It's absolutely atrocious—the horses have better accommodations than we do. But at least it's temporary."

I felt my temper rise but I kept my mouth shut. She was right—she'd be gone soon enough.

"We have to do this again," said Lucius, turning toward Charles with a big smile. He looked contented. "We must have dinner on the *Gold Coast*. We have a marvelous chef." Both men handed us their calling cards.

After a round of cheek-kissing and loud farewells, I followed Helene out of the bar. I watched her stumble, then sway, as we looked for Teddy and the Packard. But the street was empty. The cold desert wind wrapped my skirt around my legs. Sharp little stars poked through the black sky. I was pretty tight, too, but not nearly as drunk as Helene.

"Bastard," she muttered, peering down the street and shaking her head.

"He must be parked around the corner," I said with a big sigh.

"Teddy hates me," Helene moaned at the moon.

Can't imagine why, I thought.

"I'm hateful," she moaned. "Bettye the Bitch."

"Bettye?" I repeated, confused.

"Yes?" She looked up. Then she gave a big shrug. "Oh, that. That's my name." She turned her attention back to Teddy. "Where the hell is he?"

"Did you really grow up here?" I wanted her to confess it was a lie.

"No. I was born here, silly," she groaned. "No one grows up in Virginia City." She caught her toe on one of the boards and lurched forward, almost falling. "But it's a better place to die."

"Maybe you should sit down while I look for Teddy," I offered. She was a bigger mess than I'd thought.

"You do that." She collapsed onto a little bench outside a shuttered antique shop and for a second I was afraid she might just topple onto the ground. She waved me off with a limp hand.

"I'll be right back," I called. Lord, I was tired. All I wanted was to crawl into my bed.

I started picking my way down the wooden boardwalk, trying not to let my heels get stuck in the cracks and knotholes. I took a gander up the steep side street. No Packard. I glanced back at Helene, who looked for all the world like a heap of laundry. How on earth did I end up in charge of her? I walked up to the next street, and still no Teddy.

"I'm going to check up there—I think I see some headlights!" I pointed to the next street. It was probably a bad idea to put her in a car on that winding road in such a state, but we had to get back, and soon. It was way past curfew. I was upset with her, with myself, and now Teddy. This so-called Night on the Town had turned into a complete fiasco.

When I rounded the corner, the glow I'd hoped were headlights turned out to be an old neon sign with half its letters burned out. I shivered and cussed. Why the hell had I allowed her to talk me into this? It wasn't just that I had to find a taxi to take us back to the ranch. The worst thing was that I'd have to call and wake up my bosses and let them know we were coming in—no car was allowed into the Rocking B in the middle of the night. They would not be happy with me, and I could not afford to lose my job.

I hurried back into the Bucket of Blood. To my relief, Lucius and Charles were busy, chattering away with the bartender. I slipped down the hallway and into the phone booth without them seeing me.

I fumbled a dime out of my coin purse and dialed the ranch first, to get it over with. Dot answered after just one ring, which told me I was in for it. Dorothy Walker was a world-class insomniac.

"Hello, Dorothy," I began nervously.

"Who is this?" she demanded. "Do you know what time it is?"

"It's Elouise. I-I just wanted to let you know that I am with Helene, and we've run into some...car trouble."

"*Car* trouble?"

"Yes, ma'am." I tried to keep my cool. "But we'll be back soon. If you could let Stew know that we'll be coming in, so he can unlock the gate—"

Dot cut me off. "Where are you?"

"Virginia City."

"This is unacceptable," she shot back. "You know better. You know the rules!"

"I do, and I'm very sorry, ma'am," I said, and made the mistake of adding, "It wasn't my fault."

"Ha!" Dot hung up.

I stood there in the phone booth fighting back tears, then dipped my shaking fingers into the coin purse to call a cab. All it contained was a fifty-cent piece and a bunch of pennies. I would have to ask the bartender for change.

As I walked back into the saloon, Lucius and Charles, who were getting ready to leave, spotted me.

"My dear!" Lucius called. "Is everything all right?" I think they could see the expression on my face—I was close to tears. Red-faced,

I explained our situation, leaving out the part about violating curfew and getting in trouble with my boss.

"What an atrocious thing for that driver to do, abandoning two ladies in the middle of the night," said Lucius. "He should be caned!"

"I just need change to call a cab," I said, holding up the half-dollar. "It'll be fine."

At this, Charles stood up, looking very pink and indignant. "We won't hear of you ladies taking some filthy taxicab! We shall take you back to the Rocking B ourselves."

"No, please, we don't want to inconvenience you—" I tried to protest.

"I'll fetch the Jaguar," he said to Lucius, and bustled out of the bar.

"Where's the fair Helene?" asked Lucius.

"She's sitting down, just across the street." Fair she was not, at that moment. "She's in pretty rough shape. You might not want to put her in your nice car."

He smiled. "It's perfectly fine. Though a few minutes of fresh air will probably do her good."

"I'm not sure a few minutes will make much of a difference. She's pretty damn drunk."

He gazed at me. "You're certainly an interesting pair," he remarked.

"Too interesting for my taste," I replied, well aware that my interestingness was mostly due to me wearing Helene's fancy clothes. I was tired of the whole charade. "I work for Floss and Dot. I'm the ranch bookkeeper."

Lucius raised his brows. "Floss Walker is a superb judge of character."

"I don't know about that," I said. "Characters, maybe."

"Well, Nevada is full of them," Lucius replied. "To wit." Like a magician on stage, he threw on a fancy fur-lined overcoat and picked up a gold-capped walking stick that had been leaning against the bar.

It was all I could do not to just shake my head. He must have known what I was thinking. He gave me a big old smile.

"My dear, the 20th century is completely overrated." Lucius Beebe put on his silk top hat, took my arm, and we walked together out of the Bucket of Blood.

SIXTEEN

elene was not where I had left her. I stared down the street and didn't see her. Maybe she was retching in an alley. Or maybe Teddy had found her, and they'd taken off without me. I wouldn't have put it past her.

"The lady vanishes." Lucius lit a cigarette, cool as a cucumber. It was as if he had all the time in the world for this nonsense.

"Helene!" I called into the cold night air. "*Heleeeeen!* This isn't funny!"

"I think it's a little funny." Lucius exhaled cigarette smoke in a long, luxurious plume. "But she can't have gone far, can she? An inebriated woman in a Givenchy column gown and high heels?"

I didn't dare open my mouth and say what I was thinking.

"Perhaps she went downhill," he went on, as I continued to scan the main street. "The path of least resistance." He pointed at a steep side street that plunged down toward a big old church with a tall steeple.

Then I spotted the Packard, prowling toward us. I stepped right into the street, which was probably foolish, but Teddy stopped. (I would not have cared if he ran me over and put an end to the evening and my stupid life.)

He rolled down his window, and I looked into the back seat. My heart sank.

"Where on earth is she?"

"I took her to the cemetery," Teddy shot back.

Lucius chuckled. "She must've been further gone than we knew."

I pushed my head into the car window and demanded, "What do you mean, you took her to the cemetery?"

"She asked to go there. She paid me, so we're squared up. Good night."

"For heaven's sake! You can't do that!" I barely had time to step back before Teddy drove off without another word. "I'm telling Dorothy!" I shouted after the disappearing tail lights.

I tried to gather my wits before I turned around to face Mr. Beebe. I did my very best not to curse, or cry. How had I let Helene talk me into this miserable evening? All I wanted now was to be in my cabin, in bed. But I was an employee of the Rocking B and she was a guest. If I came back without her, it would mean my job. (If I still had one.)

"Did you hear that?" I stalked back to Lucius. "The nerve!"

Moonlight glazed his smooth, round face. "You cannot get good help these days," he declared, as Charles pulled up in a Jaguar. He opened the door for me. "Come on, Peach, we'll go fetch her."

I took a deep breath and tried to collect myself. It was not like me to lose my temper in front of anyone, let alone a stranger. "I'm so sorry about all this."

"About all what? We've had a marvelous evening, haven't we, Charles? It's no trouble at all."

"Where are we off to?" Charles asked, as if this were some sort of lark.

"The Silver Terrace cemetery," Lucius told him, then turned to me and explained, "the cemetery is actually several cemeteries. The Oddfellows, the Masons, the Catholics, the Firefighters...each of them has their own little hill down there."

"Oh God," I moaned. "How on earth will we find her?"

"Helene said her father was in mining," said Charles. "So we'll start with the Masons."

"She told *me* she's from Philadelphia."

Lucius chuckled. "That may be so, but it does not necessarily mean she wasn't born here."

"Sugarloaf looks lovely tonight," remarked Charles, as if we were sightseeing. The fat three-quarter moon shone on a big domed rock down in the canyon.

"Over there is the Mackay Mansion," Lucius said, pointing out a big square brick house. It reminded me of the houses in Savannah, with its fancy balconies. "Mr. Mackay was one of the original owners of the Comstock mine."

Why on earth did these fellows love old things so much? Old things had always depressed me. Even the trees in Savannah had long beards of moss, like ancient men. The aircraft factory was my first taste of the modern world. Everything there was new and shiny and clean. I loved the machinery and the efficiency and the big, bright lights that chased away all the shadows.

I cried on V-E day with the rest of the girls, but I cried because I did not want to leave the factory. I had to go back to the kitchen, just like Helene said. I never guessed that my road to freedom would have been through another broken-down old place.

But these two odd men had come to this weird, windy town to revel in the rust and decay and antiques and crumbling things. Setting up housekeeping in a town that had been dying for seventy-odd years was the last thing I would have done if I was rich.

"It's quite dangerous around here," Charles continued cheerfully. "There are collapsed mine shafts all over the landscape, hidden by brush. Most are fenced off, but occasionally an unfortunate soul will tumble into one."

I pictured myself trying to explain to Dorothy and Floss how I'd lost one of their guests down an abandoned mine shaft.

"How did you and Helene become friends?" asked Lucius.

"We...we're actually just roommates."

Charles gave a sympathetic chuckle. "That must be amusing."

I had to measure my words, since they were obviously enchanted with her. "Helene can be a very...vexing person."

"Have you ever met a great beauty who wasn't?" Lucius replied. "She has a marvelous face, doesn't she? Those hard, high cheekbones, those vulpine eyes. Like a Roman empress. Stately—and a little cruel."

Lord, I was tired of folks making such a fuss over Helene and her looks.

"Though I would have loved to see her original nose," he went on brightly. "I'm sure it was quite handsome, even if she didn't like it."

At that, I laughed. Spoken like a gossip columnist.

We turned into an empty gravel lot below the cemetery gate. To my dismay, hundreds of graves covered the hill, higgledy-piggledy, and spilled down onto other hills below, as far as the eye could see. There were a lot more dead people than living ones in Virginia City.

We all got out of the car and started scanning the cemetery. In the moonlight, the little patches of snow looked like puzzle pieces lying wrong side up. The night wind soughed through raggedy pine trees, a sound like God breathing.

"There!" said Lucius, in a hushed voice, like a birdwatcher. "Up by the bare tree."

Near the top of a little rise, we could see the figure of a woman, sitting and smoking a cigarette. The glow lit her lower face, but there were shadows where her eyes should be. She looked like some sort of specter. Or maybe the Devil herself.

"There you are!" I shouted up the hill. "Goddammit, Helene!"

She sat beneath a marble statue of a saint, the tallest thing in the graveyard. She did not answer or even react. I knew she'd heard me.

"Get in the damn car!" I shouted. She was daring me to come after her, like when Lucy was naughty and pretended not to hear me calling her in for dinner.

Well, I'd never been afraid of cemeteries. I played in graveyards my whole childhood. I stormed right in and started weaving my way through a maze of headstones and toppled statues and high weeds. Much of it was a mess, like a bunch of drunk miners had just stuck people in the ground willy-nilly.

Gravel and dirt filled the satin shoes she'd loaned me. Then I stumbled over the roots of a juniper tree and spooked a hoot owl. I could hear its huge wings beating as it flew off. Thorns snagged and tore my dress, but I didn't give a damn. I was glad I was ruining Helene's things, just as she'd ruined my evening, and maybe my life.

If I did not get fired tomorrow, I would beg Floss to move her. Or me. I would rather have slept in the goddamn barn than share a cabin with that insufferable creature for another minute.

I stumbled my way up to where Helene was sitting, smoking away as calm as you please, and just watching me, black hair blowing around and earrings tinkling like wind-chimes.

"What the hell do you think you're doing?" I demanded. "Come on. Get up." I pointed down the hill, where Charles and Lucius stood, staring at us. "See? Those nice men are going to take us back to the ranch, God only knows why."

She didn't say anything. I could see a glint that was the whites of her eyes, and the faintest little glow of her teeth in the moonlight, so I knew she was smiling at me.

"Why did I even bother?" I shouted. "I—I should leave you here!" But I couldn't. She was right, I was a goddamn Good Girl. And she knew I would come looking for her. I hated myself as much as her, right then.

Helene blew out a wreath of silver smoke that glistened in the moonlight for a moment. She crushed out her cigarette on the top of the headstone.

"Peesh," she said, her voice all soft and slurry, "allow me to introduce my father."

"Get down and get in the car!" I told her.

"I can't go."

I had lost any bit of patience I had left. I grabbed her by the wrists and tried to pull her off the headstone to her feet. She went limp and began to weep.

"Stop it!" I shouted. "You're making a spectacle of yourself."

Down the hill, Lucius and Charles were watching us like we were in a stage play.

"Is she all right?" called Charles.

"She's fine, she's just drunk!" I yelled. I turned back to Helene, who was slumped over sobbing, and wedged my shoulder under her arm. "Now stand up, dammit."

"I haven't visited Daddy in so long, Peesh," she sighed, but staggered to her feet. I peered down at the headstone where she'd been perched. In the bright moonlight, I barely made out big, squared-off letters that read, CLEARY.

"And he's been here all this time, all aloooone..." Now Helene started to heave with laughter. "He never got the shance to walk me down the aisle!" Her drunk-girl laugh echoed all the way down that rocky canyon.

"Get in that car!" I did my best to drag her down the hill, stumbling past a big grave with iron railings. A tumbleweed got hung up my skirt. I towed it along behind me, but I was not going to let go of that woman.

"My heart belongs to Daddy!" Helene brayed.

"Stop it this minute! You're going to wake up the entire town."

"The dead don't sleep!" She pointed at Lucius and Charles, standing below us in their fancy, old-fashioned clothes. "See? Ghosts!"

"Ghosts don't drive Jaguars." Exhausted, I loosened my grip. To my exasperation, she stopped to bend over a small grave and stroked a marble cherub that lay as if it was sleeping there.

"This one was a baby," she crooned. "A little...tiny...baby."

"Enough." I jerked her upright. "Can you walk?" It might as well have been a hundred miles to that damn car.

"Walk? No, but I can dance," Helene giggled. "I was going to dance on Daddy's grave, but then *you* showed up." She threw out her bare arms and started to twirl. Before I could catch her, she fell right on her behind, nearly taking me with her. I heard a loud, awful rip as she tore her dress.

"You're a good Peesh, friend," she called out in a sing-song. "Thank you for coming here to meet Daddy." Sitting there in what was left of her fancy dress, legs splayed out, holding her arms up to me, she looked like a life-size doll.

"Let me give you a hand!" called Charles, to my relief. As I stood there panting, he peeled off his jacket, handed it to Lucius, and clambered athletically up the slope.

Furious tears began to dribble down my cheeks. "Jesus God, she's a handful!"

"Don't worry, Peach." I could hear the smile in his voice. He scooped Helene up in his arms like she was his new bride. "Here we go," he said gently. "We're going to take you back to the house for some coffee."

"Coffee?" she murmured, and passed out cold.

SEVENTEEN

When I woke up the next morning, I lay there with my eyes shut for a few minutes. By some miracle, the cabin was silent. Outside, I could hear magpies fighting over the breakfast scraps. Which meant that breakfast was over in the dining room.

Which meant that I was late for work. If I still had a job.

I lurched out of bed and my reward was a big, nasty pounding sensation in my head. But Helene was gone. The sack of potatoes I'd undressed and flopped into her bed last night was already awake and out of the cabin? Her bed was neatly made. The red-and-black striped wool blanket was perfectly smooth. How on earth was that possible? Had I dreamed up the whole mess?

I yanked open the closet door to grab my blouse. I saw Helene's dress from the night before hanging there, and the one I'd worn beside it, the beautiful lace skirt torn and dirty, a little piece of tumbleweed still hanging off it. It smelled like a saloon. No, it hadn't been a bad dream. But what waited for me in the office surely would be.

My little clock read 8:11 a.m. This was bad. No time to take a shower. I pulled off my nightgown, grabbed fresh underwear, put on my brassiere, my shirt, my blue jeans, and rummaged up a kerchief to cover my hair.

The mirror reflected what my mama would call a "mess," so I circled my lips with a cheerful coral lipstick. Not much better. I found a couple of Band-aids for the blisters on my feet. Holding my breath, I tried to stuff my swollen feet into my boots. They throbbed something fierce, so I put on a pair of old plimsolls instead. Even those hurt.

I limped along the little back pathway over to the main house to avoid guests returning from breakfast. I prayed that I could get my hands on a cup of Clem's strong coffee and a whole lot of aspirin from the storeroom before I had to deal with the Boss of Bosses, Miss Dorothy Walker.

Would she hand me my walking papers as soon as I came in the door? I needed this damn job. And I was good at it. I never screwed up, I never gave a soul any reason to holler at me. Until last night. And, well, now.

Please God, I prayed. Don't let her fire me. All I wanted was to sit at my adding machine. I wanted to put things in order, add up sums, open the envelopes with guests' deposit checks—I just wanted to be around things that made sense.

"Mornin', Elouise!" came Jamie's voice. Oh Lord. The wrangler was grinning at me from the back stoop. He liked to sit there in the morning sometimes and feed the blue jays kitchen scraps. One flew up and perched on his hat, screeching for more.

"Good morning," I said, doing my best to sound "all business." I was not in the mood for any flirty nonsense. The bird let out an angry shriek as he stood up and took off his hat.

"You look mighty nice this morning, Miss Elouise."

I laughed out loud. "Nice try, Jamie. I look like nine miles of bad road and I know it."

"Nine miles of scenic highway, maybe."

"I've got work to do, Jamie." This time I didn't bother to hide my annoyance. Then his big sunny smile dimmed and I felt bad, like I'd kicked a friendly dog. "It's Friday, my busiest day in the office."

"Oh. Sure," he stammered and backed away a couple of steps. "Well, shoot. Best be getting that work done. Tomorrow's the big day."

"Tomorrow." I repeated, bewildered.

"Moving stock to summer pasture," he reminded me, then gave a little low chuckle and shook his head. "You crack me up, Elouise," he said.

The spring cattle drive. I'd forgotten all about it. Floss jokingly called it the "prom." Cattle drives—well at least the start of the cattle drives—were very popular with the guests. They were exciting and oh-so-Western. Even the dudes who'd just learned to ride would get into the act.

The last one had been a complete circus. Girls falling off horses, dogies running off down highway 395, cowboys getting mad, cowboys getting drunk, cowboys getting too friendly with the guests.

"You're coming, right?" Jamie asked.

"I was told it was compulsory."

"Compulsory!" A big grin erupted on his face at my use of such a prissy word. "It's compulsory for them cattle for sure!"

"I mean for the staff. I mean yes…I'll be there." I was stammering. That made him smile more.

"It's going to be a big one. We got the hands from Washoe Pines coming down," he said. That was a rival dude ranch up Franktown Road. "Some of my old rodeo pals from Steamboat, too."

"They for herding the cattle or the dudes?"

His face lit up with gratitude at my joke.

"Both, I guess." He smiled at me, put his hat back on. "You remember we got a big barn dance after?"

"Yes," I said. "I heard Floss and Dorothy invited boys from Sacramento. Sounds like you wranglers are going to have some competition."

"Bunch of city fellas? That's hardly competition."

"I've got to get to work," I replied. I had dilly-dallied with Jamie because I did not want to walk through that door. But now I needed to face the music.

"Well, I'll see you around, Miss Elouise." Jamie tipped his hat and sauntered off toward the barns. I stole a look at him, and noticed that his jeans fit him very nicely.

. . .

Dorothy was at her big roll-top desk, her back to me, when I walked in. Her hair was fastened in the tight ponytail she wore when she was getting down to business. The desk had belonged to her granddaddy and as usual was covered with papers—Floss liked to tease Dot that it looked like a snowman had taken a dump on it. It had been drilled into my head at the aircraft factory that mess and disorganization cost lives, so when I first got to the Rocking B, I organized the desk one afternoon when Dot was out. I had hoped to surprise and impress my new boss, but I don't think she ever forgave me.

"Good morning, Elouise," she said now, without turning around, in a tone that did not exactly match the words.

"Hello, Miss Dorothy," I replied, and started right in on my little "I'm Sorry About Last Night and It Will Never Happen Again" speech.

"Save it." Dot swiveled around and folded her arms across her chest like some sort of judge.

"Okay." I swallowed, hoping that my voice didn't reveal my nerves. I had learned as a child that the most dangerous girls on the playground were the little scrawny ones.

"What happened last night was completely unacceptable," she told me. I nodded dumbly, even though I had already admitted this in the first line of my speech.

"I'm so sorry," I said once more.

"I'm not interested in your apology," Dorothy snapped, making the word 'apology' sound downright nasty. "This is a business. I expect my employees to behave in a businesslike manner. Getting drunk with a guest and staying out all hours is not businesslike." She was speaking to me as if I were a slow child.

"I understand," I said.

"We have a curfew at this ranch, you know that, Elouise." From the way she sat smugly in her chair, it looked like she was enjoying herself. Yelling at the help was Dorothy's special talent.

"Yes, ma'am." I said in my best butter-wouldn't-melt-in-my-mouth voice.

"If you violate curfew again, you're fired. You got that?"

"Yes, ma'am," I said again, nodding. I felt a flash of relief. I still had a job! Unfortunately, Dot didn't look like she was through.

"And I will be ending the practice of letting you fraternize with our guests, Elouise," she continued. (How many times did she need to repeat my damn name?) "You will not be playing dress-up with guest's clothing and flouncing around casinos."

I began to wonder if Helene had accused me of something. That got my dander up.

"Dress-up, ma'am?" I should've kept my trap shut.

"What you did last night was completely inappropriate!" she told me. "It casts our business in a very poor light. The Rocking B has a reputation to uphold. And involving Mr. Beebe in your misadventures—"

So that was the real problem. I'd embarrassed Dot in front of Lucius Beebe.

"Helene was the one—"

"Stop talking, Elouise," snapped Dot. "Don't think I won't fire you right here and now."

I shut my mouth. I'd worked for some crummy bosses, but this little blonde Mussolini took the cake.

"Helene is a bad apple, and as a matter of fact I didn't want her here in the first place. She's a bad influence on you."

It was all I could do to hold my eyeballs down, they wanted to roll so bad. Who on earth had made sure that crazy girl got back to the ranch in one piece? I should've left her in that goddamn cemetery.

Maybe she would've obliged me and fallen down a mine shaft.

"We had a check-out yesterday," Dot went on, "so we're moving her to Room 3, here in the main house." She finished, and I saw the little bitty gleam in her cold blue eyes.

I lowered my head. I'm sure she thought I was bowing down to her, but I did it to hide the smile that was trying to take over my face. I could hear the scrape of her boots as Miss Dorothy Walker stood up out of her chair, to her full five-foot nothing, and walked out the door.

Floss and Clem, the cook, were cleaning up breakfast when I slipped into the dining room. My nerves were still sizzling like eggs on a hot griddle, but my mood had lifted. I was getting my cabin back! Sunshine poured through the old, rippled-glass windows, and as usual the place looked like a cargo plane full of breakfast dishes had crashed into the house. Maisie, wearing a gingham apron, bustled around gathering plates and cups from the tables. Though she was a paying guest, she liked to come early to help out with the morning meal, and usually stuck around to clean up afterward.

"Good morning," I said to her. "I like your apron." We were both Southern girls, but I'm pretty sure she did not own an apron.

"Good morning, Elouise." Maisie did not treat people like the Help. And that made me think about seeing her pearl necklace at the pawn shop the night before, which made me feel ashamed. Rich girls wouldn't sell Maw Maw's pearls unless things were real bad. Maybe she'd just hocked them temporarily, until her divorce settlement came in.

"Where did these fine ladies learn their manners?" groused Clem right in front of her. "I raised seven kids and our place never looked like this pigsty."

"We're horribly spoiled." Maisie laughed, shaking her head.

"You can say that again," said Clem.

"Clementine!" Floss, who'd just stepped into the dining room, made a motion like zipping up her mouth, then looked over at me.

"You want any of this?" She held up a platter with some left-over ham and potatoes. "Got any appetite?"

That told me she knew what had just happened in the office. I wondered what she thought of me.

"Yes, ma'am. Thanks," I said, with real gratitude. My stomach had not settled down after all that whisky, and I needed to put something in it. "Miss Floss..." I turned my eyes down toward the worn antique carpet of the dining room, flecked with toast crumbs. "I'm sorry about last night," I ventured. "It will never happen again, I promise."

Her expression grew serious, and she gave a little nod. "I'm sure it won't." Her voice was grave. I'd always gotten on with Floss, but right then I was reminded that she was loyal to Rocking B—and her sister. (Blood was thicker than bookkeepers, even good ones.)

I wasn't sure if I should answer, so I just stood there, my head and my feet aching, wishing I could just eat some breakfast in peace.

"You're a real good sport, Elouise," Floss gave me a funny smile. "Thank you for putting up with Helene. She was in a bad way when she showed up."

"It's fine." I gave her my best phony smile.

"We just didn't realize what a pain in the behind she'd be." Floss gave a long sigh. "Sometimes I miss the days when it was just cattle."

But cattle hadn't bought Dorothy and Floss that fine new Dodge truck, or poker games with movie stars. The divorce business had been good to the daughters of the Rocking B. Helene was a customer, and I wasn't.

It turned out to be a pleasant morning in the office, because Dot was out in the barn getting ready for the cattle drive and dance. I closed the books for April. Then Floss asked me to go with her into Reno to buy more supplies for the weekend. There would be a big barbeque after the cattle drive, and she was worried we didn't have enough beer and soda pop.

"I need an extra pair of hands," she said, by way of invitation.

That was fine by me. I did not want to run into Dot for a while, and a trip to town was always a welcome break.

"How are you doing, Elouise?" asked Floss as we headed down the driveway in the fancy rig.

"I'm fine." I stared out the truck window.

"The 'no-fraternization' part was Dot's idea," she said, as only a sister could. "Gum?" She held out a pack of Juicy Fruit. I'd noticed a while back that Florence Walker only chewed gum when she was nervous.

"No thanks," I said. "And it's fine. It wasn't my idea to 'fraternize' with that woman in the first place." I hadn't meant to add that last part, but her anxiety had made me a little bold.

"I'm sorry we stuck her in there with you."

"You had your reasons," I replied. "She's a paying guest." I thought about the day that Helene had parachuted into my life. How no one had so much as asked if it was okay.

"It was a favor for the man that helped her leave Las Vegas," Floss went on. "He's a...good friend."

"It's none of my business," I answered, very primly, but I noticed that her freckled face and chest had both gone scarlet.

"You didn't meet him when he was here, did you?" she asked.

I shook my head.

"Philippe Kiehl is pretty persuasive." She let herself smile, just a bit. I had always just accepted the fact that Floss was a spinster. She was not a feminine sort of woman, and I'd half-figured she didn't have any use for men. We had wranglers all over the ranch but she talked to them like they were her brothers. It was hard for me to imagine her flirting with anyone.

"You sticking around Nevada for a while?" Floss asked me then.

"Well...sure." I was surprised at this change of tack. I didn't want to say anything that might make her think I didn't intend to hang onto my job.

"We're hoping you want you to stay on," Floss told me. I knew she was not speaking for her mean little sister.

"I appreciate that, ma'am."

She waited a little bit before she spoke again. "Jamie's been asking after you."

My heart fell down into my socks. Had someone seen him flirting with me that morning? I did not want to get into any more trouble with my bosses.

"Don't worry," I said real quick. "I've shut him down."

"Oh." Floss looked a little surprised, and laughed. "That's not what I was getting at." She glanced my way. "He's a good fellow. He knows how to doctor cattle almost as good as the vet. He's turned out to be one of our best wranglers."

"Well what's he asking about?" I demanded. Why couldn't people just leave me alone?

"You know," she said. "We tell them not to fraternize..."

"I don't!" What on earth had he been saying about me?

"...but if you want to go out with him, we are fine with it," Floss told me, with a little smile.

Maybe it was a test.

"I don't want to go out with him. He's just a silly boy."

"That boy fought at Guadalcanal." Dorothy glanced over at me with her big bright hazel eyes. "You're a funny one, Elouise."

"Why is that so funny?" I knew I sounded kind of cross but my head was starting to hurt again and I didn't like talking about this sort of stuff with her. I felt like the ranch was just one big crazy soup of people's personal lives and emotions.

"Suit yourself," she said with a little smile. "I just thought you might like to go out with him."

"I'm sure he'd be happier rolling in the hay with one of the guests." I regretted it as soon as the words came out.

"Elouise. You know he's not like the other fellows," Floss said.

"I'm sorry," I mumbled. "I'm just not up for that sort of thing, that's all."

She nodded like she understood. Then she changed the subject again. Unfortunately, to something worse. "So how's Lucy?"

"She's fine," I managed to say. Then the words just flowed out in a stream. "Mama saw her a couple of weeks ago when she went by the place. She saw her playing in the yard with another little girl. She said her hair is real long now." (How I wished I had a new photograph of her, with her pretty long hair. Mama's last letter said it has gone blonde in the sun, just like mine at the same age.)

"That's nice," Floss said.

"Mama talked to her teacher and Mrs. Holt says that she's getting good marks."

"You must be proud."

"I sure am," I said. "She's a smart girl."

"Just like her mother." Floss turned the truck onto the highway and we headed north to Reno.

EIGHTEEN

It was bliss to have the Sugar Pine cabin to myself again. I spent Friday evening before the cattle drive devouring *The Cardinal*. I'd found the novel in the guests' lending library in the parlor. It had been a big best-seller the year before. I couldn't resist a story about a humble priest who became a Prince of the Church, even if I was pretty much done with all that Catholic nonsense.

It was nice to not feel self-conscious about reading whatever I liked. Helene had a big pile of books, none of which I'd ever heard of, most of which she'd checked out of the library in Reno after saying that the ranch bookshelves were full of potboilers and trash. She had gotten herself a library card the second day she was here, right after her big shopping spree. She was like a chain smoker, starting another book before she finished the last one.

When I'd gone over to the kitchen to filch some cookies and milk at bedtime, I found Clem still cleaning up the dinner dishes and pitched in for awhile, drying glasses and gossiping. She reported that Helene had passed the evening in the parlor with the other girls. She'd even been part of a big, loud sing-along around the piano, which wasn't like her at all. The thought of her yucking it up with the other guests when she hadn't the decency to apologize to me made me resent her even more.

I woke up Saturday morning to the sound of the wind rattling the drafty old windows in Sugar Pine. A windy day was the last thing we needed on a cattle drive. It would spook the horses, spook the stock, and put the humans in a surly mood. But it's what you get in the Washoe Valley—wind, and plenty of it.

Breakfast in the dining room ended with Dorothy's "orientation" for the dudes. We were to listen to the wranglers and do exactly what they said. Some of the girls jostled around giggling, and Dorothy got real stern with them. This was serious stuff. Dudes could get hurt or even killed on a cattle drive if they didn't mind their P's and Q's.

The summer pasture sat up in Little Valley, so we'd be driving the stock into the mountains. There were some narrow spots on the old dirt road where things might get hairy.

"Beginners, anyone not confident about your riding abilities, you'll bring up the rear," Dorothy told the guests. Then she started pairing up the stronger riders with wranglers, calling out assignments, and there was a fuss at every name she called. Girls wanted to be with certain wranglers, such as the ones they were sleeping with.

"Dammit! This is not a high school dance, ladies!" hollered Dorothy. "You ride with the wrangler you're assigned to or you can stay here."

I heard Helene's name called out. She'd been put with Connie, to no one's surprise. He was the head wrangler and she was the best rider among the guests. I was sort of hoping I'd be assigned to Jamie, but instead I was assigned the "rear guard" which was the worst place to be because of the dust.

I was worried that I might not get Kinky, so I slipped out and got to the barn early. But as soon as I got there, Jamie came over to me to say he'd gotten the pony tacked up for me. That was sure a nice thing for him to do on such a busy day, and I thanked him. He seemed a little anxious, waiting for his rodeo friends from Steamboat to show up.

The dudes poured out of the big house after breakfast, jabbering and laughing. I was glad I'd gotten ahead of the crush.

I asked Jamie if he'd seen Helene.

"Yes ma'am, she was out here bright and early," he told me, "getting some of the vinegar out of Sweet Potato."

Now a couple of beat-up trucks towing rusty old trailers bounced and rattled up the driveway, and Jamie's face relaxed.

"Elouise, come on, I want you to meet my friends," he said.

The trucks parked under the cottonwoods and three wranglers climbed out. One of them was the most bow-legged man I'd ever seen, his legs like an outline of a horse's belly. He was older than Jamie. The other two looked to be about his age.

"Elouise, I'd like to introduce my buddies," said Jamie. "This here is Randy, a team roper from Elko. We were on the circuit together for a while."

"How do you do, ma'am?" Randy gave me a big smile, one that made me suspect Jamie had talked me up a bit.

"This here is Glen. He was a saddle bronc rider back on the circuit." I noticed the big silver trophy buckle on the cowboy's worn belt.

"How do you do?" Glen was a red-haired fellow with a nose like an Idaho russet potato, both in size and texture. It looked like it had been broken a few times and burned a few times more.

"And this is Lucky, but he don't talk," Jamie grinned, slapping a tall, dark-skinned man on the back. He had long, thick, hair so black and shiny it reflected the sky, worn back in a ponytail, and coffee-brown eyes. "We met on the rodeo circuit a long time ago. Lucky, this is Miss Elouise."

He smiled politely at me, and I saw that he was missing a side tooth. One side of Lucky's face sagged a bit, and that there was a long, nasty scar above his right ear. But he was still a handsome fellow.

"Lucky rides the big steers," Jamie went on. "He got throwed one too many times. He got kicked bad by a Brahma bull and it split his skull right open. All of us were there that night."

The men nodded solemnly, but Lucky wore a slight smile.

"No one ever seen a man come back from something like that,"

Jamie went on, as if we were in the presence of a celebrity. "So he goes by Lucky."

"Hello, Lucky," I said. "Nice to meet you."

"Lucky moved here not that long ago, and right now he's looking after the haying operation at the Barkley place in Steamboat," Jamie said.

"All right fellas. Time to get these horses unloaded," said Randy, who was ready to get to work. He winked at me. "Nothing like a dude ranch cattle drive. You got twice the help and it takes four times as long."

"Hush," Jamie said to him.

"I believe it." I glanced over my shoulder at the hubbub behind us. Floss, Dorothy, and Connie were busy pulling horses in from the corral, slipping on halters, and handing them off to the guests, who led them to the railing of the corral to tack up. Pretty soon there were almost a dozen horses tied up there getting curried, blanketed, and saddled. Girls were laughing and talking too loudly. I saw Dorothy pull Bertha aside and then send her off, her face like a thundercloud. The girl was a lush and Dorothy must've smelled booze on her breath.

"You one of them dee-vor-says, too?" asked Glen, following my gaze.

"Yes I am," I said.

"Is it true what they say?"

I didn't like his tone. "What do they say?" I shot right back. At that moment I felt very protective of the ranch and our guests. I knew how hard Floss and Dorothy and the boys worked to keep us all safe here.

"Dammit Glen," Jamie said, his face turning bright red. I wasn't sure if he was angry or embarrassed. Glen just grinned in the stupid, lustful way of a man who doesn't get enough female attention but blames women for that.

"You got yourself one nice job here, Jamie," he said, but he kept looking right at me. "You let me know next time they have an opening." The way he said it gave me the creeps.

Maisie came up to us, passing out donuts from a pink box. She tried her best, but she wasn't real comfortable around the horses.

"Hello, fellas," she said in her sweet Southern way. "Care for a donut?" It was easy to picture her as a USO volunteer, which she said she'd been during the war. I noticed her Brownie camera hanging from a strap around her neck. She'd been taking snapshots of absolutely everything, driving us all a little bit crazy.

I figured a herd of women was no different from a herd of horses or cattle. Everyone in the herd knows who's weak, and who's strong. That's why Helene gloated when she saw Maisie's pearls at the pawn shop. I felt a little sick remembering that again.

All the cowboys took a donut and said thank you. Maisie moved on to the guests by the corral. Then we all watched the sneaky little mustang mare, Firefly, stretch her neck out and stick her muzzle right in Maisie's donut box. Poor Maisie gave a yelp and the box tumbled into the dust, scattering donuts willy-nilly. Firefly finished them all off, as the boys busted up.

I was glad to see Maisie laughing too.

The winter pasture was in the low country east of the ranch, close enough that the hands could get hay out to the cattle, pitching it off the back of a big flatbed pickup truck. The mama cows had their babies in the February snow while eagles and hawks and magpies made a big picnic of the leftover stuff. I will say I had a very different image of our national bird after that.

During the summer, the Rocking B's pastures were used for growing grass hay. Dorothy said they got three full crops if they were lucky. That provided the winter feed for the stock, if the winter didn't last too long. With this last big winter, we'd run out of hay and had to buy enough to see the stock through to spring. Spending her money on hay made tight-fisted Dot Walker boil. She couldn't wait to get her cattle up to Little Valley.

Now that it was May, the stock would graze up in the high meadows where it was cool and nice, coming in from the mountain sunshine to chew their cud in the shade of big Ponderosa pine trees. It seemed like a pretty swell life for a cow, even though they'd all end up on someone's dinner plate.

I had been through Little Valley, which was actually not that little, on trail rides. We had campouts for the guests up there during the summer. But springtime weather was tricky. Even now, Floss had warned, we could have a sudden blizzard. The Washoe Valley could conjure a snowstorm right out of a beautiful blue sky.

It wasn't until the beginning of the drive that I saw Helene, and I had to stop myself laughing at the sight of her on her little English saddle, riding alongside Connie with her bobbed nose in the air. I noticed a couple of cowboys from other ranches busting up too, but Connie just grinned. Sweet Potato was a cow horse and knew her stuff. All Helene had to do was give the Appaloosa her head and let her follow her instincts. Pretty soon the guest wranglers forgot about Helene's silly English tack and everyone just got to work.

It took a while to get all the stock headed in the same direction, especially the calves. They kept getting scared and running off in all the hubbub. Then they'd start bawling for their mamas and rejoin the herd. To get them up to the road to Little Valley, we had to drive them south down Highway 395 a-ways. Traffic in both directions was stopped by the wranglers.

The first part of the drive was pretty easy because there was a fence on either side of the highway, but when it opened up, the chaos began all over again. The air filled with shouts and whistles and cows bellowing and girls shrieking and laughing. Sometimes the cowboys yipped and barked like coyotes. I heard plenty of cussing, too.

The guests were excited to be on a real cattle drive, even if the ladies in my group were just bringing up the rear. Occasionally a calf would get spooked or confused and head back down our direction, but there were so many of us that she would just turn around.

Worse than the dust was the smell of cow poop. When the cattle got excited, they shat. These cattle were really excited so there was plenty of it. I decided I didn't want to be in the rear guard a minute longer.

I put my heels into Kinky and we headed up toward some cowboy-guest "teams". I noticed Glen chatting up Jennifer Waters, a very buxom girl, and giving her pointers on riding. I passed them at a little jog like I had some business up ahead.

"Jennifer!" I called, in my most "official" voice. "Can I talk to you please?"

Without hesitation, she put that horse in gear and followed me.

"Jesus," she said when we got out of earshot. "What a wolf."

We rounded a long, easy bend, and I spotted Lucky and Jamie ahead of us. They were both concentrating hard, I could see, because we were getting to a tricky part where Little Valley road got steeper and narrower. Animals could end up in a ravine. The wind blew dust down the canyon at us and I pulled my kerchief up over my nose.

Ahead of us, cattle bunched up and bumped against one another. Then, sure enough, a calf stumbled off the road, and right over the edge.

I saw Lucky point his horse down into the ravine. He leaned way back in his saddle, almost lying down against his horse's back. He disappeared too. My heart began to pound, and the whole big parade of cattle kept moving and soon we were close to the spot where Lucky had vanished.

Then up popped the calf, all wild-eyed, scrambling back onto the road, crying for its mama, with Lucky on his buckskin, right on its heels.

"Would you look at that!" I heard Jennifer say.

For almost an hour we pushed up the mountain, the cattle lowing, men hacking and spitting, and girls chatting and sneezing. It was getting pretty warm, and I had just about decided that I would not go on another cattle drive, ever, when finally we spilled out into the beautiful valley. It was like watching a river of cows reaching the sea, the way they all poured out into that bright green grass.

That was the first time I spotted Helene, who was wearing her dark sunglasses, and no hat. Maybe it had blown off, but she was smiling. It wasn't her little superior smile. It was a big old grin. Her sleeves were rolled to the elbow and a thick black braid slapped against her upper back as she and Connie loped along, joking and laughing. I had never seen her that relaxed, like she was in her element and having fun. Me, I was ready to get off the horse.

I was relieved that we'd arrived without losing any calves or dudes. It wasn't even noon yet, and the sun was still climbing into the bright blue Sierra sky.

"The spring's over here," called Jamie, who led the way toward a line of troughs that sat near the edge of the meadow.

Some of the stock who'd been there the summer before knew the way and followed his lead. The younger ones needed a little encouragement, and now that we were out in the open, the cowboys started to show off a bit for us. The guests began to hoot and clap as the men tossed a few loops over the heads of scampering calves, or cut out a heifer and let it return to the herd.

The sun felt warm on my back and I pulled out my half-empty canteen for a drink. I saw that Lucky had dismounted nearby and was checking one of the buckskin's back hooves.

"Is he all right?" I asked, and only then remembered he did not speak. I felt embarrassed. But he set down his horse's foot, turned, smiled, and gave me the "A-OK" sign.

"I saw you go get that calf," I told him. "That was something else."

He gave a little "it was nothing" shrug.

Then I heard a girl yell, and I turned to see Helene. She was waving at me wildly, like I'd just arrived on an ocean liner after being gone for a year.

Oh God, I thought. Here we go. I guess now that I was standing talking to this tall, handsome Indian fellow she'd decided it was time to make nice.

I waved half-heartedly and turned back to Lucky. That was when I noticed him staring at her. His face spread out into an expression of pure astonishment. I was glad he couldn't talk. I was glad I did not have to hear another man marvel at her goddamn beauty.

"Hyah!" I heard Helene yell at Sweet Potato, and I knew, from Lucky's widening eyes, that she was riding toward us. And for some reason I just watched his face, getting brighter by the second and also scared—no mistaking that.

Yessir, she has that effect on men, I thought.

At first, I thought the strange sound I heard had come from a calf. And then I realized that it was Lucky. He was trying to say something. I was afraid Helene would mock him, that she'd say something cruel and cutting when she heard the poor fellow try to speak.

I turned around. I had half a mind to just walk away. What did I have to say to Helene, anyway? The only thing I wanted to hear from her was, "I'm sorry."

She dismounted and let Sweet Potato's reins fall right on the ground, something no one in their right mind would do with that horse. I almost said something to her, then saw how fast she was coming toward us through the tall grass, her strides high and hard. She tore off her sunglasses. Her eyes were huge.

The sound came again, from down deep in Lucky's throat, torn to pieces by his poor, damaged brain. Was he having a fit? I looked back at him in alarm. I'd had a friend in grammar school who had seizures. I tried to remember what I was supposed to do. And then Helene's voice rang out across the meadow.

"Luuuke!" she hollered. Her voice sounded almost as raw as his.

She started running at us. Lucky lurched toward her, nearly bowling me over, and broke into a run, too. After a few strides they collided, so hard that his battered old hat fell off. She sobbed and clutched the Indian, but it was almost like she was clawing at his back, like she was a wild animal. He started crying too and gulping for air as if he was drowning.

There was quite an audience watching this strange spectacle, and everyone looked as bewildered as I was. Even Sweet Potato, who I was positive would run off, stood there and watched Helene like a worried, loyal dog.

Jamie heard the commotion and came galloping back across the meadow to see what was happening.

"What the hell?" I heard him yell. I could see he thought Lucky was hurting Helene. He dismounted with his horse still moving, pedaling the air like he was going to tie a calf he'd just roped, and ran toward the two. I saw that Jamie was getting ready to pull Lucky off Helene by his shirt collar.

"Dammit Lucky!" he shouted.

"It's okay!" I yelled, though I still wasn't sure that was true, and Jamie stopped short.

"Miss Helene!" he yelled.

But Helene did not so much as glance his way. She and Lucky sank down to the ground together, right onto their knees in the damp earth of the spring meadow. She put her hands on either side of his smooth brown face, and held him still for a moment, as if she were studying every single detail there. His face was wet with tears but he smiled at her, showing his tobacco-stained teeth.

I studied his face too, and then I realized why Lucky had looked so familiar: he had the same eyes as Helene, and his thick black eyebrows followed the same line as her perfectly plucked ones did. His lips were full like hers and his cheekbones were as high, but his skin was a deeper shade of brown, like a Sequoia tree.

Lucky kissed Helene's cheek, then touched her nose with a confused expression. I saw her face crumple then. She shook her head, and started crying harder. Even over the racket of the cows, you could hear Helene's awful sobs. I crossed myself.

Jamie glanced my way, and our eyes met. He looked over his shoulder at the group, and in some kind of silent agreement, he and I led our horses together so they stood nose-to-nose, so their bodies could shield this brother and sister from the stares of the wranglers and the guests.

PART THREE

NINETEEN

BETTYE CHRISTIAN
WASHOE VALLEY, APRIL 1952

The big barbeque after the cattle drive felt like a loud, pointless dream, the sort you want to wake up from, and can't. The sort where you're trying to get to someplace, or to someone, and can't.

As we swayed and rocked down the dirt road to the noise of other people's conversation and laughter, I wished that Luke and I had just stayed behind in Little Valley. Stayed in that meadow, with the little blue lilies all around us and the sleek garter snakes weaving through the grass and the nuthatches spiraling up the trunks of the Ponderosas. I wished that we could have just stayed there until the stars came out and the moon scaled the pines and the crickets began their song.

But we were in shock, and people in shock do what other people tell them to do:

Can you get up on your horse, Helene?

Come on, let's head back down to the ranch; there you go.

I don't remember dismounting, but I'm pretty sure it was Jamie who took care of Sweet Potato, curried her and put her away. And it was Elouise who fixed us plates of food and brought them to the long, paper-covered picnic table where we sat. We couldn't eat a bite.

We pushed the beans and the fragrant meat around with our forks, like two children waiting to be excused from the dinner table.

I was grateful that we were not sitting with people that knew either of us. We were with a group of strangers, men and women talking about the day, about inconsequential things, and laughing and clinking beer bottles and smoking.

I thought we were being politely ignored. Stories as good as mine and Luke's would make the rounds quickly here. To look at us, you may even have thought that we were not particularly happy to see one another. I was struggling with an almost volcanic joy, so overwhelming that it terrified me. I realize that people spend their lives chasing such an emotion—but I'd never believed happiness like that was possible, or even necessary. I wasn't sure there was space in my body for all of it.

Our glances kept colliding and our nervous smiles caromed off each other's. I had never before seen my brother with long hair. The boys at the Stewart School were forced to wear short, military-style haircuts—it was the first and most humiliating way that the school eradicated their "Indian-ness". Because his hair was so thick and stood up so straight, that short haircut had won him the nickname of "Badger" among his friends. But now he wore a ponytail, a thin deer hide thong wrapped securely at its base. That wasn't all—a small, carved silver hoop earring adorned his right ear.

He was proudly, obviously, Indian. After passing as White for most of my life, it was unsettling to sit there with him. It was the first time since I'd run away from the boarding school that anyone knew I was an Indian. I did not want my brother to know how exposed and afraid that made me.

Then, thank goodness, we heard the bluegrass band strike up something lively and loud, and all the guests eased themselves up from the hard benches of the picnic tables and headed off to the dance in the hay barn. Luke and I found ourselves alone.

It was like a spell had been broken. Without saying a word to one another, we got up from the table and began to walk, arm in arm. We left the grassy picnic area and turned down the sandy road behind the stable. After a few minutes, the music from the barn seemed no louder than the crickets.

We startled a taboo'o, a cottontail rabbit, as we approached a thicket of blooming antelope brush. It froze for a moment, then zigzagged up the trail ahead of us before plunging into the chaparral.

After we passed the place where it had vanished, I glanced behind and saw the rabbit doubling back, returning to the spot along the trail where we'd first seen it—a tactic Mama had pointed out to me time and time again. Cottontails might not be as clever as etza'a, coyote, she'd explained, but they could play tricks, too.

"Remember your secret rabbit drives at school?" I asked Luke. He gave a little chuckle. Rabbit drives were a tradition for tribes in the high desert: families would come together in a huge circle, walking steadily inward, flushing rabbits into an ever-shrinking center, where they would finally be clubbed to death.

The older boys at Stewart would sneak out into the sagebrush that surrounded the school to conduct their own small-scale, illicit rabbit hunts. I'd just heard stories, but never witnessed the spectacle, thank God. The boys would cook their catch over campfires they made in the canyon near Clear Creek.

I leaned against him, unable to fully believe what was happening. When Luke was shipped off to that ranch in Elko, and when his postcards slowed and finally stopped, I did not torment myself with the thought that he was still out there. Why would I? I had never seen a speck of evidence that the people I lost were anything but lost forever.

We scuffed our feet along the sandy track, and the blue-violet shadows of the mountains rested upon us like a quiet blessing. A flicker's call pierced the velvet dusk. Surrounded by the sensations of our childhood, everything in my head and heart was in an uproar.

Luke stopped, turned to me, hesitated, then touched my nose. His dense black brows rose toward the unavoidable question. From his bemused expression, it was clear he assumed I'd done it out of vanity, to rid myself of my Paiute nose.

"I cracked up a car," I shrugged, too casually. My brother shook his head, repeating the question with his eyes: *Really...how?*

I don't know why it frightened me so much to tell him the truth. Plenty of bad things had happened to us both. I still remembered, when I was eleven, how he'd beaten up a Washoe boy who had lifted my skirt in front of his friends.

"My husband," I said, my voice going a little hoarse. "Peter."

He took this news in expressionlessly, his face still, his veiled eyes unblinking. I saw a tightening in the muscle of his jaw. Then, to my relief, he nodded somberly, and took my hand like a doctor might, gentle but purposeful. As I watched closely, his finger traced letters on my palm: D-I-V-O-R...

"Yes!" I exclaimed, before he finished. "That's why I'm here. I left him a few months ago and came here from Chicago—well, from Chicago by way of Las Vegas..." I realized there was so much we hadn't even talked about.

He gave me another quizzical look and mouthed the word, "Chicago?"

"I ran away from Stewart when I turned fifteen," I explained.

His smile said, *Of course you did! I would expect nothing less.*

"But I damn well never planned to come back here," I added vehemently, and only too late realized that Luke, indeed, had come back here. He now lived and worked here.

"I ended up in Chicago, and that's where I met Peter."

At his name, the set of Luke's jaw hardened.

"It started off wonderfully." I heard my voice, almost defensive. "He was quite the romantic. And very, very wealthy. We lived on the Gold Coast, near the Palmer Mansion." Those details had been part of my script in Chicago——the hints that let others know how well-to-do we were.

His expression soured.

"You won't be quite so disgusted when I get my divorce settlement." I attempted to sound nonchalant. "I'm not like the trust fund girls here."

He gave an *oh well* shrug, and I saw what looked like disappointment in his eyes.

"Luke, the only thing I ever wanted was to be rich!" I cried. "And there were plenty of fellows out there who were willing to accept that deal. It's not as if I invented this game!"

He observed me with a cool detachment. Hard to imagine how a silent fellow could win an argument, but he seemed to be prevailing.

"I mean, what else did I have but my looks? And heaven knows, those don't last. A girl has to get while the getting's good."

He laughed, reached out, and locking his eyes to mine, tapped on my temple three times.

"Brains are a liability in a woman," I snapped. "Men don't want smart wives."

He made a face that said, *Don't be ridiculous.*

"So are you married?" I asked.

It took a moment, but he shook his head no.

"Ever married?"

A quick nod.

"And was she smart?" I challenged him. I'd yet to meet a man who valued brains over beauty.

He nodded deeply, took my hand, and wrote HOPI on it slowly.

"Children?" I asked.

He held up two fingers.

"Boys? Girls?"

He pointed to himself, and tapped his chest two times: two boys.

"Where do they live?"

He sighed, and his rough fingertip slowly spelled out YUMA on my palm. I felt as if I'd carelessly tugged on the long, dark thread that would unravel his past. I knew that I wasn't prepared for it.

"Was that before your accident?" I asked, unable to stop myself. I had hundreds of questions, maybe thousands of them. We were not reuniting as children; we were reuniting as adults, as strangers, really, with the wreckage of our lives fanned out behind us. Luke gave a shrug.

"It was over after that?"

The next look had a finality to it: *Obviously.*

I knew I should change the subject, but Luke pointed to me, and I knew he was asking if I had children.

"Thank God no children," I said vehemently, and I saw him glance down at his feet. "Oh. I'm sorry, I hope that didn't sound awful." I felt abashed at my tone, but he gave me a forgiving smile.

"Why did you stop writing to me?" I heard myself ask.

I saw the hurt in his eyes. He didn't answer right away, then pulled out the notebook. His pencil hovered for a moment before he put it away. He shrugged, and shook his head.

I thought of the dwindling postcards that had finally stopped. His perfect silence, no different than the silence that followed my mother's death.

"I thought you were dead," I said, surprised at the note of accusation in my voice.

He took out the notebook, took a deep breath, and wrote, "Wished I was."

"I'm sorry," I murmured, regretting my tone. It hadn't been his fault. And I had given up so easily—as if hope was a weakness.

Luke had guided and protected me at the Stewart School. He was the one who insisted I learn how to ride. He was the one who scolded me if I didn't get good marks or ran afoul of a teacher, even though he hated school himself.

Mother had told him many stories about Sarah Winnemucca that I had not remembered, and he would share those whenever I got discouraged. Luke had wanted me to aspire, to do something great, like her. Was it now my turn to look after him?

My brother had been shipped off to live the small and brutal life that the school had prepared him for, working on a ranch through pitiless hot summers and bitterly cold winters, an expendable cog in the wheel, toiling away for some wealthy cattleman.

"Did you fight in the war?" I asked, suddenly.

He shook his head.

"You were already hurt?"

His expression abruptly shifted; it was clear he wanted to change the subject. He took out his little notebook.

When's divorce? he wrote.

"Soon, thank God. I only have a couple of weeks left before I 'graduate'."

What then? he scribbled.

I nearly launched into my usual soliloquy: *"I'll be sipping Champagne on the terrace of a little vine-covered villa in the hills above Arles, re-reading every single Colette novel, gazing out at a pink sunset on the Mediterranean..."* but something had shifted violently inside me.

"I don't know." I heard myself say, and realized with dismay that this was now true.

Spare? he wrote.

"God no." I shook my head. Luke looked a bit relieved, too.

His pencil stub scratched excitedly. This time the letters were big, almost covering the little page: *Come with me to AZ.*

"Arizona?"

He nodded.

Job

"Where?"

Near Flagstaff, he wrote. *After rodeo season. Big ranch needs help.*

You can cook.

I laughed. "I couldn't make oatmeal to save my life."

He shrugged, and I realized that he wasn't joking. I felt the pinch of irritation. I couldn't believe that my brother would entertain such an idea. But then again, he was exactly what the White people of the Stewart Indian School had taught him to be: a ranch hand. Perhaps he thought that my education had ended when I learned to cook and sew.

You'd like Flagstaff, he scribbled.

"You've been there?"

Rodeo.

He glanced at me.

Beautiful, he added. *5 hrs from Yuma.*

"Ah." He wanted to be closer to his sons.

Your nephews, he wrote, before I could say that. I had nephews, suddenly. I had a brother, suddenly.

It was amazing that I had even recognized Luke today. I tried to recall the moment that I knew. In the glare of noon sunlight, I had seen his distinctive head, the faceted planes of his jaw and cheekbone: a manly version of the boy I'd last seen on the back of a truck leaving Reno.

I had been way across the meadow when Connie noticed my bald stare, and presuming I was like any East Coast rube at the Rocking B, teased, "Never seen an Indian in real life?" and something in me startled.

"Do you know him?" I'd blurted, unable to tear my eyes away, afraid the Indian man would disappear into the crowd again. I hadn't seen him before; he must have been riding behind us.

"Pal of Jamie's," Connie said, and loudly spat tobacco juice. "Goes by Lucky."

Lucky. Could it possibly be him? I sat riveted in my saddle, watching. Then I saw Elouise approach him. There was something in the way he reacted to her, some gesture, or facial expression—I don't even remember what it was. But that was when I just knew.

Want you to meet them, Luke wrote now.

I was seized with an overwhelming need to meet his sons, his family—our family. "Yes!" I exclaimed. Did the boys look like he had, as a child? Maybe those children could replace some of what had been stolen from us. Then a terrifying thought seized me.

"Do they still put our children in boarding schools?" I asked. "Stewart is still there. We drove past it on the way here."

Different now, he wrote, and squeezed my arm gently.

I felt it then, the sensation that my boat had been snatched by a new, swift current. The bright coastline that I had been desperately paddling toward was no longer visible. My brother and I were lashed together by fate once again. The villa in France was beginning to feel like a thing I had clipped out of a magazine a long time ago, and taped to my mirror. Looking at it now, I saw how much the image had faded, how flimsy that little dream was. There was something exciting about tearing up my old plan.

I glanced happily at Luke. I knew things that he did not. My brother had yet to realize that he was not doomed to be a handicapped cowboy who worked for wages on a ranch in Arizona. After my divorce, I would have lots of money and we would have lots of options, marvelous ones, unlimited ones.

We would come up with a new plan. How wonderful it would be to sit together and invent new lives. I could picture us all on the *Lurline*, steaming into Honolulu, his boys shouting and laughing as they chased each other down the decks, seagulls wheeling above, the smiling brown lei-makers lining the dock, ready to loop cool, moist necklaces of orchids and tuberose around our necks.

It was almost too dark to see now, so we turned back toward the ranch. The spring night was mild and aromatic, and the songs of crickets and frogs thickened the air.

Luke reached for my elbow and pointed silently. A large, long-legged toohoo'o slipped across the trail not seven strides ahead of us, with a young brush rabbit hanging limp in his mouth. That one had not been so clever. The bobcat was not particularly surprised to find us there, and he gave us a nonchalant stare. Then he vanished silently into a willow thicket.

I glanced at my brother. I couldn't tell if he was simply admiring the creature, or if he had seen something more in the glance of that cool, confident predator, because I did. A chill swept over me. To ward it off, I tucked myself against him and aimed us toward the barn.

As we approached, Floss, hurrying across the yard with a pitcher of lemonade, spotted us. Her hair had worked itself loose and she had a grin on her sweat-slicked face.

"Helene! Make sure your brother gets back to the barn dance," she called. "We're short on men."

Luke chuckled, still amused by my alias. (I'd gotten it from the empty jar of Queen Helene Mint Julep Facial Masque that had been my prized possession as a girl at Stewart. I'd used it to store buttons.)

"Come on, don't be stingy with that cowboy!" Floss declared. "Lucky, Jamie talked you up as a real good dancer, too. Now get over there and make some girls happy. And you, Princess, go make some fellas miserable."

Luke cracked up at that, and Floss hurried off.

I glanced at my brother inquiringly, placed my hand gently on his arm. I was worried at how the guests would respond to a man who could not speak.

"It's okay?" I asked, my tone hesitant and concerned. Luke knew exactly what I was asking. He shot me a scornful look that declared, *Oh ye of little faith.*

We walked arm-in-arm toward the lights of the hay barn.

TWENTY

sat on the sofa in the parlor, restlessly paging through a dog-eared *New Yorker* magazine. After the festivities of the previous day, Sunday evening was downright melancholy. Floss had stuffed seven girls into her big station wagon and taken them into Carson, to a double feature: *Singing in the Rain* and *High Noon*. Not that I wanted to see a musical (vapid cheeriness, bizarre outbursts of song and dance) or a Western (stupid, savage Indians making White people's lives miserable, before being thoroughly routed). No thank you.

Elouise and Jamie had gone to Reno for the evening. Apparently the barn dance had sealed the deal for those two. She was a good kid, and I had not yet made up to her for the horrible night in Virginia City. It was eating at me. I'd sensed that something between us had eased with my brother's arrival, but there was no disputing the fact that I still owed her a big, fat apology. It had been some time since I cared what anyone thought of me. I just didn't know where or how to begin.

Dorothy entered the parlor with her newspaper and glanced warily toward me. "Good evening, Helene," she said, and settled in on a divan at the far end of the room with the Sunday paper.

The Walkers still used the parlor as their own living room, despite the presence of the guests. They'd converted every square inch of the place into accommodations. It was a wonder they weren't renting out stalls in the barn, too. Only the Flying ME up the road charged more, but they had a swimming pool.

So here we sat, guest and proprietor. Dot had been frostier than usual after Lucius Beebe delivered me, unconscious, to her front door.

I missed Luke horribly. I was miserable, thinking about him in a nasty old bunkhouse in the middle of nowhere. All I wanted now was to be close to him. Jamie had assured me he'd help me stay in touch with Luke, since my brother had no telephone.

"Where is Steamboat, exactly?" I asked her.

"Not far," Dot said. "A little north. Nothing there but the hot springs and ranches. Why?"

"That's where my brother is."

"Well, don't get any ideas about inviting him here," Dot admonished me.

"It's not as if we can talk on the phone," I reminded her.

She heaved a big, irritated sigh. "Despite our event yesterday, only registered guests and employees are permitted on the property." It was as if she were citing the civil code of Washoe County.

"And cab drivers, and delivery men."

She gave me a thin smile. "Yes. Them, too."

"And your Tuesday poker buddies."

The resulting silence was not unexpected. But the next words out of her mouth were.

"Would you and your brother like to join this week's poker game?"

I stared at her in disbelief. "Really?"

"Happy now?"

Where had that come from? Perhaps hobnobbing with Mssrs. Beebe and Clegg had boosted my stock with the little snob after all.

Luke had demonstrated at the barn dance that he could ably hold his own in company. Nearly every ranch guest had been eager to dance with him—there was even a brief catfight over who'd get the last one. Still, a barn dance and Dorothy's poker game were two very different occasions.

"It's a fifty dollar buy-in. I don't suppose there are too many Indians with that rattling around in their pocket."

I did my best to ignore the crack. "I'll stake him," I replied.

"What are sisters for?" she said, with her little serpent's smile. "We start at 7 p.m. sharp."

"Thank you," I forced myself to say.

"Why Helene," Dorothy drawled, peeping at me over her reading glasses. "I didn't know those words were in your vocabulary."

...

Tuesday evening arrived. The sun had slipped below the mountains, but the dunes along the eastern shore of Washoe Lake still glowed in a mantle of sunlight, like a golden coastline across a sea of shadow. I spotted Luke's battered pickup as soon as he turned off the highway and started up the long drive. As casually as I could, I stood and walked down the steps of the porch. If there hadn't been guests sitting out there, I would have run to him.

Luke parked the truck near the stable and I heard the bark of rusted hinges as he pushed open the door and climbed out. I was glad he'd parked down there—it would give us a chance to converse alone before he arrived at the main house. At the same time, I felt a twinge of sadness that he knew he should park down there, with the help.

Luke was wearing a pressed shirt and stiff new jeans with a crease in them. I could see he had also polished his boots for the occasion. He looked a little nervous, his brow furrowed.

"Hey there, Handsome," I called. He grinned self-consciously.

When Luke left the Indian School he had been in the middle of a teenage growth spurt, at that awkward stage where he resembled a boy who'd been stretched. He was now easily six feet tall, lean and sinewy. Even his forearms had been carved into ropes of muscle by cowboying. (*Shoveling shit*, he'd explained.) His skin was darker than mine, and his hair, while just as black, was stick-straight. His face reminded me of Mama's, the broad flare of his cheekbones catching the light of the evening sky, his deep-set eyes almost obscured in shadow. He still wore the impassive and unreadable look he'd perfected at the Indian School.

I kissed his beardless cheek, which was nearly as smooth as it had been when he was a boy, and hooked my arm snugly into his. It was an extraordinary sensation to walk arm-in-arm with my brother. Even as children, we'd never been able to do that. My heart welled with an unfamiliar happiness.

We strolled toward the ranch house slowly, savoring the time alone. Buttery light spilled from the windows onto the veranda. A couple of guests sat on the porch swing, laughing softly, and frogs croaked in the garden. I heard Dorothy reminding the girls to check under the cushions of the porch furniture so that they would not crush the tiny frogs which sheltered there, and the guests laughing with horror at the prospect of sitting on a frog.

"Let's go say hello to the boss lady." I was still a bit uneasy about her motives for the invitation.

Luke nodded and his hand strayed to the shirt pocket, checking to make sure the little notebook was there. He saw me watching and issued an apprehensive smile.

We mounted the broad, creaking steps of the old farmhouse. The girls on the glider sang out to us as we passed: "*Hiiii*, Lucky...hi, Helene." The cowboy nickname grated on me. 'Lucky', my ass.

But Luke acknowledged them too, wearing a mischievous little smile. I'm not sure why it surprised me so to discover that my brother was a bit of a ladies' man. Maybe it was just surprising that he was a grown man, period.

We found Dorothy in the little parlor off to the side, where she held the games. The room contained a heavily carved, round pedestal table and a hodgepodge of antique chairs, with a ponderous Victorian sideboard where she set out drinks. Above that was a big, foxed mirror that had been salvaged from a wild west saloon in nearby Dayton. She wore trousers, a white man's shirt tied at the waist, and an unflattering blue-red lipstick, her favored attire for evening. She smiled up at Luke (who was a good foot taller) and extended her little hand.

"Welcome," she said. "Glad you could come."

He gave his nod-greeting and shook her hand.

"Luke, I know you're pretty handy with that pencil, but during the game there won't be time to write," she went on matter-of-factly. One thing you could say about Dorothy: she was a straight shooter.

Luke scribbled and turned the pad toward her.

Don't need to write, Dorothy read aloud. *Here's how I call.*

Luke proceeded to demonstrate how he would signal if he was to call, a slowly upturned hand extended in the direction of the player in question. Everything else in poker, I realized, was just sign language. Asking for another card. Folding. I realized with relief how simple it would be.

"Who's coming tonight?" I asked.

"One of our regulars is bringing his brother-in-law. There's a very dull state legislator. And Maisie."

"Maisie?" I laughed, but I saw Luke's eyes brighten at the mention of the girl's name. They'd shared a couple of dances the other night.

"Yes, ma'am."

"That should be like shooting fish in a barrel," I remarked.

"Then I guess we'll have plenty of dead fish," said Dorothy. "What are you drinking tonight, Luke?" she asked, stepping up to the sideboard and inspecting a highball glass with a frown. Smudged glasses were one of her many pet peeves. She set aside the offending tumbler and picked up another, glancing over her shoulder at him.

Luke shook his head.

"I've always heard that Indians can't hold their liquor," she remarked. She sounded like a visitor to a natural history museum, or a zoo. "That you're missing some sort of...enzyme?"

Luke shrugged, a diplomatic response if I ever saw one. I wanted to slap her heart-shaped face into next week.

Dorothy gave one of her rare laughs. "Hardly seems fair that you'll be the only sober one."

"More dead fish, I guess," I snapped, pasting a smile on my face. Then the phone rang, and Dorothy went off to answer it. Luke shook his head at me and smiled at my temper, circling the table with slow steps.

"Don't mind her." I reached out and grasped his hand as he completed his circuit. "She's a card-carrying bitch." My brother shrugged again. I could not tell if he didn't care or if he simply didn't want to give her stupid comment another thought.

After a moment our hostess returned. "We just lost one. Apparently he was arrested earlier today, in Utah." She chuckled. "For bigamy, I think…or sodomy. The connection wasn't very good." I watched Luke's eyes widen, and then he grinned and glanced at me.

"Let's get ourselves set up," I said to him, slipping a roll of bills from the pocket of my trousers and sitting down at the table. I'd gone to the pawn shop the previous morning and converted my diamond-and-emerald bracelet into almost two thousand dollars cash.

I counted a hundred dollars out, then offered Luke a couple of twenties and a ten. My brother's eyes narrowed, and then he frowned, chewing his lip. His eyes swung hard to me.

"It's Peter's money," I murmured. "If we win, or if we lose… he loses."

To my relief, Luke accepted his stake.

The players filtered into the parlor, one by one. The congressman, a taciturn rancher, arrived in typically Nevadan Western attire: a checkered shirt, dark blue jeans that looked brand new, and spit-polished caramel-colored ostrich-skin boots. His intricately tooled belt was inset with turquoise conchas and anchored with a large, engraved silver buckle.

Maisie hurried in, apologizing for her late arrival, and nearly collided with the Congressman. She wore a Western shirt in a plaid of soft greens and blues that set off her eyes, and her hair was in loose, shiny waves. She had a new, professional-looking camera with her, and caught me regarding it with trepidation.

"Isn't it a beauty?" she asked. "A Canon IIB. I saw it at Mr. La Grange's and I just had to have it!"

"Pearls into pictures?" I teased, but she gave an appreciative laugh.

"Yes. Maw Maw would be thrilled for me," she said, without a hint of irony, and turning swiftly to Luke, extended her hand.

"It's so nice to see you again, Luke," she enthused, as my brother shook her hand carefully, almost formally. Maisie was as lovely as a mountain bluebird, even in her wool frontier pants and cowboy boots.

"My new camera is very fast," she went on. "I'd love to take some pictures of you cowboys at work. You know—action shots."

Luke gave a brief, self-conscious smile and an amiable shrug of willingness. Maisie's face lit up in appreciation.

"Thank you, Luke," she said, then moved lightly into the room, toward the Congressman. She was swift and graceful, able to get from one place to another without creating noise or even, it seemed, disturbing the air in a room. It was an art my mother had tried and failed to teach me. I'd always sliced through rooms like a schooner in full sail, leaving a wake behind me.

"Steve Pike," I heard the congressman say, regarding Maisie briefly, but not making a move to shake hands. He was obviously the sort of fellow who considered women part of the furniture—an unremarkable fact of life, and certainly not deserving of a handshake. He had a sun-weathered, deeply creased face inset with clear, aquamarine-blue eyes, like alpine tarns set in granite.

"The Pikes have been ranching in the Truckee Meadows for generations," said Dorothy.

Without thinking, I glanced toward Luke. This assumption that we owed respect to a man whose family had been "ranching in the

Truckee Meadows for generations" set my teeth on edge. Another smug White family who'd helped themselves to the People's land and believed God himself had signed over the deed. It was probably fortunate that Luke did not look my way.

"Ah, and here's our mainstay," Dorothy called. "I'm going to have to mark you tardy, Mike." A restless, angular man entered the parlor, removing his hat, followed by a tall, heavyset fellow. They looked like they could have stepped out of a smart restaurant in Chicago, and wore expensive, well-tailored suits. Dorothy turned to us. "This is Mike Lombardo. He owns the Cottonwood Club downtown."

Mike Lombardo and Steve Pike exchanged desultory nods. It was evident that the men were already acquainted, and not happily.

"Sorry, Floss, I had trouble prying my brother-in-law here out of his office," chuckled Mike.

"All work and no play makes Jack a dull boy," quipped the big man in a booming, cheerful voice, extending a hand to Dorothy, then Steve. "Jack Storm."

"Dorothy Walker; call me Dot. Welcome to the Rocking B, Jack," our hostess said briskly. "I've heard a lot about you. Now what can I get you fellas to drink?"

Despite the pleasantries, I could see that she was all business. This was her game.

"Scotch, neat. Thanks." Storm had a fleshy, clean-shaven face, an amiable manner. His voice carried the standard-issue Great Basin twang.

"Same for me, Dorothy," said Lombardo. She poured two fingers of scotch into tumblers and handed them over. Lombardo was lean and a bit wolfish, but they were both swarthy, and their—what time was it?—7 o'clock shadow was quite pronounced.

"Any movie stars tonight, Dorothy?" Lombardo asked, grinning at me.

"This is Helene," said Dorothy. "A guest."

"Well, Hollywood doesn't know what it's missing," Lombardo declared. "You look like Ava Gardner's sister."

"Pleasure to meet you, Helene." Jack stepped toward me. He shook my hand, winked, and then smoothed his yellow silk tie, which was hand-painted with a "V" of ducks in flight.

"That's an extraordinary tie," I remarked, staring at the ghastly thing.

"Ya like it?" he grinned, and slid his hand down its length once more.

"Nice to meet you, Helene!" Lombardo gave me a poorly disguised once-over. Maybe I was supposed to notice it. He held my gaze when he added, "Dorothy, how does a fella get hired on around here?"

I issued a brief, tolerant smile. I turned toward Luke. "This is my brother, Luke Christian. He does not speak, but he does play poker."

"Is that so?" Lombardo's grin dimmed just a bit; I hoped he was now embarrassed about leering at me in front of my brother. Luke shook his hand and stepped toward Storm to shake his, too. He gave a short "nice to meet you" nod to each as he did. I noticed the Congressman's slight hesitation before shaking Luke's hand. I admired how my brother looked them all right in the eye. There was nothing deferential about his manner.

"Jack Storm," I said to the big man. "You sound like a character out of a detective novel."

"Nom de guerre," he replied, surprising me. It was obviously not the first time he'd heard such a remark. "Yep. Baptized Giacomo Pugliesi. Mama and Papa never dreamed their son would end up in the gambling business. The Pugliesi family's been growing cherries down in Smith Valley for decades."

"How will you keep 'em down on the farm once they've seen Reno?" Mike added, clapping his brother-in-law on the back. "The only cherries Jack sees these days are on a slot machine!"

Everyone but the Congressman gave an obligatory laugh.

"I imagine it's hard to get a gaming license these days with a name like *Jack-Mo Poo-guh-lazy*," the Congressman drawled, and popped a couple of peanuts into his mouth. I felt an electric tension charge the room.

Please God, not more Italians, I thought. But they were probably just a couple of local yokels, styling themselves as big fish in Reno's small pond.

"Jack's the most successful bookie in Nevada," Mike went on, unperturbed by the Congressman's dig. "Hell, he's probably the most successful bookie in the country."

Storm shrugged with exaggerated modesty and waved a thick hand.

"I've got nothing on the boys back East," he chuckled.

"That's very impressive." I remarked, noting his perfectly manicured nails. I had long ago learned not to trust any man with nails that looked nicer than my own.

"Aw, it's not like I'm a rocket scientist." Storm thumped Lombardo on the back, laughing.

"You make a helluva lot more money than any goddamn rocket scientist," Lombardo grinned. "Don't get any ideas, girls, he's happily married."

I couldn't resist peeking at Maisie, her nostrils tight above a fake smile. She glanced at me. What a couple of clowns.

Throughout this exchange, the legislator sat there with a look of mild impatience, as if waiting for an overdue train.

"This is Maisie," Dorothy announced. The debutante stepped forward and shook the men's hands without hesitating.

"First names only?" Storm teased.

"Company policy." Dorothy's smile was so brief it looked like a tic. "Our guests appreciate discretion."

"This ain't the Mapes, buddy," Lombardo told his pal. "The gals here don't wanna see and be seen."

"Exactly," said Dorothy. Next, she introduced the Congressman and a noticeable chill descended.

Storm's upper lip rolled down over his upper teeth and he fixed Pike with a strange grin. "You're looking at one of the survivors of Kefauver." He swallowed a large gulp of whisky. "Twenty-five race books before that stinkin' law passed, four after. And three of those books belong to me."

"Congratulations, Mr. Pugliesi," Steve Pike replied, his voice cool. "It sounds like you're very good at what you do."

"How many cattle are you running out there in Wells, Steve?" asked Lombardo, changing the subject. Or so I thought.

"About twenty-five hundred head, give or take," replied the Congressman.

"You ladies may or may not know about the cattle business," Lombardo continued, assuming an informative tone. "But ranchers like Congressman Pike here get to graze their stock on our public land for a pittance. Isn't that right, Steve?"

"We lease the land from the government. And that's the way it's been for generations."

"Generations of way-below-market grazing fees," said Lombardo, his voice sarcastic.

"It's amazing that we have to pay anything at all," Pike retorted. "We're in the business of putting food on America's table, using worthless desert land that no one else wants." He wasn't as cool a customer as he'd looked.

"I'll reckon that our Indian friend here might disagree with that last part," chuckled Storm, surprising me. Luke was expressionless. I felt my own face flush and I watched Pike's pale eyes narrow, fine lines fanning from the outer corners all the way across his sun-spotted temples.

"We've provided for the Indians," he replied. The men had gotten under his skin, and I didn't feel the least bit sorry for him.

"Like the Stewart School," I offered. His gaze rose to meet mine.

"Yes, like the Stewart School," Pike said, deciding I was on his side. "Our boarding school is a showplace of Indian progress."

"Our beloved alma mater." I nodded toward Luke. "Where I learned to sew. Which I guess makes me a paragon of Indian progress." I knew I was making my brother uncomfortable, but I couldn't help myself. I could not stand this self-righteous bastard, who clearly thought we owed him and the American taxpayers a big fat thank you.

"You're obviously an educated woman," Pike observed. "It seems like you learned more than sewing."

"Our mother taught us to read. And as for my education, I'm an autodidact. But yes, I also learned to cook and clean at the Stewart School."

"Maybe my wife can enroll," quipped Storm, and to my astonishment the men, including Luke, broke into relieved laughter at the joke.

"Ladies and gentlemen," Dorothy said, her timing impeccable, "Let's play cards."

I sat down, trying to get my temper in hand. Jack was placed in the chair to my right. He smelled of cigarettes and a familiar cologne that seemed too sophisticated for his vulgar racetrack style.

"So Helene, do you play the ponies?" he asked, as Dorothy began to deal.

"I ride them, I don't play them," I replied. Dorothy shot me a glance and I returned fire with my best phony smile. But Jack Storm seemed amused by my reply.

"Well all right, cowgirl," he chuckled, and toasted me with his tumbler of the scotch.

I lifted my own in return.

"She's a spunky one!" he declared to Lombardo, as if I had been placed there for his amusement. And maybe I had.

"Be careful or she'll buck you off!" Lombardo declared. I felt Luke's boot slide up against my own, as if he was applying the brakes.

"Luke, do you rodeo?" asked Storm. "That trophy buckle ain't from a pawn shop, is it?"

Luke grinned. He raised both arms and extended his index fingers to mime horns, then flipped his right hand violently over on the table, rattling the glasses and startling everyone. So Luke had a flair for the dramatic, too, I thought with satisfaction.

"Steers huh?" asked Lombardo.

Luke banged his palm against the side of his head like it was the ground, pointed to his mouth.

"You don't say?" Lombardo did not seem to realize the irony of that phrase. "Damn shame."

"Sure is," said Storm. He turned to me, and I saw that his eyes had taken on a shrewd little gleam, that the affable man now looked much more like the calculating bookie. Perhaps he thought that Luke was not all there mentally, that he would be easy pickings.

Dorothy began to deal, shooting cards in every direction, her hands moving with a hypnotic grace. "Now. As Helene mentioned, her brother Luke is mute, but his hearing is just fine. When he calls, he will do this—" she emulated the gesture Luke had shown her.

Lombardo and Storm shrugged agreeably.

"So you're Indian, too, huh?" Storm asked me, his tone friendly.

"Yes," I said, but I felt my hackles rise again.

"I had you pegged for a nice Italian girl. You sure don't talk like..." he caught himself. "Like you're from around here."

"That's because I'm not," I replied, still hot under the collar. "I'm from Chicago."

"They got Indians in Chicago too?" Storm clearly thought this was hilarious, and Lombardo joined in, laughing.

The moment the words fell out of my mouth, I regretted them. I tried to appear as if I were studying my cards, but my heart began to beat rapidly. For God's sake, these men were in the gambling business. The state of Nevada was like a small town. Giacomo Pugliesi. Nevada's biggest bookmaker. Did he know Mr. Ludovico?

"Maisie, where are you from?" asked Storm, moving on, to my relief. "That's a cute little accent you got there."

"Charleston," she replied.

"Play a lot of poker in Charleston?" he teased.

"Not much," she replied, "I'm afraid I'm much better at bridge." The men chuckled indulgently. "But Miss Dorothy is a very good teacher."

"Maisie is a natural," observed Dorothy matter-of-factly. It was the first time I'd ever heard her compliment anyone.

The girl blushed to the roots of her honey-colored hair. "I don't know about that," she murmured modestly. She glanced at her camera, sitting where she'd placed it on the sideboard. "Miss Dorothy, before we start, would you mind taking a picture of my first official Nevada poker game?"

"All right." Dorothy sighed and got to her feet. Everyone laid down their cards and Maisie hopped up to get her camera. She showed Dot where the shutter release was, then slipped behind us, placing her hands on my shoulders.

"Come on, everyone lean in," our hostess commanded. I felt Storm's arm press against mine as we posed and smiled.

"Happy?" asked Dorothy.

"Thank you," Maisie said, and Dorothy set the camera back on the sideboard. She gestured for everyone to take their seats.

"So Maisie, what are your plans after 'graduation'?" inquired Lombardo.

The eternally flustered girl did not seem to be thrown. "I've applied to college," she said, matter-of-factly. I have to admit, her answer surprised me, too.

"Going to get an M.R.S?" Storm chuckled.

I expected her to blush and stammer. But instead, she turned her pretty jade-green eyes on Jack Storm. "I'm going to study journalism."

"Well, I'll be damned," said Storm, shooting a bemused look at his brother-in-law, as if any man would find such feminine aspirations utterly comical.

"That's seeming more and more likely," I remarked.

I saw Luke's deft, calloused hands, arranging his cards, pause. Dorothy gave a deep, appreciative laugh and the men joined her. I could see she enjoyed the rough-and-tumble repartee.

"Can't imagine why she's getting a divorce," quipped Storm to his brother-in-law, jerking a big thumb in my direction.

Maisie peered at her cards and I saw a flicker of a smile.

...

"How'd you do that?" I asked Miss Maisie DuBois at the end of the evening, as Dorothy saw her disgruntled guests out to their car. Maisie had played a punishing game of poker. The men weren't exactly surly, but the jolly tone of the evening had dissolved as their losses accrued.

Pike, Storm and Pugliesi probably thought they'd been had, that Maisie was a ringer. I had enjoyed the show so much that it didn't matter a whit that she'd cleaned out the rest of us, too. Even Dorothy was remarkably sanguine.

I heard the baritone rumble of a large engine starting. I was glad that the men were leaving the ranch so early. Floss's games normally tended to run quite late.

"Maisie," I remarked, when Dorothy ambled back in. "You *are* a natural. Well done."

"Good heavens, I don't plan to keep your money," Maisie blurted, abashed. She'd already counted out three stacks of bills. She began to hand the money back to me, Luke and Dot. She blushed and stammered apologies, the old Maisie.

"You won it fair and square," Dot reminded her. "That's how poker works."

Luke nodded vehemently, and tried to hand back the money. Maisie shook her head at all of us.

"That's what I'm trying to tell you." She gave us a devilish little smile. "It's the darndest thing. I can remember all the cards."

TWENTY-ONE

My hearing date was set. The next chapter of my life was about to begin. But for the first time in months, I wasn't sure what I would find on those pages. Being reunited with Luke was a miracle, but it had delivered more questions than answers—and I was a girl who liked answers. So I did the one thing that quieted the raging, rattling thoughts in my head: I rode.

Tuesday morning I was saddling Sweet Potato in the barn when I overheard Jamie talking to Dorothy outside. They were standing by the corral that held a new horse, captured in the Virginia Range by one of Jamie's mustanger buddies. Dot had purchased him for twenty dollars the month before, gloating over the bargain, but Connie had nearly given up hope of gentling him enough for the dude string.

Picon was a blue roan, a truly handsome horse, and his summer coat was a remarkable almost navy blue. But even though he'd been gelded, he was nowhere near gentle enough for dudes. He had a bad habit of crow-hopping when he got in a mood, and he was not above biting when being tacked up. He still believed he was a stallion.

"You've got two weeks before this one heads to the cannery," Dot told Jamie.

"I think you should let Luke Moore have a go at him. He's real good with the wild horses, Miss Dorothy," Jamie said, to my surprise.

"Mustangs and Indians," Dorothy said with a dry laugh. "The Rocking B isn't a wild west show. These dude horses need to be gentle as lambs."

"He'll do it for free," Jamie added. He knew exactly how to handle Dot.

There was a little silence before she responded. "Well, if he comes out here, he better not think he's going to be fraternizing."

"No ma'am, we make sure all the wranglers know to stay out of the zoo."

"I don't trust either of them," Dorothy continued. I realized I was holding my breath, concentrating hard on making out her words. "If I see him so much as talk to one of the guests, he's out."

"Yes, ma'am," said Jamie.

It sounded like the conversation was over. I was boiling with rage…and delight. I ached to throttle Dorothy Walker, and I wanted to kiss Jamie. Luke would have a pass to get onto the ranch! We could now spend time together. We could make plans for the future.

Luke was at the barn the very next afternoon. Dorothy came down to watch his first session with Picon and stood next to the ring with her skinny arms folded, a dour expression on her face. I did my best to ignore her as she made disparaging remarks about the mustang and the prospects of training him.

"I don't want to waste feed on a lost cause," she grumbled.

She quickly bored of Luke's quiet, close-up ground work. My brother spoke patiently to Picon, rubbing his hands gently over the horse's body for close to twenty minutes, letting the mustang sniff him. Man and beast seemed to be deep in conversation.

"Good Lord," Dorothy muttered. "I hire a wrangler, and I get Saint Francis of Assisi."

"I hear he worked for free, too," I said, as she walked off.

. . .

Each day Luke arrived after his work in Steamboat was over. Happily, Dorothy had abandoned her surveillance of the project, proclaiming it a waste of her time. We began with exercise in the ring, then headed out on the trail together. Once away from the ranch, Picon seemed to relax, his gaits becoming more loose and natural. To my surprise, the mustang was polite and deferential with Sweet Potato, the perfect gentleman.

By the end of the week, Luke and I had fallen into a pleasant rhythm, an easy togetherness. I was an excellent rider now, and he was pleased about that. Maybe even proud of me.

I was certainly proud of my brother. He had a rare talent with horses, and the restless boy I'd known surprised me with his deep reserves of patience. He was a confident rider, yet had none of the swagger of the Rocking B wranglers. For a man who did battle with steers, he was incredibly respectful and gentle with horses.

But other than work as a ranch hand, what opportunities existed for him? Luke was a second-class citizen. Dorothy Walker's race prejudice wasn't the exception, it was the rule. And unlike me, my brother couldn't pass as European—nor would he wish to. His shining banner of long black hair attested to that.

Then there was the second strike against him: he was handicapped. He'd been scratching out a living between seasonal work for wages and occasional prize money. He'd worked on ranches from Billings to Salt Lake to Sacramento. Still, the only thing that bothered him about his current situation was that he was so far from his sons. He seemed excited about the Flagstaff job, and getting back to Arizona.

In one respect, our ambitions were not terribly different. We were both returning to the arena where we'd nearly died, both trying to stay atop a dangerous creature long enough to win prize money. Unlike Luke, however, I had just one big rodeo left, at the Washoe County Courthouse.

Watching my brother work so patiently and exactingly with Picon began to fill me with ideas. Luke deserved to have his own training stable, just like Philippe Kiehl. Or, if he preferred, I could buy him his own cattle spread—close to his boys.

On Friday afternoon Luke got off work early, so we took a long ride up Slide Mountain, navigating a narrow trail, crunching through the patches of snow that still lingered in the shade. We stopped at an outcropping of pink carnelian granite and sat there. Pine branches rolled and roared like waves overhead. To the west we could see the sapphire-blue water of Lake Tahoe, sun glittering off her distant whitecaps—she could be every bit as angry as an ocean when the afternoon winds kicked up. Far above us, the wind lashed the clinging snowfields, and bright, distant flares of sunlit powder exploded into the sky over Mount Rose.

A kene'e, dangling a snake, sailed out of the glare to land in a huge juniper quite close to us. We watched the red-tailed hawk as she set about eating her catch, pinning the reptile firmly under her claws as its flat, spade-shaped head hung limp over the branch. The hawk tore into the rattlesnake with her powerful hooked beak, bright golden eyes gleaming.

After a couple of minutes, the end of the snake's tail dropped into the manzanita thicket below. Luke, who'd been watching her raptly, dismounted and quietly moved into the brush to find it. The hawk remained on her branch above, watchful but undisturbed.

Luke stood and held up the snake's tail. He pushed his way out of the thicket, grinning, then knelt by a fallen pine log, where he carefully cut the rattle off with his pocket knife. He spent a moment examining it before he brought it over for my inspection. From atop Sweet Potato, I reluctantly leaned over to squint at it. He indicated that I should extend my hand. When I did, he laid the gory thing on my outstretched palm.

"It's a big one, isn't it?" I remarked. I'd seen plenty of togokwa, but never one with a rattle this large. It must have had twenty buttons. In a smooth gesture that had become familiar to me, my brother pulled out his notebook. He scribbled, then held it up.

Very old snake. Powerful.

"You count the buttons to tell the age, right?" I asked, squinting at it.

He gave me a wry smile, his head cocked, as if to say, Really? You don't know this? Then he began scratching away again.

Each button = shed. Young snakes shed a lot, he wrote. *Old snake not even 1 a year.*

"Oh." I handed the rattle back to him, hesitating a moment before I wiped the brownish-red smudge of blood on my palm against the saddle blanket.

Strong medicine. Feel it?

"Yes." I hadn't felt a thing, but I couldn't bring myself to admit that to my brother. I felt like I was standing on the other side of a canyon, the White side, observing him, the Indian.

Protection, he wrote, pointing to me, and then to himself.

Again, I nodded, and watched Luke slide the notebook back into his breast pocket. Then he dipped his hand down into the front of his shirt and drew out a little deerskin bag, attached to a slender leather thong around his neck. A medicine pouch. The soft golden chamois had been worn smooth with time. One side of the pouch had been worked in a geometric design, with tiny blue and red glass beads.

In a flash, I remembered my mother leaning over an embroidery project, blue and red seed beads in a little dish, her needle darting nimbly in and out. She'd made the pouch for him. I felt a painful tug of envy. I owned nothing that had belonged to my mother.

He loosened the drawstring and slipped the rattle inside.

"Speaking of protection," I began, hoping that the segue sounded more natural to him than it did to me, "When are you going back on the rodeo circuit?"

I had waited as long as I could to ask that question. It had been smoldering inside me but had finally burned through my better judgment.

Luke gazed at me for a long moment, then held up four fingers.

"Four…weeks?" I'd been so focused on my court date that everything beyond that seemed like a blur. But summer was barely a month away. Our lives had only just collided, and the impact had not rearranged things as much as I'd expected. Luke was returning to his rodeo.

I realized that I was running out of time. "So, do you have to pay alimony to your ex-wife? Child support for the boys?"

I watched his brow furrow. His hand moved reflexively toward the shirt pocket, then dropped back to his side. His head bobbed a single, let's-change-the-subject yes.

"Well," I said, "In another few weeks, I'm going to have more than enough money for the both of us."

As soon as the words were out of my mouth, I regretted them. A scowl tore across my brother's face like a rift. I'd never seen his eyes that dark.

"What I mean is—we'll both have a choice of what to do, where to go," I babbled, unable to stop myself. "You could have your own ranch, you wouldn't have to risk your life for prizes…"

Angrily, he rubbed his fingers together to pantomime money, and then flung his hand down, as if throwing my goddamn money on the ground. He shook his head once, very hard. He pulled the grubby notebook from his shirt pocket with a challenging glare, as if to say, *do you need me to spell this out for you*?

"I-I'm sorry," was all I could manage. In a flash, I saw the boy that I'd known at boarding school, and felt the knife-edge of his anger.

Luke climbed back on his horse. He reined Picon back onto the trail; the roan shook his head irritably and took a couple of dancing steps to the side in protest. Sweet Potato picked up on the tense mood and did a nasty spin, nearly unseating me. When I got her settled down, Luke was fifty yards ahead. I put my heels into Sweet Potato, urging the Appaloosa into a little jog.

"Hey!" I called. But my brother wouldn't look back at me. "Hey!"

I shouted, even louder.

I could see him take a deep breath, his spine straightening. But no response was forthcoming.

So much for thinking he'd want to throw in his lot with me. So much for thinking that I could bread-crumb my proud and independent brother toward the conclusion that accepting help from his wealthy kid sister was a keen idea. We were not children plotting an escape from boarding school. We were two adults who had spent almost two decades apart constructing and tearing apart and trying to reassemble painful and complicated lives. How could I have been so stupid?

We picked our way down the mountain in silence as the sun surrendered. The afternoon shadows rode alongside us, then overtook us, filling the Washoe Valley like a bathtub.

...

When the next morning dawned, it felt like spring had finally decided to unpack her bags and stay. I put on a silk shirtdress, purchased at a chic downtown Reno shop whose owner hailed from New York and traveled there twice a year to select her inventory.

I entered the main house to see Clem sweeping up the kitchen. Maisie was fussing around the parlor, looking for her camera.

"Darn it!" she exclaimed. "I'm sure I left it on the sideboard."

I was certain one of the guests had hidden the damn thing, sick of her constantly snapping pictures of everyone.

I knocked on the door of her office off the kitchen, where Elouise also sat, banging on an adding machine.

"Come in." Floss had probably registered the tap of my heels on the pine floors. Attorney and court visits were the only reason guests put on dresses and heels at the Rocking B. It felt strange to don a girdle and stockings after weeks of wearing dungarees and Western shirts.

"Your attorney appointment is at 10:30, right?" asked Floss, when she saw me.

"Yes...and I need to make a stop at Mr. La Grange's afterward, if that's all right."

"Should be fine."

At the mention of the pawn shop, Elouise looked up from her work.

"Hi, Peach," I said to her, as pleasantly as I could.

"Hello," she replied, and resumed her work. Though she had been kind to me and Luke on the afternoon of the cattle drive, we were still stiff and awkward with each other.

When I'd sold my bracelet to Mr. La Grange, I'd purchased the pearl earrings for Elouise, thinking that it would be a way to apologize for the Virginia City debacle. But as La Grange was wrapping up the velvet box, I'd realized with horror that buying jewelry to apologize for something awful was exactly what Peter did after his violent outbursts. It made me feel manipulative and ugly. So I'd lost my nerve. I'd ended up tucking the little box into my lingerie drawer.

Floss shifted in her chair and glanced at her watch.

"I'll be ready in two shakes," she told me. "You're a little early."

"I'll just wait on the porch," I told her, and headed outside, relieved to get away from Elouise's reproachful silence.

. . .

"Well, it looks like things are in order," Miriam Gonzalves, my new attorney, told me. She laid her hands atop the paperwork in my file. "Mr. Ledyard tells me that your husband's attorneys have approved the property settlement. He's drawn up the papers."

"Approved?" I repeated, dubious. "You mean, *agreed* to it?" She must be mistaken. That offer had just been our opening gambit. There was no way Peter would be willing to give me half of everything he owned.

"Well, yes." She handed me the letter from Ledyard.

"They didn't make a counter-offer?"

She shook her head. "Apparently not."

"That doesn't make sense," I told her.

"Perhaps he's remorseful."

I laughed. "Peter does not know the meaning of the word."

"Well, it's right here in black and white." She gave me one of her rare smiles. "Let's not look a gift horse in the mouth. I will draw up the Exhibit for the court. Unless you'd like to call Mr. Ledyard and discuss it?"

"No—no," I said uneasily. I sat back in my chair, my head reeling. Half of the Grafton Industries stock? Half of everything? How could it be? I'd expected I might end up with twenty percent of the stock, my car, perhaps the New York apartment, if I was extremely lucky. I'd been told Ledyard was a good attorney, but if this was true, he was an absolute miracle worker. I didn't want to jinx it.

When I emerged from Mrs. Gonzalves' office, Floss, seated in the waiting room, stared at me with apprehension. I must have been wearing an expression of pure astonishment.

"What happened?" she asked, as we exited.

"I don't quite know," I said.

...

Floss parked the ranch's station wagon on Virginia Street in front of Mr. La Grange's pawn shop. When I got out, she settled back with her newspaper.

"Take your time," she told me. I knew she appreciated being away from the Rocking B. Floss maintained a cheerful façade, but it had to have been a relief to take a break from the constant needs of her guests, the petty dramas of the staff, and the chronic friction with her sister.

I stepped inside the cool, dim shop to the chime of a bell. The satin bag nestled in my purse held my biggest prize: a sapphire collar, bracelet, and matching earrings. I'd shown the ensemble to La Grange shortly after I arrived, and he, quite impressed, had told me that he would be interested in a month or so, when he located the right buyer. He had several in mind, he assured me.

This would be a significant transaction, enough to tide me over until the settlement funds arrived. It might take a while to liquidate the real estate. I had no idea how quickly I could sell my Grafton Industries stock. There should be lots of cash in our accounts...but in the meantime, I would have expenses. And the attorneys would need to be paid.

Mr. La Grange emerged from the back room of the store with a polite, expectant expression. But the moment he saw me his face fell, and his mild gray eyes widened with alarm.

"Hello, Monsieur La Grange," I said.

"Miss Christian." He recovered some of his composure. "I wasn't expecting you."

"I've brought the sapphire and diamond set," I began, stepping toward the counter and reaching into my purse for the little satchel.

He lifted a small, neat hand as if to fend me off. "Miss Christian. I won't be able to handle that transaction. I apologize, I should have called to let you know."

"Oh," I said, taken aback. He had been so enthusiastic five weeks ago, practically quivering with excitement at the prospect of selling such rare and costly pieces.

"Actually...I won't be able to handle any more transactions for you."

"Pardon me?" I stammered. I felt my face brighten with blood.

"And I'm very sorry, but I must ask you to leave." He gestured to the door.

"I don't understand." I stood my ground and offered a reassuring smile.

He paused, measuring his words. "I can't discuss it." His voice began to quicken. "It's best if you go. Immediately. I don't want any trouble."

Trouble. So then I knew.

"Did my husband come here?" I asked. "Peter Grafton?"

La Grange repeated his entreaty. "Please. Go."

"When was he here? Just tell me, and I'll leave."

"The day before yesterday. Mr. Grafton and—another man. They took the ruby pendant."

The necklace had been my Valentine gift from Peter two years ago. An unusual, heart-shaped ruby hung from a delicate chain set with diamonds. He'd purchased it at Marshall Pierce, and presented it to me over dinner at Alexander's Steak House, his favorite restaurant.

"Pigeon's Blood red," Peter had told me with a smile. "The most precious of rubies. From Burma."

He'd insisted on putting it on me, right there in the middle of the dining room. He loved having an audience for his grand gestures. I'd managed a smile, which opened the split lip he'd given me the morning prior because he'd overheard me outside laughing with our gardener. (Pigeon's blood, indeed.)

"I'm so sorry," I exclaimed. "I hope he didn't—"

"They took it!" La Grange declared, his voice rising. "They said it was not yours to sell!"

"Mr. La Grange, that necklace was mine. It was a gift!"

The jeweler stepped past me, opening the front door. "I don't need any more trouble. Just go!" Now he pointed. And I obeyed.

I hurried to the station wagon, yanked open the passenger door, and threw myself into the front seat.

"What on earth?" Floss asked.

"We need to get the hell out of here!" I slammed the door. "Now."

"Okay." She tossed her newspaper into the back, threw the big Buick into gear, and jammed her cowboy boot down on the accelerator. The Woody shot down Virginia Street.

"Jesus, what happened in there?"

"My husband is here in Reno!" I told her.

"Well, my dear, you called it," said Floss. "The bastard's not planning to take this divorce lying down."

I looked into the side-view mirror. "He wasn't alone. I bet he was with one of the men from Las Vegas."

Floss was quiet. Was she weighing the wisdom of letting me stay at the Rocking B?

"Godammit." I slid down into the passenger seat. "I should have been more careful." I thought about the terrified look on the courtly little jeweler's face. "And I think I put Mr. La Grange in a terrible position."

Floss glanced my way as she drove right through a stop sign. "All you did was pawn some jewelry, Helene."

"But they robbed him!"

She slipped on her sunglasses. "Honey, don't waste another minute worrying about poor little Larry Granger," she told me with a smirk. "What goes around, comes around."

TWENTY-TWO

t was hard to sleep that night. I was in bed struggling through Anna and Vronsky's steadily deflating romance when I heard the sound, not far off: the unmistakable crack and crumple of metal. The continuous blare of a car horn followed. The clock read 2:11 AM.

Through the open window of my upstairs room, I heard the muffled sounds of commotion from the direction of the bunkhouse. I heard shouts, the bang of truck doors slamming, and the rumble of an engine starting as wranglers mustered to investigate. Across the east pasture, the car horn bleated helplessly. I wondered if someone had been skewered on a steering wheel.

Now that I had my own room, I'd returned to my custom of sleeping (and reading) in the nude. So I grabbed a pair of jeans, put on a shirt, and crept barefoot into the hallway. As I shut my door, I heard stirring from the direction of Floss' and Dot's rooms. I headed downstairs.

Once on the front porch I slipped to the far end, out of range of the light. From my shadowy vantage point I watched Jennifer and Bertha emerge from their cabin, chattering with excitement.

"What on earth was that?" came Bertha's sharp East Coast voice, addressing no one in particular. She stood in the moonlight, trying to tie the sash of her bathrobe, and gazing around.

"I bet someone cracked up a car out on Franktown Road!" I heard Jennifer say. "We should tell Dorothy and Floss." Then they headed toward the main house, and I stepped to the railing just as they looked up.

"Helene! What's going on?" Bertha asked.

I shook my head. "Sounded like a wreck."

A ranch truck came flying back up toward the main house. It skidded to a stop in the gravel and Stew jumped out. Floss and Dorothy burst out the front door one after the other, jackets over pajamas, boots on their feet.

"What the hell, Stew?" Dorothy demanded.

"You need to see this, Miss Dorothy," Stew said, summoning her to the pickup.

"Are the stock okay?" Her first thought, of course.

"Yes, ma'am. But we caught something in the moat."

Moat? Was that what she said? I strained to make out what they were saying as Dot and Stew got into the truck and headed back down the driveway. We heard shouts from far across the eastern pasture.

"Hello, girls," said Floss. "Might want to come up on the porch."

"What's going on?" Jennifer clutched Bertha's arm as they scrambled up the steps. "Can you see anything?" The distant car horn warbled on, but the barns and outbuildings of the ranch obscured our view of the driveway.

An uneasy feeling began to roil my gut. *Caught something in the moat*, that was what Stewart said, wasn't it?

"You girls might want to go back to your cabin 'til this gets sorted out," Floss suggested.

"Like hell we will," Bertha declared, ignoring her. "This is kind of exciting." She turned to Jennifer. "Care for a drink?"

"Sure." Jennifer and Bertha headed into the house, emerging a moment later with a bottle of gin.

"Drink?" she offered, and I reluctantly declined. Bertha took a healthy swig right from the bottle and handed it to Jennifer. Floss shook her head, annoyed.

It wasn't long before Stew and Dot returned. In the light of the moth-mobbed porch light, I saw Dorothy's face crimped with irritation.

"What's going on?" called Jennifer gaily, already emboldened by the booze. Floss descended the steps to confer quietly with Dot. Then Stew got back in the truck and rattled off down the driveway again, to the cheers of crickets and frogs. Countless small bats flickered around the garden and overhead.

Finally Floss addressed us. "Seems we caught something in the moat."

"Moat?" Jennifer gave an incredulous laugh.

"After some uninvited guests a couple of years back, Stew got an idea to turn the cattle guard on the driveway into what he called a tank trap."

Dorothy ignored us, charged up the steps, and into the house. Floss watched her go, then continued. "The boys dug out a pit about eighteen inches deep. And then Connie welded up this mechanism that could lower the grate down into it. Just a big crank and a couple of scissor lifts underneath. He was a battlefield engineer—that boy is full of surprises."

"Jeepers," said Bertha. I could tell the idea that someone might try to break into the ranch had never really crossed her mind. Her divorce was, if not amicable, mostly an administrative matter.

Inside the house, I could hear the rise and fall of Dot's voice on the phone.

"You probably never noticed that contraption out there," Floss went on. "Looks like it's just irrigation hardware. Night watch lowers it after lights-out. If someone is coming in late, they have to go out and raise it up. And it gets raised every morning at first light."

"But what about the gates? I mean, the boys lock those every night, right?" Jennifer asked.

Floss paused and listened, cocking her head. It had gone quiet out in the pasture. "Uh huh," she said, a bit distracted.

More guests wandered out on the front lawn in their nightclothes, arms wrapped tightly across their chests. The barn lights had been switched on, and golden light climbed the cottonwoods and poplars. Dorothy stalked back outside.

"Ladies, go back to your cabins, please," she called to the guests on the lawn. "We had a steer hit out on the road."

Bertha and Jennifer exchanged conspiratorial smiles and passed the bottle back and forth.

"Oh dear!" I recognized the voice as Maisie's.

"The poor cow!" cried another guest.

"Please go back inside, ladies." Dot used her most no-nonsense tone. She didn't dismiss those of us on the porch, though. I heard the bubble of voices fade away as doors shut and lights winked out again.

"Hello, Helene." Dot gave us a little nod. "Jennifer. Bertha." She eyed the bottle of gin in Bertha's hand and her mouth bunched up into a frown. "Show's over, girls, time to go back inside."

Jennifer and Bertha grumbled their way back in, but I settled myself on the glider.

"Suit yourself," snapped Dot. She took Floss by the elbow and pulled her toward the other end of the porch.

"Well, what did the catch of the day have to say?" I heard Floss ask her sister.

Dot's voice was agitated. "Told Stew he'd been invited here for a poker game. Funny, we don't usually tell guests to bring bolt cutters. The whole front end pancaked. Radiator ended up in the engine."

"Wow." Floss chuckled. "Worked even better than we expected."

"Boys nabbed two kids high-tailing it up the road," Dot reported. The sound of distant sirens pierced the cool night air. "Sounds like the Sheriff's almost here."

"Who the hell are they?" I blurted. I got up and walked over to them.

Dot shrugged. "Stew says they're a couple of punks from Sparks."

I heard footsteps approaching, and saw Elouise walking briskly toward the ranch house, fully dressed.

"What's going on?" she called, spotting us.

"Someone tried to break into the ranch," said Floss. "Crashed in the trap."

"Good heavens!" Elouise declared.

"What kind of car is it?" I already knew.

"A red Pontiac."

I wasn't surprised. "Like Mike's brother-in-law drove last week?"

"The bookmaker's car?" Dot shook her head. She looked exasperated. "I seriously doubt that."

"Well, Dot, the boys mentioned poker," Floss said.

"That doesn't make any sense." Dorothy said again. I could feel my own blood pressure rising.

"Listen, sis, you told me that those fellows lost big the other night. Didn't they leave in a snit?"

"And what? Sent some J.D.s here for revenge?" snapped Dorothy. "That's ridiculous. Jack Storm is a professional gambler, for God's sake." She emphasized "professional" as if an advanced degree was required for the job.

"But you said Maisie can count cards," Floss persisted. "Maybe they're sore."

Dorothy heaved an angry sigh. "Mike Lombardo is a loudmouth. If he had a problem, he would've told me that night. He's not going to sulk over it and then send a couple of punk kids to break into the ranch."

"I don't think it was about the poker game." My nerves sparked and spat like a campfire. "I think this is about me."

"Not everything is about you," Dot said dismissively, shaking her head.

"I was careless," I said, the words tumbling out. "I mentioned that I was from Chicago. During the poker game."

Next to me I heard Elouise murmur, "I thought you were from Philadelphia. Or was it Virginia City?"

I shot her a look and she gave me a snotty little smile.

"Why does any of that even matter?" Dorothy asked.

"They were here for me." I knew it in my bones.

"Helene, I think you need to calm down," Floss said.

"I'm serious," I told her. "My husband will not stop trying to get to me. I should leave."

"No one is going anywhere," Floss said gruffly.

I appreciated the sentiment, but she didn't have the faintest idea what, and who, she was up against.

"What on earth does Jack Storm have to do with your husband?" Dot asked with a little sneer.

"I think he knows the people my husband…does. Maybe even works for them." The sisters both stared at me.

"Helene, I think your imagination may be running away with you," remarked Dot. "That, or your bourbon."

I felt my blood start to boil. "I'm dead sober," I snapped.

"Nobody's going anywhere!" Floss glanced at her sister in annoyance. "I'm sure this has nothing to do with you, Helene. There are plenty of riled-up men around these parts that don't like the idea of a divorce ranch, and women getting their way."

Through the fine mesh of cottonwood branches, I saw blinking red lights.

"Cops are here," said Dorothy. "Floss, you and I better go back down and talk to 'em. Elouise, glad you're here. Can you call the wrecker?"

Elouise headed into the ranch house. I followed her.

"So now it's Chicago, huh?" she said over her shoulder, passing through the dark parlor. I could hear from her voice that she was peeved. She slapped the light switch and the kitchen exploded into a bright glare.

"That's where I was living before I came to Nevada." I blinked at her. "Does it really matter? I mean, my name isn't Helene, either."

"The truth always matters," she replied coldly, refusing to meet my gaze.

"I've been honest with you, Peach," I told her.

Now we locked eyes, and there was a mean little curl to her lip. "Oh, so that really was your daddy's grave?"

I nodded. "Yes."

"Such a colorful history!" Her sweet Southern drawl burned like acid now. "Such a fascinating, *mysterious* woman!"

I suppose I couldn't blame Elouise for disbelieving me. "Peach," I began. She raised a hand to silence me.

"We are sick and tired of your dramatics," she said, using the Royal We. She'd been encouraged by Dorothy's bitchery. "You nearly got me fired that night. Dragging me around town like a rag doll. So I could be your audience? So I could enjoy your performance? You were embarrassing. You were...you were...disgusting!"

"I'm sorry, Peach!" I cried. This was not how I'd planned to apologize.

"Don't call me that, dammit! My name is Elouise!" She yanked the phone from its cradle and dialed "0" with a violent twist of her hand. Standing with her back to me, she asked for the towing company. There was a brief pause, and I could hear her breathing hard. I wondered if she was regretting her outburst, but then she turned around and fixed me with bright, burning eyes. Just like that red-tail hawk ripping into the rattlesnake.

"Hello," she said to the person on the other end of the line. Her voice had gone raspy from yelling at me. "We need a tow truck down at the Rocking B on 395 in Washoe Valley. Yes. There's been a wreck. Thank you." She returned the phone to its wall cradle carefully.

"You should go back to your room," she said with icy calm. "And I don't care what Floss and Dorothy said about you leaving. You should pack your things."

"Go to hell," I said.

TWENTY-THREE

The next afternoon I was sitting on the porch, exasperated by how long Tolstoy expected me to hang on after Anna threw herself in front of that train. I heard a car and watched as Jack Storm rolled in, driving a brand-new Pontiac Chieftain with a Reno dealer's paper license plates. There was no way I would give him the satisfaction of seeing me scurry inside. I stayed put.

"Afternoon, Helene! Heard you girls had a scare last night!" he boomed, mounting the front steps. "Just came by to apologize to you ladies for all the hullabaloo."

I fixed him with an unblinking stare. "I'm sure the Walkers will be touched, Mr. Pugliesi."

"Please. Call me Jack," he said, with a grin. "I should never have left the keys in the car. Damn shame you can't do that anymore. Reno's changed."

"It certainly has." I lit a cigarette to quell my nerves. "A criminal element seems to have moved in."

"Must've been something!" he remarked, gazing back down the driveway.

"Not really," I said—as coolly as I could manage with my heart lodged in my throat. I prayed that he would go inside to look for Dot. "Shame about your car," I added.

"The silver lining is I got a brand new one," Pugliesi gloated. "She's a beaut, isn't she?"

Having cracked up a car myself, I knew that insurance companies didn't hand you a new one the next day. But I knew who would: Peter Grafton.

"Oh, she definitely is a beaut," I said. And suddenly, without even trying, I remembered where I'd first heard Jack Storm's hail-fellow-well-met voice. On that quiet morning street in Bishop. It belonged to the man who'd accosted Philippe Kiehl out of nowhere, making small talk about the horse in the trailer. "Moe Gladstone", connoisseur of fine horse-flesh, was actually Giacomo Pugliesi, bookie.

It all came back: the expensive suit, the yellow tie, the Basin-and-Range twang. He'd been sent from Reno to intercept us.

"Want to come out for a spin?" Pugliesi trotted out that grin again.

My heart began to jackhammer. "I'll let you get on your way. You should probably go check on your friends and see how they're recovering from their injuries." The grin stayed fixed on his face, but there was a disquieting flicker in his gaze.

"Friends? Not hardly. Those were just some juvenile delinquents who decided to go on a joy ride."

"With some joyful bolt-cutters."

"Who knows what they were up to." Pugliesi shook his head, as if we were both on the same side. "Kids these days, right?"

Dorothy stepped out onto the porch at that moment. I watched her stiffen.

"Mr. Storm." Her tone was formal. "To what do we owe the pleasure?"

"Miss Walker—Dorothy—I can't tell you how sorry I am about all this." He removed his tan fedora.

She eyed him warily. "Your car was stolen. Which obviously wasn't your fault."

"Well, like a knucklehead, I left the keys in it," he said, repeating his cockamamie story. "Foolish'a me. That must have given everyone a helluva fright. In the middle of the night and everything."

"It cost us some sleep," she replied. "But so do the bears." Now she glanced at me. "It was neighborly of you to come by."

Pugliesi recognized that he was being dismissed. "Well, thank you for being so understanding." He replaced his hat and touched his hand lightly to the brim. "Ladies." He returned to the Pontiac and started it up.

Dot and I watched him go.

"I don't trust him." I said. I wanted to see how she'd react.

"Oh, they're all like that," she replied dismissively.

"Like what?" I turned toward her. I needed to see her eyes.

"Full of shit." She wouldn't look at me, but followed the cloud of dust billowing behind the Pontiac.

"He was behind the break-in."

"You're still on that?"

"My husband knows I'm here."

Dot sighed. "Helene, it's close to your hearing date. It's pretty common for girls to get jumpy."

"Do I look jumpy?" I demanded, standing up.

"You don't exactly look relaxed."

"Well, I have a very powerful husband who seems to have made friends with some mobsters," I told her. "And Mr. Pugliesi is in a... related business."

"Christ, Helene. Not everyone in the gambling business is a gangster. And not everyone with an Italian name is in the Mob." Then came her coup de grace. "Just like not everyone who's an Indian is..."

"Is what?" I folded my arms and cocked my head.

"...backward and bloodthirsty," Dot said. She was a tiny woman—I could have tossed her off the porch with one hand. But she stalked right past me and banged through the screen door.

I watched her vanish into the gloomy foyer, the report of her boots fading away into the office. Every muscle in my body yearned to go after her, to spin her around and slap her right into next week. To split her lip the way Peter had split mine. I wanted to hear her whimpering apology. It was as if she were daring me to prove her right.

"Fuck you and the horse you rode in on, Dorothy Walker." I said it to the door instead, etching my words into its worn white paint so that every time she passed through, it would curse her anew.

…

The following evening, Luke managed to get out to the ranch. Then he broke the news to me: he and Glen were headed to a big rodeo in Phoenix in less than two weeks. After that, he explained, they'd be heading to Albuquerque, then up to Boise, and Billings. The season was beginning.

"What about the job in Flagstaff?" I asked.

"In between," he replied. "Then full time."

I was devastated. How could he just run off and leave me again? I could barely sleep, and first thing in the morning I went out to the barn to find Jamie. I needed him to talk some sense into Luke.

"Miss Helene, Lucky is the stubbornest man I know," he told me. "I hope you don't mind me saying this, but no one is going to change his mind. Bull riding is his life. It's a hard thing to explain."

"Obviously," I groaned.

Jamie fell quiet, and I realized I was being cross with the wrong person.

"I'm sorry," I said with a sigh. "I don't understand it."

He gave me a little smile. "Here's what I think, Miss Helene." He looked off into the east toward the Virginia Range, parsing his words carefully. "Your brother is a warrior. And there's not much call for braves these days in the US of A. Bull riding may just be as close as that man can get to being one."

I stood there, speechless. Luke's friend might just be right. He knew my brother far better than I did. It embarrassed me to be so blind. I added Jamie Jansen to the growing list of people whose wisdom I'd underestimated.

Luke was busy cutting the first spring hay out in Steamboat, so I had to spend the last days of my residency on my own. After living in terror of my husband for almost ten years, what was another few days? A goddamn eternity. It seemed unthinkable that just a few weeks before, all I had desired was solitude.

Wednesday afternoon I was back on the porch, trying to read Reno's silly excuse for a newspaper and finally giving up. A cup of coffee sat next to me, untouched and cold. What I really wanted was a bourbon, but I hadn't had a drink since that night in Virginia City. I watched a flatbed truck rumble in from the lower field, black and white collie dogs perched nimbly atop fresh bales of grass hay.

A whistle sounded across the pasture; I saw a little cloud of steam wafting up from the Virginia & Truckee's grotty old steam train as it passed through the Washoe Valley, on its way from Reno to Minden. It was the same grotty old steam train that had plied the same route during my childhood. Rocking B guests—the same girls who, back home, attended the opera and symphony—filled flasks with whisky, got on horses, and went down to cheer and wave as the engine took on water from the tank that was the sole remnant of once-bustling Franktown.

To them it was another charming relic of the Old West, but every time I heard that whistle I gritted my teeth. The V & T train had stopped at the Stewart Indian School to unload mountains of coal and wood chips, which were burned by the school's enormous boiler. This provided the steam heat for the buildings through a network of underground pipes.

The worst work assignment the boys at Stewart could be given was shoveling fuel into the furnace, so it was a popular form of punishment among the orderlies. Luke was sent there so many times, and attacked the piles with such fury, that his lanky body grew strong—too strong. And because there was no way to break Luke's will with physical punishment, the preferred discipline for my brother's transgressions became humiliating "work" like cleaning toilets with a toothbrush.

The screen door's hinge complained and Elouise stepped out of the house. "These came for you." She held out two envelopes, her expression inscrutable. I hesitated, then took them from her hand. Without another word, she headed off across the lawn and through the aspen, toward the Sugar Pine cabin.

To my relief, one envelope bore the return address of Red Rock Stables, Las Vegas, and the other was a heavy, dove-gray envelope, its flap embossed with the names Beebe & Clegg.

I had been intending to pen a note of apology to Lucius and Charles, and had even started one a couple of times. Each time, I just felt mortified. I couldn't even remember all the things that I needed to apologize for.

To my surprise, inside was an invitation to dinner on the *Gold Coast*, the men's private railcar, for the following evening. I had apparently been absolved.

Please extend our invitation to the charming Peach, as well, it said.

Not likely, I thought. I sorely needed the distraction—and the inspiration. They were such bold, unapologetic characters, living by their own rules. Most of all, they were a reminder of a bright, stimulating world that I had once been part of and would be able to rejoin soon.

Heartened, I opened the letter from Kiehl. It was neatly typed on a piece of plain light blue paper, and rather brief.

Dear Friend,

I hope you're doing well in Reno, and are close to achieving your freedom. There was a bit of unpleasantness after Philippe returned, but it is all sorted. We are fine here and very busy. Susan's health is improving and she has started to ride again.

Philippe has gone to sign papers for the purchase of our new ranch in New Mexico. In two weeks, we are all moving to a beautiful area in the north, close to Rinconada, along the Rio Grande. I hope you will come to visit us when you are able, and stay as long as you can.

Warmly,
Ingrid

I don't know why I was so surprised that Ingrid had written the note. I read it over and over. "Unpleasantness"? What had happened at Red Rock Stables? Philippe hadn't mentioned anything about plans to leave Las Vegas. Was the "unpleasantness" why they were leaving? Had I brought this on them?

Then I discovered something else in the envelope: a little snapshot of Susan. She was smiling shyly, wearing that silly wig that I had given her, standing close to Ingrid, who was kneeling. Ingrid was beaming, relaxed, caught mid-laugh. She looked pretty—almost girlish—and virtually unrecognizable as the cool, intimidating Valkyrie I'd met.

I turned the photograph over.

She won't take the damned thing off, Ingrid had written on the back, in a lovely, looping hand. I examined the picture again. Susan's eyes, as children's eyes often did, seemed almost too large for her face. They were burning with curiosity, ready to devour the world.

I read the letter once more. "We are all moving"? Not "We are both moving"? Was Ingrid referring to Susan? What had happened in this last month? Had the girl's remaining family died?

I slipped the letters back into their envelopes and headed to the only place that guests could make calls, the "phone booth". It was a converted pantry downstairs, with an old-fashioned black phone that sat on a small, rickety desk. The blotter had been doodled on by countless guests. There was a squeaky, uncomfortable Edwardian dining room chair that looked, and felt, as if it had been tossed off a truck. The phone booth had clearly been appointed in this manner to ensure no one would stay in there for long.

I wrote my name on the little chalkboard that hung outside, and paced the hallway as Jennifer cooed and giggled through a call with her "spare", who'd just arrived in Reno and was staying at the Mapes. (The previous week after dinner she'd insisted on modeling her unflattering, off-the-rack wedding dress for the guests. I couldn't help myself; I offered to do some alterations for her. She nearly broke my ribs hugging me in thanks.) When my turn came, I settled into the chair, and dialed the phone number on Lucius's invitation.

To my surprise, a woman answered. "Beebe and Clegg residence," she announced. Her voice was crisp, carrying a faint English accent—probably affected.

"I'm calling to RSVP to Mr. Beebe's dinner invitation," I told her. "This is Helene…Christian." It felt strange to say my once-and-future surname aloud.

"They've been expecting your call. You'll find the *Gold Coast*, the Messrs. private railcar, on the siding at the Virginia & Truckee depot in Carson City. Anyone there can direct you to it."

I hesitated. How would I get there? I certainly wouldn't be having Floss drop me off in the station wagon. And after the Virginia City debacle, I could hardly ask Teddy. Taking a taxicab seemed much too risky now. By now, my husband (or Pugliesi, or Rick) would have spread bribes through every taxi company in town, for "tips" on the comings and goings at the Rocking B. And no one would've thought twice—it was the way Reno worked.

"Would it be possible for the Mssrs. to send a car to the Rocking B Ranch for me?"

The secretary (or whatever she was) paused just long enough to let me know I had overstepped. "I'm sure…that can be arranged," she replied.

"Thank you." There was no point trying to explain my impertinent request. "Goodbye."

I replaced the heavy receiver on the old black phone and sat there for a moment, contemplating a loose bit of wallpaper that looked like it had been peeled back by a fidgeting guest. I was no stranger to "private varnish", as aficionados of elegant private railcars referred to them. Peter's company had two Pullmans fitted out before the war as rolling offices for its executives; each included an office, a parlor, a dining room, bedrooms, berths for servants, and a galley kitchen. They were paneled in the same lugubrious mahogany as the Grafton Industries headquarters in Chicago. Peter was too impatient for train travel, though, and preferred to fly.

We had traveled together in a Grafton Industries Pullman car just once, to New York. The car was staffed with a Negro valet, a waiter, and a chef; Peter treated them all with cool disdain. It was a dreadful night, shut up in that train car with him. He insisted on loud, rough, unpleasant sex. The following morning at breakfast I watched him glancing up from his newspaper to study the poor waiter's face. I knew he was hoping to catch him looking at me, which would have been my fault. And then there would have been a row. But the waiter was occupied with an issue in the kitchen, and my husband's little set-piece was foiled.

Where was Peter right now? Probably sprawled in the biggest suite at the Mapes, or throwing his weight around at the Riverside. He normally bought out an entire floor for himself and his retinue, which included secretaries and valets. Attorneys trailed behind him, like goslings eagerly following the Goose That Laid the Golden Egg.

Since the break-in, every cell in my body had oscillated with his presence. It was as if I was treading water in the ocean, feeling all the creatures lurking in the gloom below, studying my threshing legs and wondering what I'd taste like.

I dialed the long-distance operator, who connected me to the Kiehls' stable. I sat there, my nerves buzzing along with each ring. But there was no answer.

"Miss?" inquired the operator. "Shall I keep ringing?"

"No, thank you." I hung up the phone, surprised at the depth of my disappointment.

TWENTY-FOUR

'd seen girls walk out of that tiny phone alcove with every possible human emotion on their face—everything from glee to shock, bewilderment to despondency. I took a moment to compose myself.

Maisie caught my eye from her favorite perch, an old velvet-covered settee by the radio, and put down her magazine. She stood and approached me hesitantly.

"Are you okay, Helene?" Apparently, I didn't appear as composed as I'd hoped.

"I'm fine."

"Have you by chance seen my new camera?" She'd been asking everyone. Repeatedly.

"Sorry, no." The girl gave a small, abashed nod, then returned to her settee. But my eye drifted toward the game table, where some guests were playing gin rummy. And something occurred to me at that moment.

"Maisie!" I called. "When was the last time you saw it?"

She hurried back to me. "The night of the poker game. That was a brand-new roll of film."

"We took a group picture with it," I said.

"Yes, Dorothy put it on the sideboard before we sat down to play." She lowered her voice and added, "And you know I have a very good memory."

"It was sitting next to the booze bottles."

She blinked slowly and glanced around the parlor, as if assessing everyone's probability of being a thief. "I'm just fit to be tied," she whispered. "I can't believe anyone here would take my camera."

"Maybe we've got a kleptomaniac in this little repertory group," I said.

Maisie scanned the room again with a slight shake of her head. It was a typical evening. Guests sat in small knots playing cards, chatting, and reading. Bertha slumped in an overstuffed chair, fumbling with her needlepoint, two empty highball glasses on the side table next to her. It was a homely, peaceful "Little Women" sort of scene, if you didn't know that everyone was there because their lives had fallen apart.

"This is ridiculous," Maisie muttered. "I guess I'll have to go back to that damn Brownie. No one seemed to be tempted by that."

"You're too good a photographer for that contraption," I told her. Floss had enlarged a couple of Maisie's photographs from the new camera and set them up on the mantle. They were not snapshots, but something more sensitive and observant—the farrier nailing on horseshoes, wranglers calf-roping in the morning light. She had a knack for capturing people in action. "You have an excellent eye," I added.

"You think so?" she asked. I could see in her expression that she thought I might be teasing her.

"Absolutely," I replied. "You could do it for a living."

"Thanks, Helene," she said. "That means a lot coming from you."

I smiled at her. "I feel like a tiger pacing in a zoo," I said. "Do you want to take a walk?"

"Sure." She looked surprised at my invitation. "I could use some fresh air."

We headed out the front door, our boots thumping down the planks of the wooden steps.

"When everyone else settles down after dinner, I want to climb the walls," she confessed. "It's the worst time of the day for me."

"Me too. Especially because I've knocked off the booze."

Maisie rolled down the sleeves of her Western shirt. It was hard to imagine her as a Charleston debutante, now. I'd noticed that she had shed a lot of her flutteriness; even her knee-jerk apologies had diminished.

"Cool tonight," she observed.

The ranch was already blanketed in the Sierra's shadow, but the pale turquoise sky, oblivious to the darkening land below, would remain light for another hour. We started down the long gravel drive at a rambling, after-dinner pace, scuffing pebbles. The wind, as ever, pursued us.

It seemed like all the things that White people had built in Nevada followed straight lines—the roads, the fields, the fences, the irrigation ditches. The land had been sliced and diced into squares and rectangles. One of these ditches, sandwiched between the road and the pasture fence, burbled pleasantly alongside us as we walked. Crickets tried out their first tentative songs of the evening. A pamogo began to croak. (This had been happening with increasing frequency, the longer I was there: my brain would just substitute a Numu word for the English one.)

Maisie and I paused to admire the pasture full of glossy horses, quietly grazing in the lush spring grass. There were buckskins, bays, chestnuts, sorrels, paints, and Bombshell, a gorgeous Palomino that all the new dudes wanted to ride (until they discovered that the handsome gelding was a hopeless plug.)

Sweet Potato saw me, whickered, and ambled in my direction. I loved the satin-skirt sound of her strong legs sweeping through the grass. She put her head over the fence and I scratched under her forelock gently, then behind her large, soft ears. I wished I'd remembered to bring her something—a carrot, or one of Clem's oatmeal cookies.

"She sure likes you," observed Maisie, from a cautious distance.

"She just needed a rider who didn't try to dominate her," I said. Once Sweet Potato trusted me, she showed the most heart of any horse I'd ridden, and more willingness. She'd ford a stream, jump a log, with no hesitation. We had become partners. I didn't want to think about life without her, without our daily rides. It was the only time I felt fully alive, and fully myself.

We continued down the long driveway, past the stock pond. The wind strummed its surface, revealing its twisting, occult shape. We startled some ducks, who lifted off into the air, enjoying the easy loft of a hawk. After a wild spin above our heads, they tumbled back to the water, clamoring like kids getting off the tilt-a-whirl at a carnival.

The smells of wet soil and growing things filled my nostrils, stirring something deep in my memory. Tamano, spring: as a little girl, it had been my favorite season. Spring was when the snow melted, when the tanabe (what Whites called desert peach) sent forth their delicate flowers and their sweet perfume. It was when the precarious world I'd navigated with my mother felt hopeful once again.

I heard the one-note clarion of the atsabana and saw the flash of its amber tail and spotted breast as the flicker alighted on a fencepost. Mama used to tell me a story about these birds—that the Creator had made all the other birds first, and patchworked the atsabana together from leftover parts of six other birds. I didn't know if this was a Paiute story or the product of her own poetic imagination.

"Oh dear." Maisie interrupted my rumination. "This must be where the car crashed."

Scattered across the driveway were little bits of glass, pale blue and twinkling, like fragments of the sky fallen to earth.

We glanced at one another, and I could see in her eyes that Maisie was still afraid that the boys had come to take revenge for her poker victory.

"Maisie," I said. "You're going to be okay. They were here for me."

She blinked, disbelieving. "You? Why?" she asked.

"I'm pretty certain Mr. Pugliesi helped my husband find me."

I swallowed. "That night at the poker game, I let it slip that I was from Chicago. Peter's people knew I was in Reno, because someone spotted me at the Riverside..." I stopped. The less she knew, the better it would be for her.

Maisie frowned. "Didn't the sheriff say it was some...teenagers?"

"Yes it was. The big boys don't like to get their hands dirty." I could imagine the chain of command: Peter, Rick Russo, Giacomo Pugliesi and finally, a couple of would-be kidnappers, hired on the cheap. "But they're not going to try anything like that again. They overplayed their hand."

"They seem to do that a lot," she said, and we both laughed.

We crunched our way through the broken glass. The long timothy grass alongside the cattle guard-turned-tank trap had been trampled flat. Water purled in the irrigation ditch, flowing away across the pastures, toward Washoe Lake. If you didn't know better, you'd think you were in paradise.

"Are you worried about your divorce hearing?" asked Maisie. "Do you think your husband is going to be there?"

"Yes." I had been brooding about it—I was so close to the finish line. But I wasn't kidding myself. Getting divorced from Peter was not the same thing as getting away from him. At least I wouldn't be cornered here, with my wings clipped.

"So what are you going to do after this?" Maisie asked, with sincere curiosity.

"I'm not really sure anymore."

"Because of your brother?"

I had to smile at her insightfulness. "Yes." I was pretty sure Maisie was sweet on him. "How about you? How on earth did you end up in this zoo?"

"The usual reasons, I guess. I married my high-school sweetheart right after graduation, and then we both grew up," she said. "We turned into different people."

"Any children?"

"Thank heavens, no," she aimed her boot at a pebble and kicked it down the road. "I'm not really sure I should be a mother anyhow."

"Why is that?" I asked, surprised.

"It just feels like a trap to me." She cringed, then chuckled. "That sounds pretty horrible, doesn't it?"

"Not at all," I reassured her.

"I want to see the world," she said. "Maybe then I'll feel like settling down and having babies."

"I'll just warn you, it doesn't have that effect on everyone," I laughed.

We followed the ditch another hundred yards, down to a little metal diversion gate that hung from a rope. It was closed, forcing the water to take an abrupt left turn. From there, it flowed across the northern hayfields of the ranch. There was an eddy by the gate where the water spiraled.

We stopped and stared. Floating in a trap of brown foam and leaves was something that looked very much like a photograph.

I squatted by the ditch and leaned forward over the cold, swirling water. Up close I realized the ditch was deeper than it looked. I reached toward the photograph, but it bobbed just beyond my fingertips.

"Try this." Maisie handed me a piece of tumbleweed that the wind had pinned to the pasture fence. Using it I raked the photograph to the edge, and fished it out. Shaking off the water, I wiped the scum onto my jeans, and smoothed it flat.

"Is that what I think it is?" asked Maisie.

It had faded, but the image was still recognizable. There we sit, smiling obediently around the poker table, Maisie beaming like Miss America. Though the ink was barely distinguishable, in the waning light I could make out the embossed X that had been inscribed on my chest with a ballpoint pen.

I handed Maisie the photograph. She stared at it for a moment, then ran her finger over the X as if to confirm that it was really there.

"Oh, Helene," she murmured, looking into my eyes. She handed it to me. I turned the snapshot over, and by squinting I could just make out the words BETTYE CHRISTIAN AKA "HELENE" scribbled on the back.

"What does it say?"

"My real name and my alias."

I shivered hard. Another gust of wind careened down off the mountains, nearly snatching the photo from my hand. The lights of the ranch flickered behind the distant cottonwoods. I felt exposed as hell out there. A good shot could pick me off from the road.

"Come on," I said to her. "Let's get back." I slid the photo into my back pocket, turned on my heel and started walking back. Fast.

"What are you going to do with that?" Maisie scrambled to catch up to me. "I mean, that's evidence, isn't it?"

"Evidence of what?" I walked faster.

"Shouldn't we show that to the Sheriff?"

"Nothing good is going to come from bringing this up with the Washoe County Sheriff," I said. "You saw how tight he is with Dorothy."

The 'investigation', as far as I had seen, consisted of the Sheriff sitting on the porch with Dot over a neighborly cup of coffee. He hadn't spoken with any of the guests. To call his approach desultory would be an overstatement.

"But what does that prove, Helene?"

I was torn between charging back to the house and stopping to spell it out for her.

Maisie caught up to me, reached out and seized my arm.

"Oh, Helene! She wouldn't."

"Then how the hell did they find out?"

"I can't imagine she'd be mixed up in something criminal. I mean, they're respectable members of the community. Why would she?"

From the moment we met, my gut had told me that Dorothy Walker did not want me on her ranch.

"What's her favorite thing in the world?" I asked.

"After cows? Oh, that's easy. Money. She's always carrying on about how much things cost, how they should raise their rates…"

"Exactly," I said. "So if there was a price on my head…"

Maisie's voice quickened with excitement. "But if she was in on it, why did those boys end up in the moat?"

"I bet she didn't realize how far they'd take it," I said. "Or that they'd try to break into the ranch to get to me. If this got out, it could ruin their business. She would not have signed up for that."

"But you know, ever since she found out about your brother…" her voice trailed off. She knew she was entering dangerous territory. "She doesn't think you belong here. I've heard her talking when I'm helping out with breakfast."

"She's made that abundantly clear to me," I said. I'd been a fool to share my suspicions about Pugliesi with Dorothy. "Maisie, you can't tell anyone about this."

"I won't," she said. "You can trust me, Helene."

We parted quietly. She headed off to her cabin and I climbed the steep, narrow stairs to the second floor. I could see a band of light under the door to Dorothy's room and quickly slipped into my own.

I switched on the wobbly little milk-glass lamp by the bed, put on my glasses, and studied the photograph. But it told me nothing I didn't already know. Yes, it was evidence of a bungled attempt to grab me. But the fact was, I'd been in danger for weeks—even during the times when I forgot about it. And I was still in danger. Situation normal, all fucked up.

Thanks to my blunders, the bastards knew exactly where I was. But thanks to their blunders, they now knew that I knew. Ironically, I was probably safer at the Rocking B now, even if Dorothy Walker had tried to sell me out. She wasn't a fool; she wouldn't try again. The wranglers were now on high alert. The conniving bitch would have to put a bullet in my head herself to get that reward.

Peter had to be loving every minute of this. But we both understood that his game of cat-and-mouse had reached its finale. He must have "agreed" to give me half of everything because he was confident I would be dead before the divorce.

. . .

The next morning I called Mrs. Gonzalves. To my annoyance, she didn't seem overly concerned when I informed her that Peter was in Reno, and that I believed someone working with him had tried to abduct me from the Rocking B.

"Mrs. Grafton, I understand this is a very unsettling time for you," she began. "But even if your husband attends your hearing, you're going to get your divorce. That's why you're here in Nevada."

"Yes, but the property settlement—it's bogus," I insisted. "He didn't think I'd live to get my divorce decree."

"Well, he signed it," she said. "We'll be entering it as an exhibit at the hearing, but as far as the law is concerned, the settlement is complete."

"Not if I'm dead!"

"Bettye." She uttered my name with deep patience. Her skepticism brought me back to my senses. "He wants you back, not dead. That is how men like Peter behave."

I'd already arranged for Mrs. Gonzalves to handle all my financial affairs. Her office would be my legal address and my divorce settlement funds would be sent there. Once I'd left Nevada, Peter would have no address at which to find me.

My married name was another piece of baggage I couldn't wait to discard, though my maiden name wasn't much better. There were few people in the world who were less Christian than I. (Then again, despite all the paintings portraying him with limpid blue eyes and porcelain skin, Mr. Jesus Christ was from the desert, too. He might very well look like an Indian.)

I had already cleaned and loaded my Colt. I'd purchased bullets on one of my shopping trips to downtown Reno, and had been doing some target practice during the afternoon rides with Luke. Though he was bemused by my tiny pistol, he'd helped me sharpen my skills. I wished I could have carried a more powerful weapon, but the beauty of the little Colt was that it was easily hidden in a handbag.

After all the running, all the waiting, it was almost time. There was no way Peter or Rick or Pugiliesi were going to stop me. I would get my divorce. I would get my money. And I would leave the goddamn state of Nevada for good and all.

TWENTY-FIVE

There was no better way to conclude my sentence in Nevada than dinner with Lucius Beebe and Charles Clegg. I desperately needed the distraction. I told Floss that Mr. Beebe was sending a car for me that evening, but I let her think I would be dining at his home in Virginia City. She seemed pleased, almost relieved, that I was going out, and especially that I wasn't stewing about the break-in anymore.

Remembering my hosts' formality, I'd chosen an evening gown I'd purchased when I first arrived, in the palest celery-green watered silk. I piled my hair atop my head, Gibson-girl style. (A bit more modern than their favorite era, but close enough.) I slipped the Virginia City madam's jeweled bracelet onto my bare wrist. I opened my beaded clutch and nestled the Colt into the satin lining, and then lay a handkerchief over it, along with my compact and my lipstick.

When I heard one of the wranglers opening the gate closest to the ranch house, I looked out the window. Into the yard below crept a magnificent Rolls Royce Silver Wraith. So much for not attracting attention. As I descended the stairs, trying to tiptoe, I was met with the murmur of voices in the living room, followed by the unmistakable sound of footsteps on the porch; some of the girls had stepped outside to gawk.

"Oh my gosh, Helene!" exclaimed Maisie, as I tried to slip past her at the foot of the stairs. "You look so beautiful! Can I take a picture of you?" She was holding her old Brownie.

"Sure," I smiled. "How about here?" I stopped and posed with the clumsy portrait of Grandpa Walker that hung in the entryway, and she snapped away.

I brushed past other guests as I hurried outside, hoisting the floor-length skirt of the dress to keep it out of the dust.

"Helene!" called Bertha from the porch. "Hot date?"

A handsome, clean-cut young man, who looked to be about the age of a college student, stood by the open rear passenger door. He wore a chauffeur's uniform, replete with a jaunty cap.

"Miss Christian?" he inquired politely.

"Hello," I said with a smile, climbing inside. I pulled my skirt to safety, smoothing it against my legs. He shut the door and got into the driver's seat.

Had it been a mistake not to take a cab? Plenty of guests did, and no one would've batted an eye. This distinctive car had made a bit too much of a splash, smack-dab in the middle of a gaggle of bored women thirsty for gossip. Well, what was done was done. If Dot was in league with Pugliesi, at least she believed that I was heading to the Piper Mansion in Virginia City.

"Lovely evening, isn't it?" the chauffeur said.

"Yes, it is." I could sense the fellow, who was hardly more than a boy, struggling to stay quiet. No doubt he'd been instructed not to say anything else.

I leaned forward as we reached the ranch gate, catching his eye in the rearview mirror. "Do you mind turning left here?"

His young brow furrowed. "Oh, Miss, the *Gold Coast* is down in Carson City."

"Yes, I know," I said, offering an ingratiating smile, "But would it be possible to drive past the Bowers Mansion first? The girls told me it's lovely at night." If anyone was still watching from the ranch house, they'd see the Rolls turn north on 395, as if heading toward Virginia City.

"Uh, sure. I mean—certainly."

I turned to look out of the rear window. No headlights behind us. Good. I settled back into the soft, leather-upholstered seat.

The Bowers's Italianate pleasure palace came into view. It had been built by a former mining-camp laundress whose customers often paid their overdue bills by signing over claims. Her Comstock fortune was the sort my father had dreamed of but never found. Close to the end of my time at Stewart, we older girls had been taken out by train one Saturday for a picnic on the grounds of the "resort" that occupied the former Bowers family estate.

As an avid student of wealthy people, I'd hung on every word spoken by the tour guide. To my disappointment, it turned out that Eillie Orrum Bowers had met with an ignominious end, finishing her days as an itinerant desert fortune-teller. The Comstock had been a brutal mistress for her, too.

"Would you like me to pull over, Miss?" the chauffeur asked.

"No, that's fine," I said. "Thank you for letting me sight-see."

"They made a swell county park out of it," he said, as he turned onto the highway. "With a swimming pool and everything."

That explained why I'd heard Dot bitching that the Bowers Mansion was being maintained by her tax dollars. It seemed that the Walker clan, who'd built their farmhouse around the same time, had a family tradition of contempt for the nouveau riche pile.

Soon we were climbing out of the Washoe Valley, the Rolls Royce engine purring voluptuously. I resisted the urge to look out the rear window again. The trip to the depot felt like it took forever, but when I consulted my watch, I saw that 'forever' had taken all of nineteen minutes.

I regarded the roundhouse and the jumble of cars sitting on the siding with dismay.

"Please, allow me to escort you." The young man opened the door and helped me out of the car. "It's a bit tricky in places, Miss," he warned, taking my arm carefully as we picked our way across the rails.

It was easy to spot the *Gold Coast*; even in the waning light, the handsome railcar gleamed. Not a speck of desert dust was in evidence: it looked like it had been polished mere moments before. Charles, clad in an immaculately tailored cutaway dinner jacket, stepped out onto the car's rear platform and waved to me. I waved back. Tonight it would be 1872, not 1952. It would be a relief to step into their eccentric fantasy life for the evening.'

Charles helped me up the steps and dismissed the chauffeur.

"You look absolutely lovely, Helene." He opened the door into the parlor. Lucius, wearing a similar dinner jacket, jumped to his feet, took my hand and kissed it.

"Welcome to the *Gold Coast*, my dear," he smiled.

"It's fabulous," I told him as I gazed around, astounded.

To call the appointments lavish was an understatement. And in keeping with their manner of dress, the décor was giddily ostentatious: Victorian Bordello meets Venetian Palazzo. Murano glass chandeliers hung from the coffered ceiling. The car's windows were swathed in heavy velvet draperies dripping with bullion fringe, and thick Oriental carpets covered the floor. I heard soft classical music playing from a phonograph and recognized Debussy's La Mer. (Naturally they would listen to the Romantics.)

"We're delighted you could join us," Charles said. Then he seemed to remember that Elouise was missing. "Miss...Peach couldn't come?" He glanced toward Lucius.

"Unfortunately not," I smiled. "But she sends her regrets."

"What a shame," said Lucius thoughtfully, but a little smile played across his face, as if something marvelous had just occurred to him. "Why don't we have a cocktail in the parlor?" Then he turned to Charles.

"Would you mind fetching the—" he began, and Charles instantly understood his request and bustled away down the hallway.

Lucius showed me to a low, velvet-covered slipper chair—the perfect seat for my evening gown. The silk skirt spilled prettily around me as I sat.

To my surprise, a Negro steward—older than the driver but every bit as handsome, and clad in a crisp dark uniform—appeared now, like an actor who'd been hovering just offstage.

"Ah, Mr. Tucker," smiled Lucius.

"Good evening, Mr. Beebe," the steward said, as if he had arrived from some remote wing of a manor house. He wore a soft, enigmatic smile and carried a bottle of Champagne on a tray, which also held delicate rose-colored antique glasses edged in gold.

"Mr. Tucker, this is Miss Christian." I'd never known someone with servants to introduce them, and it surprised me.

"A pleasure to meet you, Miss Christian," Mr. Tucker responded, meeting my gaze with clear, mirthful brown eyes, as if we were both in on the joke of all this make-believe.

"Likewise," I said.

"We never miss a chance to pop a bottle of bubbly," declared Lucius, taking the bottle from the tray. He slipped off the foil and unwound the wire cage. The cork fired unexpectedly and ricocheted off the ceiling.

"Oh!" I startled, my hand flying to my chest. Mr. Tucker had not so much as flinched, his tray of glasses level and rock-steady.

"You must be a veteran." I gave a self-conscious laugh, feeling my face color. It was clear to anyone watching that I was nervous as a cat.

"Yes, ma'am." Mr. Tucker's playful smile remained unchanged.

"And still in the line of fire!" chuckled Lucius, carefully filling three shallow glasses. He peered at me sympathetically as he handed one across the table. "My dear, if we had a foxhole in this parlor, I think you would have jumped into it. Are you all right?"

"Oh, yes." I forced out what I hoped would sound like a carefree laugh.

Charles returned now, holding some papers.

"Ah!" He took one of the glasses. "Lovely. Shall we have a toast?"

"Do let's," declared Charles. "To provenance and providence!"

"To provenance and providence," I echoed, along with Lucius. With care, I clinked my pink coupe glass to theirs. "What sort of toast is that?"

"The toast of a historian," Lucius said.

"I can't tell you how happy we are to have you here this evening, Helene," Charles told me. I noticed that both men looked extraordinarily excited, as if ready to burst. Mr. Tucker had exited the parlor as soundlessly as he'd arrived. "And actually, it's rather a good thing that it's just the three of us."

"Why is that?" I took a tiny sip of the perfectly chilled Champagne. It was the first alcohol I'd had since our night at the Bucket of Blood, and I feared that it would go straight to my head.

The men exchanged glances.

"The evening we met, you made a rather extraordinary statement," Charles said.

"I believe I made a lot of extraordinary statements that night." I smiled nervously, as my curiosity turned to apprehension. "And I must apologize for them all."

"No, no," Lucius smiled. "That's not at all what I meant." He glanced up as Mr. Tucker returned to offer us a tray of exquisite-looking canapes. "And forgive me, because this is a very personal question. But I'm asking because I am a historian. If that makes sense."

Both men seemed perfectly relaxed and convivial, though they were clearly waiting for my assent. All sorts of thoughts ran through my head.

"Go on," I said, and Charles beamed.

"When we went to...pick you up at the cemetery," he began, selecting a canape, "you told us that you had gone there to visit your...father."

I felt the blood drain from my face. "I was terribly drunk," I managed.

Lucius reached over and gently patted my hand, then took a canape and popped it into his mouth, waiting for me to continue.

"Good heavens, I don't remember saying that." I gave an unconvincing laugh and declined the hors d'oeuvres with a little shake of my head.

"It's not our intention to make you feel uncomfortable, my dear." Lucius' face creased momentarily with concern, then switched to an expression that looked suspiciously like delight. "But you unwittingly presented two avid historians with a tantalizing mystery, right in our own backyard. So naturally, our curiosity was piqued."

I glanced from him to Charles, who looked like a boy about to unwrap a birthday present.

"When Elouise found you, you were sitting on...a headstone."

"Yes," I said. "That was mortifying."

"An apt choice of words." Lucius chuckled, enjoying my accidental pun.

Charles shot him an affectionate little glance of warning. His voice dropped to an intimate, gentle register. "Daniel Cleary was your father, wasn't he, my dear?"

It was a shock to hear the name spoken out loud—the sort of shock you feel in your solar plexus. My eyes fell to my lap. Suddenly it seemed the only sound in the room was the symphony, which had entered an early, anxious passage. Strings fluttered nervously, flutes began a repetitive motif, followed by the ting of a triangle, sharp, striking bells, and frantic glissandos on a harp.

I nodded once. The two men exchanged glances. Then Charles placed a very old wedding portrait on the cocktail table. The clean-shaven groom, who was sitting, had short dark hair neatly parted on the side, with a slightly rakish forelock. You could see the determined set to his jaw. He had a short, round Irish nose but his lips were full.

Was this my father? His eyes were pale and blank, in the way of old photos. I searched his face for my own, and found little resemblance: maybe the shape of my hairline—perhaps my chin.

Then I studied the woman standing behind his chair. Mrs. Cleary had fair hair styled in a high Edwardian coiffure festooned with curls and a fancy comb. She had a pretty but severe mouth, plump cheeks, a dainty chin. She had a stern and sensible face, a woman you would cross at your peril were you her servant. Like a woman who would not hesitate to toss a harlot out of her house.

"Have you ever seen this photograph?" Lucius asked. I shook my head no. I couldn't stop staring at it.

"This is Daniel Cleary and his wife Margaret, at their wedding in 1905."

"Is this all right?" interjected Charles, his voice soft.

I shrugged. "You've gone to some trouble, I see."

"No trouble at all. This is what historians do," Lucius said. Then he produced another photograph, which by its appearance was recent. The photo had been enlarged to an eight-by-ten-inch print. It showed a hand-written document, a log. Storey County birth records from St. Mary's Hospital.

"Margaret Cleary gave birth to two of her four children at the hospital," Charles said. "Her last child, Eleanor, was born in 1912." He pointed to a line on the log, waited for a moment, then took the photograph and placed it on the table. He picked up another.

In it, a freckled, fair-haired child in a sailor suit sat on a wooden chair in front of a painted backdrop of roses. He turned it over so I could see the inscription on the back, in faded blue-black ink: Eleanor Anne Cleary, age 6.

"So what's the point of all this sleuthing?" My remark did not come out as offhand as I'd hoped. I was growing increasingly worried about the purpose of their little show and tell.

"You're certainly not Eleanor," said Lucius, with a smile.

"I'm so sorry you went to all this trouble to tell me that."

Undaunted by my sarcasm, he produced another enlarged photograph, this time of a page from what appeared to be a diary.

"This was Margaret Cleary's household journal," Charles explained. "It managed to make its way to the Virginia City Historical Society. She was extremely detailed, and it is one of the best accounts we've yet seen of domestic life here in the early 20th century."

Lucius leaned forward and pointed at the picture. "Here, on March 1, 1917, she records the hiring of a servant named Mary Christian."

At the sound of my mother's name, I flinched involuntarily. I picked up the photograph gingerly. That was not all that the meticulous Mrs. Cleary had written in her household journal. In her tidy hand, she had added, "a widowed Indian squaw".

TWENTY-SIX

Squaw. My mother, reduced to that ugly little slur.

"Helene?" Charles murmured.

I knew before he showed me what he would produce next: the record of my birth at St. Mary's hospital in April, 1919.

I blinked slowly and then let my eyes remain shut. The symphony had reached its most familiar theme, where the gorgeous piano sways between a sort of heavenly reverie and those unforgettably odd, almost dissonant notes. It was a perfect reflection of my emotions.

"This is your story?" asked Charles, breaking the silence. I opened my eyes.

"It's part of my story," I replied.

"We didn't mean to upset you," said Lucius, "But you must understand, your mystery was just...irresistible."

"I'm surprised you found this so fascinating." I could hear my voice, querulous and hard. "It's entirely unremarkable. My mother was a domestic. My father was her employer..." I stopped.

Both men sat staring at me, rapt.

"I'm not sure what's so mysterious and irresistible about that. My father forced himself on his servant, and she bore a bastard child. It's not just unremarkable, it's...common."

They sat there contemplating me with what I presumed to be pity.

"Is that what she...told you?" Lucius inquired carefully. There was something in his expression that let me know he had more to say.

"It's obvious," I snapped.

"I'm not so sure that it is." Lucius' brow furrowed. He glanced again at Charles, then cleared his throat.

"Oh? Did Mrs. Cleary explain all about that in her marvelously thorough household journal?" I felt a hairpin poking into my scalp and resisted the urge to tear it out.

"No." Charles deliberately sidestepped my anger. He spoke with lawyerly precision. "By the time of her husband's death, she had already left Virginia City with their children. They had returned to Boston."

"Not all the history in this town resides in its archives and records," said Lucius. Then he allowed himself a little smile of self-satisfaction. "As a matter of fact, there is quite a lot of it to be found in establishments like the one where we met."

"Saloons?" I snorted.

"More precisely, saloonkeepers," said Lucius. "One in particular has been most helpful."

"I thought you were historians." What was with these men? They were like a couple of magpies, digging up shiny bits of other people's lives and carrying them off to their nest for their own amusement.

"Well, I'd never deny being a tosspot, but my dear, oral histories are a perfectly legitimate resource," Lucius countered, drawing himself up in his chair, unshakable in his authority, like some sort of great professor.

"Well spill, then," I challenged him. "Let's hear what the local saloonkeeper thinks he knows about my mother and father. I can't wait."

Lucius ignored my provocation. "The gentleman we spoke with, Mr. Edward Fish, has been the proprietor of the Silver Chandelier Saloon since 1911. At the time he made your father's acquaintance, he was a young man, but he remembers him quite well. Apparently Daniel Cleary cut a striking figure in town. Mr. Fish described him as tall and spruce, with copper hair, riveting hazel-green eyes and—

what were his words?—'Large, even teeth'."

The better to eat you with, I thought.

"He was one of the latter-day Comstock mine operators," Lucius went on. "An Irishman, obviously. The Clearys came to Virginia City from Boston, but that was decades after the boom here had ended. Your father bought his mine for an inflated price, even so. He was a bit gullible, says Mr. Fish, and given to fits of over-generosity, as most Irishmen are, when he was in his cups. This did not prove to be a good combination for the Cleary family finances."

I shrugged.

"Mr. Fish remembers him as a persistent, optimistic, rather sunny fellow. And Cleary did have a modest little strike at the beginning, enough to buy the house and send for his family. Then he spent the next seven years slowly going broke. Six years into the debacle, his wife packed up the children and returned to her family in Boston."

Lucius sat back in his tufted velvet armchair. Charles then laid a fragile, yellowed newspaper clipping on the table between us. It was from the newspaper they now owned, *The Territorial Enterprise*, but it was dated September 13, 1918. It appeared to be an article, a gossip column perhaps, about a performance at Piper's Opera House. Lucius placed an immaculate finger next to a paragraph listing the attendees.

"...Mrs. Jacob Van Der Brock wore a simple gown of sky-blue silk. This was the first time that she has been seen in public without her widow's weeds since laying her husband to rest last year in the Masonic Cemetery. Mr. Daniel Cleary attended the concert with Miss Maria Elena Cristobal, a petite beauty said to be the daughter of a Spanish Grandee and Peruvian princess. Rumor has it that our once-grand Piper's Opera House will shortly become a Motion Picture House...

"So?" I sniffed.

"Daniel Cleary did not attend this concert with his wife," Lucius said.

"You just told me that she left him," I replied, growing impatient with their slow-motion revelations.

"Look at the woman's name," Lucius urged.

Despite myself, I peered again at the clipping, the name Maria Elena Cristobal.

"We think that Maria Elena Cristobal could very well be Mary Christian," Charles blurted, unable to wait.

"Really," I muttered.

"The name Cristobal means 'follower of Christ' in Spanish," Charles said.

I loosed a sigh of exasperation. But still, I tried to picture it—my mother arm-in-arm with my father, walking into a concert to admiring glances. The images would not form. All I could see was Mama's weary face, suspended over an ironing board or a washing machine, and the ghostly photograph they'd shown me of Daniel Cleary, stiff and unsmiling as a corpse. None of it made sense together. She had never told me stories about him. All she had shared with me was his name, the fact that he had another family, that drink had been his undoing, and that he had died.

The daughter of a Spanish grandee and a Peruvian princess. What utter nonsense. But then again, for a White man in Nevada to attend an event with an Indian woman on his arm, while not unheard of, would certainly have been outrageous in 1918.

"You have to admit, it's intriguing," Lucius said.

"Does your Mr. Fish recall meeting any Peruvian royalty?" I retorted. To my surprise, they both smiled broadly.

"No," allowed Charles. "But he did remember that it was quite a scandal in Virginia City when Daniel Cleary's wife and children left."

"A scandal," I repeated, and gave a sigh. "That's all you have?"

"Well, we've just started our research," Lucius said.

"How many other saloons are left to visit?"

He gave a deep, hearty laugh. Neither man seemed fazed by my dismissal, not even disappointed. Nor were they offended by my skepticism. It was as if they were two missionaries, trying to convert someone who had yet to see the light, but extravagantly confident in their ultimate success.

"We also found a death notice for Mary Christian in the Nevada Appeal archives," began Charles, after a moment's hesitation. "And that pointed us to the coroner's record." There, he stopped. I knew why.

"We were told about the condition of her remains," I said.

"Apparently she was identified by the Bible found with her."

I startled. "What?"

The priest who'd told Luke and I about Mama had never told us that her Bible, her most prized possession, had been recovered. That old priest was so set on proving to us that our mother was damned to hell, he'd omitted that inconvenient fact. But how else would anyone have known who those forlorn remains, high up on a mountain, belonged to? What I would give to have it, to see her handwriting!

Then a thought occurred to me that made me feel almost sick.

"You're not planning to write about this, are you?" I groaned. I'd read Lucius' column in the new *Territorial Enterprise*. It was the last thing I needed or wanted, to be some sort of historical curiosity, another weird denizen of Virginia City, to join the ranks of the town's "colorful" eccentrics and tragic failures.

"No—I mean—we would never write anything without your consent, my dear," Charles replied quickly. "And it's an unfinished story, isn't it? We would love to hear more of it. From you."

"My story is in my past, which is where I prefer that it stay."

"I am sure this is painful," allowed Charles. "And we're sorry if we upset you—"

"But through our research, we hope to provide enlightening new...information, to you too," Lucius added.

"I don't want new information," I said. "The old information is bad enough."

A silence fell between us.

"Your father's death raised some interesting questions," Charles began again, a hopeful note in his voice.

"Unless he left me a fortune, I would like to change the subject, if you don't mind." The light and distracting evening I'd needed so desperately had turned out to be anything but.

The two men looked at one another again, then back at me.

"Of course, my dear. I'm sorry if it feels like we ambushed you," Charles said, in a resigned tone that suggested their presentation had concluded. "Perhaps we can talk some more another time."

"More Champagne?" Lucius interjected, but I could see he was disappointed by my reaction. He managed to compose himself, and added a bit stiffly, "We must give you the full tour of the *Gold Coast*. We have been remiss."

"Thank you, a tour sounds lovely." It was a graceful way to end the awful conversation.

Charles stood and helped me up from the low chair. Then, with mounting enthusiasm, the men led me through the railcar, pointing out details and finishes and explaining the provenance of the antiques and artwork that adorned it. The Gold Coast was a rolling museum. But I could not manage to stay with the conversation; my mind was zig-zagging from past to present. Then Mr. Tucker announced dinner, and we sat down in a formal dining room.

"Claret, my dear?" asked Lucius, proffering a cut-crystal bottle.

"Just a splash."

The steward arrived with our first course. He ladled a delicate consommé from an ornate porcelain tureen. Good. I could manage to swallow that.

"The menu tonight is a replica of a formal dinner from the International Hotel in Virginia City in 1873," announced Lucius. "With a few adjustments made for ingredients one can no longer find. Our poor chef thinks we're barking mad."

"We *are* mad," Charles replied, and lifted his glass.

"To our guest, a true native daughter of the Golden West," pronounced Lucius. We clinked glasses.

To a half-breed bastard daughter of the Golden West, I thought. I was an exemplar of everything that was wrong with the "golden" west: a product of the unwanted union between a greedy and ambitious man who raped the earth first, then my mother—a woman who was one of the last vestiges of a dying people. And here I sat, decades later, with two men who wanted to play make-believe and re-enact the terrible era, as if it were a children's fairy tale.

I sipped soup from a monogrammed silver spoon and listened to the lively banter between Charles and Lucius. They began chattering about a trip they were going to take in the *Gold Coast*, to New York.

"We'll be moving her up to Reno tomorrow," explained Lucius.

"But we don't leave until Friday evening," Charles added. "There's always a bit of bother getting her into position on the siding. Then she'll be coupled to the City of San Francisco, and we're off to Chicago, first." He began to expound on the art of train-car coupling.

It descended on me, then, the sensation that had dogged me my entire life: the feeling of being trapped, a fox with her foot in a snare. As a girl, I had believed with a religious zeal that as an adult I would be free to do as I pleased. I knew better now.

What would happen to Luke and me? If nearly dying hadn't done it, how on earth could I convince my stubborn brother to give up his dangerous avocation? Maybe miracles were different now. Maybe they were not intended to provide happy endings. And if all I got out of it was a happy beginning, well, that was miracle enough. I might still be at war, but I had a comrade-in-arms, at long last.

With effort, I returned my attention to my hosts. They were now gossiping with abandon—tonight's victim was Lana Turner, in Nevada for her divorce—and giving me significant looks every now and then, as if I were in on the fun. And then a thought struck me.

"You're taking the *Gold Coast* to New York?" I blurted, interrupting them.

"Yes," said Lucius, with a wry chuckle.

I mustered a smile. "As of Friday afternoon, I will be a free woman. And I was planning to travel to New York, too. I'm booking passage on the Queen Elizabeth to Le Havre, spending a few days in Paris, then heading to the south of France for the season."

"Helene!" declared Lucius, his face almost childlike with surprise and delight. "We'd be thrilled to have you join us."

I pretended to equivocate. "I'm afraid I have more than the usual baggage," I said hesitantly.

"Oh, there's plenty of room," he replied.

"Actually...I meant that you might think twice about letting me hitch a ride."

"Nonsense," said Charles.

"My husband has been trying to find me. I was going to get divorced in Las Vegas, but I had to come here when he discovered where I was. I thought I was safe at the Rocking B. Until last week. There was a break-in. I believe he attempted to have me abducted."

"My dear!" declared Charles, and Lucius gave an audible gasp. "You should have told us!"

"It's just so sordid," I sighed. "And so...embarrassing." I wrung my hands in my lap for good measure.

"This is outrageous!" Lucius thundered. "What on earth happened?" His face had turned an impressive shade of pink.

"There were two young hoodlums arrested at the ranch last Friday night. They were foiled, but the car they drove was wrecked." I glanced from one to the other. "The car belonged to a well-known bookmaker, a man named Jack Storm." I paused, but there was no sign of recognition on their faces. "He also goes by Giacomo Pugliesi." Again, blanks. "I met him at the ranch, at Dot's poker game last week. They arrested two boys, who everyone keeps calling 'juvenile delinquents.' The police said they were out for a joyride in a stolen vehicle."

"But clearly, you don't think so?" Charles leaned forward.

"No. I'm certain they'd been hired by Mr. Pugliesi. The following day, near the place they crashed the car, I found a discarded photograph that the...trespassers left behind. A picture of me. With my name written on the back."

They both stared at me in near-disbelief, and I could see them tingling at the thrill of it all. A damsel in distress! Attempted kidnapping! It was pure catnip.

"So I believe that, when I leave Reno after the divorce hearing, avoiding the standard means of transportation would be...prudent."

"What is your husband's name?" asked Lucius.

"Peter Grafton. He's an industri—" I began, only to be interrupted.

"Grafton? The most aptly named man in the United States? Oh, my dear." Lucius fixed me with a look of profound sympathy. "You should have said."

"You've heard of him?" I asked, surprised.

"I've heard of every millionaire in the country," Lucius replied, "And I've met most of them. In this day and age, alas, they're usually dull people—rarely worthy of their wealth. But Mr. Grafton is a memorable one. A particularly vile breed—a war profiteer." He paused to gauge my expression. "And if you don't mind me saying—a tick lodged in the neck of the American taxpayer."

"I don't mind at all," I assured him. (Not that I'd ever been terribly concerned about milking the poor American taxpayer—I had a ledger full of Accounts Receivable.)

"J. Edgar is absolutely furious with him," noted Charles, with an intriguing note of familiarity.

"What are they saying?" I asked.

"You weren't aware? *Forbes* ran a piece last month," Lucius said. "Your husband's business troubles have come under quite a bit of scrutiny."

"He was in some hot water before I left."

"Dear girl, the water has reached a rolling boil," exclaimed Lucius, leaning toward me. "Peter Grafton is being accused of fraud. Massive fraud."

So Peter's corruption had finally caught up to him. But as I sat there, a sensation akin to defensiveness rose in my breast. Peter was a monster, indeed. But it was something else to be the wife of a monstrous public figure. I was doubly grateful not to be in Chicago anymore, where the stain of his character would have transferred to me. There were no innocent wives in such stories. Even my disappearance probably smacked of conspiracy now.

"Before I left, Peter was called to two different hearings in Washington, D.C.," I told them. "He hired a gaggle of new lawyers. And each time he came back in a foul mood. He loved to rant about corruption in government, about lying politicians. When he wasn't boasting about them accepting his gifts."

"This is extraordinary!" Lucius declared.

"So you see, smuggling me out of Nevada might be a risky proposition. I'd hate for you to get tangled up in such a mess." (Nothing like a little reverse psychology.)

"I am mad about messes!" Charles immediately began to think out loud. "Helene, they may well be looking for you aboard the *The City of San Francisco*, but no one has to know you're on the *Gold Coast*. She'll be on the siding hours before the train arrives. You can slip aboard as soon as you're done at the courthouse."

I gave them an apprehensive look. "It's a grand idea," I acknowledged. "But I'm afraid I won't be traveling alone."

"Oh?" Lucius glanced at Charles. "My dear, you haven't succumbed to the charms of one of those strapping young wranglers, have you?"

"Hardly." I looked carefully from one to the other. It was now or never—I had to ask. "My brother is traveling with me."

"Your brother?" they said in unison. I enjoyed seeing the confusion on their faces. These brilliant historians didn't know as much about me as they thought.

"Luke was born on the reservation," I said, seeing how avidly they sopped up these new details. "His father was Jack Moore, a Washoe lumberjack. My brother is several years older than me."

"Well well," said Lucius. "Mrs. Cleary mentioned a 'widowed Indian squaw' in her journal. But there was no reference to any child."

He had spoken the slur aloud: squaw. He had cited that woman's household journal as if it were the foremost authority on my mother's life. As if Mrs. Cleary wasn't simply adding my mother's body to her household inventory. My mouth tightened in anger, and I watched alarm rise in Lucius's eyes. "My apologies. Please, go on," he said.

"My brother was playing ball with his friends not far from the house when they snatched him, and two other little boys as well, and took them to the Stewart School."

"The Indian Boarding School?" asked Charles.

"Are you familiar with that history?" I demanded, before I could stop myself. I saw Charles glance uncomfortably at his partner. "Not very familiar," he admitted. "The school is still in operation, isn't it?"

"Indeed it is," I replied. "I'm sure the term 'boarding school' conjures up a very different image for you than it does for me," I went on. "Indian children were not *enrolled* in boarding school. We were taken from our families and incarcerated. We were used as forced labor."

No, these men weren't interested in that sort of history. They were in love with the glamorous Old West that had been dreamed up by White people. The Old West of steam trains and bustles and beaver hats, laughing whorehouse madams draped in red velvet, of gold strikes and shootouts and stampedes. Of painted, war-whooping Indians who were always vanquished by the end of the movie. Not our Old West, the one of erasure, of epidemic, of kidnapped children and stolen homeland. The Old West of slow and certain doom.

The parlor had fallen silent, save for the serene ticking of the grandfather clock, and the soft creak of footfalls in the galley.

"Not one of our nation's proudest moments," murmured Charles, at last. Lucius nodded gravely.

I couldn't help but laugh. "Over half a century is a hell of a 'moment'." I held his gaze long enough to see something shift in his expression. Had I ruined my chances of escape? It didn't matter. I wasn't going anywhere without Luke.

A dense, uncomfortable silence followed, and I broke it myself.

"My brother is a rodeo cowboy," I continued, in a calmer voice. "He is a bull rider. He had a terrible accident a couple of years ago, in which he received a severe brain injury. He's recovered from most of it, but he's lost the ability to speak."

"I'm so sorry, Helene." Charles' voice was quiet. "How terrible."

Lucius kept his eyes fixed on me as if he didn't want to miss a single second. I felt like I was on stage.

"Luke didn't receive proper medical care after his accident." I tried to settle my voice back down into its normal contralto. "But I'm in a position to help him, and I—I have to."

"Certainly," said Lucius.

"My plan is to take him to a specialist in New York. A brain surgeon that I've read about, Dr. Francis Egan."

At this, Lucius sat up. "Dr. Egan teaches at the New York University Medical School," he told me with authority, clearly glad that the conversation had returned to matters on which he could opine. "He's brilliant."

"If anyone could help your brother, it would be him," Charles agreed, his kind eyes shining with sympathy.

"That's what I...I hope," I stammered. This plan had been playing out in my head, where it had seemed perfectly plausible, even though I had not so much as made a phone call, the barest hint of a start.

Now, when I talked about Dr. Egan, I sounded like a child talking about Santa Claus.

I was awash in guilt and confusion. My brother would be deeply humiliated if he knew what I was saying. And even if the brilliant Dr. Egan agreed to see him, would Luke really permit me to drag him to New York? I suspected that he'd fight me tooth and nail. But whatever the price, I had to try. Mama would have wanted this. And Luke would come to realize that I had only his best interests at heart. Maybe not right away...but he would.

I saw Charles direct a glance at Lucius. I watched the silent conversation in their eyes. Then Lucius rose to his feet. He thumped his palm on the dining table, as if gaveling closed a meeting.

"Absolutely," he declared, "You and your brother are coming with us!"

TWENTY-SEVEN

I hitched up the skirts of my evening gown and mounted the front steps of the ranch house. Crickets raved in the lilac bushes, and my pulse seemed to throb to the same rhythm. A sudden, shuddering yawn shook my whole body. I realized for the first time just how exhausted I was.

I believed Lucius Beebe's heart was in the right place, but I wasn't sure that his mouth was. Could a gossip columnist really keep such a juicy secret, an irresistible scandal-within-a-scandal? I turned to watch the Silver Wraith's headlights as they washed the long driveway, all the way back to Franktown Road.

"Welcome back," came a voice from the gloom behind me, and I nearly jumped out of my skin.

"Jesus!" I exclaimed. There sat Elouise on a porch glider, alone in the dark.

"Wow," she said, standing. "You're pretty dolled up. Costume party?"

"Something like that."

"Smoke?" she offered cheerfully. After days of giving me the cold shoulder, what was with this strange, chipper mood of hers?

"Sure."

Elouise came over to offer her pack of cigarettes. I stood there as she lit one for me, her face not far from my own. Then she stepped over to the porch railing and glanced across the dooryard to reassure herself that we were alone. In the distance, moonlight silvered the calm water of Washoe Lake. She turned back toward me.

"Did you have a nice evening with Lucius and Charles?" she asked. She knew where I'd been.

"Yes." I decided to leave it at that.

"I didn't get back 'til a little while ago myself. Jamie, Luke and I went to the Halfway Club for spaghetti."

That took me by surprise. The restaurant was a rollicking joint halfway to the summit on Mount Rose Highway. She'd spent the evening with my brother? And I hadn't been invited? I felt a sharp twitch of jealousy.

"Is that so?"

"We had some laughs." She exhaled. "I had no idea your brother was such a hoot."

Luke—a hoot? This time my jealousy felt like the jab of a goat-head thorn. But I stayed silent. When I finally glanced her way, I saw that her breezy tone belied a pensive expression.

"I think I owe you an apology," she said. The tip of her cigarette glowed brighter as she took another long draw.

"You don't owe me anything," I said.

"Luke told us about your mother."

My body quivered like a plucked string. How could my brother, normally so reticent, make such a terrible mistake?

"That does sound like a hoot," I said coldly.

"It was my fault," she added quickly. "I was asking. You know, after that night in Virginia City, and then this crazy break-in...I was curious. I had no idea what you'd been through—"

"There's a reason for that," I snapped, cutting her off. "It's none of your damned business."

I knew I was being a brute. She fell silent. But I was not going to stand there so this ignorant White girl could feel sorry for me. I felt her eyes burn right through my silk gown. She could see the half-breed child in the flour-sack dress and worn-out boy's shoes. She could see Student #24 scrubbing pots and pans in the cafeteria of the Stewart School. Well, I didn't need pity, especially from White-trash, workaday Elouise. Anyone on earth would have chosen being a Chicago socialite over a dude-ranch secretary.

"I'm leaving Friday, after the hearing," I told her. "Lucius and Charles are going to take Luke and me to New York on the *Gold Coast*."

"Oh?" she said quickly, and I relished the surprise in her voice.

"They invited us," I went on, glad that I had one-upped her. "It's all arranged."

"But, Helene...I mean, the rodeo season is just beginning...I can't imagine Luke would want—"

I cut her off. "There are excellent doctors there. I've been in touch with a well-known physician, an expert in brain injury."

Elouise shook her head in consternation. "Helene, forgive me— but I just don't think Luke wants to see another doctor."

"What the hell would you know about that?" I demanded. "I'm talking about a nationally renowned neurosurgeon who has helped thousands of patients. Why wouldn't he?"

"Well, from what I can tell—"

"From what I can tell, he's *my* brother," I snapped. "Just because he pals around with your boyfriend doesn't mean you know a damned thing about us."

To my surprise, she stood her ground. The ember on her cigarette brightened again. She exhaled softly. "I just think you should ask him if it's what he wants, that's all," she said.

"I think he'd like to be able to speak, like any normal human being!" I struggled not to shout. "Or do you just think Indians should be seen and not heard?"

"That's not fair," she said. It was hard to imagine that only a month ago I'd made this girl cower with a few well-chosen words.

"No, what's not fair is that my brother didn't get the medical care he deserved!"

"You're right, Helene." I could hear her wrestling her voice into a reasonable tone before she came at me again. "But what matters now is what *he* wants...isn't it?"

"A plate of spaghetti and a bottle of Chianti and now you're an expert in what my brother wants. You're a regular head-shrinker, Elouise."

She tossed her cigarette to the porch and ground it out with the smooth sole of her boot. Then the gloves came off.

"Take him all the way to New York? What if you don't hear what you want? What if this fancy doctor can't help Luke?"

"Then he's no worse off than he is now."

"Says you."

Oh, I'd had quite enough of her. "Why don't you mind your own business, Elouise?" I crushed out my cigarette on the railing and flung the butt into the lilacs.

"I need you to listen to me, Bettye." At the sound of my real name I turned. "We've figured out a way to get you out of here," Elouise told me. Her voice was clear and cool, resolved. For the first time I could picture her in that Savannah aircraft factory, ordering a crew around.

I felt my exasperation crest again. "I just told you, I have a way to get out of here."

She was quiet, but it was the quiet of waiting. I could practically hear the wheels turning in her head.

"Well, let's hear your brilliant plan," I challenged her at last. "Hot air balloon? A flying horse? Or do we just put in a call to Superman?"

"We can't talk out here. Come on." Elouise reached out and took my moist, trembling hand in her dry, steady one. I let her lead me down the steps and across the lawn.

TWENTY-EIGHT

"You ready for today?" Floss asked brightly. I'd arrived at breakfast late, as usual, and Clem was cleaning up the dining room with her customary scowl. Dorothy sat at the small dinette in the kitchen, studying a seed catalog.

"Lots to pack," I said by way of excuse. "Morning, Dorothy," I added, and when she didn't bother to answer, I added, "Going to miss me?" Just to needle her.

"Oh yes, Helene," she said, her sarcasm on full display. "I've issued extra handkerchiefs to everyone. We will all miss you terribly."

I was ready. I had asked Floss if she would mind buying me two new suitcases when she went to Reno the day before. She returned with ugly brown Samsonites. I'd folded all but one set of my Western clothes and left them on my bed, a donation to the Rocking B's lending library. I'd also sneaked into Elouise's cabin and hung most of my dresses in her closet. I stuffed the things that were left, higgledy-piggledy, into the Samsonites.

I could hear Elouise in the back office, the solid clack of her typewriter keys. Floss found me a couple of slices of toast and put them on a plate.

"Clem, get Helene some coffee, for heaven's sake."

Clem shot her boss an irritated glance and stopped her cleanup to fetch a cup for me. I thanked them both and alighted on the edge of a kitchen chair opposite Dorothy. I tried to force down some buttered toast but my mouth was horribly dry. I swallowed some coffee.

"How are your nerves?" asked Floss. "You ready for your big day?"

"I could use a cigarette," I replied. She picked up a pack from the kitchen counter and shook one out for me.

"It's very simple—your lawyer does all the work. You'll do just fine." Floss assured me, leaning back against the counter and folding her arms. "Just make sure Jamie remembers he's driving you," Floss said. I could feel Dorothy's attention snap to, though she hadn't moved an inch.

"He remembers, I saw him on my way over." Jamie was taking me to court that morning in his pickup truck. Maisie had mentioned casually that she'd like to come, telling Floss that she wanted to see what the hearings were like, in order to get herself prepared for her own day in court. They would be in the ranch station wagon.

It was not exactly a secret that I was heading to court this morning. In fact, it was public record. Pugliesi and anyone else who might want to stop me could be waiting along our route. So we decided that Jamie and I would leave a whole hour early; I told Floss that I had to meet with my attorney at her office first. But the real plan was to take a circuitous detour to Reno: we'd drive east out Highway 50, take the winding road through Six Mile Canyon, up through Virginia City, and back down Geiger Grade into south Reno—a big, long loop. Once on the outskirts of Reno we'd take side streets to the courthouse near the Truckee River.

"Will your brother be meeting us there?" asked Floss. I felt badly for her already. She had no idea what a lousy day she was in for.

"No," I said. I glanced over at Dorothy, and I could see she was listening, not reading. "Peter is likely to show up. Luke might blow his top, and we don't need a scene. The last thing I need is for the bailiff to arrest my brother in the middle of the Washoe County Courthouse!"

"Good thinking," Floss said. She slipped on her glasses and squinted at the notebook she kept on the counter. She kept meticulous track of all the guests' comings and goings as well as train and airline schedules. "And you'll be catching *The Spirit of San Francisco* this evening?"

"Yes and no," I said, and paused for dramatic effect. "We'll be traveling in Lucius Beebe's private railcar."

At the mention of his name, Floss's mouth dropped open and from the corner of my eye, I saw Dorothy's head rise like a cobra's from its basket.

"Mr. Beebe sure seems to have taken a shine to you," Floss chuckled. I could tell she reveled in these little moments, when interesting people collided with one another in unexpected ways.

"We are kindred spirits," I said. "We had an absolutely marvelous dinner together this week, and when we found out we were heading in the same direction...well. It seemed like fate."

Dorothy gave a little snort, unable to contain herself.

"I have friends in high places, too, Dorothy," I said cheerfully, unable to resist. At that, I stood and left the room.

As the door shut behind her sister, Floss sat herself down on a kitchen chair and gave a low, deep laugh. "Dammit, Helene, just when I was starting to feel sorry for you."

"I still have to be very careful. Can we drive to the train station afterward separately? I'm just worried about Peter."

"Well, sure," she said, grimacing a little. "It's not as if the ranch wagon is incognito, with those big old Rocking B's painted right on the doors."

"Exactly," I said. "I need to stay light on my feet."

"How 'bout I head over to the station and drop your suitcases off with the porter right after your hearing? He'll get them to the *Gold Coast.*" Then she leaned toward me with her quick, reassuring smile. Her hazel eyes were bright with resolve, reminding me of the day we met, when she took me in. "And I'll wait there until you get on that goddamn train."

Floss had saved me the trouble of suggesting exactly that. As unwitting accomplices went, she was aces.

. . .

Jamie grinned as he opened the passenger door for me. I was wearing a deep indigo-blue wool suit, and stared into the truck's dusty interior in dismay. I hadn't thought to bring a lint brush with me.

"Pardon the dust, Miss Helene. It ain't no Rolls Royce, but it'll get us there," the wrangler said. I set a Ferragamo pump awkwardly onto the running board and pushed myself onto the broad bench seat. Jamie glanced away politely as I swung my legs into the cab, then handed me back the valise, which I settled by my feet in a confetti of alfalfa and stray rolling papers.

"Looks like rain," I said. An understatement. Huge thunderclouds were crawling over the Sierra, dragging dull blue shadows behind them. The Washoe Zephyr whipped the pines into a velvet-throated roar, like the sound of a distant crowd cheering in a stadium. A front was pushing in. The timing could not have been worse.

Jamie looked up. "What's a little rain, anyhow?" He flashed me one of his easy grins, which looked a lot less easy than usual.

"I just don't want to spoil my hairdo," I smiled.

We were both thinking the same thing, and we both knew it, but I think it helped us both to go through this little exchange. Then Jamie slammed the heavy passenger door with a hard clang. He'd run the heater to warm up the truck, and the cab smelled of saddle soap and gasoline. It took me right back to Philippe Kiehl's horse trailer. I felt claustrophobia clutch at me and tried to push away the sensation.

I had come too far to panic now. We had a good plan. It just unnerved me to have so many people involved in it. A few weeks ago, even enlisting a single co-conspirator, someone as discreet and adroit as Philippe Kiehl, had tested the bounds of my trust.

"You all set?" Jamie asked, and I nodded once, as emphatically as I could. There was no turning back now.

I took one last look at the ranch house and through a scrim of wind-blown dust saw the unmistakable, tiny figure of Dorothy Walker at the porch railing. Like a ship's captain standing there on her deck, she surveyed the sea of grass that rolled across the Washoe Valley. She did not give us so much as a glance. Instead, she turned her neat blonde head and spat into the lilac bushes at the foot of the porch. Seeing that, and certain that it was for my benefit, I felt a fresh fury rise in my chest, incinerating the fluttering moths of anxiety.

"Go to hell, Dorothy Walker," I said.

"I'm pretty sure she's in charge of hell," Jamie replied.

We reached the highway and turned south toward Carson City. Jamie pushed down on the accelerator and the old truck responded with a lusty roar and a surprising burst of speed. At my expression of surprise, he laughed out loud.

"I souped up the old shit bucket," he confessed. "In case we needed to make a quick getaway."

We flew south on the two-lane blacktop, through lush green pastures full of grazing cows and shiny black calves.

"So you and Elouise..." I began. Teasing the cowboy would help get my mind off what we were about to do. To my delight, he blushed deeply.

"Me and Elouise," he repeated at last, nodding and allowing himself a smile.

"She's a great girl, Jamie," I said.

"Yes ma'am." He gave me a little sidelong look. "I knew from the minute I laid eyes on her that she was the one for me."

"Love at first sight?"

"I guess so," he said with a shrug.

What did that feel like? I'd never believed in true love. And I'd certainly never believed in Fate—that is, until I found Luke here. So maybe there was hope for True Love, too—but I doubted it.

"She has a good head on her shoulders," I told him. "And a very pretty one, too."

He glanced at me again. "Can you keep a secret?" he grinned.

"Sure." I knew what he was about to say.

"I'm going to ask her to marry me."

"That's wonderful, Jamie!" I told him. "I'm so happy for you."

Jamie and Elouise—they made sense. I could picture their life together on a Nevada ranch, with their brood. Yet it was ironic to hear this young man planning to do exactly the thing I was planning to un-do in less than one hour.

Well, not exactly the same thing. I hadn't married Peter for love, I'd married for money, for security, for the feeling of belonging that had eluded me my entire life. I wasn't the first girl who'd come up with that scheme, but it made me feel, for the moment, as if I might be a completely different species than this starry-eyed kid.

"We're going to get married here, I mean legally and everything, but then I want us to have a nice church ceremony in Savannah, so she can have her mama and Lucy there."

"I think she'd really like that, Jamie," I said.

"I'm ready to have my own family," the wrangler continued. "I can't wait to meet that little Lucy."

When I brought my dresses to the Sugar Pine cabin that morning, I'd peered at the framed photograph of Elouise and Lucy closely for the first time. She'd put it back out after I moved to the upstairs room. What a heartless idiot I'd been. I'd put it in the drawer to assuage my own discomfort at having to look at a photograph of a loving mother and her child.

The sun now pushed its way through a hole in the brooding clouds and a brilliant pool of light illuminated one of the bright green fields. I stared out the window at the rich and bountiful land that had supported my ancestors for centuries, with trout and ducks and cattail pollen and grass seeds and pine nuts. Now that I was leaving again, I saw it all as if I were a young girl: spring in full bloom, wild iris bending in the wind, the meadows dotted with their trembling, pale blue petals, and streams pouring their icy snowmelt water into broad, shallow Washoe lake.

To anyone who'd trudged across the Great Basin to the east, and survived its final test, the Forty Mile Desert, this land must have felt like their rightful reward. And we Paiutes were willing to share it, at first, because that's what we did. The idea of land belonging to any one person was simply incomprehensible.

But my ancestors had no idea how many Whites would show up. By the time they realized the Whites had no plans to share—had plans only to take steadily more—it was too late. Now the People's land lay behind barbed-wire and white-washed plank fences of ranches like the Walkers'. Signs that warned against hunting, fishing, or trespassing were nailed to fence posts. It hurt my heart.

"You just sit back and relax, now," said Jamie.

TWENTY-NINE

J ust before we reached Virginia City, to Jamie's surprise, I asked him to stop at the Silver Terrace Cemeteries.

"Are you all right?" he asked nervously. He probably thought I was carsick from the twisting drive up Six Mile Canyon, or that I had lost my nerve entirely about going to the hearing.

"I'm fine, Jamie," I said. "I'll just be a minute." I opened the door and carefully stepped down.

"I'll keep the motor running," he offered.

"Would you mind turning it off?" I asked. Jamie hesitated, then silently relented. He glanced out the window at the dark, sagging clouds—his way of telling me that we didn't have time for this. The air was thick and smelled like rain.

"I'll just be a minute," I said.

I opened the sagging, rusted metal gate and entered the cemetery. Pieces of toppled headstones littered the ground, half-obscured by weeds and sagebrush. Taking a deep breath, I picked my way up the hill, toward the marble angel that crowned the Masonic graveyard. I would never have found my father's grave without her, after so many years. She was an easy landmark to remember, but she belonged to a much grander plot above my father's modest granite marker.

As I approached, I realized for the first time that the statue had no wings—my childhood memory, not surprisingly, had proved unreliable. She wasn't an angel after all, but a barefoot woman in a bell-sleeved cassock, gathered at the waist by a slender cord. She had a cascade of exquisitely carved stone flowers draped over one arm. Between slender fingers, she held a delicate stone rose, extending her offering toward my father's grave.

Who was she, then? Probably a saint. She had a firm jaw and full, sensuous lips, deeply bowed. A long, strong, straight nose. It was a face that would inevitably be described as "classical". In the shadowless gray light, her lowered eyes beneath their heavy lids seemed thoughtful. If her lovely face, her delicate hands and feet, had not been the pale gray of statuary marble...if they'd instead been brown, and the lush twists of hair that rolled back from that face had been black...she could resemble my mother.

I followed her gaze, down toward the headstone at my feet. I reached out and touched the cool granite, wishing that I had something to leave there. "I don't expect I'll be passing this way again," I said to my father. "But it looks like she's taking good care of you."

Jamie had the truck running before I reached it. As soon as I got in, it began to pour.

...

As we approached on Virginia Street, I could see the tarnished metal dome of the Washoe County courthouse, slick with rain. The windshield wipers on the old truck could barely keep up with the deluge. If rain on your wedding day was good luck, what was rain on your divorce day? Every inch of my body trembled and a maddening tic caused my eyelid to twitch every few seconds.

"I think there's a flask in the glove box if you need a little liquid courage," Jamie offered.

"I'm okay," I told him. (Had I actually stopped drinking?) Even Mrs. Gonzalves had suggested a mild tranquilizer. But I needed my head clear and my reflexes sharp.

"I'm going to drop you off as soon as I see the rest of them on the sidewalk. Then I'm going to park around the corner on Court

Street," he said. "When you're done, come out the back entrance, and you'll see the truck. I'll be looking for you. Okay?"

"Okay." I opened my purse and lifted the handkerchief, as if the Colt might have disappeared somehow.

"Is that a gun?" Jamie asked, surprised.

"Yes sir," I said.

"I don't think they let you take guns into the courthouse."

"Who's going to know?" I doubted that anyone, even here in the Wild West, would search a lady's handbag.

"I s'pose you can try," he shrugged.

"I'll just play dumb if I get caught."

"That, I'd have to see to believe," Jamie said.

We had timed it well. Floss had found a parking spot across the street from the courthouse. Jamie halted the truck in the middle of Virginia Street, as we had planned, and as soon as they saw us, Floss and Maisie got out of the station wagon and started to cross. Maisie wore a smart tan suit and heels, with a hat pulled low over her face.

I squinted toward the slabs of Sierra granite that made up the courthouse steps and its towering Corinthian columns. I would walk into that building as Peter Grafton's wife, and not very long from now, I'd walk out as Elizabeth Christian, free woman.

Thanks to the gusting wind and the rain, there was no one loitering outside. Reporters usually hovered around the courthouse like seagulls at a garbage dump, hoping to catch some celebrity divorce in flagrante. I took a long breath, the moist air strange and thick in my lungs.

"Thank you, Jamie," I said, turning to him.

"It's nothing," he replied reassuringly. "Eight seconds, Miss Helene," he added, and clenched his hand tightly before his chest like he had climbed onto a rodeo bronc and grabbed the bucking strap. "Just gotta stay on for eight seconds and you'll be fine."

"Here goes nothing," I said, getting out. I headed to the curb, where Floss was standing. She took my arm, pulled me underneath her umbrella, and walked me quickly up the steps as rain pelted us. Maisie was close behind, struggling with an uncooperative umbrella.

"Wow, you picked a hell of a day to get divorced," Floss said, pushing open the heavy door. "Looks like you're leaving just in time. Apparently winter's doing an encore."

Mrs. Gonzalves was standing just inside, holding her briefcase. Next to her hovered her legal secretary, Rebecca Winters, a recent graduate from the law school at the University. Mrs. G wore a drab brown suit and her customary oxfords. I mustered a smile.

"Good morning, Mrs. Grafton," she said briskly. "How are you?"

"I'm fine," I replied.

"Good morning, Miss Walker," she said to Floss. They shook hands.

"Nice to see you again, Mrs. Gonzalves," Floss said. "Hello, Miss Winters. Don't you look pretty today."

I tuned out the small talk, staring over Mrs. G's head, scanning the busy, broad hallway. There were a lot of people in the courthouse. To my dismay, that included a noisy gaggle of reporters. A moist fug of wet wool, cigarettes and Aqua Velva hung in the space.

"That fellow's the stringer for the *New York Daily News*," said Floss, indicating one of them with a discreet tilt of her chin. "He's been on the divorce beat for years."

"I don't think anyone has caught wind of your hearing," said Mrs. Gonzalves. "And we're in luck. There's a very pregnant B-movie actress getting divorced this morning."

"Is he here?" I asked her.

My attorney hesitated, scrutinizing my face before she spoke. "Not yet."

I nodded, inhaled deeply, and drew my shoulders back. "Okay."

"Shall we?" Mrs. Gonzalves turned and walked briskly down the long hall. We dutifully followed her. When we reached the door, it opened and a couple of men straggled out, deep in conversation. Rebecca grabbed the handle and held it open for us.

"I'm going to find the ladies' room. I'll be right back," said Maisie, just as we had planned, and hurried off.

"Good Lord, I think her nerves are worse than yours today," remarked Floss in a perplexed voice, as the rest of us filed into the waiting room. Nearly all the seats were filled.

"I didn't expect an audience," I muttered, dismayed.

"The hearings are so closely scheduled, people just sit and wait their turn," Mrs. Gonzalves replied. She glanced at me. "You cut it a bit close."

Floss gestured for the one open chair, but I shook my head. I felt better standing.

Then the waiting room door opened, and a man in a dark suit entered. He glanced around, then behind him, and gave a nod.

In walked Peter. Three other men followed him, and suddenly the stuffy waiting room was as full as a Plaza Hotel elevator car. My heart began to pound, but it was impossible to look away.

His attorneys wore virtually identical dark gray suits. They were all nearly the same height—and none were taller than him. They looked for all the world like groomsmen at a wedding.

Without a word, and very casually, Floss, Rebecca and Mrs. G formed a little semi-circle in front of me and Floss fixed her eyes on mine, trying to get me to ignore Peter and his entourage. But my body was rigid, and I found my gaze once again on him. It felt like if I took my eyes off him for a second, he might suddenly be on me.

To our relief, the bailiff stepped out. "Grafton!" he called, and held open the door to the private hearing room. My God, it looked small. Most of these Nevada divorces, Mrs. Gonzalves had explained, were not contested, and it was rare that both parties occupied the intimate confines. Usually the wife was dispatched to Nevada to take care of things, since the husband would not want to take six weeks off work.

"Ladies first," said Peter's attorney. To my relief, Peter was behaving as if we weren't even there.

We stepped into the courtroom and I glanced nervously around. It was small, but held the usual things: the judge's bench, a witness stand, and tables for the attorneys, witnesses and clients. There were just a handful of chairs in the gallery.

Mrs. Gonzalves approached one of the tables and set down her battered leather satchel. She pulled out a chair for me.

"Here we are," she said, placing Rebecca to my left, and Floss nearest the aisle, since she would have to testify first.

It was hard not to compare my motley crew to Peter's group. A frumpy middle-aged lady lawyer, her wisp of an assistant with the gravitas of a shopgirl, and fresh-off-the-ranch Florence Walker in the same ill-fitting suit she wore every time she was heading off to court with a guest.

Then Peter turned toward us—casually, as if he was waiting in a hotel lobby, not a courtroom. I began to sweat profusely in my rain-soaked wool suit. He met my gaze and aimed a smile at me—the mocking, knowing, awful smile I knew so well. I felt like I was going to be sick to my stomach. I had imagined this moment so many times, imagining the fierce, composed expression I would wear, but all I could do was look away.

Mrs. Gonzalves busied herself organizing her papers, then took a look at my face.

"How are you doing, dear?" I heard her murmur, but I couldn't reply. How was I doing? I was sitting in the same room with the man who had tormented me for seven years. I was seeing his face for the first time in over six months. The man who nearly killed me, who still gave me nightmares. Who looked, as always, like he knew something that I didn't.

Mrs. G turned to Rebecca. "Alka Seltzer," she said in a low voice, sounding like a surgeon issuing orders to a nurse in the operating room. The secretary quickly produced a packet from her handbag and poured a glass of water for me from a pitcher on the table.

I shook my head no and she stopped. "Please—just water," I whispered. Peter would love to see me gulping Alka Seltzer.

The funk of my damp wool suit unexpectedly broke the spell, yanking me back to a memory: Springtime, the sheep pen at the boarding school. Luke and I sitting atop the wooden fence smoking the cigarettes he'd just rolled.

I desperately wished it had been possible for my brother to come to court. I wanted him here. I needed his strength. But Luke was right where he should be, making ready for our escape from Nevada. I thought of the brown suitcases filled with my things, sitting in the back of Floss' station wagon. I thought of Lucius and Charles, heading for the railroad siding where the *Gold Coast* sat waiting for the afternoon arrival of the *City of San Francisco*, after its winding passage through the Truckee River canyon.

Mrs. Gonzalves began busily removing papers from a folder, pulling out the Exhibits. I glanced over and saw one of the photos she'd enlarged: me with two black eyes, my lips split and ragged. My nose spread across my face, an angry, swollen pulp. Peter had kicked me as I lay on the bedroom floor, the room gyring around me like a carnival ride, gagging on my own blood.

I looked into my own eyes and a dead, haunted woman stared back. A hot wave of indignation flooded me, washing away my anxiety. Every cell in my body began to vibrate with fury.

"Sweet Jesus," breathed Floss.

Now I could not take my eyes off Peter, who'd assumed his familiar, casually contemptuous posture. He looked like a Roman Emperor lounging on his dais in the Coliseum, ready to lazily thumbs-down a wounded gladiator. He glanced at his watch in a brief but ostentatious display of irritation. Who the hell was this penny-ante Nevada divorce court judge, to keep the mighty Peter Grafton waiting?

I seized that moment. I pushed my chair back and stood, drawing a soft, startled exclamation from Mrs. Gonzalves.

"We're about to begin!" she whispered to me. "Bettye! Sit down!"

But I'd already slipped behind her chair, and I started toward the table where Peter sat.

"Bettye!" she hissed. "Come back!" Rebecca reached for my sleeve and missed.

I stopped in the aisle, staring at the men at the table. His attorney glanced up at me and frowned, then Peter turned to look. When our eyes met, I took a deep breath and opened my mouth.

"You will never hurt me again," I said. For a moment Peter looked perfectly dumbfounded. Then he began to laugh.

My words had come out in Numu.

"Please go back to your seat, Mrs. Grafton," one of the attorneys said, at the very moment I felt Rebecca's hand taking my own.

"What sort of gibberish was that?" Peter gave a loud, theatrical sigh and shook his head. "Sounds like she's drunk again."

Rebecca drew me back to my seat and I didn't resist. I'd said what I needed to say. Even if he didn't understand the words, I was certain he knew exactly what I'd said.

I was done being his victim. I'd made it here, to this arena, and I was getting my divorce. He was being made to answer for his misdeeds in public. Everyone would know exactly who Peter Grafton really was. And he couldn't do a thing to stop it.

The door to the judge's chambers opened, and I settled into my chair between Mrs. Gonzalves and Floss, feeling strangely calm. I could feel my witness staring at me, dumbstruck.

"You are full of surprises, Helene," Floss said.

Mrs. Gonzalves touched my arm and leaned toward me. "You never told me you were Paiute."

"Neither did you," I replied.

She gazed at me evenly. "The Ancestors are with you today," she said, her voice low and confident.

"All rise," declared the sergeant at arms, and we stood. Peter got to his feet with the sort of studied indolence with which he might greet a fellow country club member he didn't care for. The judge settled himself on the bench with a brisk-yet-bored demeanor, as if there were a competition between these men to demonstrate how little either wished to be in the room. Mrs. Gonzalves had told me Judge Givens granted dozens of divorces a day in his production-line courtroom.

"Let's get started, shall we?" he said, slipping on little half-moon reading glasses. "We're running late today and I haven't had lunch yet. First, Mr. Richards will swear in witnesses who are giving testimony today. Everyone else, please be seated."

A tall, imposing officer of the court stepped forward to swear us in. He began with Floss, whom he recognized, permitting a half-smile to crack a face that could have been carved from granite. Next, he addressed me.

"Please state your name."

"Elizabeth Christian…Grafton," I said. I could see the court stenographer tapping quietly away on her machine. It was that detail, rather than the entrance of the judge, that made it all real for me. This woman would be recording everything. Peter's "extreme cruelty" would be a matter of legal record.

"Do you swear to tell the truth, the whole truth and nothing but the truth, so help you God?"

"I do."

When Peter stood to be sworn in, I scrutinized him. He looked the same—the picture of health, just the right amount of tan, rowing-club shoulders as broad as ever, posture as effortlessly commanding. Was there a little more gray in his hair? If so, it only added to his presence. Everything about him shouted that he was a man accustomed to getting his way. Even the casual way he swore his oath suggested that the whole affair was barely worth the effort.

I looked at the judge, wondering how this act was playing with him, but his face was expressionless. I'm sure he'd seen plenty of Peters in his day, men trying to show everyone that they were still in charge, even when they weren't.

I heard the door to the courtroom open and shut behind us, but I didn't take my eyes off my husband. As I watched him sit back down on the sturdy wooden chair and cross his legs, I thought about my plan. We'd gone over and over it the night before. Luke knew what to do, Jamie was just outside the back entrance of the courthouse in his truck, and Maisie should by now be in the ladies' room, ferrying my change of costume in a shopping bag that Jamie had concealed behind a trash can the previous evening.

The divorce hearing turned out to be a remarkably dry and straightforward transaction. First Floss was called as a witness; she got on the stand and testified that she knew me, that I lived at the Rocking B Ranch, and that she had seen me at least once in every twenty-four-hour period for the last six weeks.

"The plaintiff will take the stand," the judge intoned, and I stood. I was sworn in, just as Floss had been.

"Where do you reside?" the judge asked.

"At the Rocking B Ranch," I replied, "In Franktown, Nevada."

"When did you come to Nevada?"

"Ten weeks ago," I replied. "But I have resided at the Rocking B for the last six weeks."

"Have you any other home or place of legal residence?" He asked.

"No," I said.

"When you arrived, was it your intention to live here indefinitely and make Nevada your home?"

"It was," I said. "Yes."

"Is this still your intention?"

"It is," I said. It was a lie as old as the Nevada divorce racket itself, a lie that had been told by a cavalcade of movie stars, East Coast bluebloods and minor European royals before me.

"You're stating the grounds for this divorce as extreme cruelty?" asked the judge.

"Yes, your Honor. I'd like to provide the court with an Exhibit." Mrs. Gonzalves rose and handed the photographs to the court clerk.

In the state of Nevada, Mrs. G had explained at our first meeting, there were nine conditions that provided grounds for divorce, any one of which was sufficient. They included my personal favorite, extreme cruelty, along with insanity, infidelity, abandonment and even impotence. Though it was not even necessary to document my grounds—my statement alone would suffice—I had wanted it on the record. I wanted the world to know just who Peter Grafton was. The press would have a field day with it.

"Mr. Grafton physically assaulted my client, on more than one occasion," my attorney said in a voice utterly scrubbed of emotion. She returned to her chair.

The judge glanced up at me, as if to confirm that I was the same woman in the photographs.

"This assault, documented in the photographs, broke my client's nose. She required reconstructive surgery," added Mrs. Gonzalves.

Even as he studied the photographs of my bloodied and battered face, I did not see the judge's expression change. But I noticed a movement from the corner of my eye and saw Peter whisper something in his attorney's ear. Then Peter turned around in his chair. As we all watched, he smiled at a beautiful blonde now sitting in the gallery.

She could not have been more than twenty-five, and wore a stunning pale yellow suit with a robin's egg blue blouse of silk crepe de chine. Her lips were painted a lush, deep red, and when she smiled back at Peter, her perfect white teeth gleamed. The heart-shaped pigeon's-blood ruby pendant rested just below her throat.

Peter was the very picture of sangfroid, wearing his Saville Row suit, a crisp white shirt, a salmon-colored silk tie and pocket square. All that was missing was his boutonniere and her corsage. Peter was going to marry her as soon as our hearing was over. There was no waiting period in Nevada. They could walk straight to the county clerk's office and tie the knot before the ink on the divorce decree was dry.

The judge handed off the photographs to the court clerk. "Let the record show that the Court has received photographs depicting Elizabeth Grafton's injuries from an alleged assault by Peter Grafton," he stated in a monotone.

My eyes were riveted on the girl. Didn't she realize that she was next? I watched her aim the pearly smile at Peter. She was a gorgeous girl, the best money could buy. Just like I had been.

"How does the defendant respond to these allegations?" the judge asked. One of the attorneys stood.

"The defendant denies each and every, all and singular allegations," he proclaimed. "Furthermore, the plaintiff has perjured herself. The injuries shown in the photographs are the result of a car accident that the plaintiff had while driving under the influence of alcohol and sleeping pills."

"That's a lie!" I said.

"Order!" declared the judge. "Mrs. Gonzalves, please make sure there are no more outbursts from your client, or I will hold her in contempt."

"Yes, Your Honor," responded Mrs. Gonzalves. She turned to me. "Bettye," she said in a very low voice. "Keep your cool. You're getting your divorce no matter what he says." The door to the courtroom opened behind us and I could hear a rising hubbub echoing from the hallway past the waiting room. The judge looked up, his brow furrowed.

"Are these gentlemen your guests?" he demanded, clearly annoyed. I turned and saw Rick Russo and Giacomo Pugliesi filing silently in and sitting down in chairs next to the door. I wasn't sure if I wanted to laugh, burst into tears, or scream—maybe all three.

"No," said Peter's attorney, visibly confused. "Our apologies, your Honor."

"Bailiff, please show these gentlemen where they can wait outside." The Judge gave a long sigh.

I saw Peter glance back over his shoulder. So this was how he was going to play it? The bastard had such a flair for the dramatic. He would waggle his fiancée in front of me, then let me know that I was still utterly fucked. These men would finish me off while he was getting married.

I thought about the gun nestled in my purse. I thought about Jamie, hovering at the back entrance of the courthouse, ready to hustle me away as soon as this was done. Did I have a prayer of making it outside?

I clutched Mrs. Gonzalves' hand under the table. "That was the man behind the break-in at the ranch," I told her in a low voice. "Giacomo Pugliesi. The big one. He goes by Jack Storm. And the other one is a criminal from Las Vegas. Rick Russo. He's the one who held me prisoner, and tried to turn me over to Peter."

"Are you sure?"

"Yes!" I hissed.

"I know, Bettye, it is suspicious," she allowed, in her maddening, calm way. "But there's really nothing we can do right now unless they threaten you in some way. Let's concentrate on what we have to do here."

"I just don't want to be dead five minutes after my divorce!"

She squeezed my hand. "Before we leave the courtroom, we'll speak to the sergeant at arms. He will get you a Sheriff's escort out of the courthouse."

"And then what?"

Mrs. Gonzalves angled her head toward the judge, urging me to refocus.

"I find that your grounds for divorce meet the legal requirement of the state of Nevada," he intoned. It was over.

I'd done it. I'd divorced the bastard. I'd "graduated".

"Congratulations!" Floss thumped me on the back. I wished I felt more relief, but the business of staying alive had taken precedence.

There was not so much as a peep from Peter's attorney. The judge began to write out the decree, and I allowed myself a glance at my now-ex-husband.

To my surprise, Peter's composure had vanished. He sat hunched over, urgently whispering with his attorneys, gesturing toward the door. His smug, varnished face was bone-white.

"Something's up," I murmured to Mrs. Gonzalves.

Now the judge lay down his pen and looked up at Mrs. Gonzalves.

"And this is your settlement Exhibit?" he asked.

"Yes, your Honor," said my attorney.

I sat up straighter. From the corner of my eye, I saw Peter do the same. His little row of perfectly matched attorneys sat there, like blackbirds flanking a big, brooding raven on a telephone line.

Peter Grafton was about to pay for what he'd done to me.

"Let's make sure everything's in order," said the judge, and he began to review the Exhibit.

Then the judge's face registered, at last, just who was sitting in his courtroom. He looked as if he'd caught a whiff of something rotten.

"You're *that* Peter Grafton?" he asked.

"Yes I am," said my ex-husband.

"Well you've had a helluva week," commented the judge dryly.

"I've had better," Peter replied with a stiff smile. He didn't look like such a cool customer now.

His attorney stood up. "Your Honor," he said. "While the terms of the settlement stand, we regret to inform the Court that the Graftons' assets have been seized by the United States Government."

THIRTY

My ears filled with a strange roar that might have been blood rushing, might have been the hubbub of voices outside the courtroom. I couldn't focus my eyes. I felt like I had after one of Peter's assaults—not yet sure of how badly I'd been injured. Was I going to vomit? I reached out for the table, trying to steady myself. I felt Rebecca's hand gently alight on mine.

"Are you okay?" I heard her ask. "Here, try to drink some water." I couldn't see, let alone hold, the glass she attempted to hand me, and she set it back down.

The judge began to speak. I tried to make out what he was saying, but it was just a drone, the sound of bees around a hive. Other voices, men's voices, joined the drone. Then I heard Mrs. Gonzalves thanking the judge, another gavel rap.

"Is it over?" I rasped.

"Yes," came Mrs. Gonzalves' voice. "We're done."

"And he doesn't have to...?" I couldn't even say the words.

"We're going to look into it." Mrs. Gonzalves placed a hand on my shoulder, but she didn't sound confident at all. *Look into it?* I knew Peter. This was checkmate.

Images, forms, people now began to sway and shimmer back into focus. I saw Peter and his three attorneys, standing together in a little knot of dark suits at the front of the emptying courtroom. I wanted to scream. There was nothing I could do about this now, I knew. I tried to force myself to think about our escape plan.

"You can pick up your divorce decree in a few minutes," said Mrs. Gonzalves, "At the clerk's office upstairs."

"Can you do it?" I croaked.

"Of course," she said. "I can mail it to you, if you prefer not to wait."

"I won't be waiting. Can you give my photos to the reporter from the New York Daily News?"

"Are you sure?"

"Yes," I said.

Now Floss extended her hand to me. "I'm going to go drop off your suitcases at the station. I'll see you...over there."

I didn't want her to see me like this—humiliated, vanquished. And Floss didn't know the half of it. The swashbuckling escape that Elouise, Jamie, Luke and I had cooked up two nights ago now seemed like some childish lark.

What had I expected? These men were determined to crush me, to dispose of me like some trash that the desert wind had blown against their feet.

The devastating words spoken by Peter's attorney echoed in my head. But I could not surrender to despair. If I wanted to live to fight another day, I needed to get out of this building. Fast. What I had to do next would require all my focus.

"You're going to be fine." Floss smiled and gave me a hug. "It ain't over til it's over."

She wasn't kidding. It wasn't over by a long shot. There was a gauntlet of vicious bastards to navigate before I got out of Reno.

I glanced back toward Peter's entourage, which had tightened into a small knot. They surrounded Peter, two of them still conferring with him urgently as they started to walk, prodded toward the exit by the enormous, scowling bailiff.

"Ladies," boomed the bailiff, "It's time to go. The next case is starting."

Outside the courtroom doors, the ruckus in the echoing marble hallway was growing steadily louder. Floss, Rebecca, and Mrs. Gonzalves moved in front of me, and we shuffled toward the exit behind Peter's group.

My mind raced. Where the hell was Rick? The door to the waiting room stood open now, but I couldn't see him. Then, closer to the hallway, I spotted Pugliesi, chatting up Peter's girl. I could hear his forced laughter, and saw the girl staring toward Peter, wearing the unmistakable *save me!* face of a woman desperate to get away from an overbearing man. But Peter didn't seem particularly interested in her at the moment. Not far from Pugliesi hovered Maisie, eyes like daggers.

Peter's retinue moved through the courtroom door, then into the waiting room, wavering uncertainly, as if they were wondering which train platform they should be heading toward. Then Peter turned around, stalked back toward us, and fixed me with a hateful stare. I knew the look all too well.

"You bitch!" he declared loudly, jerking his chin upward, a gesture that had always reminded me of some mythical horned beast. "Look what you've done!" It was one of his favorite refrains, one of Peter Grafton's Greatest Hits.

The fresh group of people in the waiting room stopped chatting and murmuring and fixed us with eager, horrified stares.

"That's quite enough, Mr. Grafton!" To my surprise, Rebecca's sweet, girlish voice had become the clarion of an irate grammar school teacher.

"Peee-ter!" bleated his girlfriend, as if she were afraid we were hurting her precious fiancé. Peter stood there, rigid and shaking.

"And what exactly did I do?" I shouted. I had witnesses, at last, to his monstrous behavior. Red blotches erupted on Peter's face. His big jaw thrust forward. When one of the attorneys tried to take his arm and pull him back, he angrily shoved the man aside.

Reflexively, I stepped back. He wouldn't hit me here, would he?

Peter Grafton was a monster, but he wasn't a stupid monster; he wouldn't lay a hand on me in a courthouse, in front of reporters. The bailiff pushed forward through the scrum, leaning in like a referee separating boxers in a clinch.

"Move along!" he told Peter gruffly. "You all need to clear out. Now."

"Come on," one of the attorneys urged, and finally pulled Peter away from me. His awkward group began to rumble toward the exit.

"Bitch!" my ex-husband shouted over his shoulder. I looked into his metal-gray eyes, shook my head, and gave him a mocking smile. It was an Academy Award performance—my legs were about to collapse under me.

The sergeant at arms tapped me on the shoulder and pointed toward the door. "You too, ma'am," he said, and I obeyed.

I waded into the maelstrom. The commotion in the lobby rose, rolling toward us like an ocean wave. I found myself awash in the wake of Peter's little flotilla and felt eyes tugging at me. I heard flash bulbs popping.

That's Peter Grafton's ex-wife!

It was terrific theater, wasn't it? Forget theater, this was church. The unholy lifeblood of Reno...drama and scandal, romance and catastrophe. How could I have been so foolish to think I could, with another clever costume change, disappear as easily as a magician's assistant?

Peter's girl elbowed her way toward him and tried to throw her arms around his neck, but he stiff-armed her like the halfback he'd once been, and she stumbled back, shocked at his brutality. I heard her give a little gulping sob of surprise and dismay.

"We're leaving!" I heard him declare—as if they had a choice.

Yes, this is your knight in shining armor, I wanted to say. *Save yourself.* The child would be married to that bastard in another hour, but now she trailed after the men, head down, humiliated.

We shuffled through the doorway into the lobby. I knew Rick Russo was out there, waiting for me. Ready to finish what he'd started in Las Vegas. The swelling tide of people jostled aside Maisie, Rebecca and Mrs. Gonzalves. Suddenly I found myself alone in the crowd. The marble hall seethed with activity, all of it surging toward the big man who'd just emerged. Reporters held up cameras. Others waved for his attention, shouted questions.

"Mr. Grafton!" hollered a reporter.

"Hey Grafton!" shouted another. "Over here!" A flashbulb exploded a few feet away.

I clutched my purse to my side and ducked my head. It was time to focus on getting out of that building alive. My first objective was the Ladies' Room on the lower level. There I'd change into the clothes Maisie had stashed in a janitor's closet: jeans and boots, a man's sheepskin jacket—and most importantly, a cowboy hat—then wait until the coast was clear. At least this change required far less artistry than the one in Las Vegas. Then, the theory went, I'd just walk out the back door and get into Jamie's truck, unnoticed.

The moment I stepped into the courthouse scrum, I felt a hand seize my arm. I knew who it was without looking, even before I heard his voice in my ear.

"Move!" Rick commanded me. He knew better than to drag me away. Like a skillful dance partner in a crowded nightclub, he swept me into the thick of the chaos swirling around Peter.

"Let go of me!" I yelled, but my voice flew away into the hubbub, swirling into the towering dome above us, along with the shouts of reporters.

My heart smashed wildly inside my chest, trying to batter its way out. I knew what came next. Rick and Pugliesi were going to drag me out of the courthouse, throw me into a waiting car, drive me out into the desert, and put a bullet in my head.

I could not let him take me out of the building. If he managed to do that, it was all over.

Now we were almost directly behind Peter, close enough that I could smell the nauseating tang of his sweat and his leathery after-shave, the smell of countless terrifying nights in our Chicago house. The din of voices overwhelmed me and the rapidly popping flash-bulbs left my eyes half-blinded by bilious green clouds.

Rick suddenly spun me, dropped my arm, and grabbed my purse from my other hand. Oh my God—the gun. He had not forgotten it was in there, not since that day at the Sands. He didn't need to drive me into the desert, he was going to kill me with my own little Colt, in the middle of this melee.

I screamed. Rick wrenched away my handbag, pulled out the Colt, and let my purse drop. We were so close together that the hand-bag fell against my chest, and I clutched it to me like a useless shield. Then I realized he wasn't holding onto me anymore, and I threw myself sideways, lurching against a reporter.

"What the hell, lady?" shouted the man, trying to push me off him. I was unable to regain my balance, unable to fall. The threshing legs of the crowd looked nearly as dangerous as the gun I could see in Rick's hand. He held it low, knowing I couldn't escape, confident he'd get a good shot at me. We were still moving, bodies surging for-ward but somehow clinging to Peter, like jetsam surrounding a great, sinking ship. I screamed again.

I caught half a glimpse of the ceiling, the light fixtures twirling overhead, and then Rick's hand, now waist-high, close to his body. Aiming the revolver. Firing it three times into Peter's back. It made a sound no louder than the flash bulbs popping around us.

Then Rick opened his hand and let the gun drop, making no move that would draw attention to himself. Peter lurched forward, falling like a tree over the reporters who'd been facing him. A mo-ment's pause, then shouts, terror. His girl was shrieking, hysterical, kneeling beside him, pawing at his clothes.

"What happened?" someone shouted.

"Grafton had a heart attack!" yelled a reporter. More shoving ensued, and flashbulbs began to explode again with redoubled speed. They were taking pictures of Peter's body, face-down on the marble floor, and the crouching, keening girl.

Then Rick pulled me upright. "Are you all right?" he cried, in the voice of an anxious husband. Bewildered, I nodded, and to my utter surprise, he hugged me to him. Then, into my ear he said, "Fucking welsher deserved what he got. Merry Christmas and Happy Birthday, Bettye." And he let me go.

"I'm going to call an ambulance!" he shouted, pushing his way out of the circle. "Step aside! We need a doctor!"

"Someone shot him!" I heard a woman scream, as a bright pool of blood began to bloom from Peter's body. And there, next to his ankle, lay my little Colt.

"There's a gun!" a man yelled.

The throng exploded like a covey of quail panicked by a diving hawk. People fled blindly in every direction. I was nearly knocked to the floor again. Stumbling out of the fray, I looked around for Rebecca and Mrs. Gonzalves, but they had disappeared. Sheriff's deputies charged into the hallway. It was now or never. I kicked off my shoes and sprinted for the basement.

PART FOUR

THIRTY-ONE

ELOUISE BERNARD
WASHOE VALLEY, MAY 1952

After everyone left to drive to the courthouse, I invented a bookkeeping problem with the cattle, telling Dot in a nervous voice that I'd messed up the inventory of winter calves. It was the perfect distraction—the sort of thing that obsessed her. She was pretty damned angry when I told her I also had a migraine headache and needed to go to lie down.

"Well, that's convenient," she snapped. "Leave me with your mess."

"I'm sorry, Miss Dorothy, this headache is real bad." I grimaced and squinted. "I can't even focus my eyes."

"Oh, for God's sake," she huffed. "Give that to me." She snatched the ledger right out of my hand. "We're going to have a talk about this later, Elouise."

The hell we are, I thought to myself. Doing my best to appear miserable instead of scared to death, I slouched off through the downpour toward my cabin. When I got out of sight of the main house, I made a beeline for the barn. All of a sudden the freezing cold rain turned to big fat hailstones and I had to sprint the final few yards.

Hail roared against the barn's metal roof like someone was pouring gravel on it. Despite the racket, Luke's cowhorse Dusty stood easily inside, tacked up and ready to go.

"You there?" I called softly, and Luke stepped out of the shadows with a little half-nod. He'd hauled Dusty over a couple of days back, when the farrier was here. It was the perfect excuse. We'd told Dorothy the trailer he'd borrowed had a bad axle, and asked if she'd mind letting him leave Dusty there at the ranch until it got fixed. (She'd made me charge him three bucks for feed, the tightwad.)

I walked up to Luke and gave him a big smile, which I knew looked pretty unconvincing. He sat himself back down on a bale of alfalfa.

"Y'all ready?" I asked.

He nodded and offered me a cigarette, which I declined. I watched him flick his ash into an old coffee can.

"You find the slickers?" Stew asked, coming out of the tack room. Luke patted the folded yellow ponchos on the bale next to him. Then he started to put a shower-cap-looking thing on his cowboy hat, to protect the nice Resistol from the rain.

"Hey, Elouise," Stew said. "Everything okay over there?"

"I think I've got Dot occupied for now," I told him.

He stepped over to Sweet Potato and cussed softly. The mare turned her head, exposed her teeth, and tried to nip his behind, but the cross-ties brought her up short.

"She's ticked off by this heavy pack saddle," Stew grumbled. "Helene spoiled her with that little-bitty English thing." He could blame the mare all he wanted, but I'm sure our nerves were getting to her.

"You hear?" he said to me. "They're saying it might snow."

"What on earth?" I glanced quickly at Luke. "It's May, for heaven's sake."

"That's the Sierra," Stew said. "I seen it snow every month of the year here in the Washoe Valley. Once even on Fourth of July."

I resisted the urge to say what I was thinking: They should be out of here by now. The hail had let up but the rain was still beating on the barn roof. My ears almost hurt, I was listening so hard for the sound of Jamie's truck. I checked Dusty's panniers one more time, counting the same eight sandwiches and two thermoses of coffee. I'd snatched half a pan of Clem's brownies, too. It was more than enough for a day's ride.

I checked my watch again. It was just after two p.m. and the sun wouldn't be setting until well after six p.m., if it even managed to show its face again.

Luke stubbed out his half-smoked cigarette. He stood up and walked to the barn door and stared out into the rain.

"Maybe things didn't start on time at the hearing," I said. Then I shut my damn mouth.

In fine weather, it was a long but pleasant day's ride to Glenbrook, an old lumber camp turned resort on the east shore of Lake Tahoe. Some of the guests would go over the mountain and spend the night at the Glenbrook Inn. The resort got a lot of the Hollywood types, since it was in Nevada too. Red Wolf Ranch sat on a big meadow maybe half a mile from there, out past Spooner Lake.

A couple of days ago, Dot had received a note from "Bob Mitchell", introducing himself as a breeder from Pleasant Valley who wanted to acquire her Appaloosa. Friends had told him what a fine specimen she was, he said. I was giggling when I scribbled it out in my cabin, using the block letters men favor.

Enclosed in the envelope was a money order for one thousand dollars, a ridiculous sum, which Bettye had provided. Pleasant Valley was getting known for fancy horse farms, and we wanted Dot to think this Mr. Bob Mitchell was a rich sucker.

It's my job to collect the mail from our post office box in Reno and sort out the ranch business from the guests' personal mail, so it was easy to slip it in with the other stuff. Since we didn't have enough time to mail the letter, I had carefully drawn on a postmark copied from another envelope. I was proud of my handiwork, but boy was I nervous as I sat at my desk the day she slit it open with her penknife. Then she muttered, "Well, I'll be damned," and gave a little laugh.

"What?" I asked innocently, as if there might be a problem.

"Nothing," she sniffed, which told me she'd swallowed it hook, line and sinker.

When I stepped out of the office I overheard her call the barn and tell Stewart she'd sold Sweet Potato. A while later Stewart came in and let her know that he had arranged to take the horse to the Mitchell farm and that he'd trailer Luke's horse back to Steamboat in the same run.

"It's about time we got rid of that nag," Dot told him. "The nerve of that red-skinned bastard, helping himself to our hospitality. That's just how They are—give 'em an inch and They take a mile." She snorted. "And I don't want that low-life bum to set foot on this property again. Am I clear?"

"Yes, ma'am," Stewart had said, in the obedient monotone the wranglers took with Dorothy. I guess being in the military had given him practice hiding how he felt about his superiors. I pushed hard on my typewriter keys to cover up my shaking hands.

That little story meant Stewart would be leaving the ranch with an empty trailer, but there wasn't a very good view of the driveway from the main house. Because Stewart bossed the wranglers, if any of the boys noticed that and found it peculiar, they'd say something to him first—and he'd tell them to keep their traps shut. So when it looked like rain this morning, we were pretty happy—no one would be outside. As long as it didn't come down too hard and cause problems, rainy days were a rare opportunity for the boys to take it easy.

Suddenly I heard the familiar *burr-upp* of a truck speeding over the cattle guard. I poked my head out of the barn and saw Jamie's pickup bouncing toward us.

He pulled up as close to the barn as he could and shut off the ignition. Then the passenger door swung itself open as if by magic, and

Helene unfolded herself from where she'd been curled up on the seat.

She climbed out of the truck wearing her frontier pants, the wool Pendleton shirt, cowboy boots, and an old sheepskin jacket. Her hair was stuffed up inside a wool watch cap. She picked up the cowboy hat from the floor of the truck where it had fallen. She didn't exactly look like a man, but she sure as hell didn't look like Helene. As soon as we hustled her into the barn she gave Luke a big hug.

She'd left that morning not a hair out of place, wearing a beautiful blue suit that set off her complexion, and a pair of high heels that had cost about what I'd spend on a month's rent, back home. She looked like a queen.

"Let's get you going," I said.

"So everything went off without a hitch?" Stew asked her. Jamie shot me a very pointed let's-not-talk-about-that-now look.

"Not quite." Helene said. "I actually lost count of the hitches."

"All's well that ends well?" I offered hopefully.

"Peter's dead," she said.

At first I thought I hadn't heard her right. Then I thought she was kidding.

"What on earth?"

"Shot to death with my gun." Good Lord, she was serious. I looked from her to Jamie, but he just looked down at the ground.

"What the hell?" I couldn't believe what I was hearing. "You shot him?"

"Calm down. It was my gun, but I didn't do it," she said. "Russo, the man from Las Vegas did."

"But I thought they were in...cahoots!" Now I was completely confused.

"He called Peter a welsher."

"A welsher?"

"The bastard must've refused to pay them for finding me." She smiled at me. "No honor among thieves."

"Oh my God," I groaned. Murder? Jesus Christ. What a mess we'd gotten ourselves into. I tried to catch Jamie's eye again—I wanted him to reassure me.

"No one is going to say a goddamn word about this," Jamie said, instead. His tone was sharp. "Understand?"

We all nodded silently.

"It'll blow over," he told us. "This is Reno. But Bettye and Luke need to get the hell out of here. And the rest of us need to keep our lips zipped."

Helene—Bettye—patted Sweet Potato's neck, and set to adjusting her stirrup. "Jamie's right, we need to make tracks."

"But why would you leave now?" I jabbered. "If your husband's dead, he can't hurt you!"

"It was my gun," she repeated, as if I were dense.

"But you're innocent!" I protested.

"You really think anyone would believe that?"

I just stood there with my mouth open, speechless. She was right, I knew. It didn't matter if she was innocent.

She was fussing with the stirrup when I heard her say, "There's not going to be any money, Peach. No big fat check."

Now Luke looked quickly at his sister.

"Why on earth not?" I was feeling indignant all over again. "You said he'd agreed to everything in the settlement—"

"Uncle Sam got there first," she said. "His assets were seized. Our assets."

"But..." I started again. "That's not fair!"

"Oh, Peach," she sighed, and stepped toward me. Her eyes were warm. "Haven't you heard? All's fair in love and war."

That just made me start crying. Then Luke came up and shook Jamie's hand, and Stew's. He uttered two sounds that we all knew were *thank you*.

He took out his little notebook, scribbled something, and showed it to me.

Good luck at college, he wrote, to my surprise. I wiped my face and tried to smile. I guess Jamie had told him I was going to try to get into the University of Nevada. I'd been helping some of the guests with their legal paperwork, and I had taken a shine to it. I'd decided that I wanted to study law.

After all that, I was surprised to see that Luke looked relieved and light. Like a big burden had been taken off his shoulders. I could see he was eager to get going.

Bettye gave me a long hug, which shocked the daylights out of me. She'd never done anything like that before. She stepped back and put her hands on either side of my face and stared right into my eyes. Hers were getting all shiny with tears, too.

"Elouise," she told me, "You are a lifesaver." It was the first time in weeks that she'd called me by my real name.

The corrals were filled with puddles of muddy water. The dude horses huddled in their little lean-to sheds looking miserable. It was definitely not the sort of day for a trail ride, so there was not much danger anyone would come out to the barn in that downpour, unless a guest was headed to the hayloft for a rendezvous with a wrangler. But we still had Dot to worry about, for a few more minutes at least. She had a nose for strange goings-on at the ranch.

Stew threw on his own slicker and headed over to the ranch house to make sure no one was outside. The guests would be reading by the living room fire and gossiping over their gin rummy games. Clem would be grousing about boning rainbows for the Friday night trout dinner. And Floss...well, she would be getting back from Reno soon, anxious, confused, and feeling like she'd failed. I tried to imagine the conversation that she would have with Dorothy that night.

I was pretty sure that Dorothy would think that meant Mr. Pugliesi and his friends had succeeded, that everything had gone according to plan. I felt dizzy just thinking about the tangled web we'd all woven.

Then I looked up toward the mountains and noticed a filmy white veil blurring our view. It hung just a couple hundred feet above the ranch, and ended in a neat line, like it had been hemmed.

"Is that snow?" I asked Jamie anxiously.

"It should let up soon." He sounded like he was trying to convince himself too. He put his arm around me and squeezed me tight to his side.

"Well, the good news is no one is going to be following us up there." Bettye said, trying to sound brave and blasé. She looked at Luke. "You ready?"

He gave a little thumbs-up. He didn't seem worried at all. In fact, Luke seemed more comfortable than I'd ever seen him.

"You got your topo map and compass, right? Just in case?" Jamie asked, and Luke rolled his eyes.

"Oh that's right, you're an Indian. That stuff is just for amateurs."

Luke and Bettye put on their rain slickers, slow and careful so they didn't spook the horses, and mounted up. Jamie stepped out and took a peek around the corner of the barn.

"Okay, Stew just gave me the high sign from the front porch," he called back.

Luke gave Dusty a little nudge with his boot heels and he headed out of the barn without hesitating a second. Bettye and Sweet Potato followed him, drawing up alongside as soon as they reached the sandy road that ran along the foot of the mountain. I could see that despite the rain the big mare was ready to go, happy to have her mistress on board. She swiveled her ears back, waiting for instructions.

Bettye put her heels into the Appaloosa's sides. Then the golden horse and the spotted horse took off at an easy lope, toward the trail that would take them up to the summit and, if they were very lucky, all the way to freedom.

THIRTY-TWO

The rain fell harder after dinner, and Floss hadn't returned to the Rocking B. I did my best not to think about what all that damn water was doing up in the high peaks, where it was freezing cold.

When I went to the house to get some dinner, sneaking into the kitchen to avoid Dorothy, The guests were in quite a mood after being cooped up all afternoon. A couple of girls poked their heads into the kitchen, wanting to know if the Friday evening trip to the Nugget was still on. I had to tell them that I didn't know. Floss usually drove the gang to Carson in the station wagon, but neither was at the ranch. They reminded me of spoiled children, but after a while, they quit their grousing and all went back to reading magazines and playing cards.

Passing the office door, I heard Clem ask where Floss was.

"She probably went shopping," Dot said, as if it was perfectly normal for her sister and a guest to miss dinner and go AWOL on a stormy night.

I hadn't known before I came here that there were White people in the West who hated Indians the way people in the South hated Negroes. But that's how it was in Nevada, especially Reno. There were "Whites Only" signs everywhere, just like back home. In the Walker family photo album in the parlor there was a picture of crosses being burned, labeled "Peavine Initiation 1925". It was in there alongside photographs of picnics, a new Dodge, and Dot and Floss when they were little girls.

It seemed like the worse people had been treated—Black folks being kidnapped from Africa and turned into slaves or Indians being driven off their homelands and killed and starved—the more the people whose relatives had done those terrible things just plain hated them. I suppose they had to come up with reasons why they were entitled to the land or the labor they stole.

When Dorothy Walker had called Bettye a "troublemaker" I just assumed it was because she ignored the rules and complained about nearly everything—though we had plenty of guests like that. I'd seen some real troublemakers in my short time at the Rocking B, gals that would have a feud (even an honest-to-God hair-pulling fight) with another guest. Some made scenes or seduced wranglers that "belonged" to other girls. And after that awful night in Virginia City, I had decided that Dot was right after all.

But I knew better now. And I knew that Dorothy Walker was up to no good. I felt it in my gut, the same way I had known when George was cheating on me.

The previous morning I'd heard Dot on the phone making arrangements to attend a cattle auction, laughing and joking with someone like they were old pals. Laughing and joking like she never did. She sounded as happy as a lady who'd just spun the roulette wheel at the Nugget and won herself a jackpot.

It got dark, but still no Floss or Maisie. Stranger yet, there wasn't a mention of them from Dot. And while I'd just been worried about Bettye and Luke, now I started worrying about them, too. Floss could have smashed up her car or got caught in a flash flood, which was common in the desert when there was a sudden heavy rain.

I was worried enough to venture into the dragon's den, the office. Dot was preoccupied now and seemed to have forgotten all about our dust-up.

"Have you heard from Floss?" I asked her, though I was certain she hadn't.

"They must've gone out to dinner." But I could see that she was starting to get a little nervous, too.

It was about an hour later that a car door slammed outside, and we heard fast, hard footsteps on the porch. In came poor Floss, Maisie trailing behind. I had just come out of the phone nook, where I'd called the train station and confirmed that the *Spirit of San Francisco* had left the station—on time, for once.

They looked like crazy women. Their hair and courtroom suits were all wet. Their shoes were ruined.

"What happened to you?" I asked. Floss hardly glanced at me. Maisie's mouth was clamped shut.

"Is Bettye here?" Floss demanded.

"What?" I did my best to look confused. "Isn't she on the train?" Time to start trying for my Academy Award.

"Maisie, you should go change out of those wet things," Floss said. Maisie caught my eye, gave me a little nod and walked back out of the main house like she knew what was coming next.

Floss waited until she heard the front door close, then turned back to me.

"Where's Dot?" she demanded. I had never seen her in such a state. Guilty did not begin to describe how I felt.

"I think she's in the office."

Floss blew past me like a hurricane. She shoved the office door so hard that it hit the wall. I followed her to the threshold, desperate to hear what had happened at the courthouse. I hovered just outside, shaky and excited.

"Where the hell is she?" Floss asked, and I heard Dot's chair squeak as she turned around from her desk.

"Where the hell is who?" Dot asked, all irritated.

"You know who!" bellowed Floss.

"Quiet down. You're going to scare the guests."

"Scare the guests? That's a laugh!" Floss shot right back. "You're going to ruin us, you know that?"

"Oh really?" The chair squeaked again, telling me Dorothy had stood up. "That's rich."

"Bettye Christian never made it to the train station," said Floss. Her voice was shaking with anger.

"Well who told you that?" No one would give Dot a role in a school play, let alone an Academy Award, for her acting.

"Lucius Beebe told me that," said Floss. "I waited there until the train left. Bettye and Luke were not on it."

"Who cares?" Dot snorted. "She's not our problem anymore."

"You know damn well she was supposed to be traveling with Lucius and Charles on the *Gold Coast.*"

Dot's tone got testier. "She must have changed her plans."

"Her luggage got on, but she didn't. How do you explain that?"

"Give it a rest, Florence."

There was a short, unnerving silence. "You don't know what happened at the courthouse today, do you?" Floss's voice went all low, but I could still make it out.

"I don't know why you want to get so involved in a guest's—"

Floss cut her off. "Bettye's husband was shot dead right outside the courtroom."

"Don't be ridiculous!" snapped Dot.

"And no one can find Bettye," Floss continued. "She has up and vanished. So it looks like we'll be getting another visit from the police."

There was a short silence, which meant that Dot was thinking things over. "That woman was bad news—I knew it from the beginning." She didn't sound very surprised. "That's the last time we let anyone like that stay here."

"You know who I think is the real bad news?" Floss demanded. "Your pal Mr. Storm, or Pugliesi, or whatever his goddamn name is. He was there at the hearing today—sitting there fat and sassy, like he owned the place. Why was *he* there?"

"How would I know?" I could hear Dot's voice getting tense. "He's not my 'pal'. He was probably just there to gawk at the circus. That woman and her husband are notorious."

"*Were* notorious." I could tell Floss was struggling to reconcile what had happened that morning with what she had come to believe about Bettye: that she was a good person who'd gotten the shaft.

"This'll be bad for the guest business," Dot finally remarked. I knew where she was going with that. She resented the dude ranch operation, felt it was beneath her dignity. She liked to tell everyone she was a "cattlewoman".

"Is that all you can think about right now?" Floss yelled back. "Your reputation?"

"You should spend a little more time thinking about it yourself," Dot hollered. "Dad didn't work all his life to have his ranch turned into some sort of home for alcoholics and adulterers and...savages!"

There was a sudden scuffing of shoes and an angry little yelp.

"You let go of me!" Dot shrieked. Their voices carried out into the hallway.

"Something happened to Bettye Christian!" Floss cried. Boy, I felt sorry for her, and guilty besides. I longed to tell her the truth, though that wasn't much better. "Those bastards tried to get to her a couple of weeks ago right here on our property! And you helped them!"

"You better damn well quiet down before you stir up the guests." Then Dorothy laughed—the coldest, meanest laugh. "Though I'm fine if we go back to being a cattle operation."

"Like hell we will!" yelled Floss. Then Dot flew out the door and into the hallway so quick I barely got out of her way.

"Hello, Dot," I held her gaze longer than I ever would have dared before. She was way smaller than me but still scary as a rattlesnake.

"Eavesdropping?"

"You ladies were talking awful loud." I did not drop my eyes.

(Since when had I become so reckless?)

To my surprise, she just brushed past me and climbed the stairs. I waited until I heard her door shut, and I went into the office.

Floss was sitting at her desk, her face in her hands. I wasn't sure if she was crying.

"Floss?" I dropped my voice so as not to startle her.

"What." She was in a terrible state. She didn't look up.

"I have something to tell you."

"Elouise..." she began wearily. She wanted to brush me off.

"Please," I insisted. "Floss, you need to hear this."

She turned and looked at me. Her face was pale and fearful.

I lowered my voice. "All I can say is…you don't need to worry."

"Elouise, if you're mixed up in this, so help me…" Floss stood up so suddenly that I took a step back.

"You have to trust me. Please. Bettye didn't ever intend to get on that train."

"What the hell?" growled Floss. "Then where on earth is she?"

"She had another plan." I could not confess that Bettye and Luke were riding into the jaws of a Sierra Nevada blizzard.

"Did that plan include killing her husband?"

"No!" I said. "The plan was to disappear before he could kill *her*."

"Well, he was shot dead right after her hearing, right after she found out she wasn't going to get a dime from the son of a bitch." Floss glanced at the office door.

I knew I should keep my mouth shut, but I just couldn't bear to leave it at that. "You've heard the stories about Mr. Grafton. He must have a lot of enemies."

She stared at me, mulling this over for a moment. "When the police come, I think it's best if you don't say anything about Bettye's plans," she told me. "They interviewed me and Maisie at the courthouse, but I expect they'll want to talk to everyone here."

"Sure." The prospect of lying to the police scared the holy hell out of me.

Floss' eyes flickered up toward the ceiling and then back at me. "She meant to disappear how?"

"Bettye's with her brother," I offered, hoping that would help.

"Did they take a car instead?" she asked.

"I think so," I said. It was the most plausible explanation, after all.

"So…" she studied my face. "It was a double-cross?"

When I opened my mouth to speak, she held up a hand to stop me. "You know what? Don't say anything else." She pushed the wet hair off her forehead with both hands. "I had a helluva day, Elouise. That woman gave me ten heart attacks."

"She said to tell you she was sorry, and goodbye." I needed her to know that.

She tried to stop me again, and I kept going. "But she didn't trust Dorothy."

"Took me 39 years, but it only took Bettye six weeks to figure that out." Floss gave a big sigh, and kind of hugged herself with her long arms. "Well hell. Maybe I'll be able to sleep tonight after all."

I started to walk out of the office, and then I stopped and turned around. "I think Dorothy is planning to buy a mess of cattle at the auction in Winnemucca next week," I said, real quiet.

Floss cocked her head like the ranch dogs did when they heard coyotes in the distance.

"What?" Her face got sharp. "Like how many?"

"Sixty-eight head is what I heard her say on the phone this morning."

She stood there for a moment with her mouth half-open and took that in.

"I'm not sure how she plans to pay for them," I added. "We don't have that kind of money in our checking account, even with our last batch of deposits."

"That is certainly news to me," Floss finally said.

THIRTY-THREE

Jamie was worried and heartsick. He and Stew rode up the mountain the day after the storm, as soon as the weather settled. But there was too much snow, and they had to turn around some ways southwest of Little Valley.

They went back out again a few days later. Both boys were good trackers, but they didn't find any sign of Bettye and Luke or the horses. If they'd gotten lost in those mountains, there was no telling where they'd ended up. No one would even begin to know where to look.

The Red Wolf Ranch, where Bettye and Luke were headed, was owned by people that Bettye's friend Mr. Kiehl knew. It was where he was heading when he dropped her off here six weeks ago.

Mr. Kiehl was very businesslike and seemed to know what he was doing. Before he agreed to help, he asked to speak to each of us in turn. When I got on the line with him he just asked me questions about where I was from and who my people were, like you would at a cocktail party. But I guess I passed his test. He told us that the Red Wolf ranch owners would stay mum about any riders passing through and any horse trailer that might show up.

Now, this was all before a notorious man was shot and killed in the middle of the Washoe County Courthouse and Bettye became the most wanted woman in Nevada. If the folks at that ranch had met Luke and Bettye, whose pictures were now everywhere, they must have thought they'd been snookered.

The gossip and speculation at the Rocking B lasted for days and days. I was a ball of nerves. A lot of the girls thought that Bettye had been killed and buried out in the desert, or sent to the bottom of Pyramid Lake tied to a bag of rocks. Others insisted that they knew she was a murderess. They ate it up when the detectives came to interview everyone. Even girls that hadn't given her the time of day wanted to tell the officers things they had supposedly noticed about her.

I'd thought long and hard about what I would say when it was my turn. I could not just play dumb. I told the lead detective about the break-in, about Mr. Storm's car crashing in the moat, and Maisie's stolen camera and that photo with the "X" and Bettye's name written on it. I didn't say I thought it was an attempted kidnapping. That would have made me sound like a hysterical female. So I was glad to hear the detective suggest this idea to his partner.

"Do you think she might have killed her husband—her ex-husband, I mean—in self-defense?" asked the detective, who reminded all the girls of Rock Hudson. He showed me copies of the photographs of Bettye with the broken nose and black eyes, which made me sick to look at.

"She told me she was afraid of him," I said. "But the girl I knew wouldn't hurt a fly."

The second detective just chuckled. He seemed convinced of her guilt. "The gun that was used to kill Peter Grafton belonged to her."

"Good heavens," I said, and made a squeamish face.

"Were you aware that Elizabeth Christian was actually an Indian?" he added.

"No." I had to bite my tongue. It was all I could do not to ask him why the hell that mattered. Maybe an Indian with a gun was still a frightening idea for a modern-day Western lawman.

"She was an escapee from the Stewart Indian School," he told me, referring to a piece of paper he had in a folder. "In fact, it appears she lied about her identity for years. Apparently even her husband didn't know."

"It seems unlikely that the Walkers would have accepted a guest with that kind of background," pointed out the lead detective.

"Probably not," I said, thinking of the picture of the burning crosses on Peavine mountain.

...

The Walker sisters hadn't spoken to each other since the day of the hearing. Dorothy made herself scarce around the office, which was fine by me, but Floss's mood stayed glum. Clem moved to Sacramento to look after her mother, so we hired on a new cook and housekeeper, Ellie, who talked too much. I never expected to miss a grouch like Clementine, but I did.

It took several weeks, but gradually the fuss around Peter Grafton's murder died down. All the guests who'd been there at the time had moved on, and the story left with them. A new crop of dudes had arrived for the high season and the Rocking B settled into its summer routine. Funnily enough, Dorothy's new cattle had vanished right along with the ranch's most infamous guest.

The center of my life shifted. I spent all my free time with Jamie. And after a while, even he and I barely talked about Bettye and Luke.

I missed Maisie, and we wrote to each other. She was having some grand adventures in New York. Her letters always included photographs she'd taken of the city—crowds of people in a subway station, or a traffic cop in the middle of a sea of cars. I never told her that those pictures made me realize that I never wanted to live in a city.

Jamie and I had started talking about the future. I was crazy about him, but I never felt that funny, dizzy feeling, the thing that I used to think was love. It kind of sneaked up on me. I woke up one morning and realized he was the one. He thought it was awful funny that it had taken me so long to figure that out.

In June he took me out to Lovelock, east of Reno, to meet his mama and daddy and five sisters. They invited us over for Sunday dinner. I was awful nervous, but everyone was real nice to me. Mama said that a boy who grew up with five older sisters would understand women, and probably make a good husband.

Jamie proposed to me up at Castle Rock on a beautiful clear day when Lake Tahoe was bluer than I had ever seen it. We decided to get married at Christmas. He told me he wanted to be Lucy's daddy. He also wanted us to have a few kids of our own, and our own place. He'd been saving up his wages for a little ranch.

Savannah seemed like a faraway place to me now. I'd gotten used to the desert and the big, empty West. I realized that Nevada could be home. If she would let us, I wanted to move Mama out to Nevada, too. I thought she'd like Lake Tahoe and the beautiful Truckee River. But I was probably getting ahead of myself.

The first order of business was to get my daughter back. I would have to sue for custody. So I went down to Mrs. Gonzalves' law office and asked if I could work as a secretary part time, in the evenings after I was done at the Rocking B, in exchange for legal services. I told her I was planning to study law at the University, and when she heard that, she offered me a full-time job on the spot. Her assistant Rebecca was getting married.

Two dollars and seventy-five cents an hour. I couldn't believe my ears. I could finally quit the damned Rocking B and get out of that crazy place. I could have my own little apartment in downtown Reno. I kept saying, "Are you sure?" until she told me to stop.

"Elouise, I'd be lucky to have you. You're a very intelligent and capable young woman." That was the very first time anyone had told me that, let alone a person as successful as Mrs. Gonzalves. I smiled the whole way back from town.

When I got to the Rocking B, I walked straight into the office. I gave the Walker sisters two weeks' notice, with that big smile still on my face.

THIRTY-FOUR

CONGRESSWOMAN ELOUISE JANSEN
CARSON CITY, NEVADA
NOVEMBER 1988

Scott walked into my office looking nervous. "Ma'am? We're running late," he said.

He had shaved and put on a clean white shirt for the ceremony. I was glad that short hair was back in fashion for young men, so I no longer had to tell my aide when it was touching his collar. He'd even gotten the knot right on his narrow black tie. If I hadn't known better, I'd have guessed it was 1958, not 1988.

"Give me a moment, Scott," I said to him. Everyone knew I was a stickler for punctuality, especially when there was media involved. But as long as I'd looked forward to the day, I found myself reluctant to make my final walk down to the Assembly for the retirement ceremony.

"Actually, ma'am, I forgot to give this to you earlier. It came in today's mail." His voice was apologetic. For the first time I saw that he held a small package in his hand.

"Thank you." I set it on my desk. The package was wrapped in creased brown paper that had been re-used, a humble note that brought a smile to my face. On it the sender had written "Congresswoman Elouise Jansen" in spidery, feminine handwriting.

I had worked with constituents for three decades, the first as my husband Jim's right hand, and then two more on my own. Little old ladies loved to send me gifts—like a red, white and blue crocheted toilet paper cover, or a handmade quilt with the Nevada state seal pieced into the center. Years ago they would tell me, in the little card or note enclosed, that I reminded them of their daughter.

By most standards, I was now a little old lady myself. Maybe I would mail handicrafts to my congressional representatives someday. Neither of the kids had the slightest interest in the family business. (Lucy was too smart for it. Jim Junior was too practical.)

"See you in a moment, ma'am," Scott said, and stepped out into the corridor. I set the package on my desk and walked to the mirror to put on my lipstick, the bright one I only wore when I was going to be on television. I gave my hair another quick spritz of hairspray. It was my TV hair, too, the light-brown helmet you always saw on older female politicians. (Blonde was for Texans and bubblehead reporters.) Of the many pleasures of retirement, the one I was looking forward to the most was letting my hair go gray. Or white. Or whatever the hell color it was, now.

As I turned to walk out of my office, my eye fell on the package again. It might be the last gift I received as a member of the United States Congress. Why not open it? I sat down at the desk, held the little box, and tore away the paper.

During my 20 some-odd years as a legislator I had received a lot of strange things in the mail, much stranger than crocheted toilet paper covers. Occasionally something threatening (a gift-wrapped dildo with a note telling me to go fuck myself) and once, just once, something dangerous (a live baby rattlesnake). But this box from New Mexico with the little old lady handwriting on it just didn't look dangerous to me.

But wouldn't it be ironic to open something deadly on my last day in office? I could almost hear Jim, who'd sat in this very chair, at this very desk, warning me to be more careful.

Inside was a plain cardboard box, also taped. I slipped my finger under the yellow, brittle tape, which gave way without resistance. This little box had obviously been sealed up for years. Inside sat a pristine blue velvet box in a nest of crumpled newspaper. It was held shut by a tiny gold clasp. A jewelry box.

Well, now we're talking, I told myself. (Not that I could ever have accepted a gift of jewelry, but as they say—it's the thought that counts.)

I shook away the newspaper. I lifted the tarnished clasp and opened the blue velvet box. When I saw the antique pearl earrings lying in the yellowed satin, my hands began to shake. I set the box down on the desk and just stared at them for what seemed like forever. The design was unmistakable. There was a tiny ring of diamonds above each perfect pear-shaped pearl, and a filigree of gold openwork. They were a bit smaller than I remembered. But just as beautiful.

I heard a soft knock on my office door.

"Ma'am?"

"One minute, please!" I managed.

I sifted through the wrapping and found nothing else—no note, no card. I snatched at the brown paper and stared at the return address, as if it might tell me something different now.

E. Cristobal, it said. And there was a post office box.

My hands were trembling so violently that I could barely tug the earrings out of their little slots. I stepped over to my mirror, took off the chunky, brushed-gold earrings that I'd picked out that morning, and replaced them with the little pearl drops. They were not right for a Congresswoman's retirement speech, or for my Reagan-red power suit. They were Victorian, for heaven's sake—delicate and old-fashioned.

Pearls are for good girls, I could hear Bettye Christian say, with that mocking lilt in her voice, as I'd admired the earrings in a Reno pawn shop that long-ago night.

I smiled at my reflection. No one who knew me now would possibly describe the Honorable Elouise M. Jansen that way.

THIRTY-FIVE

ELOUISE JANSEN
TAOS, NEW MEXICO
SEPTEMBER 1989

drove my rented Ford Taurus down into a canyon, following a half-paved road that meandered along the Rio Grande. September had turned the cottonwood groves lining the river into a mosaic of yellow and orange leaves.

I was pretty certain I'd gotten myself lost, but I wasn't too worried. Driving around in the middle of nowhere was nothing new to me. I'd visited plenty of my constituents on hell-and-gone ranches in Nevada, relying on sketchy directions that involved an odometer and a good eye for landmarks like red mailboxes or abandoned tractors.

Soon enough, though, I spotted the promised iron-truss bridge over the river, and up I went, out of the canyon. I drove through rolling, open land studded with pinon pine trees and junipers, what we Westerners call "piju". The soil was a mysterious shade of pink.

Finally I saw a gate, and a weather-beaten wooden sign with routed, white-painted letters reading, *River Ranch*. The gate sat open in a way that suggested it was rarely closed. I felt relieved as I turned in and drove up the hill toward a cluster of buildings.

As I got closer, I saw a wooden barn and riding ring atop a natural mesa, and sitting on a gentle rise beyond that hunkered a typical New Mexican house. It was a low rectangle, plastered smooth, and it had shutters painted a chalky, forget-me-not blue.

A woman started walking toward me from the breezeway of the barn, where she'd been grooming a big bay horse. She was thin, with snow-white hair pulled into a braid, and a kind of regal look despite a limp. But it wasn't Bettye. I turned off the engine and got out.

"Welcome, Elouise," she greeted me, with the hard-to-place European accent I'd heard on the phone. "I'm Ingrid. We're so glad you could come." She had the palest blue eyes I'd ever seen, made paler by her deeply tanned, freckled face.

"Please. Call me Lou."

I extended my hand and shook hers. She had an awfully strong grip.

"You found us on the first try?"

"Pure luck," I said, glancing back at my dust-covered rental car.

"Beth is out in her studio. Shall we go find her?"

Ingrid led the way to another square, flat-roofed building behind the house, with peeled pine logs sticking out near the roofline. One side was covered with a huge, many-paned window that looked like it came from an old factory.

"Beth!" Ingrid called in the open door. "Elouise is here!"

We stepped inside. A kiva fireplace took up one corner, its hearth set with colorful tiles. Coals glowed inside it and the air smelled of pinon smoke. The rough wooden work table in the center of the room held pieces of fawn-colored leather and all sorts of tools and scissors and patterns.

"Come in, come in!" called a familiar voice. A woman with long, salt-and-pepper hair appeared from around the corner. All I could do was gape at the sight of Bettye Christian.

We were both shorter, though I was still far shorter and broader in the beam, and I had more wrinkles. My hair was cut short because I'd grown impatient waiting for the old dye to grow out, but my salt-and-pepper was not as crisp as Bettye's. Abundant white strands sparkled in her thick, raven hair. Damn her, I thought. She still looks fantastic.

"Peach!" she cried, using her old nickname for me. She embraced me and kissed my cheek. "It's so good of you to come all this way!"

When I'd written her my thank you note for the earrings last year, I wasn't even sure I'd get a reply. Then, out of nowhere, a short note arrived, in that same spidery handwriting—an invitation to visit. I could not pass that up.

"You look wonderful," I managed to say.

"So do you," she said.

"I'm going to let you two get reacquainted." Ingrid turned and left us alone in the studio. As you do in a friend's home, I made enthusiastic remarks about how lovely everything was.

My eyes went immediately to a row of large black and white photographs on the walls. The first I noticed was of a man, sun-freckled, standing casually next to a very large horse. He had a clear, confident gaze, and a little smile played at the corners of his mouth. An unlit cigarette was between his lips.

"That's a wonderful photo."

"You know the photographer," she said.

"Who?"

"Maisie Cornell."

I stared at her and laughed. "Maisie was here?"

"About ten years back, I saw her in Santa Fe. The museum was having a show of her Vietnam photographs from the sixties and seventies."

Another Nevada legislator had given me a coffee-table book of Maisie Cornell's war photography, which sat on the coffee table in my office. I was told more than once that it wasn't appropriate to display it in my office. (I was not of a mind to consider the truth inappropriate. It stayed there.)

"We got her out here to the ranch for a few days, and that's when she shot these photographs. This one is Ingrid's brother Philippe. The man who got Luke and me out of Nevada."

I glanced over my shoulder at her. "Is he still...alive?"

"Oh yes, very much so. Philippe moved back to Alsace, where he and Ingrid were born, not that long after this was taken," she told me. "He was a riding instructor, and authored a couple of excellent books on horsemanship. A Jewish girl he'd known in his hometown before the war—a girl he thought was dead—tracked him down through his publisher and..." she gave a little shrug. "I'd always pegged him for some sort of ascetic, almost a monk, but he turned out to be quite the romantic. He and Ingrid were extremely close, but he finally realized that she did not need him to look after her anymore."

I moved down the row of photographs, admiring each in turn. One in particular, of a lovely young Indian woman, struck me.

"What a beautiful girl," I said, stepping in front of it.

"That's Susan." Bettye's voice softened with affection. "Our daughter."

"You have a...daughter?" I knew there was a look of surprise (well, shock) on my face.

"An adopted daughter." After the tiniest hesitation she added, "Not that it makes her any less of our daughter."

Who did the pronoun "our" refer to, I wondered?

"Susan is Ingrid's and my daughter," she said. I hadn't been here five minutes and Bettye, true to form, had thrown me a curveball. "Her tribe, they were Shoshone, lived close to the test site, the one outside Las Vegas," explained Bettye. "She lost most of her immediate family to radiation sickness, at a very young age. She adored animals, and insisted on being a vegetarian even as a little girl, so she wouldn't eat rabbit. And that saved her life, because those rabbits had become radioactive from eating plants at the test site."

My heart sagged. "Oh, God," I said. I remembered the deep, impotent guilt I used to feel when I would receive a call or a letter or a visit from a tribal representative, telling me about the way his people, or her people, were being ignored or abused by the government. I thought of the inane and inadequate phrases I used to parrot when I was first in office, before I'd stopped coloring between the lines.

"How did you meet Susan?" I asked. Such adoptions were very rare.

"She was working at Philippe's old stable in Las Vegas as a young girl. She fed the horses and cleaned stalls in exchange for lessons. And she was an extraordinary rider. With Philippe's coaching, she made the Junior Olympics equestrian team." Bettye's voice was warm with pride.

I looked at the portrait of Susan, and into her frank, challenging eyes. I'd spent a lot of time fighting with the DOD and the DOE about cleaning up the radioactive waste in the Nevada desert. It had won me a bit of a reputation as a troublemaker in my party. I'd brought tribal leaders to Washington, D.C., year after year, to tell their stories. And now the DOE wanted to ship more radioactive waste to an area near the old Nevada Test Site, Yucca Mountain. But that would be a battle for my successor to fight.

"Susan's a large-animal veterinarian and works with the tribes here in New Mexico," Bettye continued, to my relief. "She married a ridiculously handsome Navajo, a water rights attorney. They have a beautiful family in Albuquerque. So we have three grandchildren, close by."

She pointed out a photograph sitting on a bookshelf. A smiling boy with long black hair, who appeared to be the oldest, flanked by a laughing girl. Another tiny girl sat confidently on his shoulders, one fist in the air.

"Do they ride?" I was already sure of the answer.

"Oh yes," she said. "We are Horse Indians around here."

Seeing my gaze move toward something that resembled a small puppet theater under construction, she said, "I teach classes in the children's arts program at the Pueblo cultural center. Right now we're creating these ofrendas for the Dios de los Muertos celebration at the church."

It was one of the tabletop altars that honored the dead during that Mexican celebration. Among the objects was a familiar plastic figurine of a longhorn bull, the same Breyer model that had crowned Jim Jr.'s bookshelf in junior high, alongside his 4H trophies. The ofrenda also held a coiled bit of frayed sisal rope, a worn suede pouch with some red and blue beads barely clinging to it, and a vivid blue rock—recognizable to my collector's eye as Sleeping Beauty Mine turquoise.

"It's always their favorite project of the year," she said, and probably noticed the surprised expression on my face, because she added, "Dios de las Muertos is not about mourning and sadness. It's a celebration of the dead."

"How many dead people could a child know?" I asked, and immediately wished I hadn't.

"Well, if you're a Native American child, chances are good that you know quite a few," she replied evenly. "Our students have an ample supply of dead friends and relatives."

To my relief, her expression was kind. Then I noticed a sketchbook sitting on her main work table. "May I?"

"Of course."

I opened it to a beautiful watercolor rendering of a coat. "Is this yours?"

"Yes it is."

The coat was a handsome hybrid of Native American textiles and a chic European silhouette, with the padded shoulders that I haven't been able to bring myself to wear, because I wore the first version.

"You're so talented!"

"Thank you." Her smile was sincere. "I have a small boutique in Taos, called Red Willow. We feature Native clothing and jewelry designers, and it raises money for our kids' program. I hope you'll get a chance to visit."

"I wouldn't miss it," I told her. This retirement thing was such a new experience. If I wanted to stay in New Mexico for a week, I could. I could visit Taos, and see Bettye's boutique, and I could see the school where she taught if I wanted to.

"Come on, let me get you something to drink," she offered. "You must be thirsty. Iced tea? Water?"

"Tea, thank you." My head was buzzing with questions.

She dropped ice cubes into pretty, hand-blown blue glasses and poured the tea in.

"Come out to the garden." I followed her through a set of French doors to a terrace paved with huge, buff-colored flagstones. Lavender edged the terrace, and hollyhocks nodded gently in the high desert wind. A few late-season rose bushes were in the final days of bloom, their yellow petals sifting to the ground.

"This is lovely." Two comfy rattan chairs, cushions upholstered with bright Navajo blankets, sat overlooking a mown meadow. On one chair, an enormous tabby cat dozed.

"Come on, Buddy," said Bettye, nudging him awake. "We have a guest." Buddy the cat gave her a look of disdain, slowly poured his fluffy bulk off the chair, and slipped into the lavender.

"He may bring us a lizard, just fair warning," she told me with a laugh.

I took in the patio, the gently sloped hillside above the studio, and the remains of an orchard, where ancient, grizzled apple trees still held some fruit. A hammock hung between two of the trees. It was a charming spot, the sort of place where a person could while away an afternoon with a good book.

Bettye gestured to one of the chairs and sat down on Buddy's. A carved Moroccan-style table between the chairs was stacked with art and design books, and on top sat another sketchbook.

"You know, you turned me into a clothes horse," I scolded.

"Thanks to your hand-me-downs—those gorgeous things you left behind for me."

Jim had always fretted that I dressed too nicely for my role as the political spouse, but I refused to wear the prim, frumpy dresses expected of me. But over time he realized that his picture showed up in the papers far more often when I was there with him, wearing something chic. And when I ran for his office after he got sick, people already knew who I was.

"I'm glad to hear that," Bettye told me. "USA Today ran a picture of you in that cobalt-blue Blass suit at your inauguration. I saved it."

I smiled. I thought of Bettye seeing me in a newspaper, here in New Mexico. So she had known I was a Congresswoman from the very beginning.

"Oh God. I spent a fortune on that suit," I cringed.

"Smart to pick the same colors as the Nevada flag. The gold scarf was a clever touch."

I laughed, unable to believe she'd remember such details. "I got some flak."

"Pssh. That just tells you you're doing something right!" Bettye waved her hand in the air in her old, familiar gesture of imperial scorn. Maybe she was aware of it too, because she glanced down at her lap, and began fidgeting with a large antique turquoise ring on her right hand. Her knuckles were knobby with arthritis.

"So…" I started.

THIRTY-SIX

"I can't tell you how happy I was to hear from you," I said. "To know...that you were alive. It took me a few minutes to connect the dots. The name 'Cristobal' threw me at first."

"An old family name." Bettye said with a mysterious smile.

"It rang a bell. I dug up those old Territorial Enterprise stories that Lucius Beebe wrote." I told her. "The State Archives had them on microfiche."

"A reverse treasure hunt."

"Maria Cristobal. Your mother."

"Yes. I took her surname—or her alias, if you will. And Ingrid had already started calling me Beth. Voila, a new identity. I'm a non-person. Makes life remarkably simple."

"But you have a business—how does that work?" My attorney's brain was already trying to work out the logistics.

"Oh, we have a little corporation. Ingrid is the sole shareholder." Her tone was dismissive. "You know all about that sort of thing."

"I do." I had chased plenty of ghosts during my law practice, mostly vanishing fathers, absconding husbands. And I'd helped more than a few battered wives to disappear, to begin lives in new states.

Abruptly, she changed the subject. "You closed the Stewart Indian School."

"Oh. Yes. Eight years ago. All those masonry buildings had seismic safety issues, there wasn't enough funding..."

"Jesus, knock it all down. Build a tract of ugly new houses right on top of it. Or a golf course." Bettye laughed. "Call it 'Indian Meadows'."

"You may be surprised to hear this, but the Stewart School became a real source of pride for the Native American community," I told her. "There are many alumni who want to see it turned into a cultural center and museum."

"Good for them," she said. It was time to change the subject again, as if she was working from an agenda. "You're on your own now?" Unlike most people who asked me that question, her tone wasn't moist with sympathy.

"Yes," I said. "And I'm not interested in re-marrying. Sure as hell not interested in dating. I'm way too old to learn new tricks. I've got Jimmy—Jim Junior—nearby, and my grandkids. Close, but not too close. Just the way I like it. Just the way my daughter-in-law likes it." There weren't too many women you could admit this stuff to, but I knew Bettye wasn't about to judge me for it.

"What's next?" she asked.

"I want to travel." I'd been on codels, trips with congressional delegations, all over the world. But this was my very first trip just for myself.

Bettye nodded. I sensed it was time for us to get into the real conversation.

"I'm so sorry you had to...hide for all those years," I told her then. "Based on the way you went on about France, and how much you said you hated the desert, I never would have looked for you in New Mexico."

A smile played over her face. "Ingrid loves the desert," she shrugged. I could see that she was testing me a bit.

"Well, you deserve to be happy," I said.

"I am happy," she responded, turning the ring on her finger. "We have a wonderful life."

I finally worked up the courage to ask about her brother. I had seen his picture on the ofrenda. "And Luke?"

"He's gone," Bettye said. "Alzheimer's started when he was just 52."

At that moment, a pair of mourning doves plunged recklessly out of the sky, fluttering noisily into the pinon pine behind us. I felt like the wind had been knocked out of me. "I'm so sorry," I said.

"It was the head injury—or injuries—according to the doctors." There was sorrow in her eyes now. "He kept rodeoing until he was just too busted up to continue. It was how he wanted it, though. Luke was never going to be an old man."

I'd attended many funerals and memorials, and heard plenty of eulogies where someone was said to have "burned brightly." But Luke Moore had glowed like banked coals turning themselves steadily into ash.

"The day after he passed," Bettye went on, "A golden eagle, the biggest one I've ever seen, came and sat up in that dead cottonwood—over there," she pointed toward a tree whose smooth white branches looked like sun-bleached bones reaching into the sky. "For the entire day. He sat there until sunset, and flew off. He never came back."

I nodded. I'd heard a lot of these strange bird stories over the years. A hummingbird in the house the day after a loved one died. A hawk flying directly at a widow's car as she drove to the cemetery, grazing the roof with its claws. I'd come to chalk these accounts up to the Lord's "mysterious ways," which just seemed to grow more mysterious the older I got.

Then Bettye smiled. "But my brother, bless his heart, supplied me with two wonderful nephews, Lester and Charlie. They live out in Tucson, and they abandon their children here for a few weeks every summer. We built a bunkhouse for the kids." She stood up. "Come on, let me give you a tour."

She linked her arm in mine like we were a couple of old pals. We began to walk slowly, and for the first time, I could tell that her balance was a little off. The sunshine dimmed as another big cloud rode in from the north. The air went cool.

We started up a little gravel path that ran between some rabbit brush in full bloom, tufts of yellow-gold flowers vibrant against the dull green foliage. Bettye pointed out a series of mosaic stepping stones made by her students; a riotous collection of fanciful bluebird houses on poles, also created by children in her art program. She was moving swiftly into the present, but I was not quite done with the past.

So I stopped and took her hand firmly in mine. "Beth. I really want to hear how you did it," I said. "How you escaped."

There had never been a plan to get word to us when they were safe. The whole idea was that none of us would know what became of them—for our own protection. "Plausible deniability", they called it in politics.

"Lucius Beebe published a whole story about your divorce, about Peter, and your mysterious disappearance in the Territorial Enterprise," I told Bettye. "They serialized it, for God's sake."

She chuckled, meeting my gaze warmly now. I wasn't sure she was going to say anything else, but she finally gave a little sigh. "We spent two nights in the mountains."

"Two nights? That must have been...terrifying." I released her hands.

"Well, it was for me. Luke didn't seem bothered by it. If anything, it almost seemed like he was enjoying himself. He told me he'd been sent out in worse weather, when he worked on the sheep ranch in Elko as a boy.

"When it started getting dark, I was on the verge of panic. But Luke put me to work building a lean-to on the leeward side of a big boulder, with pine branches. It was May, and the horses didn't have their winter coats anymore. They were as unprepared for that snow as we were. Luke pried the shoes off the horses, so the snow wouldn't ball up in their hooves and make them lame."

She hesitated. "Our mother died of hypothermia. In those same mountains."

Pretty much all of what I knew about her life had come from hearing her drunken tale in the Bucket of Blood, and the yarn that Lucius had spun in his newspaper. I'd always presumed he'd taken plenty of dramatic license—though the parts I'd been witness to were certainly not short on drama.

"So that story was true?"

"Yes." She pushed at a tall spike of a pink hollyhock, then let it spring back. "It seemed like we were going to meet the same fate. Like God was playing one final joke on us.

"It was beautiful and clear by noon the next day—remember? Bright blue sky. But the snow was just too deep, and the trail had completely vanished. We hadn't brought enough food for ourselves, or the horses. But Luke thought we should let the sun do the work for us, rather than exhaust the horses trying to break out. So he went out, shot a couple of rabbits, and made us dinner." She laughed. "I hadn't seen anyone dress a rabbit that quickly since my mother."

She glanced at me, her eyes bright and a little challenging. "That night, I dreamed about her. She walked up to an enormous juniper tree, and stood next to it. This tree stood all by itself, high on a knob of granite. It looked like it had been ripped in half by a lightning strike years before, because it had two crowns. I told Luke about the dream the next morning. And even though we'd lost the trail, we started looking for a two-crowned juniper. It didn't take us long to spot it.

"We rode up to that tree, stood and looked around. And then I spotted a little glint. Luke got out his binoculars and it turned out to be a weathervane on the roof of a barn. We finally got to the Red Wolf just before nightfall, completely exhausted from breaking trail in the snow."

She squinted across the garden, toward a rough granite birdbath settled in a large round clearing of coarse pink gravel, ringed with old, woody lavender. "Sweet Potato and I had another sixteen years together."

As I watched a robin splashing in the shallow basin, I wondered if that might be the spot where she'd laid her beloved horse to rest.

"We still have her daughter, Sweet Thing, but she's almost twenty-eight now. Retired." She glanced at me. "An old girl, like us."

I smiled. I watched her refocus on the barn below us, and followed her gaze. Ingrid was carrying a saddle out to her horse. She glanced in our direction, as if she knew we were watching. Bettye raised her arm in a wave. Ingrid gave a little lift of her chin.

"And that one is going to die with her boots on," she said.

I thought of my best friends Gloria and Mary-Grace, and how we liked to talk about starting a commune for old ladies who refused to behave like old ladies. We planned to have plenty of good wine and a suicide pact.

"We had frostbite, but we were otherwise okay," Bettye said now.

"Frostbite?"

"I'm short a couple of toes," she remarked, almost casually. At my startled reaction, she added, "Oh, they were pinky toes, useless little things. We didn't realize the frostbite was as bad as it was for a couple of days. You know...bits start to turn black. When we got down here, it was off to the hospital, and off with..." Bettye grinned mischievously and pantomimed chopping.

"Oh!" I cringed, squeezing my eyes shut.

"So Ingrid and I have matching limps," she went on brightly. "We cut quite a figure in town, gimping about."

I managed a chuckle. "How did she acquire hers?" I asked.

"Philippe and Ingrid were part of the French Resistance."

"Good heavens." I squinted toward the woman saddling the horse outside the barn. (I suppose I should've expected something dramatic. This was Bettye, after all.)

"Her leg was broken during one of their operations," said Bettye. "Shattered her tibia and fibula."

I stared in astonishment at Ingrid Kiehl, bustling purposefully around her barn.

"But I still can't keep up with her." Now she brushed her hands, dusted with golden pollen from the hollyhock, against her pants. "It was meant to be temporary, Luke and me staying here in New Mexico with Philippe and Ingrid. But they'd just bought the ranch, and it was kind of a mess." She sighed. "It felt good to just pitch in, to work with my hands. I got quite good at stringing barbed-wire fences. And a week turned into a month and so on."

Her gaze swept out over the silvery Rio Grande, returning with the noisy flight of two magpies, who alighted in one of the apple trees.

"It felt safe here," she said. "I'd never experienced that feeling. Ever."

I reached out, squeezed her hand, and let it go.

"And I had fallen in love."

Not planning to stick my foot in my mouth again, I waited for her to continue.

"Susan was special—a brilliant little girl, extremely brave," Bettye said, slowly shaking her head. "And...these two lovely people were trying to come to her rescue."

"Trying?"

"Well, it was what Ingrid and Philippe knew how to do. During the war, they rescued people: they brought them from a dangerous place, to a safe place. They were brilliant at it. They rescued me and Luke."

"And that's what they did for Susan?" I asked, hopefully.

"For the most part, yes..." she said. "They saw something tragic— this lovely child, their friend—who'd lost her entire family. The reservation land was poisoned with radioactivity, unsafe. It made sense to Ingrid and Philippe, to see if they could get her out of there. And they did. At that time, such things were acceptable. But the 'rescue' didn't go well. By the time Luke and I arrived here, Susan had essentially stopped speaking."

"Oh." I winced.

"I will never forget the night we arrived here. We drove from Lake Tahoe straight through, Philippe and Luke switching off. By the time we dragged ourselves into the house, it was very late. But Ingrid was waiting up for us, by the fire. And I guess the commotion woke Susan up.

"Susan and I had met just once before, at their ranch in Las Vegas, and I had given her a silly present, spoken to her in Numu. But she recognized me. Her eyes went absolutely huge. And I…I don't know why, but I just held out my arms and she ran to me." Tears bulged in Bettye's brown eyes, threatening to spill down her cheeks. "She started chattering at me in Shoshone, which I can barely understand. But even you would have known what she was saying, Elouise. The next morning Ingrid told me that Susan hadn't said a word in close to a month, that she and Philippe had been utterly desperate."

The high desert wind lifted her hair from her shoulders. Her eyes brightened, sharpened.

"It's strange how things work out," I said.

"Yes. It seems that we were needed here, as much as we needed to be here."

I knew she wanted to tell me the rest of her story. It had taken people like Scott, my aide, to show me that one of God's most Mysterious Ways was the way he'd wired up the human heart. I'd never been close to a gay person before Scott.

"Tell me about Ingrid," I said.

Bettye gave me an appraising look and finished off her tea, setting the glass down on the little table to the chime of ice cubes.

"On Christmas Eve, our first winter here, we all piled into Philippe's truck and went to Midnight Mass at the Taos Pueblo. Susan was out of her mind with excitement about being up that late.

"The farolitos—those little paper bags with candles in them?—

were all glowing on the rooftops, around the square. Susan had never seen them before—she was utterly enchanted. You know what it's like, watching a child having a magical experience. I think it opened up my heart."

"Yes," I said, thinking of my grandchildren clutching my hand, as we watched in awe as the space shuttle launched at Cape Canaveral.

"So we went to the San Geronimo church. You probably haven't seen it, but it looks like it could have been created by children, out of clay—it has this simplicity, this humbleness. Now, I hadn't been inside a church since I'd gotten married. And that was Holy Name Cathedral in Chicago." She laughed and gave a mock shudder. "But this church was different. It was intimate. It has the most beautiful, brightly painted altar. There were hundreds of candles, and incense, and music—it was just so lovely." She hesitated. "The church was chockablock with people, some tourists—but mostly people who looked like my brother and me and Susan. And there we sat with these two peculiar Alsatians, so far from their homeland.

"I remember looking down the pew at these people...at Luke, and Susan, and Philippe, and Ingrid. And I realized suddenly that I was looking at my family. It was the first time in my life that I was actually happy. And at that very moment, Ingrid turned and smiled at me and... well." Bettye's deep brown eyes shone. "I realized that I was in love."

I reached out for her hand again, and squeezed it. We sat there for a moment, not speaking.

"So, what made you decide to get in touch now?" I finally asked.

She smiled. "Don't worry, I'm not dying. I found your earrings when I was cleaning out our basement last year. It seemed like such a pity that I'd never had the nerve to give them to you. But we both know there's no statute of limitations on murder. It was probably still a foolish thing to do, getting in touch, but..." her voice trailed off.

At this, I couldn't help but smile. It was strange to think that I knew something she didn't. "I may have a bit of news for you," I said.

She glanced my way. "News?" She gave a brief, cynical snort. "I do hope that you're going to tell me that Dorothy Walker is dead." Good Lord, she could still look ferocious.

"Yes, she's been gone for years. But that's not the news I meant." Bettye scrutinized my face.

"Does the name Michael Bartosz sound familiar?" I asked.

She blinked slowly. I could see that she was taking her time, trying to figure out if acknowledging this was a good idea. I didn't blame her. So I proceeded matter-of-factly, as if her memory might just need to be jogged.

"He worked for a crime boss named Gianni Ludovico, originally from Chicago, who was trying to set up shop in Las Vegas back in the early fifties. A Bugsy Siegel wannabe." I sat back and waited.

"Mike was the fellow I originally came to Nevada with," Bettye finally said. "A gorgeous slab of beef. Not a lot between the ears, but wonderful between the sheets."

"Well, in the mid-seventies, Mr. Bartosz ended up at San Quentin with a fellow named Richard Russo." I watched her eyes narrow a bit. "Apparently they were former colleagues." She gave a cautious nod.

"Seems Mr. Bartosz had an old beef with Mr. Russo," I went on.

Bettye's lips parted, then pursed into a little smile. Her eyes began to dance.

"He gave Russo up for the murder of Peter Grafton. In exchange for a reduced sentence."

She threw her head back and laughed. So did I. It was a long time before we stopped. When we finally caught our breath, she held out her hand.

"Come on." She drew me to my feet. "We have to tell Ingrid." And we started toward the barn. Bettye's step might have been uneven, but it was quick; on those long legs she was like a tall ship cutting through the heaving ocean of wind. Then she stopped, where the path dipped down off the rise.

Ingrid was astride the big bay horse, whose ears were pricked back toward his mistress, his black tail switching in excitement. Past them I could see a wall of huge slate-colored thunderheads, trailing wisps of rain like a torn hem hanging from a big gray ball gown. Below the ranch, the river was the same brooding color, but the wind had stirred up little white riffles on its surface.

"Ingriiiid!" called Bettye, but the wind whisked away her voice.

As we watched, Ingrid rode right into a big puddle of sunshine that made her white hair glow bright as an angel's. Then, just like I'd seen Bettye do many years before, she kicked her horse into an all-out gallop, and they flew together down the pink sand road toward the Rio Grande.

"We'll have to tell her at dinner, then." Bettye turned back to me, her face still alight. "I hope you're planning to stay."

"I'd love to," I said.

THE END

THE BETTER HALF

TOPICS & QUESTIONS
FOR DISCUSSION

THE BETTER HALF

TOPICS & QUESTIONS FOR DISCUSSION

Conversation Starter

Who would you cast as Bettye, Elouise, Luke and Peter in a film of The Better Half?

Divorce

1. If you've ended a marriage, do you think you might have been a migratory divorce seeker in the 1950's? Why or why not?

2. If you've spent some time in a residential setting with a group of women, (college, vacation, religious retreat, etc.) what was your experience like?

3. Why do you think many women find it hard, or even impossible, to leave an abusive relationship? Why do you think Bettye was able to do this, during an era where she would have had little social support for her decision?

Indian Schools

1. If you already knew about the history of Indian Boarding Schools, how did you find out? If you've recently learned about them, how did you find out?

2. What was most shocking to you about Bettye and Luke's experiences at the Stewart Indian School? How did those experiences shape their respective destinies?

3. If you were to meet a former student of an Indian School, what question(s) would you like to ask them?

4. Why do you think supposedly "well-meaning" people create damaging organizations or initiatives?

Character

1. What role did her personal image and fashion play in Bettye's survival strategy?

2. Why do you think Bettye begins to remember Numu words, later in the story?

3. What was the most surprising aspect of the character Elouise? Why do you think she followed the career path that she did?

4. Was there another character you thought might assume a romantic role later in Bettye's life?

5. Do you know any eccentric characters, like Beebe and Clegg? What are their obsessions or odd/interesting behaviors?

6. Why do you think the Walker sisters had such different personalities? Do you think "nature" or "nurture" plays a bigger role in shaping our personalities?

AFTERWORD & ACKNOWLEDGEMENTS

When I moved to Northern Nevada in 2015, like most non-Native Americans, I'd never heard of an Indian Boarding School—or the nationwide boarding school system that existed from the late 19th century into the mid-20th century. When a new museum and cultural center opened at the Stewart Indian School in Carson City, my adopted hometown, I became a little obsessed with the subject. As I talked to locals (the ones who *didn't* move here from California) I heard stories of relatives who were forced into the boarding school, as well as relatives who attended Stewart voluntarily later in the 20th century, and remember their alma mater with pride.

But there's no disputing the original mission of the Indian schools: to force assimilation of Indian children into white society, no matter the cost. And the cost was very, very high. We are told that half the children who attended these schools did not survive. Stewart, like virtually every other Indian School, has its own cemetery. It contains both marked and unmarked graves—perhaps 200 of them, though many children who became very sick were sent home to their families to die.

I'm also a painter, and I begin every novel inspired by a specific landscape, after which my characters "arrive" to claim that setting. Walking the Stewart campus, looking at the dormitories, exploring the sagebrush steppe of our high desert, and hiking the mountain trails, that sense of place grew stronger and stronger. I knew my protagonist would have to be up to its challenges. The mountains and the desert are not forgiving places. My heroine would not be forgiving, either.

Things have changed in the few short years since I began this project. As I write this, Deb Haaland, the Secretary of the Interior, a member of the Pueblo of Laguna and our first Indian Cabinet

Secretary, is conducting a "Road to Healing" listening tour across the country, hearing from survivors and descendants of the Indian Boarding Schools. Soon after her confirmation by the U.S. Senate on June 22, 2021, she launched the Federal Indian Boarding School Initiative, described by the Department of the Interior as "a comprehensive effort to recognize the troubled legacy of federal Indian boarding school policies with the goal of addressing their intergenerational impact and to shed light on the traumas of the past."

Profits from the sale of this book are being donated to:

**National Native American
Boarding School Healing Coalition**
2525 E. Franklin Ave., Suite 120
Minneapolis, MN 55406

As a White author I did my best to ground my novel, a thriller about a woman of Paiute and Irish heritage, in accurate historical events. I undertook my research in a spirit of curiosity and respect. If I got anything wrong, I offer my sincere apologies.

This book is a work of the imagination, and most of the characters are fictional. Many authors describe being "chosen" by their protagonists, and once the very fictional Bettye Christian tapped me on the shoulder, there was no turning back. Her voice—inspired by a grande dame I once knew who had been an MGM chorine in the 1940's—came through loud and clear.

I can't imagine being stuck writing strictly from my lived experience. I hope authors continue to let curiosity, imagination, passion, and empathy inspire their writing.

It's undeniable that conventional publishing offers very few seats at its rarefied table, which has excluded many marginalized would-be storytellers. But independent publishing has changed almost everything. My story didn't have to get past any gatekeepers, and it isn't supplanting someone else's. It's simply another book on the shelf (or on your tablet).

I ask that readers decide for themselves if I've done justice to my subject matter, and judge my work on its merits. I hope this commercial thriller will spark curiosity in readers in its subject matter.

I took the liberty of including several historical figures in my story. First and most important is Sarah Winnemucca, the Northern Paiute tribal leader and social justice crusader. While not an active character in my story, her influence is felt by my protagonist and her mother. Sarah gave lectures and performances across the country to raise awareness of the plight of her tribe, and her book, *Life Among the Piutes, Their Wrongs and Claims*, is one of the most important accounts of American Indian history ever written. A heroic bronze statue of this Native woman, who also served as an Army guide and interpreter, stands in the rotunda of the Nevada's Historic State Capitol.

I also included two fascinating men, Lucius Beebe and Charles Clegg, unapologetically gay life partners who supercharged the literary and social scene of mid-20th century Northern Nevada, particularly post-war Virginia City. Beebe, the society writer responsible for coining the term "cafe society", brought a frontier version of his social scene to Nevada when he decamped New York.

Beebe and Clegg were authors, photographers, historians, railroad enthusiasts, and bon vivants. They wore period clothes and lived high on the hog. The couple's books on railroad history are still essential works for collectors. Mr. Beebe's witty, irreverent writing inspired his dialogue in this book. (Where else would I have discovered the fabulous word, "tosspot"?) The extraordinary private railcar that Lucius and Charles owned, *The Gold Coast*, is on display at the California State Railroad Museum in Sacramento. It was a delight imagining how they would have interacted with the glamorous and intriguing Bettye Christian.

. . .

I owe much of the inspiration for this book to Sandra McGee, who with her late husband William "Bill" McGee, wrote the seminal history of the Nevada Divorce Ranches, *The Divorce Seekers*. Bill was a young wrangler on a tony divorce ranch from 1947 to 1948, and his colorful tales of life on the Flying ME in Washoe Valley—just minutes from where I live now—provided me with a rich and very entertaining portrait of one of the most renowned of these establishments. Clark Gable was indeed one of its frequent guests—but just for rest and relaxation.

The Divorce Seekers, which has been re-issued in a commemorative edition, is the bible of the Reno Divorce Colony, which was a 20th century American cultural phenomenon. As frothy as descriptions of this era tend to be, the bottom line was that Nevada enabled women to escape unhappy or abusive marriages long before the era of "no-fault" divorce.

Sandra McGee is a tireless researcher with an encyclopedic knowledge of this era, and spent a great deal of time here in Northern Nevada interviewing local historians. Most of the people who remember this era are no longer with us. Sandra kindly permitted me to excerpt a transcript of a mid-century divorce hearing from her book.

I also thank my beta readers, including Suzinn Weiss, Denise Carter Wells (who deserves a second thank you for her meticulous proofreading), Robin Rowe, Susan Rutherford, Steve Cappelini, Pepper Hume, David Wilson, and Miya MacKenzie, for their valuable feedback. I'm also grateful to Stephanie Guillen for her Indigenous perspective on my story and its characters.

I also thank my parents, Beverly and Ronal Borgman, who encouraged my writing from a young age, and my supportive siblings Patty and David. Finally, I'm so grateful for my wonderful husband Mark Coates, whose crazy idea it was to move to the Eastern Sierra.

ABOUT THE AUTHOR

The Better Half is the second novel by P.W. Borgman, an author and artist who tells stories about the lives of women in the American West. She is a graduate of the University of California, Santa Cruz and lives in the Eastern Sierra Nevada, near Lake Tahoe.

Visit the author at PWBorgman.com